The Silent Places

SARAH MELLOR

Harper
North

HarperNorth
Windmill Green
24 Mount Street
Manchester M2 3NX

A division of
HarperCollins*Publishers*
1 London Bridge Street
London SE1 9GF

www.harpercollins.co.uk

HarperCollins*Publishers*
Macken House,
39/40 Mayor Street Upper,
Dublin 1, D01 C9W8, Ireland

Published by HarperCollins*Publishers* Ltd 2026

Copyright © Sarah Mellor 2026

Sarah Mellor asserts the moral right to
be identified as the author of this work.

A catalogue record for this book is available from the British Library.

HB ISBN: 978-0-00-871625-7

This novel is entirely a work of fiction. The names, characters and incidents portrayed in it are the work of the author's imagination. Any resemblance to actual persons, living or dead, events or localities is entirely coincidental.

Set in Sabon LT Std by Amnet

Printed and bound in the UK using 100% Renewable Electricity by
CPI Group (UK) Ltd

All rights reserved. No part of this publication may be reproduced, stored in a retrieval system, or transmitted, in any form or by any means, electronic, mechanical, photocopying, recording or otherwise, without the prior permission of the publishers.

Without limiting the exclusive rights of any author, contributor or the publisher of this publication, any unauthorised use of this publication to train generative artificial intelligence (AI) technologies is expressly prohibited. HarperCollins also exercise their rights under Article 4(3) of the Digital Single Market Directive 2019/790 and expressly reserve this publication from the text and data mining exception.

To Eleanora, our shining light

Ta scadoo yn vaaish cheet gys dy chooilley pheiagh
The shadow of death comes to all

Manx saying

February 1981

1

The courtroom gasps.

From the left-side public bench: cheers, claps, and at least one fist pump. From the right-side: a long, sorrowful wail.

Leigh slams her way out of Liverpool Crown Court, intending to get as far away as possible from the cheers and the tears and the shock; intending to get as far away as possible from the crumpled face of Gail Harding's mother, Nikki.

She bolts out of the back entrance onto St John's Lane, opposite the multi-storey car park her own mother once stood on the ledge of, pretending she was going to throw herself off. On her turn towards town, she boots an empty can of Cresta, which lifts off her toes like a football, hurtling through the air and landing with a clang.

As if in tune with her rage, the baby in her belly gives her a massive kick.

When she reaches Lime Street, Leigh looks back at the steps of St George's Hall, towards the cluster of placards calling for justice for Duane Harding, the child-murdering tosser who will shortly be greeting his supporters as a free man, dressed in his court outfit of dad cardigan, tan slacks and spectacles, the very picture of harmless. She turns away and bolts through the crisp, sunny afternoon, heading in no particular direction, wanting to get lost in a crowd. Passing the travel agents, she sees her own dark shape reflected in the window: a stick figure with a distended stomach, dressed in an unlucky green suit, worn to court today to watch the almighty balls-up of the acquittal.

As Leigh marches through Williamson Square, dodging seagulls and men clutching beer cans, she decides it has all been a dream. What just happened didn't happen because it can't be so. It can't be that a man who killed a nine-year-old girl and hid her body has just walked out of the court room to gulps and sobs from little Gail's family and knuckle-bumping from his, not least his new wife.

The baby puts the boot into her stomach, two hard kicks that make her wince. She has let Gail's mum down three times now, she thinks: once by failing to find her daughter's body, once by failing to get a conviction, and now by storming out of the courtroom. It seems fitting that Leigh is being kicked from the inside, the baby punching the parts she can't reach herself.

She finds herself on the main shopping street without knowing how she got there. She feels a burning need to tell someone, anyone, what has just happened. She rushes over to a group of women's rights campaigners and stands, immobile, in front of the stall, while a woman wearing a pea coat over peasants' clothing arranges leaflets in a fan: *women unite*. Leigh's words get caught in her throat. She hopes the woman will see the sweating, heavily pregnant woman and ask her what's wrong. She doesn't. Leigh takes off again – this can't wait – over the new paving towards a blob of blue: a police officer, heavy and hot in his uniform, neck bent towards his radio. He'll do. She'll report it to the police. Injustice! State-sanctioned murder! But then she remembers she *is* the police, and that the police are fascist agents of the state, so she doesn't bother.

Running out of steam, Leigh rests her hand on the side wall of Marks & Spencer. She has a pain in her breastbone, indigestion from the toad in the hole she'd shared with her mum last night, eaten on their knees in front of *That's Life*. She peels her shirt away from her belly and watches people moving around on Church Street. Here she has found the crowd she was looking for, although, echoing the mob outside St George's Hall, a fair number of them are holding placards. Placards waved by students calling for a right to walk the streets after dark. *'Take back the night. Take back our lives.'* Placards held by the Socialist Worker's Party, calling for an end to the totalitarian regime. *'Say no to a police state. Police state? No!'* And a fella wearing a sandwich board, proclaiming that the end of all things is at hand. That's more like it, Leigh thinks. She wants to shake his doom-mongering hand for capturing the mood so succinctly.

She must get her own placard, she thinks. Mount a one-woman protest against life and all its bollocks. *'Say no to murdering tossers. Murdering tossers? No!'*

Or how about, simply, *'Bollocks'*.

Leigh stands in the winter sun – overheated, clammy, assaulted from the inside – and squeezes her eyes together, trying to stem the angry tears.

Without a conviction, there's little chance of ever finding Gail's body.

At this reminder of an unlocated body, she suddenly senses her brother behind her shoulder, standing silently in her blind spot. She knows he isn't really there – it's been seven years since he went missing and she's not daft – but at some unspecified time in the past year, she's started to imagine James dogging her steps, a looming presence with dull eyes who shuffles his bare feet along the pavement next to her. This never used to happen. Since she finally accepted that he isn't coming back, they have entered a new phase.

James has no placard and neither does Gail Harding, because they are The Disappeared. (Although if Gail could have one, she's pretty sure it would say *'Loser'*, and be pointed at Leigh.)

'Are you all right, love?'

Leigh is surprised out of her breakdown by a woman wearing a headscarf over a blue rinse. Her eyes twinkle with kindness; someone's favourite nan. The woman holds out a pair of hands and Leigh takes them helplessly. The hands are strong and capable and lead her towards a bench she has no desire to sit on. 'You stay there, love.'

Leigh decides to do what she's told for half a minute. James has left her side now, perhaps attracted by the sight of Woolworths, where he used to buy records with his pocket money every Saturday. She watches the woman disappear in the same direction and decides to make a move before she attracts any more unwanted Liverpool nan attention. She wonders if she can make it to Chinatown, but the road there seems long, as far as the road to John O'Groats.

As she heads in the direction of Bold Street, Leigh runs into another protest – a group of fellas marching down Ranelagh Street with serious faces, sweating in shirts and ties, holding white paper on sticks. *'No to closure. Jobs, not dole.'* Everyone calling for something, everyone rallying against unfairness: the women against violence, the socialists against the brutality of her colleagues, the desperate men against losing their livelihoods. Leigh understands it all: just a short distance away, outside Liverpool Crown Court, a murderer is walking free and there's no justice in the world.

2

She finds Des in the Golden Yuen, at a window table that doubles as a makeshift office when he wants to get out of the flat he shares with his mum and sisters; a flat Leigh has tried to picture herself living in and failed. The restaurant is a safe haven where he can work uninterrupted and hide from people who want to kill a copper, of which there are a growing number in the city.

The air in the Golden Yuen is smoky and still. The curtains are slightly drawn and the sun is on the other side of the street, illuminating the boarded-up restaurants and broken windows of Nelson Street: Liverpool's Chinatown has seen better days.

'No case to answer!' she shouts at the silhouette in the corner.

Leigh stands helplessly in the middle of the room, sweating under her eyes. It's so dark out of the winter sun she's momentarily blinded.

'You're joking?' Des says, materialising out of the haze to stand in front of her. 'What happened?'

'He got off scot-free, that's what happened.'

'He's obviously guilty,' Des says, shaking his head.

'He killed her, I know he did!' Leigh shouts, and begins to cry.

This is so unlike her that the restaurant owner, Mr Tam, appears out of the back and helps Des manhandle her into a chair. Leigh enjoys being feeble for a few moments before freeing herself by punching Des on the arm.

'That judge,' she says, 'I don't know how he's going to sleep at night.'

She fixes her eyes on Des through the blur of sunshine. He is grinding out his cigarette in the ashtray, his brow crumpled with concern.

'I told you he'd get off,' Leigh says, in the manner of being proved right from an earlier argument.

Des is still shaking his head.

'It does happen with circumstantial evidence, I'm afraid,' he says. 'It's unfortunate, but we always knew it would be difficult to get a conviction without a body.'

'Circumstantial?' Leigh says, wanting an argument to let off steam. 'He didn't call the police when she went missing. He didn't even look for her because he was too busy driving around, trying to find a place to dump her body.'

'He did act rather strangely,' Des says, sounding unsure.

Leigh is seemingly the only person in the world who is 100 per cent certain of Duane Harding's guilt.

'Anyway,' Leigh says, checking an imaginary watch on her wrist, 'the upshot is that the murdering tosser will be on his way home for his tea around now. Or going on a bender at the Penny Farthing with his stupid band of stupid supporters and his stupid new wife.'

The presence in court of Duane Harding's new wife, Clara, had influenced the judge, Leigh is sure of it. Softly spoken and dressed in paisley, her fragrant presence had done much to shore up the preposterous idea that her husband was innocent.

'It's bollocking, wanking bollocks,' she concludes and Des agrees that it is.

'Would she like some tea?' Mr Tam, who for some reason is still hanging around in his own restaurant, asks Des. 'Tea's very calming.'

Des smiles, nods and offers profuse thanks, then looks at Leigh and pats his lap. She pops one foot on his thigh and he takes off her shoe and rubs a swollen ankle through sweaty socks. Mr Tam returns with a teapot and a small cup and sets it down in front of her. He picks up a fan and gives it a flutter in her face. In the Golden Yuen, she can have anything she wants. In the Golden Yuen, she is treated like a queen.

The baby turns in the cramped space and settles down to sleep.

'How did Gail's family take it?' Des asks.

'I don't know. I didn't hang around long enough to find out.'

The last she'd seen of Gail's mum, Nikki, before they went into court, she'd been smiling through tears and nerves, carrying a stuffed yellow dog the size of a small child: her daughter's childhood toy.

'I should go back,' Leigh says, suddenly yanking her foot back and twisting, getting her belly wedged against the table.

Des catches her hand.

'There'll be other people looking after the family. There's nothing more you can do, I'm afraid.'

Leigh thinks he means she's already done enough. On her way into the courtroom, she had been harangued by Duane Harding's supporters. They'd accused her of targeting an innocent man, harassing him to the point his life was ruined. With the conviction hanging over him, they claimed, Duane Harding couldn't get a job, his home had been vandalised, and he'd received death threats. She had no way of proving Duane harmed Gail and disposed of her body and she knew it.

Leigh knew no such thing. But the evidence presented in the prosecution's opening statement had sounded flimsy, and they may as well have been speaking the defence, for all the good it did.

'You put everything into this case,' Des says. 'You couldn't have done more to get him convicted.'

That's right, Leigh thinks, she couldn't. As acting detective inspector, she'd worked hard to nail a case no one else thought stood a chance of getting to trial.

And now all her effort has led to failure.

Her last hoorah before going on maternity leave and becoming a penniless unmarried mother.

Leigh is slumping, losing energy now the anger is waning. She sinks down in her chair, disappointment setting in, presents her other foot to Des. She undoes her flies and pulls her waistband down below the bump, from which a spread of toes is visible through the stretched skin. It's the weirdest thing ever, having an alien in her belly. She has relentless indigestion and zero temperature control. She can no longer lie on her stomach. She can no longer get in and out of doors without a series of manoeuvres.

The owner appears again, holding a telephone and pointing to the receiver – a work call for Des. Mr Tam only makes it to the middle of the room because the cord won't stretch any further. She watches Des at the counter, handsome in blue, shirt sleeves rolled up and his hair grown longer, covering his big ears. She gazes around the restaurant. The tables are set with tablecloths and chopsticks, but there's no smell of food being cooked. The street outside is deserted and it's doubtful that any customers are expected this weekday lunchtime, despite the menu advertising *'Business lunches served Monday to Friday 11.30 a.m. to 2 p.m.'*. Leigh picks up a menu, which is held together with yellowing Sellotape and rusted staples. Interested in the banana fritters in syrup, she turns to the desserts section at the back.

The alien wakes up and gives her another kick.

Des's call doesn't last very long – updates on an investigation into an assault in Liverpool city centre – but the upshot is he has to go to Admiral Street, the Toxteth police station where he's been based since his promotion to detective inspector with local CID. It's a move from serious crime that Leigh feels responsible for, although Des seems confident enough in his new role. He's the only male in a family of four women, and the oldest child. This gives him a certain glow but with it comes responsibility, *non-negotiable* responsibility – to his mum, to his sisters, to work, to Leigh and the baby. He has to get up at 5 a.m. to fit everything in because there aren't enough hours in the day for him to fulfil his non-negotiables, never mind anything else. As a result, she hardly gets to see him.

Or maybe it's that she's feeling left out. Apart from the court appearance, she hasn't got any cases, except for a deathly dull stake-out which her DCI is reluctantly letting her work on. She spends her days (9 – 5 only) relaxing horizontally in the recliner seat of an unmarked Ford Capri, eating packets of fizzy cola bottles and complaining about boredom, while her unfortunate partner keeps a look out for money exchanging hands on a street corner.

When Des arrives back at the table, he pulls a handkerchief out of his pocket and leans across to wipe her face. Then he puts a hand to her forehead to test her temperature, as if she's sick.

'How are you feeling?' he asks, nodding towards the alien in her stomach, the tiny heel which has replaced the toes. Leigh sees that her make-up, self-consciously worn for court, has come off on his hankie, which is covered with a horrible tan smear.

'You're very hot,' he says, touching her forehead again. 'Did you walk all the way up here from St George's Hall?'

Leigh must have done, but she can't remember much of the journey, only the chants of desperate men fading into the distance.

'If you don't mind me saying so,' Des starts.

'Go on. I know you're going to say it anyway.'

'I think you should probably go home and rest.'

This is a sensible idea. Leigh is going out with her friend Alice tonight and she could do with some rest before hitting the shebeens for a final time before the baby arrives in less than three weeks. And her bedsit on Canning Street is only a short walk up the hill; a bedsit widely deemed unsuitable for a mother to be, never mind a baby, consisting of not much more than a bed and a sink, and with a shared bathroom she can't get into at the best of times. She's still living there because the other options are worse – sharing a cramped flat with Des and his family, or living with her mother. But she dismisses the idea of going to her bedsit – she doesn't want to be alone with her thoughts. And besides, she's enjoying the attention.

'Or you could go to my mum's for a lie-down?' Des suggests.

Another reasonable suggestion – the Chung family's first-floor flat is only two doors down and she can always rely on a warm welcome. She briefly imagines Min, Des's enthusiastic mum, offering her tea, dim sum leftovers, and the opportunity of yet another perusal of the clutter of baby equipment in her hallway: Min's on standby to take over after the birth when Leigh decides to dump the baby. Leigh likes Des's mum, she really does – Min didn't hold it against her when she turned down her son's marriage proposal – but resting is not what she would be doing there.

'Can the baby have soup?' Mr Tam asks from the counter, trying to get rid of one of the three soups of the day advertised on the front page of the menu.

'The baby will get what she's given,' Leigh says.

They have no idea whether it's a girl or a boy, but Leigh and Des are unanimous in their prediction: the alien is a miniature Leigh – why else all that kicking and punching?

Des orders the soup, just to please the owner and make a contribution to his failing business, and he orders banana fritters, just to please Leigh. Then he gulps down Leigh's untouched tea to avoid offending Mr Tam.

'Fritters have run out,' Mr Tam says, returning to the room shortly afterwards.

'You're getting soup whether you want it or not, I'm afraid,' Des says, bursting into a smile.

She looks at his lovely face and sees her own face reflected back, a version of herself she never sees when she looks in the mirror. The person reflected in Des's eyes is a wondrous being possessed of rare beauty and a good heart. But she is a mirage, an imposter, a mere trick of the light.

'I'm sorry you're having to deal with all this,' Des says.

'I'm fine,' Leigh says, 'I love putting my heart and soul into getting a conviction, only for all my evidence to get thrown out before the trial even starts. I also love being overworked, underpaid and generally hated as fascist bizzy scum. In short, I love my job.'

She is counting off the days to her maternity leave. Reaching the time when she can get away from the thankless task of being a police officer is her number one goal.

Des leans towards the adorable face of the imposter, who must be giving him an encouraging smile, because he is holding her hand and gazing into her eyes. She feels a drop of sweat fall from her forehead as she entwines her fingers with his. Their lives are in chaos, their future undecided, and they are at an impasse: his family frowns on them living together, Leigh frowns on being forced into getting married and is digging her heels in. She smiles back at him through the sun beams and dancing dust, her lovely boyfriend and father of the alien. Despite the unplanned pregnancy, the embarrassing marriage proposal, the long list of non-negotiables; despite *everything*, Des Chung is still her favourite person in the world.

Five Months Later
July 1981

3

Her first day back at work, and this.

Seven o'clock in the morning, a red sun rising, a day's work already done seeing to the baby, and Leigh is careering past a leaning traffic light and two burned-out cars, heading towards an urgent call-out – a stabbing in riot-torn L8, a disturbance at dawn, a woman screaming like she was being murdered.

She had recognised the address straight away.

Leigh strides towards the Victorian terrace, the smell of acrid smoke filling her lungs. She jumps over what looks suspiciously like a school javelin and then crunches her way through shattered milk bottles to reach the house on Devonshire Road.

Only to find local CID has beaten her to it.

'Hello,' Leigh says, in the tone of a hostile question. 'What are you doing here?'

Des swings his head around in surprise at the sound of her voice.

'Oh,' he says, making a mock cringe. 'Did you get the call too? I'm afraid we must have doubled up.'

'No, really,' Leigh says, 'what are local CID doing here?'

She is on the backfoot, ready for a fight. When the call had come through, in a confused, second-hand manner amid the chaos, Leigh had thought the job was hers, and hers alone. No one else had been available to come with her, owing to a hefty number of officers lying in hospital beds with singed eyebrows and bandages around their heads.

'Are you on your own?' Des asks, looking around for her DCI Stan Pearce, who she'd left a message for back at Walton station. 'How did you get here?'

'Hitched a lift in a jam butty car.'

The traffic cop's face had been pressed to the windscreen as they drove through Toxteth, looking skywards towards what's left of Upper Parliament Street and frequently wincing as if he was dodging a petrol bomb.

'It is rather dangerous around here,' Des says, glancing behind him at the smoky street.

Leigh stares at him. Is he saying that because she's the mother of his child? Or does he mean it's too dangerous for a woman? Women officers hadn't been allowed to take part in the frontline policing during the rioting, but, to Des's mind, it's okay for Leigh to work in serious crime because all they do is watch their colleagues getting pelted with stones on the television, which, to be fair, was what she had done last night.

'You're here, aren't you?' she says after a pause.

'We did get the call-out,' Des says, wearing his grim cop face, the same face he greeted her with this morning when she dropped the baby off at his mum's. 'I'm not sure why the call went through to Walton, too.'

'Ooh, serious crime!' says the tall fella at his side she presumes is his new partner. 'The big boys are here, are they?'

Leigh sighs loudly. This isn't going to be easy. No one wants serious crime butting in.

Not least her ex-boyfriend.

'Yeah, well,' Leigh says. 'It *is* serious, from what I've heard.'

'This is DC Callum Jenner,' Des says, before glancing down at Leigh's chest – she's wearing a shirt he's yet to collect from her bedsit and he's noticed.

Leigh gazes up at Des's new partner, a person she is more than a little jealous of, and their eyes lock. She's seen him before, numerous times in fact, on nights out at The Porto on Victoria Street. He's the star of the dancefloor, last seen wriggling his arse to 'Funky Town', into the face of a fella smoking a joint the size of a sausage. It's clear from his expression of raised eyebrows and pursed lips that he recognises her too; although, given that he is new, not in the context of being the mother of his DI's baby. He has a face like an imp and his eyes have a malign sparkle to them.

She likes him already.

Leigh and Des both make to go inside at the same time, shoulders bumping. There's a brief pause as the three of them stand on the top step leading to the front door. The remnants of graffiti have faded but are still visible on the outside wall: MURDERER. Leigh stares at Des, trying to communicate her deepest thoughts through telepathy. *Told you, told you, told you.* It was only a matter of time before he killed again.

'They had a chance to lock him up,' she says out loud, 'and they didn't take it.'

'Think he would have been safer being locked up,' DC Callum Jenner pipes up behind her.

Leigh is wrinkling her nose in confusion as Des puts a hand up to stop her walking into her own crime scene. She tries to sidestep him but he stands in her way, a position she knows, from experience, will be hard to shift him from.

'Before you go in,' he says, 'you should know that this isn't what you think it is.'

Leigh attempts to move under his outstretched arm. This is exactly what she thinks it is.

'Yeah, yeah, yeah, but I got the call-out,' she says.

But she's no longer an acting DI, merely a detective sergeant, and she couldn't pull rank even if she wanted to.

Leigh steps over the threshold into the familiar hallway. She's been here before, many times. She knows the layout of the rooms. She knows the insides of the cabinets and cupboards and wardrobes; she knows what's underneath the floorboards and the paving stones in the back yard. She knows this ground-floor flat inside out because she'd been here when it was ripped apart.

The uniform shoots her a look of surprise.

'They've sent a girl, guv?' he asks Des.

'DS Borrowdale,' Des says, valiantly, although he's still wearing his grim cop face.

Leigh is irritated when he gives a nod of assent to the uniform – permission for her to enter on his say so as a senior ranking officer. The uniform points to the closed door leading off the hallway. Leigh puts on a pair of latex gloves before opening it and stepping inside.

In the kitchen, the blinds have yet to be drawn on the new day. The room is in darkness, save a square of sunshine shining in through a cat flap. It takes a few seconds for Leigh's eyes to adjust to what she is not expecting to see: lying twisted in front of the oven is the body of the child murderer, Duane Harding. She takes in the WPC, bending down, talking in a soft voice, before her eyes move sideways. And there, kneeling on the floor, wearing a long nightdress patterned with cherries and blood, is Duane Harding's new wife, Clara.

4

The WPC has been trying to prise Clara Harding off the floor for half an hour now and they're considering using force.

Leigh shakes her head at Des – *hold off* – intending to have another go herself. She leaves the two CID officers at the door and approaches with determination. The WPC had been gentle at first, cajoling their suspect up with kind encouragement, but things have taken a turn and they are now involved in a physical altercation. The policewoman is being pulled this way and that, staggering too near Duane Harding's body, in danger of contaminating the scene.

'You need to get up now, Clara,' Leigh says, looming over her.

When she gets no response, she indicates to the WPC to let go and squats in front of Clara, seeking out her eyes.

'It's Leigh, the police detective,' she says. 'Remember me?'

Leigh fears she remembers her all too well.

Clara puts her head between her legs.

'Can you hear what I'm saying?'

The slender woman on the floor moans. She sobs and she rocks. Her head remains buried in her husband's chest.

Clara has fortitude, Leigh thinks. She's determined she's not going to move.

A one-woman protest against the world.

Leigh draws herself back up on her feet, preparing to give the order to drag Clara away, or for Des to give the order – she has no idea who's in charge here. But they need to move her soon because the scene of crime officer has arrived. The ambulance crew are waiting outside, but they're still missing the pathologist, due to roadblocks. There's still no sign of her DCI, Stan Pearce, and Leigh is already losing hope on that score.

She joins a silent Callum at the door while Des has a go.

'I'm so sorry to have to ask you this,' he says, kneeling next to Clara on the floor. 'But you do need to move away, if you feel up to standing.'

Even in full charm mode, Des gets nothing back.

'I know this must be difficult and I'm very sorry to have to prise you away like this, but if you don't mind? It really would be for the best.'

Clara Harding turns her face towards him. Leigh's eyes widen as she sees, for the first time, that she is hurt. There is a fresh bruise under her left eye and a recent cut to her mouth.

'I can see you're injured,' Des says urgently. 'Shall we get you to hospital?'

'Who hit you?' Leigh asks, and gets a reply from the WPC.

'When I got here, she told me that she'd disturbed an intruder in the early hours,' she says. 'Said he punched her in the face and ran out the front door.'

'Description?' Leigh asks Clara, and is again replied to by the WPC.

'Male. Big and broad, wearing black and a balaclava.'

A loud buzzing noise starts from somewhere in the house, making everyone jump. They relax after a few seconds when they realise it's an alarm clock, going off in one of the bedrooms. The cat flap springs open and a big ginger tom, alerted by the signal for breakfast-time, clambers through it and starts furling its way around Des's legs. The appearance of the cat – or Des's charm offensive – seems to do the trick. Clara Harding stands.

She is clearly in shock, shivering, despite the foil blanket now around her shoulders. The injuries to her face look fresh.

'No handcuffs,' Leigh orders.

She's not under arrest – yet.

'He'll need his breakfast,' Clara says. 'You need your breakfast, don't you?' she asks of the cat.

'We'll do that for you,' Des says.

'She needs to get checked out at the hospital,' Leigh says, hearing the rustle of paper shoes as the SOCO moves into the room.

'He has half a tin of Kattomeat,' Clara says as she is led away.

The uniform in the hallway shakes his head. The ginger tom steps through his owner's blood, leaving paw marks on the tiled floor.

'Can someone get that frigging cat out of here?' the SOCO shouts.

After making a big fuss of the cat and depositing it in the back yard, Callum goes upstairs to get fresh clothes for Clara – they'll need to bag her nightie as evidence. Des steps into the back room to talk on his radio, trying to find a solution to the problem of Leigh being here. She hears him say: '*We've got a situation here.*'

Left alone, and still waiting for Stan to show up and take charge, Leigh circles the body, squats down, and rises to her feet again. The last time she'd seen Duane Harding flashes through her mind: fist-bumping a friend, inside Liverpool Crown Court. She stares down at the man she so desperately wanted to put away. His eyes are open and the expression on his face is one of shock. He was obviously taken by surprise.

Leigh glances around the room, at the plugs out of their sockets in preparation for going to bed last night, the two mugs with fresh teabags inside, ready for the start of the new day. The tops are spick and span, empty except for the mugs, a saucer of uneaten cat food and an office document tray in the corner full of felt-tip pens. The Hardings' knives are in a wooden block by the side of the oven and look intact.

Now the scene is all hers – or is it? Who knows? – she finds she is in a panic. She remembers to keep clear of the body so the SOCO can do his work, but her checklist doesn't get much further than that. Beset by brain freeze, she watches through the window as Clara is led out of the house to the waiting ambulance, accompanied by Callum and the WPC. Their frail suspect is now wearing a summer dress and sandals Callum had plucked out of the wardrobe. The nightie is already bagged up.

Overwhelmed by so much to do, Leigh stays at the window, gazing out at the uniforms guarding the scene. The streets are filling up now and the police officers are sitting ducks in the morning sunshine. One of the officers keeps glancing over his shoulder, dogged, as he is, by a shaggy-haired fella with a film camera who's got wind of something afoot. Yesterday, an anonymous phone call had come through to Walton station saying a police officer was going to be shot. Leigh moves away from the window, suddenly fearful that an unseen gun is aimed at her. The possibility of Kai growing up without a mother flickers through her head as she turns back to the crime scene.

She plucks her notebook from her pocket and finds her pen has run out of ink. She circles the room. Her brain won't work; interrupted, as it is, every 10 seconds or so, by a voice telling her to think. The voice has the same tone as her mother and berates her for being a bad mother for going back to work and leaving her baby behind. As she has done numerous times this morning, she looks down, expecting to find Kai attached to her by a sling. She can still feel the warmth of his little body, against her chest.

'What are you thinking?' the baby's father says, materialising in the room behind her.

'He's been stabbed,' Leigh says.

'You don't say,' Callum says, appearing back in the flat.

Leigh swings around to give the DC the daggers.

'What's the plan?' Des says brightly.

'Give me another minute and I'll tell you,' Leigh says, although many minutes have already ticked by.

She scrapes her pen in zigzag lines on her notebook to get it working and then drops to the floor again, ostensibly to look for anything foreign to the scene but in actuality to stare at the floor tiles: pink and black geometric shapes which make her eyes go funny.

'We need to search inside and out for the murder weapon,' she says eventually.

She waits for Callum to make a smart-arse remark. His silence is worse.

'And we need to get the uniforms going door to door,' she says, suddenly thinking of witnesses. 'Talk to the neighbours – find out whether they saw anyone coming in or out.'

'What? Through the clear view they would have had through the flames and flying bricks,' says Callum, whom she is rapidly going off.

'Well, there's no point in putting more uniforms on the streets to reassure people because L8 is already flooded with them,' Leigh says, raising her voice, 'and there's no point using road blocks either because the roads are already blocked.'

'It doesn't look like anything's missing from the other rooms,' the DC says, 'nothing's been disturbed.'

'Can I make a suggestion?' Des says, about to make one anyway. 'It could be something simple, a robbery disturbed. The perp takes his chance while the riots are raging, comes across Duane Harding and it all goes wrong. Clara finds him and becomes distressed.'

'A druggie after money to feed their habit?' Callum offers.

'Or a member of the one in ten, desperate to feed his kids.'

'One in ten?' Des asks.

'UB40's new song, *I am the one in ten*. That's how many people are unemployed.'

'And a starving thief just happened to find himself in the flat of a child murderer?' Leigh counters. 'All they'd have to do is walk into the nearby supermarket and take something off the shelves.'

The shops had been looted over the weekend, windows smashed and stock cleared out.

'The front door was open when we got here, sir,' the uniform says, an unexpected ally in the hallway. He's taken his helmet off and his hairline is patched up; dissolvable stitches sitting on top of a swelling – he was obviously caught up in the violence over the weekend and has come straight back to work.

Leigh walks to the doorway and looks down at the hallway floor. There are faint footsteps on the parquet, the imprint of a heel, traces left by a shoe or boot heading to the kitchen. Des, standing close to her now, also has his eyes down.

'Duane Harding could have opened the door and let our perp in,' he says.

'Or maybe Clara found out her husband had been lying all along and lost it,' Leigh says. 'We should talk to her as quickly as possible, get a fresh full search of the house, there might be new information about Gail.'

'Preliminaries first? Where would you like to start?' Des asks, still giving a good impression of not being in charge.

Leigh's brain is starting to work again but she feels like she's taking part in a test at training school. 'Get the neighbour who called it in down to the station to make a statement,' she says.

'Because dragging him through Toxteth is a really good idea,' Callum says.

'That's up to serious crime,' Des says, a familiar note of steel creeping into his voice.

Leigh knows it's childish to feel a frisson of triumph but she feels it anyway. After graciously relenting to taking the neighbour's statement in his own home, she suggests they take a good look around the flat. She hears the uneven click of Des's shoes on the parquet floor as he follows her into the hallway and feels a pang. How can she miss a man who wears heel taps on the bottom of his shoes? She doesn't know. She just can.

Shortly afterwards, the three of them are staring at a message scrawled on the wall, just inside the front door. They'd missed it on their first foray into the flat because the door had been open and the uniform had been standing in front of it.

'"Sorry, had no choice",' Leigh says, reading the graffiti out loud.

'Is it fresh?' Des asks next to her.

'Looks like it,' Leigh says, moving closer. 'Maybe Clara fancied vandalising her own flat.'

'That's likely,' Callum says.

Leigh ignores his sarcasm and they all sniff as Des puts a finger on the letter S and examines the red smear left behind.

'I really don't think Clara Harding would write on her own wall,' he says, 'not if it was a crime of passion.'

'Scrawled on the wall hastily as the perp was leaving?' Leigh asks.

'It's a bit of a risk,' Des says. 'Taking your time to write on the wall, either before or after you've killed someone.'

'There are felt-tip pens in the kitchen,' Leigh points out, 'they could have grabbed one from there.'

'Whoever it was felt they needed to explain themselves,' Des says, swinging around as he hears the pathologist coming through the door.

'We need to get the photographer in here,' Leigh says.

Leigh glances over the DC's shoulder, towards where Duane Harding's car had been parked when Gail went missing; where a cadaver dog had barked during the search two years ago. A hollow feeling runs through her as she thinks of Duane Harding, lying dead in the kitchen. She can't get up an ounce of sympathy for him. All she can think of is the little girl who disappeared and how the chances of finding her body are now gone forever.

5

'How was Kai this morning when you left him?' Des asks in a cool tone after the pathologist has shared the opinion that the blood has come from stab wounds to the torso and Duane Harding has been dead for around four hours. 'I had to rush off, I'm afraid.'

'His usual laidback self,' Leigh says. 'He didn't make a murmur when I handed him over. Just went like this ...'

She gives Des a loopy smile, intended to replicate the baby's toothless grin. She has learned, over the past five months, that when it comes to nature versus nurture, nature wins every time. Kai barely cries. He sleeps through the night. He is as polite as his father. He'll soon be asking her if she minds if he burps, or saying he's sorry to disturb her if he wakes her up in the night. Which he almost never does.

She'd had to wake him up this morning.

'Mum was excited,' Des says, sounding anything but, 'she's been up since half past four, preparing for his arrival.'

Leigh smiles. She knows this isn't an exaggeration. Des's mum Min is a sweet woman for whom catastrophe is always around the corner. She had been serene in the first few months after losing her husband a couple of years ago, but the anxiety had crept up on her when she realised she was going to have to live the rest of her life without him. First it was crowds she became afraid of, then it was anywhere she couldn't escape from, then it generalised to everything on earth. The roof falling in. The sky falling in. Kai's head dropping off.

Leigh trusts Min with the baby's life.

'She's sterilised everything in case the plague sweeps through Nelson Street,' Des says. 'And she's moved the bedroom wardrobe into the hallway, ready to barricade the door if the rioting starts up again. How was he at your mum's last night? Did he settle?'

'I think I managed to protect him from lasting emotional damage,' Leigh says, 'but only time will tell.'

Late last night, she had called Des on the Chung family's newly installed telephone to let him know that she and Kai had been forced into staying with her mother; a temporary arrangement after being driven out of her bedsit on Canning Street by the nearby rioting.

As they knock at the property next door, glancing around them for danger, Leigh thinks of Kai, existing in a parallel universe in Chinatown. He is a wizened wizard of a baby, with a comb-over which stretches in two strands over his bald head. The little prince, they call him, or at least they used to when Des said more than pleasantries to her.

'Kai will be asleep now,' Leigh says, feeling a surge in her chest.

'He'll be fine,' Des says, turning to look at her and then immediately losing eye contact.

This is how their conversations go: polite enquiries as to whether Kai has eaten or slept or burped or smiled; conversations that are hot and cold but mainly lukewarm, punctuated by small pockets of time when Des forgets he's angry with her.

An hour later, they are walking through Granby, over the two-lane boulevard, heading towards the Welsh Streets. The sun is hot on their heads and the earth is scorched beneath their feet. Leigh storms ahead of Des and Callum, as if they've had an almighty row. She can hear cranes squealing and big engines running – the rioters had only been dispersed as dawn broke and the clean-up operation has already begun. She saw the first workmen on her way to the scene this morning, getting an early start before the tarmac began to melt beneath the wheels of their trucks.

Plenty of people in L8 want to talk to them – the owner of a little supermarket with empty shelves wants to tell them he's ruined after the looting (but from whom secret softie Callum still manages to buy a tin of cat food); a man in a bright woollen hat, misjudging the mood, wants to dance with Leigh; and a bunch of kids sitting on a wall want to know if they're from out of town and to share their thoughts on the scumbag racist Liverpool police.

But no one wants to talk to them about their murder enquiry, not even the Hardings' immediate neighbours, where they had started their efforts nearly an hour ago. The neighbour who called in the disturbance had said he heard raised voices, a woman screaming, at around 4.30 a.m., nothing before that because it was too noisy outside. The nearby neighbours who had answered their doors said they hadn't noticed anything unusual, taken up, as they had been, with worrying about their homes being burned down and their family members being teargassed. Since then, the three of them have fanned out in a circle, getting further and further away from any likelihood of finding a witness.

When Leigh describes the suspect to the owner of the local funeral parlour – '*Male, big and broad, wearing black and a balaclava*' – he laughs in her face.

Towards lunchtime, Leigh stands next to a café with smashed windows, squinting into the sun, looking around for Des and Callum and trying to squash the urge to buy a can of the Tizer she'd given up during pregnancy. She spots the two of them moving slowly up the street under the shadows of burned-out buildings. Des is limping slightly, as if his shoes are full of stones. Since being shot in the leg a couple of years ago, during a case they were both working on, his leg often hurts. But he usually only allows himself to limp on his days off, having grimaced his way through the fit for work medical last year. He rights his gait as he crosses the road and manoeuvres around a car tyre and a large sheet of corrugated iron; literally putting his best foot forward, dressed in a perfectly pressed navy suit, exercising his non-negotiable right to be strolling through a war-torn Toxteth on a muggy July morning.

There's a bit of a stand-off between Leigh and Callum as to who gets the unwanted job of feeding the Hardings' cat – they daren't touch the saucer Clara left out in case they contaminate evidence. It is a stand-off Leigh wins, although it's a close-run contest. Callum reluctantly heads back to the flat to find the ginger tom.

Leigh and Des wait in Des's Allegro, the interior of which is practically at boiling point. A bug clings to the passenger window and refuses to budge when she tries to wind it down. Leigh keeps her eyes trained on the road and in the wing mirror, nervous someone will come along and stuff a petrol-soaked rag in the tank. She glances at Des, handsome in an apricot-coloured shirt she hasn't seen before, and then drinks in the familiar surrounds of the Allegro. It's hot and smoky in here, but being in the car is like meeting up with an old friend: the aroma of stale tobacco mixed with the talcum powder Des always smells of. The only addition from the good old days, which ended five months ago, is the carry cot in the back seat, ready for when Des drives the baby to the park on Sunday mornings.

She expects them to talk about the case, to speculate like they used to, but they sit in awkward silence. Des won't talk to her about the end of their relationship, nor, it seems, anything else. There's still no sign of Stan, and Leigh hasn't a clue where he is; probably nearby at Admiral Street station, terrorising the lower ranks into mounting a counter-riot, run ragged in a way her former boss DCI Murphy never was, preferring to sit in his office puffing a pipe.

Leigh can only partially open her window, for bug welfare reasons, and she isn't going to beg Des to talk to her, so she gets out and stands on the pavement, watching as Callum's lanky frame disappears inside the front door of the Hardings' flat, holding an empty tin of Choosy out in front of him. The verge is full of stuff that people lobbed out of their flat windows last night. Leigh spies a bicycle wheel, a lamp, bottles and cans, and a carpet of household rubbish which has spilled out of bags. Apparently, a police officer was injured when a giant cactus in a pot landed on his head.

On the street, the curtains of the houses are still shut to keep the midday heat out, but the pavements are getting busier. Youths dressed in black combat gear, looking as if they're at war, mingle with sightseers who've come to glimpse the devastation for themselves. There are reporters too; a film crew setting up and the same shaggy-haired man with the Super-8. On a nearby wall, a boy sits on the kerb, cricket stumps under his arm. From a doorway, the beat of Roots Reggae starts to pound.

Toxteth is heating up.

A group of young fellas pass by, pushing a shopping trolley filled to the brim with spoils from a nearby store. Leigh pretends she hasn't seen them and gets back in the car – she's more cautious with her safety since becoming a mother. She matters more now, she thinks, if only as a food source.

'What do you think of Clara's story about the intruder?' she asks Des when she's slammed the door.

'It is rather convenient,' he says, raising his eyebrows without looking in her direction. 'It means there's zero chance of finding him.'

'Ballies are definitely the headwear of choice around here,' Leigh says, eyeing a lad wearing what looks like a woolly hat with eye and mouth holes cut out of the material.

The conversation is over quickly and they lapse into silence again.

Callum is an age feeding the cat.

6

A few minutes later, Leigh is at Admiral Street station, staring at a scrum of dark-suited fellas, in the middle of which, unseen to her eye, is someone yelling his head off. The content is unclear, owing to the volume and machine-gun delivery, but Leigh catches the words, *'gangland'*, *'bleeding liabilities'*, and *'fucking eejits'*.

She has finally located her DCI.

The scrum parts and the exploding meteor that is Stan Pearce bursts out and shoots freefall into the incident room, his gnarled face seriously red and his lips white with spit. He sweeps past her and then comes to a violent stop and turns.

'Where the bleeding hell have you been?' he shouts.

Leigh was going to ask him the same question. If Des hadn't been at the crime scene, the murder investigation would have been without an officer with the authority to oversee it.

'I left a message at Walton,' Leigh says, folding her arms. 'I was called out to a murder first thing.'

'Murder!' Stan shouts. 'We haven't got time for a bleeding murder!'

Despite being yelled at, Leigh feels the corners of her mouth twitching. She rights her face to explain, as best she can to a raging bull, the events of that morning.

Stan's mouth falls open when he hears the name of the victim.

'You what? Why wasn't I bleeding told about this?' he shouts.

Leigh stares at him, marvelling at his endless capacity to be unreasonable. His salt and pepper crewcut is damp, and beads of sweat are swinging from his forehead. He's a hefty fella and she's concerned he's going to have a heart attack. She babbles more scant facts about the murder but there's no two-way conversation with Stan, you just have to get your words out before he moves onto something else.

Leigh isn't fast enough.

'Get the wife charged and then get back here,' he orders. 'We'll sort the resulting carnage out later.'

She opens her mouth to speak.

'It'll take you all of five bleeding minutes.'

With that, he storms off, depositing a few drops of sweat on her face.

'Welcome back,' Leigh mutters under her breath.

The major incident room, set up in Toxteth to police the riots, is packed with bodies, some standing, some sitting, some leaning, most suffering in the heat; a workplace staffed by the walking wounded of the Merseyside force, her colleagues from the serious crime squad, and the here-to-sort-it faces of officers drafted in from other parts of the country, some from the Midlands and some from as far away as Surrey. The atmosphere is one of adrenalin-fuelled excitement, undercut with fear – they lost control of the streets last night, looting is still going on and more unrest is expected later. There are even rumours of terrorist involvement from, among others, the Libyans, the IRA, and the Russian Secret Service.

Leigh is surprised the police station is still standing.

'All right, love?' a crime squad detective greets her, as if he's only seen her yesterday. Another familiar face raises his eyebrows and fixes his eyes on her belly. Leigh scowls at them, reacting to the silent thoughts she knows they're having about both messing up the Gail Harding case *and* being a bad mother. Neither of them asks how she is, or enquires after Kai, although Leigh had proudly shown his photograph to an enthusiastic secretary on the way in.

She looks around for Des and Callum, both of whom disappeared the minute they got here. She hears the sound of Stan's voice shouting orders above the din, and thinks she needs to get an answer from him about who's taking on the murder case, no matter how busy he is. And she needs to point out that Clara Harding has been admitted to hospital and it will be some time before they can get to speak to her. Despite Stan's bulldozer ways, she's grown to respect him over the two years she's been working in serious crime. Although he's still an almighty pain in the arse, he'd supported her the most in the case against Duane Harding. He may run the gamut of emotions from A to A – agitation to anger – but once, in a rare moment of sensitivity, he'd told her about a case that had stayed with him; his discovery of a little boy's battered body when he'd been a PC. The six-year-old had been dead on arrival at the hospital.

Leigh sips from the can of Tizer she's treated herself to, waiting for her chance. Her ears are assailed by the noise of the chatter in the room and there's an overpowering smell of flowers coming from a bouquet on a desk, no doubt waiting to be taken to the wives and mothers of the injured. Next to the flowers, swinging on office chairs and throwing scrunched up paper balls at each other, are two plain clothed officers who are so young they've still got teenage acne. A fella with his head bandaged makes a noisy entrance and is greeted with a barrage of stupid jokes – he was the officer who'd been hit by the flying cactus on Princes Road. Another fella from a place she's never heard of introduces himself and calls her '*duck*'. Leigh's eyes snag on a person who stands out from the crowd. She's wearing an emerald green dress and is surrounded by a group of attentive fellas.

For once, Leigh is not the only woman in the room.

Despite her trying to get Stan's attention on numerous occasions, gestures he must surely have seen, it's a while before he arrives in front of her, awaiting confirmation that this inconvenient murder has gone away. She braces herself to tell him she hasn't got it sorted in five bleeding minutes.

'Has the wife confessed?' he snarls, although it's been less than five minutes since she last spoke to him.

'We don't know whose case it is, boss,' she blurts out. 'Serious crime and local CID both got the callout.'

'We're only just going to talk to Clara Harding now,' Des says from behind Leigh.

Stan groans. There's a loaded silence while he breathes dramatically to show his displeasure. For some time now, Stan has had it in for Des. *'Are you all right, love?'* he'd asked her when she was pregnant, *'I don't believe in what's he's doing. Fellas should do the right thing.'* Leigh has tried to put Stan right on a number of occasions, but he isn't the listening type; his lizard brain can't compute that she is the one who's refusing to get married.

'Put pressure on Clara Harding to confess,' he orders Leigh.

'Um,' Des says, 'there's a problem with that, quite a big one, actually.'

'Problem?' Stan counters. 'What bleeding problem?'

'It's probably the case that Clara Harding didn't do it.'

Stan splutters.

'If it's *probably* the case she didn't do it, she can't have bleeding done it then, can she?'

Leigh and Des wait. They both know Stan thinks on his feet. And right enough, he gives the nod – his usual way of issuing a summons. They follow him out of the room and into a meeting room; a small, windowless space up the corridor from where the major public order investigation is taking place.

'I don't give a shit who murdered that bastard,' is Stan's opening line. 'But I want this tied up, fast. It's a serious crime case but we're all run ragged and all our DIs are coordinating efforts on the streets. I've thought this over,' he continues, although Leigh very much doubts that. 'Chung's the only person of that rank so he's seconded back to serious crime for the duration.'

Des is standing next to him, but you wouldn't think it – all Stan's words are spat out at Leigh.

'You,' he says, jabbing a finger at her. 'You deputise as you know the previous case.'

Stan disappears in a puff of smoke and Leigh turns to Des, expecting him to start confiding his feelings about the encounter, like he used to in the good old days.

'Stan probably thinks our case is gangster related,' she tells him as they set up camp. 'Everything comes down to mobsters for him.'

'Um, Duane Harding didn't have gangland connections, that we're aware of,' Des says seriously as he takes a seat.

Leigh wants to say that she was joking, based on their experience of Stan from a past case, when he was single-minded in his pursuit of the wrong suspect.

But Des doesn't remember in-jokes. He just remembers her betraying him.

7

Over the next few minutes, they are joined in the meeting room by a smirking Callum, one of the paper-throwing, acned lads, and two of Stan's cronies from the Godfather squad, so called by Leigh and Des because of their resemblance to the film's cast. Leigh swears under her breath when she sees them, not least because her break up with Des is the subject of her colleagues' gossip. One of them is a carbon copy of Stan but not as bombastic, or as good at his job. The other is a slapdash fella who's the type to run out of a burning building before you. She'd had the misfortune of working with him on the Gail Harding case. Apart from being permanently late and never being where he said he'd be, he'd been a vocal critic throughout the investigation, making it clear he thought Leigh had the wrong person. ('*Duane Harding comes across as a nice fella to me,*' he'd said at the time, '*it's the wife I don't trust.*')

Briefing his team with a quiet but stern voice, Des is impressive. Leigh takes a seat and watches him as he talks through what she and Callum already know. He doesn't look her way. He doesn't check anything out with her. She is not invited to contribute. It's as though she's a distant work colleague who holds little interest for him, or just someone he used to know, but not that well.

Her gaze shifts and she takes in the small group gathered around the meeting table: a trainee detective, eagerly making notes, a sarcastic DC with his eyebrows raised, two resentful Godfather squad detectives with their arms folded, and herself, a woman who would rather be walking in the park with her baby, surrounded by bird song. They are quite the team, the few who can be spared, although others who could have been spared probably hadn't wanted to be landed with a dull old murder when there's glory to be had in bringing down the Russian mafia.

'Identity has been confirmed,' Des is saying. 'Duane Harding, aged 32, unemployed, but used to work as a mechanic at Richardson's garage.'

He runs through the charges previously brought against their victim, stressing – too strongly to Leigh's mind – that he was acquitted.

'The pathologist has yet to report fully,' Des continues, 'but preliminary findings show the time of death was between four and five in the morning. The victim was stabbed at least five times. There were no defensive wounds to the victim's hands and the blood was confined to the kitchen floor.'

Leigh listens to Des speak. She has always liked his voice – the well-mannered enunciation mixed with the heavily accented edge of the Liverpool streets he comes from. She notices now that his speech is almost entirely without the pleases and thank yous and if you don't minds he's tried hard to shed since his promotion. His hands still dance the way they've always done when he's self-conscious, but for the most part, he's cool and efficient, a high-end fridge-freezer from the back pages of the Littlewoods catalogue.

When she gets the chance, Leigh must tell him he comes across as a little cold.

'Forensics are searching the flat, inside and out, but so far,' Des continues, 'the murder weapon is missing. Clara Harding is in hospital, suffering from shock and injuries to her face, so we'll talk to her as soon as possible. She remains a suspect but she claims she intercepted an intruder.'

After describing the intruder and the footprints in the hallway, Des pauses to pass a photograph of the graffiti around, a move which prompts an almost exact re-run of the speculation they'd voiced earlier in the Hardings' flat. The trainee, whose name is Kevin Sajjad, puts his hand up to ask a question but nobody invites him to speak.

'It's not the first time the house has been graffitied,' Leigh says. 'Someone daubed murderer on the front of the house.'

But no one is listening to her. Their heads are all turned towards the out-of-town woman officer in the green dress. She's walking past the window with a group of fellas trailing behind her like a gaggle of geese. Des smiles across and waves and she waves back.

'There was another job called in yesterday,' says Stan Mark II. 'Flat in L8 robbed by a druggie. The victim was a young girl with a baby, unmarried mother, her handbag was snatched from the kitchen table. Some low mark taking advantage of the rioting.'

'Worth looking into,' Des says, the fade of a smile still on his face.

'What?' Leigh says, abandoning her intention to repeat what she said about the graffiti, 'you think that's our perp?'

'Our victim might have fought back,' Mark II says, 'stopped the druggie getting at the leccy tin.'

'What?' Leigh repeats. 'And then he stopped on the way out to write *Sorry* on the back wall?'

'You're right, of course,' Des says, addressing the Godfather squad members. 'This could be nothing to do with the crime Duane Harding was accused of. We need to be careful about jumping to conclusions.'

'So, a child murderer just happens to get stabbed during a botched burglary?' Leigh asks, incredulously.

She stares at Des, willing him to look her way. But it turns out he isn't even someone she used to know.

'We've already done some preliminary door knocking,' he says, 'but with the situation in L8 at the moment, that proved tricky. Nobody saw anything. If it was premeditated, during the rioting was the ideal time to strike.'

Des is certainly thorough, and his coldness is mesmerising, but it's hot in here and Leigh suddenly feels weary. The blinds are shut to keep the sun out but it's having the opposite effect of trapping the heat inside. She's exhausted and craving the touch of her baby. If she feels this way after only a few hours away from him, how is she going to face the days and months ahead?

'Thinking back to the charges against Duane Harding ...' Des says.

'Charges which were thrown out,' the slapdash fella says, glancing at Leigh.

'... it could be we're looking for someone who might want to take revenge, or got someone else to take revenge on their behalf. We need to consider every possibility as to who that might be.'

The list is endless, Leigh thinks, with her name at the top.

'Detective Sergeant Borrowdale was involved in the original case,' Des says. 'Who might be possible suspects, do you think, from the people you spoke to as part of the enquiry?'

Leigh perks up at the sound of her name, pleased at last to get an acknowledgement of her existence.

'Number one – Clara Harding,' she says. 'If she found out that Duane Harding had been lying about what happened to Gail, she might have snapped.'

'List of potential interviewees?' Des interrupts. 'If you don't mind? We've got no indication as yet that Clara Harding found anything out.'

'Yeah, yeah, yeah,' Leigh says, thinking it's wrong to turn the victims of Duane Harding's crime into suspects. 'There's Nikki, Gail's mother, and we could talk to Nikki's grandparents,

Dolcis and Matty – they brought her up. But they're not likely suspects. He's ill with prostate cancer, she's frail.'

They are people who have got old before their time.

'Oh well, that exonerates them, then,' Callum says.

'And her brother, Warren,' Leigh adds, ignoring the DC. 'To rule him out.'

At this, the slapdash fella, who has so far spent the briefing sloped sideways in his chair, shuffling his moccasin shoes, sits up.

'Didn't Nikki Harding's brother assault our victim outside the courtroom?' he asks.

Warren had lost control when Duane Harding had winked at him on the steps of St George's Hall. Leigh doesn't think this makes Warren a suspect. She would have gone for him too.

'The charges were dropped,' she says, 'and I'm telling you now he wouldn't have killed Duane Harding, none of the family would – they're all desperate to find out where he hid Gail's body.'

'Huh,' the slapdash fella says, sloping back down again. 'I reckon we should interview all the other suspects in the kiddie's disappearance.'

'There were no other suspects,' Leigh says.

'Can we focus, please?' Des asks as the slapdash fella shakes his head in a way that infuriates Leigh.

'Where's Gail's real dad?' Callum asks.

'Dead,' Leigh says. 'Cancer, years ago.'

'Shall we start close and then fan out?' Des says. 'I think we should start the interviews with immediate family, but we do need to be sensitive.'

He looks around the table for someone sensitive and bafflingly decides on Callum to speak to Gail's great-grandparents – a judgement no doubt made on the basis that the DC had searched for a neighbour to look after the Hardings' cat.

'We'll need to talk to Duane Harding's family, too. They've only just been informed so again, go easy, but try and find out what they know about his past weeks and whether he felt under threat in any way from vigilantes. We need to trace Duane Harding's last movements. There has to be a "why now".'

Des lists the jobs that need doing, a wish list that has Kevin scribbling even more furiously, even though no one's told him to write anything down. Des wants to know the type of shoes the perp was wearing and where they could have been bought from. He wants someone to go and see the young woman who was robbed by the druggie. He wants someone to go and talk to Duane Harding's ex-workmates and friends. And, when the situation in L8 has calmed down a bit, he wants another round of door knocks in the area – including neighbours, shop owners and publicans.

There are far too many jobs for the amount of people around the table.

And the Godfather squad officers don't look happy at all – as experienced detectives in serious crime, they consider door knocking, and just about anything else, to be beneath them.

'DCI Pearce says other officers are on hand, if needed, but resources are currently diverted elsewhere so it is going to be us knocking on doors, if you don't mind,' Des says, the qualifiers sneaking back into his speech when he sees the look on their faces.

Leigh stands, smooths down her crumpled trousers and waits for Des to find out what job they're going on. As the DS on the case, she expects to be partnered with him and she's hoping he'll defrost a little once they're out and about together. She looks expectantly at his face as he comes towards her, but as he gets near, he turns away to brief Callum on going with him to talk to the pathologist. Her gaze stays focused on Des for a few moments. His shirt sleeves are rolled up and his glossy hair is falling over his thick-lashed eyes. He's very good looking, she thinks. It's a shame they've never met before.

8

After work, Leigh takes the woodland path through Calderstones Park, smiling down at the bundle attached to her chest in a sling. Kai is peacefully asleep, radiating old man's wisdom. She drinks in the beauty surrounding them: a magnificent sun is sinking behind the monkey puzzle trees, an unseen wood pigeon is calling from the tree tops, and the woodland path is bathed in golden light.

Magic is in the air.

For the past five months, Leigh has been running on happiness: a searing joy that comes from nowhere but is connected to merely being alive. For the past five months, she has been free of the misery of people's lives, free of being haunted by Gail's disappearance; free, too, of the grief about her brother that was always waiting for her in the silences. Since Kai was born in February there have been no silences because she has never been alone. She has lived her life permanently accompanied by a tiny being, a soft, mind-emptying shield against pain. In the past five months, and despite the break up with Des, a massive fall-out with her dad, and her mother's mere existence, her thoughts have been less. And without thoughts, she has been happy.

But one day back at work and, already, something inside her head is altered. She has begun to think again – about her relentless search to find Gail's body, about her obsessive determination to bring Duane Harding to justice.

About Des, keeping her at arm's length with his polite hurt.

Leigh hears twigs breaking beneath her feet as she walks along the dirt track through the trees, ducking to negotiate her way through outstretched branches. Once on open ground, a dog overtakes them and bounds ahead. Its owner emerges from a copse of ivy-clad trees and smiles. People have never smiled at her so much as they have over the past five months, although most of them, if not all, are smiling at Kai and his sweet baby beauty. Having never paid attention to anyone else's baby, Leigh now enjoys it when people coo at hers. Even if he seems to have bypassed her genes altogether in favour of Des's side of the family, causing some people to look from the baby's face to hers and back again. Outside the Spar last week, one woman had assumed he wasn't hers. '*Aw,*' she said, '*someone on our street's got one of them too; they adopted it from an orphanage in Mongolia.*'

Kai has been smiling since he was six weeks' old; a definite smile, distinct from the grimace of a windy belly. Now, he smiles when he wakes up. He smiles when he looks at her face. He smiles for no reason whatsoever. Leigh is amazed. When she was pregnant, she'd imagined a girl built in her image: a scowling, screaming ball of fury with a topping of witchy hair; a little monster who kept her awake at night by slamming her fists into the sides of the crib. Beryl the Peril, here on earth to make her mother's life a misery.

But what she got instead was a baby with a happy and tranquil soul; a wise old man, born at the age of 100 years old and come to teach them all the wisdom of this world.

As a consequence of Kai's temperament, the feared takeover by family more equipped to nurture than herself has not happened. Leigh has surprised everyone, including herself, by being quite good at it. And the loss of the freedom she's always so badly craved also hasn't happened. With Kai, she is freer than ever. She carries him in a sling across her chest, so all she has to do is strap him to her and go. He is as light as a pin cushion, as easily transportable as her own body. '*Why don't you use the pram, Leigh, like a normal person?*' her ever-helpful mother had asked. '*You look all hippy dippy.*'

Leigh sees prams as instruments of women's oppression. This way, the *hippy dippy* way, means Leigh and Kai are inseparable, conjoined twins, attached at the chest.

She never wants to put him down.

And yet, not only had she handed him over to Des's mum this morning, there had been long periods of the day when she had forgotten about him, aware only of a persistent but vague ache in her chest where the amputation had occurred. When the time came, too quickly, she hadn't wanted to go back to work at all, but what choice did she have? Her maternity pay had run out after just seven weeks and she was barely surviving on statutory pay.

Leigh arranges thin strands of hair over Kai's cradle-capped scalp and slips her fingers over the shine on his forehead, over which Des's mum has rubbed baby oil. Leigh is so lucky to have Min, who fed her delicious steamed fish before she left. Having breathlessly survived the first day looking after her grandson, she was full of stories about what they'd done together.

Leigh gently grabs one of Kai's miniature feet and jiggles it around, luxuriates in her missing body part being restored to her.

Maybe she won't go back to work tomorrow, she thinks. Maybe she'll sign on the dole and Kai can become just another burden on the welfare state, as the song goes.

She walks to the lake, where fishermen sit in silence. She stays there for a while, looking out at the sinking red sun, greeting ducks walking about on the concrete path in the hope of being fed. Leigh lifts Kai out of his sling to share the wonders of the bird world with him, although she doubts he can see that far.

'Duck,' she says. 'Quack, quack.'

Over the past five months, strange noises have started to emit from Leigh's mouth, words that previously would have caused her to put her fingers down her throat. These noises are frequently repeated, and often feature questions which she then answers herself. *Is that a duck? Yes it is! Is that a goose? Yes it is!*

In the past five months, Leigh has had a personality transplant.

Kai laughs without teeth. He's not interested in wildfowl. His gaze is fixed on her face and he's smiling at her as if she's a wondrous thing, just as Des used to before she sabotaged their relationship with one last fling at the Burundi Club. She'd been upset about Duane Harding's acquittal, she'd been intent on wrecking her own happiness.

She doesn't know why Des can't forgive her.

'*How do I know you won't do it again?*' he'd said when he'd split with her. '*People always repeat the same patterns, it's human nature.*'

A tennis ball lands at her feet and she kicks it back to a spaniel, fixated on its toy in the same way her baby is fixated on her face. She lifts Kai back into his sling and exchanges a conspiratorial smile with the mother of a crying baby who passes by, pushing an instrument of women's oppression. Leigh glances into the pram and sees a tiny bawling face.

She smiles down at Kai.

'Crying is for babies,' she tells him.

Leigh is more than a little smug. She'd heard the tales of horror at the only mother and baby class she'd ever been to – babies who stayed up all night, babies who cried all the time, babies with the devil inside of them. Leigh has experienced none of this.

Leigh has been free.

At the white mansion house, the café is shut for the night and the detritus of a hot day is left behind in an overflowing bin. She gazes up at the purple horizon behind the building and sees a lone young bird singing boisterously on its chimney top. Kai makes a sound that's just as sweet and Leigh gets that soaring joy again.

9

The joy starts to slide away when she turns into Dunbabin Road, and disappears almost entirely when she arrives at the doorstep of her childhood home.

'Where have you been?' her mum says from the kitchen. 'The baby shouldn't be out at this time of night.'

Leigh hesitates in the porch, reluctant to go inside. Kai has slept all the way from the park and is still fast away now. Still, she'd underestimated the length of the walk and the sky had turned black on the way. She doesn't tell her mother she'd taken a detour on her way back from Min's, although the grass on her shoes gives her away, as does the whiff of dog muck she must have stood in. She hangs onto the door frame, slips her shoes off in the porch and steps inside.

With a sour face, her mum moves quickly across the room to the doorway, arms outstretched. Her expression changes when she sees the top of Kai's head poking out of the sling. She moves a fingernail gently across his bald head; a fingernail, Leigh notices, which is manicured and painted the colour of candyfloss. Leigh frees the baby from his straitjacket and hands him over. Kai immediately starts to cry, protesting at the rude awakening.

'I haven't seen you all day, have I?' her mum says, putting her nose to the baby's bottom and inhaling to check Leigh has changed his nappy. 'You haven't seen your Nana all day long, have you? Aw, did you miss me? Did you miss your best Nana?'

Her mum point blank refuses to look after Kai while Leigh goes to work, but Min looking after him isn't the solution she had in mind. The solution she had in mind was for Leigh to stop working and get married.

Leigh leaves her to it and goes into the living room, still wearing the sling. The lights are blazing, there's a stench of nail polish, and the ashtray is full. She wanders over to the mantelpiece to look at the photograph of James. Tomorrow would have been her brother's 25th birthday, an event which, for the past seven years, has gone unmentioned and uncelebrated. Emotions start to run through her as she stares at his smiling face and then the melancholy feeling becomes a residue, replaced by pleasure at the photograph of Kai, looking cute in his blue cap. She can hear her mum talking to him in the kitchen, communicating with her through the baby.

'Did she keep you out in the cold and the dark? Did she? Aw, keeping you out until this time of night. Are you cold, sweetheart?'

Leigh sends her eyes skywards. It's certainly not cold in here – the living room must be nudging a hundred degrees because her mum never opens the windows. She takes off the sling and sits awkwardly on the edge of the settee, wondering how she's going to last another night at her mother's.

She peels her socks from her sweaty feet and listens to her mum's happy voice. When she'd been pregnant, the only emotion her mum had expressed was shame. On and on she'd gone about Leigh not being married and what would people think and how it was unfair on *the child*, as she referred to the baby. *The child* would be bullied at school and it would have enough to contend with without that. '*What do you mean?*' Leigh had demanded to know. But she'd known what she meant.

But that had all changed when her mum clapped eyes on Kai for the first time. Her face had turned from stone to putty and Leigh swears she shed years in the matter of a few seconds. She is completely delighted with him. She proudly parades him up and down Dunbabin Road, past the houses of the neighbours whose judgement she feared, suddenly proud to be part of a multi-racial family. She has even read a book about China.

'He's beautiful! Beautiful!' her mum exclaims from the kitchen.

Kai is still grizzling with the inconvenience of being adored, but her mum goes on making contented murmurs, sounding happier than she's been in years. Her new, improved mood is a welcome change from depressed, which she has been ever since James went missing and Leigh's dad left for another woman. Up until recently, when she wasn't in a hospital ward, she spent her days on the settee and didn't even bother to change out of her grubby nightie. She never left the house, unless it was to try and kill herself in a public place. But over these last months, and particularly recently, the improvements have come thick and fast. The house is cleaner and tidier than it once was. She has stopped eating the slabs of toffee that made her teeth stick together. And she has even altered her appearance, painting her fingernails the hideous pink colour and making regular visits to the hairdresser for a perm and set.

'You've tired him out,' her mum says, coming into the room with the baby in one arm and a prepared bottle in the other. 'It's not all about you now, Leigh.'

She may have changed her appearance, but her tongue remains as acidic as ever.

Still, Leigh is grateful for the bottle, a little act of giving that doesn't go unappreciated. While she waits for the milk to cool, she pulls Kai onto her. He fixes her with his granddad gaze, staring right into her soul. Leigh turns away from her baby's intense gaze to the screen: a tribute programme about John Lennon, everyone still reeling six months after his death. When she's finished feeding him, she sits the baby up and gently pats his back. Her mum glances over to check progress and they both cheer when he burps.

After 'Imagine' plays over the final credits, the news comes on.

'Put him down now, Leigh,' her mum says. 'You'll ruin him, hanging onto him all the time like that. Put him upstairs in the crib.'

Leigh doesn't move. Kai goes to bed when she goes to bed. He gets up when she gets up. She attempts to quell down irritation but it locks her neck, making her muscles tight. She stares at the television screen as familiar faces from the station pass in front of the camera and finds herself thinking of Trey, one of the two friends who had been on the camping trip with James when he disappeared. The last time she heard, Trey was still living in Toxteth and she wonders how he's doing. Leigh hasn't kept in touch with James's friends – bearing witness to them moving on in life is too painful. Geoff, her brother's best friend, lives in Chester now and she hasn't been in contact with him in years, and the last time she'd seen Trey, he was angry and didn't trust her because she was a police officer. She wonders if he ever thinks of James. She scours the crowds on the television, wondering if Trey was one of the people throwing Molotov cocktails at the weekend.

When the endlessly replayed footage of the riots has ended, the newsreader re-appears to say the police fear more violence will erupt over the coming days.

'A friend of mine said the whole skyline was lit up on Saturday night,' her mum says.

'What friend?' Leigh says.

Her mum doesn't know anybody. The only friend she had was Brenda, who ran off with Leigh's dad.

'I do have friends, you know,' her mum says.

'First I've heard,' Leigh says, not taking her eyes from the television, where the footage is back on again, showing rising smoke from petrol bombs.

'Yeah, well, you never take an interest in what I do,' her mum says, puffing on a cigarette.

'You're blowing smoke on Kai's face!' Leigh complains, cradling the baby's head to stop him breathing in the fumes.

That's it, she thinks. That's definitely it. She's going back to her bedsit just as soon as the last Molotov cocktail has been thrown.

Later, after Kai's bath time, Leigh is lying on the top of the bed, a sweet-smelling baby on her belly, when she senses a change in the atmosphere. She goes on gazing at the ceiling, but she knows he's there: a big fold in the blanket, bulked up next to her.

Her brother, James.

In the summer of 1979, when Leigh and Des had still been a couple, they'd visited the Isle of Man and gone to the bay her brother disappeared from when he was on a camping trip with friends. She'd walked along the beach where James had gone for a walk on the night he was last seen. They know he went for this walk because he'd stopped on his way from the campsite to talk to a couple on the path, saying he was going to look at the stars. Leigh has long wondered whether he was going to meet a blonde girl who had apparently caught his eye; a Dutch girl called Anke, his friends said, who has since been untraceable.

The idea of the pilgrimage to the island she was born on was that Leigh would finally accept the likelihood that James had had an accident in the bay, and could then move on with her life. When she'd got home, on the advice of Min, she'd assembled a memory box she could open when she felt sad; a box containing the paltry selection of mementoes she had of her brother. This hadn't worked. Over the following two years, she found out that James could not be contained in one spot. As soon as she started to come to terms with his death, he began appearing, sidling up alongside her or following her around, dragging his feet. She knows he's a figment of her imagination, confined by her memory to the rooms of this house. In the year after James went missing, Leigh had gone to a bereavement group and learnt that it's common for people to see their dead loved ones, or to smell them, or hear them, or simply feel their presence. Although she'd never gone back to the group – a woman she'd once arrested had been among their number – she'd been grateful for the knowledge. It had helped alleviate some of her doubts about her sanity. And then Kai came along and James went away, having been, all along, no more than a thought conjured up by her fluid mind.

Now, she finds he hasn't gone away at all. He's been hanging out at Dunbabin Road all along.

Leigh doesn't turn her head – she can't anyway as Kai is lying on her chest – but she can see her brother's sandy bare feet reaching the end of the bedclothes, the ankle which bears a scar from falling out of a tree while being stoned as a teenager on Sefton Park. She lies still, pinned to the bed by a baby. Being a figment of her imagination, James doesn't speak, not even to mention his birthday tomorrow.

Out of the corner of her eye, she sees him make their secret sign: a warning their dad is on his way up the stairs, or their mum is on the warpath, or that boring Mr Higginbotham from next door is afoot. It's the sign they always made when they weren't in a position to speak but needed to communicate a warning: a thumbs-down, the digit pressed against the side of the nose, squeezing one nostril.

'Kai, meet your uncle James,' Leigh says madly, indicating to the left side of the bed.

The baby gurgles, as if she's said something funny.

'James,' she says, still not turning her head towards the apparition, 'this is your nephew, Kai.'

Her brother turns on his back and clasps his hands around his neck: lazing on a sunny afternoon. Leigh finds his response a little immature. There was always an age difference of four years between them, but that gap has widened since 1974 and there are 11 years now. She's 29, but he's still 18.

This isn't the brother who followed her around town when she was pregnant – the thunderous presence with dull eyes – this is the James of her memories: happy go lucky, impulsive, a little careless, with an unfortunate liking for Lynyrd Skynyrd. This James exists in an entirely different timeframe. To him, it's still the eve of his 18th birthday in 1974 and he's looking forward to a long summer before his first term at university; he's looking forward to going on a camping trip with his friends and then getting away from Dunbabin Road and living his long, happy life.

He goes on tapping his foot, hogging the bed, hitching up his denim cut-off shorts. He doesn't realise, this James, what has already been lost.

10

On a dark and bitter November Monday in 1979, they had searched the Hardings' flat, looking for a burial place. They had torn up the floorboards and dug over the back yard, desperate to find Gail's body.

Leigh had stood on the Toxteth street and watched as officers closed the road and unpacked the excavation equipment. It had taken them two days to get a warrant, based only on Duane Harding's zero concern about Gail's whereabouts.

She would have torn the place apart with her bare hands, if she could.

Leigh had waited in the back yard and watched as a police dog pulled towards Duane Harding's car in the back alleyway. She had stepped forward when the shiny black spaniel started to bark and the handler gave her more lead. But the dog had only turned away and sniffed in another direction.

The search had lasted all day and continued until darkness fell and they'd had to use flashlights to pack up. The floorboards were drilled, concrete was removed from the yard and the ground excavated underneath. The entire area was dusted for fingerprints, handprints, palm prints and footprints.

The search went on for the next day, and the next and the next, through rain, hail, sleet, and a burst of sunshine on the Thursday.

Leigh had gone every day.

At regular intervals, Duane Harding's friends and family had turned up to screech that Nikki was a fucking liar and Leigh was a fucking bitch, and Stan had frequently waved reporters away. They had requested a news blackout but a search operation on this scale had been hard to hide.

A number of items were retrieved, including a white Alice band, a used condom, and a bar of soap with a nail mark in it. All were sent for examination in the laboratory and all were found to have no direct connection to Gail's disappearance.

By the end of the week, the press had lost interest, the roads had re-opened, the officers had packed their dogs and pickaxes and shovels into vans and everyone, including Leigh, had gone home.

Her second day back at work and she's back, assigned by Des to take another look around before she travels up to Crosby to visit Gail's mum, Nikki.

The forensic fellas are all in the kitchen, having concentrated their overnight efforts around the area where the stabbing took place on Monday morning, and are quietly engaged in searching for clues. The kitchen blinds are open now, giving Leigh a clear view of the evidence so far collected in bags. She briefly casts her eyes on the spot where Duane Harding had been lying. The swirly floor is marked with black crusted blood. The saucer of uneaten cat food remains untouched, and there's no sign of the ginger tom.

She nods at the boss of the forensics team, a fella she'd had a one-night stand with yonks ago and who still has the hots for her.

'Found anything?' she asks him.

'Like what?' he asks, grinning at her.
'Like a key, or a bunch of keys.'
'Still on the search for his lock-up?'
'Certainly am.'

He's alluding to Leigh's dogged but unsuccessful search for a second location two years ago, during which she had examined maps and drawn a circle around the area between their only suspect's home and work.

'I'll let you know if we find anything that leads us to that little girl,' he says.

Leigh graces him with a smile – not everyone thinks she was wrong about Duane Harding.

She snaps on a pair of latex gloves and heads into the main bedroom, thinking that's the most likely place Duane Harding would hide something incriminating; in the drawers, perhaps, or under the bed. As she enters the room he shared with his wife, she notices the duffel bag straight away, lying open on the floor. Leigh peers inside but it's empty. Her eyes move past the unmade bed to the table on the left. Nothing there but a collapsed pile of spare change and the alarm clock that had gone off on Monday, giving them all a start.

She goes over to a man's dressing gown hanging on the back of the door and puts her hands in the pockets. She opens the wardrobe – organised into a his and hers sides – and peers at Clara's dresses on hangers and the jumble of sparkly shoes and sandals at the base. On the other side are Duane's shirts and trousers. She goes through all the pockets, fixated now on searching for a key.

Before Duane Harding's arrest, they had put him under surveillance, watching him for days and nights in the hope he'd lead them to where he put Gail's body. They'd tried concentrating their enquiries elsewhere, in the hope he'd think the heat was off him and get careless. If she hadn't been on maternity leave, Leigh would have continued to keep tabs on him after he was acquitted.

But, as it was, he'd had the past five months to get lazy and leave a vital clue behind.

Leigh glances out of the window, checking all is calm outside. The Bishop of Liverpool has made an appeal for peace, as have community leaders, but at least 60 people are making court appearances today and the local residents have been further upset by police raids on their homes. She marches across to the dressing table and starts rifling through the drawers. In the top drawer – men's socks; in the middle drawer – jumpers, and in the bottom, the dad cardigan and tan slacks Duane Harding wore to court. She feels in the pockets and under the clothes and then looks down the sides of the dressing table.

Nothing there, either.

Leigh crosses the landing and takes a quick glance in the bathroom, where the original search had been concentrated. Duane Harding had told them that Gail had had a bath that night and then gone to bed. The bath had been scrubbed clean when CID arrived the next morning and follow-up forensics showed no signs of a struggle or blood. Leigh fixes her eyes on the bathtub. He'd used a hell of a lot of bleach for a routine clean. She's pretty sure Duane Harding harmed Gail in here. Then he messed up her sheets to make it look like she'd slept in her bed, wrapped her in a never-recovered garment cover, and carried her out to the boot of his car. He'd left the back door open to make it look as if the little girl had left of her own accord.

And then he'd gone to bed and slept like a baby.

Leigh opens the door into the room that once belonged to a nine-year-old girl with her whole life ahead of her. Gail's room has been cleared out – there are marks on the floor where bed wheels used to be, the blue carpet lighter in colour where her wardrobe once sat. There is nothing of Gail in here, or, for that matter, anywhere in this flat – no photographs, no drawings she did at school, none of the books she enjoyed reading – her last day had been spent at Toxteth Library with her mum. Duane Harding hadn't kept one single memento of the stepdaughter he claimed to be fond of (he always stopped short of 'loved').

The mood in the Hardings' living room is one of aspiration, an inexpensive opulence achieved through loud flowery wallpaper, and the careful placement of mock silk cushions. Clara's touch is everywhere – the décor has changed since Nikki's time, when it was a jumble of mismatching fabrics and paint colours. The curtains now have gold sashes and the glass coffee table has furniture coasters under its legs to protect the parquet floor. Although the fire is a mess of grey coals, a table lamp with a dark red shade has been left on, making the room look cosy.

Its homely feel makes Leigh feel sick.

She puts her hands on the top of the settee, inhaling the aroma of a take-out bacon buttie wafting in from the kitchen. And then she goes to the book shelf and opens a wallet of photographs which have been developed at Boots. All the snapshots are of Duane and Clara, standing together beside a turquoise swimming pool, palm trees surrounding it. He's wearing a tight pair of striped trunks, his waistline bursting over the top, the folds of skin glistening in oil; she's in a slashed-neck swimsuit in orange. Leigh feels sickened he'd taken a holiday, sickened that he'd been able to enjoy life since being released from custody. '*Where is she?*' she hisses at his image. '*Where is she, you fucker?*'

Leigh wishes she was in charge of this investigation. If it was down to her, she'd have the floorboards ripped up and the walls torn apart again. ('*I can't put a sergeant in charge of a DI, can I?*' Stan had hissed when he'd materialised by her side this morning, '*but you're running it, you're running him. And his bunch of girlies.*')

Stan obviously doesn't know Des very well if he thinks that's what's going to happen.

Leigh looks towards the back door: Duane Harding's exit point for carrying Gail's body out of the house. His footprint, size 8, faint, but there, was found just outside. The defence said that proved nothing – a man has every right to step into his yard when he feels like it. She turns back and examines the spines of the few books on the shelf – glossy books on war that look unread. She's in the process of taking them out one by one and shaking them when she hears one of the forensic fellas say, '*Guv*,' and Des appears at the door.

'I've been through the bedroom, there's no keys anywhere,' she tells him.

'Sorry? Keys?'

'To lock-ups he might have taken Gail to.'

'If you don't mind me saying so, you are meant to be looking for evidence which helps us solve Duane Harding's murder,' Des says. 'Did you find any of that, by any chance?'

'There's an overnight bag on the bedroom floor, nothing in it,' she says, indicating to the bedroom with her eyes. 'It looks like a woman's bag. She might have been in the process of leaving him.'

'We'll take the bag as evidence,' Des says, glancing out of the window to a view of grey dust. 'Although, of course, she might have been getting ready to de-camp to a safer part of the city.'

Leigh nods, unconvinced, even though she'd been forced to do the same and flee to Dunbabin Road. For the first time in weeks, Kai had been awake during the night and couldn't be comforted; a turn of events for which she blames her mother.

'Any news on when we can speak to Clara Harding?'

Des shakes his head.

'Nothing much from the pathologist that's new either,' he says. 'The stab wounds were random, rather than aimed at a particular part of his anatomy, so no expert. Our perp's unlikely to be a hitman.'

'Any keys in the pyjamas Duane Harding was wearing when he was murdered?' asks Leigh, who has a one-track mind.

Des says *'No'* silently as he looks around him.

'Callum's gone to see Nikki Harding's brother, Warren,' he says.

This mention of a brother pulls her in a different direction. But Des has obviously forgotten, because he doesn't mention it's James's birthday today.

'The other two are in Toxteth,' he says, referring to the Godfather squad fellas, 'visiting the young woman who was robbed by the druggie.'

Des had persuaded them with flattery, saying he needed men who weren't afraid of fronting up hostility.

'And Kevin?'

'Um, I'm not entirely sure. He did seem to be making a lot of notes when I left the station.'

A brief smile; a brief warming?

'I'm going up to Crosby to talk to Nikki now,' Leigh says, taking advantage. 'Want to come?'

'Oh,' Des says. 'I thought, if you like, I'll cover for you? I can do the interview. I'll drop you at mum's and you can spend some time with Kai.'

Leigh gives him a hostile stare.

'I tell you what,' she says, 'why don't you go to your mum's and spend time with Kai and *I'll* do the interview?'

Des doesn't answer, which further infuriates her. Her search over for now, she exits the flat through the front door, determined to carry on with the investigation. With every step she takes, she feels like a bad parent, and she hopes Des does too.

11

Still in a huff, and with her old Mini out of action, Leigh gets the train to Crosby and the caravan park near the beach where Nikki Harding now lives. She walks the quarter of a mile or so through the drizzle towards the coast, and then stands, feet descending into sand, face pressed against the window when Gail's mum doesn't answer the door.

Leigh can see a shadow, moving around inside.

'Do one!' Nikki shouts, 'I've got nothing to say to you.'

'It's me,' Leigh says, knocking on the glass, trying to avoid the cobwebs where spiders are madly spinning.

The shadow moves closer to the window – Nikki double checking that Leigh's not a reporter, come to bother her about her former husband's murder.

'Aw, sorry, Leigh,' Nikki says as she opens the rusty door. 'I had all sorts knocking yesterday.'

'There's no news about Gail,' Leigh says, which is what she always says first, in case Nikki's hopes are heightened by her arrival.

'Aw, it's nice to see you, anyway.'

'You've heard?'

Nikki nods, and then gives Leigh a hug.

'Aw, how's the baby?' she asks.

Nikki is a person who meets you more than half way. Everyone, from the court ushers at St George's Hall to her loyal band of friends from schooldays, described her as lovely, inside and out; a former Miss Liverpool with square shoulders, a smattering of freckles across her nose, a sunny smile of milk teeth, and an air of vulnerability about her. Leigh finds it difficult to believe anyone was persuaded by Duane Harding that Nikki was involved in Gail's disappearance, but persuade them he did: she had a shocking amount of abuse from people who didn't know her, including a steady supply of poison pen letters accusing her of being, at best, a bad mother and, at worst, the murderer of her own child.

The caravan rocks as Leigh mounts the steps and turns left into what could be described as the living room – a table and two bench seats either side that she has to squeeze herself into. Next to a photograph of Gail, her long wavy hair the colour of a sunflower, there's a collection of faded happy mottos dotted around on the walls. '*Do what makes you happy.*' '*Yes you can!*' '*Weak wills wilt*' – one for Leigh. In the corner of the bench is Gail's beloved yellow dog, its head bowed due to a lack of stuffing and its fur matted through years of love. Next to it are some of the books Gail loved – *Frog and Toad are Friends*, *The Runaway Rabbit*, and a school text book, covered in the florid wallpaper Leigh remembers from the Toxteth flat when Nikki lived there.

Leigh likes the caravan. It's a place of sanctuary, like her own bedsit, but with a view of the sea, and today, a big cloudy sky which threatens rain. She understands why Nikki feels happier here, away from prying eyes, away from daily reminders of what might have happened to her daughter.

'You've heard?' Leigh says again as Nikki busies herself putting a kettle on the boil to make tea. 'He was murdered, stabbed, at home, in his kitchen.'

She's trying to find a way in without being insensitive. But Nikki is still talking about babies, sharing a heartbreaking reminiscence of how Gail used to sleep face down and she had to get up numerous times in the night to roll her onto her back. Leigh watches her smiling face, feeling treacherous for coming here to ask questions.

'Listen, Nikki,' she says. 'We have to look into it like we do everything else. We're talking to everyone.'

'Aw, I know,' Nikki says, carrying the mugs to the table and sitting down opposite. 'It's not your fault.'

'I have to ask you about it, so we'll get that bit over with and then we can have a chat.'

She can't seem to bring herself to ask if Nikki has an alibi for the early hours of Monday morning. 'Do you know of anyone who'd want to harm Duane?' she asks instead.

Nikki gives a big harrumph.

'Most of Liverpool?' she says.

'What about her real dad's family?'

'They never had anything to do with Gail.'

'Listen, Nikki,' Leigh continues. 'I feel bad for asking, but our detectives have gone to talk to Warren. Has he had any contact with Duane Harding since he was acquitted?'

Nikki's face reddens. She looks away. She shakes her head. And then she bursts into tears.

'I just wanted to know, that's all I wanted,' she says tearfully. 'Do you think Duane told anyone where she is? Someone else?'

'I don't know,' Leigh says, watching Nikki's face closely. 'I'm working on it.'

'She's here now,' Nikki says, looking up beside her. 'I keep seeing Gail next to me. And I keep hearing her voice, saying mum, like it's passing through my head.'

Leigh sits forwards, both hands around the hot mug of tea. She understands completely the tendency of the living to imagine the dead are with them – it happened to her only last night. For a moment, she pictures imaginary James squeezing in beside her, clutching *Free Bird* by Lynyrd Skynyrd and making his secret sign. She shakes her head and the thought is gone – there's only room for Gail's ghost in the confined space of the caravan.

'I'll never find her now,' Nikki says, smile gone, tears pumping out.

'I won't stop looking for her,' Leigh says. 'I promise you. I'll never stop.'

Nikki squeezes out of the bench seat, mug in hand, and pours the tea away in the sink. She reaches across, takes Leigh's mug from the table and does the same. And then she stretches up to a cupboard above her head and retrieves a full bottle of vodka. She plonks the bottle on the table, along with the two empty mugs. She always wants to go over it all again, and that's all right with Leigh.

Nikki hadn't felt like going out on the night of the 28 September 1979. She'd got out of the habit since she'd married Duane – he got so jealous, it wasn't worth the hassle. But it had been the birthday of one of her oldest mates and she hadn't wanted to hurt her feelings by saying no. They'd gone to the She Club on Victoria Street, a place that attracted an older crowd and had a reputation as a pick up joint. Nikki had planned on going home early, but not many had turned up for the birthday celebrations, so she stayed.

It was nearly three o'clock in the morning when she finally got home, worse for wear. She threw her shoes off and fell into bed in her nightclub gear, Duane asleep by her side. He was definitely asleep, because she remembers he was snoring. She woke up at dawn, thirsty and in need of a wee, and peeked into her daughter's bedroom, which was just across from the toilet. Gail's bed was empty. Nikki started calling her daughter's name, thinking she must have got up and gone downstairs. But she wasn't too worried at that point, so she went ahead and had a wee and drank some water, and then went to find Gail.

That's when she saw things she hadn't noticed last night. The light was on in the living room and the back door, usually locked, was ajar. There was gravel on the carpet just inside. Nikki went into the back yard to see if Gail was there but she wasn't. The yard door was shut, but unlocked. Duane's car was parked where it always was, in the back alleyway.

The first thing she did was check all the other rooms in the house. Then she went into their bedroom to shake Duane. He complained about getting woken up early, and then sat up in the bed and said to stop making a fuss, that Gail would be somewhere. As far as he was concerned, he'd run Gail a bath last night and then she'd gone to bed – her bedsheets were messy, as if she'd slept in them. The bathroom was spotless, but then it always was, Duane was a clean freak and always scrubbed the bath after anyone had used it.

Panic mounting, she ran around the neighbours' houses, knocking everyone up. When she discovered no one had seen Gail, she ran back to tell Duane, who was boiling a kettle for coffee and lighting his first cigarette of the day. She said she was going to call the police but Duane told her not to. He said that Gail would turn up in a minute and Nikki was overreacting, like she always did.

'How are you going to explain going out last night and leaving her?' he asked. 'They'll get the kiddies social onto us and everything. What are you going to say?'

'What do you mean?' Nikki said, the fear of God in her.

'If they find her, they'll say it's you.'

'What do you mean, if they find her?'

Duane had shrugged it off, saying he didn't mean it like that.

Back in the caravan in 1981, Nikki continues the story Leigh has heard many times before.

Duane changed his tune then, said Gail must have wandered off and he'd go out looking for her in the car. He said to hold off calling the bizzies until he was back. Nikki said she'd go with him, but he told her to stay local while he went further afield. Some of the neighbours were out on the street by that stage – it was around 7 a.m. on the Sunday morning – and they were brilliant, searching the neighbourhood and looking in their outhouses. They persuaded Nikki to call the bizzies, which she did, but, even then, she feared Duane would get in a mood about it because he'd told her not to.

Her husband never came home until teatime. He said he'd had to go into work because of an emergency.

'If only I'd never gone out,' Nikki says now. 'I knew, I *knew*, but I believed him when he said Gail would be fine with him. He even got annoyed with me over it, said he couldn't believe I didn't trust him.'

Nikki's only crime was to be taken in by a master manipulator, Leigh thinks. That was the judge's crime, too, and the crime of Duane Harding's supporters, his new wife Clara, and some of Leigh's colleagues in the station, who believed she'd got the wrong man.

'I knew something bad would happen before it happened. I had a bad feeling all night. But I still stayed out.'

Rain starts to splatter against the windows as Nikki's head slumps against her chest, causing her long hair to dip into the mug of vodka. And then she pulls her chin out of her chest to look at Leigh.

'I didn't want anyone to harm Duane,' she says, 'I just wanted him to tell me where he'd put my Gail.'

Leigh nods thoughtfully, the fact it's James's birthday today on the tip of her tongue. Her and Nikki have always got on; they had bonded over missing loved ones at a time when Leigh had few people to talk to about James. Her job, her pregnancy, her life in general (but mostly her job) had meant she'd lost touch with most of her old friends. As a result Leigh had confided in Nikki, a little too much: about her difficulties in her relationship with her mum, about James, about the untraceable Dutch girl Anke, about how she'd sabotaged her relationship with Des by sleeping with a scumbag without a name after a night out in a Toxteth drinking den.

In return, Leigh had acted as a beacon of hope for Nikki, clutching at straws to bring her stories of missing children who had turned up alive. She'd hidden bad news too – a girl's body had been found in woodland in Wales only last year, another child's body had been recovered from a burning house; more girls and women murdered than should be possible without an international outcry.

Leigh feels the words building up inside her and has a brief argument with herself – she's tired, she hasn't eaten, she's driving, she's on duty – and then thinks, *Fuck it*, and holds out her mug.

'It's my brother's birthday,' she says, an announcement she's been holding inside all day. 'He would have been 25.'

Leigh begins to talk, and by the time she's finished, the sky is dark, rain is pounding on the roof, and water is streaming down the windows. Recognising her first chance to let her hair down since Kai was born, she holds out her mug for more vodka and Nikki pours. They are getting drunk now, and won't stop until they are.

12

Nikki is asleep, her head slumped on a table scattered with crumpled tissues, as Leigh finds the door, misses the steps and lands hard on the sandy grass in the rain. She's intent on getting back to Liverpool but not sure how to go about it. In the fading light, and the incompetence that drunkenness brings, she's become clueless about how to catch a train or bus. Maybe she can sleep in Nikki's caravan, she thinks – but what about the baby?

Leigh's feet descend into the dunes as she makes her way clumsily towards the lights of the houses along the promenade. She walks along the beach for a short stretch, crunching on razor clams, disturbing rooks feasting on washed-up sea creatures. The tide has gone out and even though it's a long way to the sea, she can hear the rumble of small waves. Leigh gazes at a freighter sailing at a snail's pace towards the cranes of the docks and then she looks across to the caravan and thinks again about the letters Nikki got, some of them calling her heartless for smiling on her way into court.

Straight away, Duane Harding had tried to manipulate the situation so Nikki would get the blame. When he came under suspicion, he'd told Leigh she was looking in the wrong direction, that she should be looking at Gail's mother, because he certainly was. He went on and on about time discrepancies, saying his wife came back earlier than she actually did. But Nikki's alibi held up – she was with her friends all night.

And that was only the beginning. Over the course of the investigation, he planted ideas he hoped would lead everyone to believe that Nikki was a certain kind of person: a mother who'd initially had problems bonding with her daughter; a mother who went out on the lash and who copped off with other fellas. Nikki was a difficult woman to cope with, he'd said, with a sad little smile.

'I tried, I really did.'

Leigh hadn't had her bollocks placard with her at the time.

If it had been anyone other than Nikki, lovely, kind Nikki, who won't clean her windows in case spiders are disturbed, Leigh would have seen his point: you have no memory of getting in at night and when you wake up, your child is missing. But this was Nikki, and Leigh didn't see his point.

She turns her back on the beach and heads in the direction of the high street. Leigh has never doubted Nikki's version of events, all through the mud-slinging and the accusations and the anger. And she still doesn't. But this afternoon, she'd seen her hesitate, and then redden, at the mention of her brother, Warren. As Leigh weaves her way towards the lights of the town, she wonders why Nikki is lying to her.

Inside the telephone box she finds on autopilot, she calls Des, finding she can coordinate her fingertips magnificently, although it takes a few goes to get through, including wasting 2p on a wrong number.

'Leigh!' Min says breathlessly when she answers. 'Oh, oh! We've been so worried! Where are you?'

'I'm in Crosby,' Leigh says, trying to sound sober. 'I'm going to be late.'

'We've been so worried!' Min repeats. 'It's dark outside! You didn't phone!'

'There wasn't a phone …' Leigh starts but it seems too complicated to explain. 'Sorry,' she says instead, but Min has gone and Des comes on the line.

'I'm going to be late,' Leigh repeats, slurring slightly.

'You're already late, actually,' Des says, although not unkindly.

'I've been talking to Nikki, I've been with Nikki.'

'Yes, I can hear,' Des says, no doubt wanting to hide from his mum that his ex-girlfriend has abandoned her baby to get lathered – in case Min hadn't already noticed.

'I'll be back soon,' she says, 'half an hour.'

'How are you going to get back?' Des says as the pips go.

'Walk, I'll walk,' Leigh shouts into the earphone. 'I'll be half an hour, tops.'

She doesn't intend to hang up, but her magnificent coordination fails her. She misses the coin slot, and the phone goes dead.

Oh well, Leigh thinks. Never mind.

In reality, the journey by foot from Crosby to Liverpool is much longer than half an hour. She has been walking for that long already and has only just reached the roundabout leading to the main road into the city. Unsteady on her feet, she tramps along the dark roadside, her way lit only by a crescent moon that sporadically disappears between clouds. A solitary car drives past at speed in the opposite direction, its windscreen wipers being switched on as the rain starts again. But apart from that, there are few vehicles at this time of night, just an empty dual carriageway she may well be walking down forever.

It crosses Leigh's mind that her dad's new fancy house isn't far from here. The thought makes her pick her pace up. Alan, as she's come to call him, hasn't been in contact since they had a massive fallout over her being pregnant with a Chinese man's baby. Leigh is so angry with him she doesn't care if she never sees him again, although she misses her half-brother Garry. She'd sent him a card and present for his fifth birthday but hadn't received the usual round-robin thank you note back.

The rain gets harder. Her shoes are rubbing against the sides of her feet and she needs a wee. Leigh's earlier pleasure in being drunk gives way to a feeling of defeat. She considers just lying down in a hedge and giving up. But then the rain eases and makes way for another sound – the hiss of tyres on the road, the purr of an engine. There's a flash of light and the headlamps of Des's Allegro slow behind her and come to a stop.

Des leans across and pushes the passenger door open so hard it clangs on the pavement. Leigh falls into the passenger seat with a thump and hears a loud scrape as she yanks the door out of the curb. She careers over to one side, her head out of the car, and is pulled back by a strong grip on her arm. She swivels her head to smile at Des. He is a sight for sore eyes, in his toothpaste-bright white t-shirt which contrasts with his hair. He doesn't look at her or speak. He sets off straight away, his mouth set in a line, displaying that familiar quiet, simmering anger that is worse than shouting. Leigh, on the other hand, is all talk, deciding it's a good time to tell him again about her hopes that forensics will discover a key in Duane Harding's flat.

'He could have left the key to the look-up, I mean lock-up,' she says, a small titter acknowledging that the wrong word came out of her mouth.

Des will be interested in this, she knows, so she talks drunkenly, and at length, about where this lock-up could be. Her voice is loud, her jacket is fluted behind her and her feet are pressed awkwardly against one of Kai's crib mattresses on the floor. As she spouts forth, she vaguely notices that her legs are cramped. The passenger seat has been moved and is no longer in the right position for her long legs.

'I do think it's probably best if we speak about it in the morning,' Des says, slowing to light a cigarette.

'I want to talk about it now!' Leigh complains, and realises she's forgotten to remind him it's James's birthday today – she hasn't even given him her excuse for getting drunk! But she doesn't say this because she thinks she may have already told him. Confused, she stares at the windscreen wipers, which seem to be moving in the opposite way to their usual direction of travel.

Leigh turns to look at Des again, to gauge his reaction. But she soon forgets about that and drinks him in, gazing at him like he's a photograph. She still fancies him like mad. And she is nothing but a fuck it drunk. So, she puts her hand on his thigh. Des firmly removes it. She puts it back again and squeezes, enjoying the feel of his leg muscles. He slaps her hand lightly and says nothing.

'Spoilsport,' Leigh says. 'You're no fun. You used to be fun.'

'Shall we just get back?' Des says. 'You can stay at your bedsit, Kai can stay with me tonight.'

Leigh hiccups in reply.

'Tonight!' she declares. 'Tonight, we would have been celebrating James's 25th birthday!'

'Sorry?'

'I told you!' she says. 'He would have been 25 today.'

Des swings his head towards her, suddenly listening. But Leigh has allowed her eyes to close for a few moments and that's all it takes for her to lay her head on his shoulder and be out for the count.

13

Her third day back at work, and Leigh sleeps through the alarm.

It takes her a few seconds to prise open her eyelids, which seem to have been glued together during the night. And then it takes her another few seconds to realise that she's in her bedsit on Canning Street. A glance at the bedside clock tells her it's after eight o'clock. Shit. She's meant to be dropping Kai off at Min's right now. And where is the baby? Leigh staggers out of bed and heads for the crib.

A few more seconds of sheer terror.

And then she remembers she stayed here alone last night after getting drunk in Nikki's caravan. Her terror turns to mortification. Only three days in and her routine is falling apart; only three days in, and she's in danger of proving everyone right.

Leigh springs into mechanical action. She puts her hands in front of her to guide her as she heads out of the bedsit and down the flight of stairs to the shared bathroom. She knocks her shoulder against the door when she finds it locked and lurches back to her bedsit.

Any pleasure she felt from being drunk yesterday has evaporated; any relief she might have felt from being back at her bedsit has been replaced by guilt. The room is a mess, the solitary table cluttered with bottles, nappies, Kai's Great Uncle Bulgaria cuddly toy, an expired light bulb, a biscuit tin with money for the rent inside, and a rotting tangerine. Her conscience groans with the load, her previous joy buried under a mound of placards, all of them protesting about her. *'Say no to bad mothers! Bad mothers? No!'*

Leigh's head starts to pound as she opens the chest of drawers in search of clean knickers. She eyes the telephone she's had installed since Kai came along, wondering whether to call Min and apologise. There are so many things for her to feel bad about, she doesn't know where to start. Apart from abandoning her baby last night, she has the uncanny impression that she missed James's birthday night out; as if he'd gone for a few drinks with his mates Geoff and Trey in Casey's Bar and she hadn't shown up. In reality, she'd intended to light a candle, look at the stars, do something small but significant that would mark the event. She glances at the giant telescope in the corner. It's one of the only mementoes she has of her brother's existence, rescued by Leigh when her mum cleared the house of everything belonging to James soon – too soon – after he disappeared. She doesn't have time for more than a glance – she's going to be very late for work – so she puts her thumb on her nose and taps, making their secret sign. As if that's enough, as if that will do for the brother she forgot about because she was too busy getting hammered and making a pass at her ex-boyfriend.

Leigh cringes as she remembers her failed attempts to pull Des down onto the mattress last night.

There's only one pair of knickers in the drawer and she doesn't know where the others might have got to. Buried under the pile of baby clothes in the corner, perhaps. She goes to the drying rack to collect a clean body suit for Kai. The only one on there has a hard front crusted with milk. Unable to find a clean top to put on, she grabs another of the shirts Des left behind. As she pulls it over her head, she notices the pint of milk she'd put on the windowsill before she'd left at the weekend. It's probably curdled by now.

Beset by poor coordination, Leigh bangs her hand against the door frame as she makes her way into the kitchen. She opens the bottom cabinet where the mice family live and grabs a can of Tizer. The warm fizzy drink relieves her thirst, but the effect is ruined when she finds a half-empty packet of Toffos on the side and crams four into her mouth in quick succession.

Feeling the opposite of refreshed, Leigh leaves her bedsit for Chinatown, passing by her clapped out car which has gone unfixed for months. She's longing for Kai's touch and intent on seeing him before she goes to work, even if it makes her later than she already is. The sunlight hurts her eyes as she takes big strides past the Anglican Cathedral. By the Yuet Ben restaurant, her feet get caught on melting tarmac. When she looks down, she finds it's not the liquefying road that's tripped her up – a discarded placard has snapped beneath her feet, its cardboard turned brittle in the sun. Even though the marker pen has faded and the placard is splattered with the remnants of a Chinese takeaway, she can still read the writing, its message is loud and clear: kill the fascist pigs.

Leigh finds Min on the street outside her flat, standing in the shade, jiggling Kai up and down. They are surrounded by birds – Des's mum is feeding brown bananas to the pigeons with her free hand.

'Here she is!' Min says when she sees Leigh, her expression one of pure delight – who knows what Des told her about where Leigh had been. 'Here's Mummy!'

Min has a beaming smile, like her son's; like Kai's, in fact, although his is gummy and minus the two sets of gleaming teeth. The baby shrieks with excitement and rolls to the side with his hand extended, reaching out to her. Desperate to hold him, Leigh takes him from Min's arms and bends to kiss her on the cheek, immediately turning away so she can't smell her breath – she'd left her bedsit without brushing her teeth.

'Mummy has been working all night at her job as a police officer, a very important job!' Min tells the baby. 'She protects us from bad men!'

Min is sweetly excited that Leigh is a detective, so it was a good lie Des had told her.

'Bananas for the pigeons,' Min says, by way of explanation, although none is needed.

'Quack, quack,' Leigh says, getting her birds mixed up.

'And soup for you,' Min says, handing over a plastic bag.

'Oh,' Leigh says, as the heat from the carton bangs against her thigh and scorches through her jeans, 'thanks.'

'Oh!' Min says, misreading her hungover face. 'Have I done the wrong thing?'

'No! It's great!'

Min's brow furrows as she has a new worrying thought.

'The soup's hot, very hot. It might burn the baby. Hold it away from you when you carry it. And let it cool down or it will burn your tongue. Oh, I shouldn't have made soup, I'm a silly billy to make soup in hot weather.'

'It's great,' Leigh says again. 'Don't worry, Min.'

Leigh continues to reassure Des's mum that the soup is a really good idea. They walk together to the end of an eerily quiet Nelson Street, Min carrying the soup, Leigh smothering Kai with kisses; sorry kisses, I'll make it up to you kisses, I'll soon have two weeks' leave kisses.

She swears the baby rears his head back at the stench of her breath.

'Your mum phoned last night, worried about where you were,' Min says when they are about to part. Leigh groans inwardly. She forgot her baby, she forgot her brother and, oh my Lord, she forgot her mother.

'I told her you were working at your very important job.'

At the end of the road, Min waits patiently while Leigh puts her hand on the baby's back, luxuriating in the touch. She reluctantly hands him back, all three of them speaking rapidly at the same time, Leigh thanking Min profusely, Kai babbling gobbledegook, and Min wanting to know when she's going to sleep after working all night. Because she'll be tired, and if she gets too tired, she won't be able to do her job, and if she can't do her job, she'll have no money to look after the baby ... and so on until perpetuity.

The woman is a Godsend, Leigh thinks as she waves goodbye. If she'd accepted Des's embarrassing proposal, if the engagement ring hadn't been returned to the catalogue, Min would be her mother-in-law by now. And Des would be related to her own mum, the kind of mother-in-law who is the butt of comedians' jokes.

It's a wonder he asked her to marry him in the first place.

Leigh's thoughts stay on Des as she quickly walks to work. She hadn't thought their separation would last but, here they are, months later, and he's still keeping away from her and being careful not to stand too close.

'Why can't he just get over it?' she'd asked her friend Alice, shortly after the break-up. To which Alice, known for her bluntness, had replied: 'You turn down his marriage proposal, you refuse to move in with him, even though he's prepared to go against his family's wishes to do it, and then you sleep with someone else. He is probably going to be upset.'

'I'm still not seeing it,' Leigh had said.

14

'I've been held up with other things,' Leigh says, by way of an explanation she doesn't have to make to trainee Kevin, the sole detective in a meeting room that stinks of coffee and nicotine. 'What did I miss?'

Kevin half stands, half sits, half stands again, unsure of rank etiquette and what he's supposed to be doing in the presence of a DS no one takes any notice of.

'I'm compiling information on the knife our perp might have used,' the lad says, pink-faced with pride.

'Good for you.'

'It's probably a boning knife, soft grip soft handle, steel blade, it could have come from any catering supply company, though. It's common. I'm going to start on the shoe tread next.'

Kevin races through the rest of it, telling her that Callum hadn't been able to locate Nikki's brother, Warren, but the Godfather squad fellas had pulled in the druggie who'd robbed the flat of the young mother. This hadn't been too difficult because said druggie had been hanging around the streets, out of her mind on the brown stuff she'd bought with the stolen money.

He saves the headline for last.

Clara Harding has been discharged from hospital, and they're bringing her in for interview right now.

Leigh leaves Min's scorching soup in the meeting room and finds Des hanging about in the corridor outside a downstairs custody room, no doubt waiting for Clara.

'Kai was fine,' he says, his eyes narrowing as he glances down at the shirt she's wearing, the second one of his she's had on in three days. 'My mum was up with him during the night a few times though.'

'Your mum was?' Leigh says, noticing his well-rested face and immaculate appearance.

Des is wearing a black suit in temperatures which will hit 90 by midday. It's a look designed to give him the gravitas he thinks he needs as a detective whose face doesn't fit. There's a tiny white spec on the collar of his shirt, most likely made by baby sick.

'My mum did rather insist,' he says, a little sheepishly.

He won't say anything about Leigh missing the briefing. Although having the irresponsible mother of your son on the murder squad isn't ideal, he knows she isn't a slacker.

'I'm sorry I forgot it was James's birthday yesterday,' he says.

'I forgot to mark it,' she says, getting unwanted memories of trying to kiss Des last night. 'I meant to do something, I'm not sure what, but that didn't happen.'

Des pulls a face, indicating he understands why.

'Were you all right at the bedsit last night?' he asks. 'No trouble?'

He's more concerned than she is that everyone knows a copper lives on Canning Street.

'You look tired,' he adds, before she's had a chance to answer. 'You can go home to your mum's, if you like, be with Kai.'

'I heard about Clara, from Kevin,' Leigh says, shaking her head, wondering why he keeps making her feel like a bad mother for coming to work.

'Callum has gone with uniforms to escort her in,' Des says. 'We thought the interview was best done at the station under caution. We're not arresting her. The evidence doesn't warrant it – the front door was open, she had injuries consistent with an intruder assault, and there's the graffiti on the living room wall.'

Leigh wonders who is included in the 'we' he is referring to. Isn't she on the murder squad too?

'I'm in on the interview?' she asks, but it comes out as a statement, not a question. She's hoping Clara will tell them what she knows about Gail now that Duane is gone.

Des nods in a resigned manner.

'The physical evidence is in from the Hardings' flat,' he says, 'but nothing much more came of the talk with Duane Harding's family. Although his dad in particular had a lot to say about an innocent man being accused of a terrible crime and how that was to blame. He even suggested our perp might be you.'

'I was at my mother's that night and morning,' Leigh says, enjoying being teased but also thinking of her mother. Knowing her, she wouldn't back up her alibi.

'He's rather bitter and, of course, grieving, but he did say something interesting.'

'Really? What's that?'

'He said Duane had promised new evidence of his innocence.'

'Did he say what it was?'

'No, he said he wanted to keep it a secret until it was sorted, but it hints at motive, if someone wanted to stop that coming out.'

'What a load of rubbish,' Leigh says. 'Duane Harding was his son. He'd say any old bollocks.'

'Gail's grandparents were more helpful, but they didn't shed any light on our perp. What did Nikki Harding say yesterday?'

'Nothing much. I'll write the report up this morning but there's not much to write. She was shook up, upset …'

Leigh is about to make an excuse for them both getting lathered but her head is pounding and she hasn't got the energy.

'We haven't spoken to her brother, Warren, yet,' Des says.

'I know, Kevin said,' Leigh says, thinking about Nikki not telling her the truth yesterday. 'But there's absolutely no way Warren would have killed Duane Harding without finding out where Gail is.'

'He's got the physical strength. He fits the description. It could be he lost his temper when Duane wouldn't tell him where Gail's body was. Maybe it got out of hand. He's got a drink problem, and a motive.'

Nikki's brother Warren is rough and ready, a labourer on a building site, when he's sober enough. He's a bit of a handful, but Leigh has a soft spot for him. He'd been vociferous in blaming Duane for his niece's disappearance, and she'd persuaded him to stay away from the bottle long enough to go on television to make an appeal.

'He wouldn't have brought his own knife, in that case, wouldn't he?' Leigh says. 'If it was an argument that got out of hand.'

'That's a good point, actually,' Des says.

'Glad I actually made a good point,' she says as she squeezes past him on her way down to the evidence room.

In the basement, the forensics fella has his back to her, taking photographs for the file.

'Anything for me?' she asks, making him jump.

He leans across and snatches one of the exhibits from the table.

'Look what I found,' he says, dangling a bunch of keys and smiling triumphantly.

'Where did you find them?'

'In a tool box under the kitchen sink. They were buried under a set of screwdrivers.'

'Front door? His car?'

The forensic fella shakes his head.

'They don't fit any of the locks in the flat, tried them all. These don't look residential to me, more likely for a commercial place. This crucifix key here,' he adds, moving forward to stand too close, 'they're usually for a garage door. The keyhole you're looking for will be shaped like a cross.'

'Brilliant,' Leigh says. 'I need to sign them out straight away.'

Finding Des is still waiting for Clara Harding in the corridor, Leigh shakes the bunch of keys in his face.

'Look what was in Duane Harding's flat,' she says. 'This key, the crucifix one, it's for a garage door.'

'Oh,' Des responds, looking less than impressed.

'It might lead us to Gail,' Leigh stresses. 'We need to check all lock-ups in the area again, on the way from Duane Harding's flat to his work.'

'If you don't mind me saying so, it's not really our focus,' Des says.

'It'll take my mind off James,' she says, when Des says 'Um' again and his eyes dart up the corridor. 'I'll lead it. I'll organise the search.'

When Des continues to stare over her shoulder, Leigh swings her head to follow his gaze, expecting to see Clara Harding but finding herself almost face to face with the out-of-town woman officer, the one the men in the station are calling the Bolsover Beauty, owing to her coming from some place in the Midlands and being good looking. She's in her early 50s, perhaps, with deep blue eyes, alabaster skin and luscious nut-brown hair. Her name is actually DI Josephine Bennett, and she's wearing the green dress again. In her presence, Leigh is reminded of the shampoo, hairspray and perfume her mum has started assembling in the bathroom at Dunbabin Road.

'Detective Inspector Chung!' the woman says, in a teasing manner. 'Always lovely to see you again.'

She touches him on the arm and cocks her head to one side so her shiny hair falls on one shoulder.

'Josie!' Des exclaims, beaming at her.

He doesn't introduce Leigh, and 'Josie' doesn't acknowledge her – she's one of those inspectors who have no time for the lower ranks. Leigh leaves them as they begin to talk pleasantries about how she's finding Liverpool. As she makes her way into the murder investigation room, she glances back, considers the woman's height, and wonders if she's the right size for the altered passenger seat in the Allegro.

15

There were as many people who said Duane Harding was a nice fella as believed he would harm a child, describing him as a modest, hard-working man who was dedicated to his family. When Leigh had first interviewed him, he had been quietly spoken. He had worn that sad little smile. She had disliked him immediately.

His supporters, however, said he was the best stepfather anyone could wish for and anyone who said fucking different was a fucking liar. They supported him to the hilt. And so, too, did his fragrant wife Clara, who now greets Leigh and Des in the downstairs interview room with a look of alarm, followed by flickering eye contact. Her teeth are chattering, even though the room is baking hot. The doctor who'd finally discharged her had explained, in medical speak, that her symptoms were moderate and she could go home; although home to Devonshire Road isn't where Clara will be going any time soon. She's lost contact with her family, apparently, and staying with friends.

Des introduces them both, although Clara has been interviewed by Leigh many times before.

'Clara?' Des says, sitting down next to her. 'I realise this is going to be difficult for you, but we do need to ask you a few questions.'

'Do you understand?' Leigh asks.

Clara doesn't respond. She trembles. She is porcelain that would break if you touched it. Her hair, a halo of fuzzy fair curls, is dark with sweat on the hairline. Her left eye is swollen and both eyes are ringed red with prolonged crying. She's wearing a jacket the same colour as the body suit Leigh had dressed Kai in this morning – pale blue, over a matching dress which looks as though she's made it herself from a Simplicity pattern. She looks like a child, girlish, in the same way Nikki seems young for her age. Duane Harding was obviously drawn to women who seem helpless. He'd chosen Clara from a number of deluded candidates who had written him fan letters when he was on remand.

'Do you understand, Clara?' Leigh asks again.

Clara says nothing. Despite her play act of vulnerability, she's still employing the fortitude she showed when campaigning for her dead husband's release. After the man she married had been charged with murder, Clara had been as adamant Duane was innocent as Leigh was adamant he was guilty. Clara blamed Nikki for making her new husband's life a living hell by agreeing to give evidence against him. When he was on remand – during which time Nikki had divorced him and he'd proposed to Clara – she'd organised a petition, collecting 342 signatures of fools who claimed he was innocent. She raised money to pay for a good lawyer. She gave interviews to newspapers, which were published under headlines such as *'The Man I Love is Innocent'* and *'Wrongly Accused'*.

Leigh would have done her for perverting the course of justice if she could.

'Clara,' Des says, sitting forwards. 'We do have to ask you about what happened.'

'It will be better for you, in the long run,' Leigh snaps, 'better for your defence.'

Des shoots her a look. They'd had a brief conversation about the interview in the corridor, Des focused on the present murder enquiry, Leigh stressing the importance of finding out if Duane Harding told Clara where Gail's body is. ('*If you don't mind me saying so,*' Des had said, '*we're supposed to be gathering evidence for the case we're actually working on.*')

'We'd appreciate it if you could talk us through the events of early Monday morning,' Des says now.

'You were at the scene, so you don't have an alibi,' Leigh says. 'It's cut and dried. Unless you tell us differently.'

'If you could tell us more about the intruder wearing the balaclava,' Des says, 'that would be greatly appreciated.'

They've never had to play good cop / bad cop, their roles are dictated by their personalities.

'Did Duane confess to hurting Gail?' Leigh blurts out, causing Des to turn her way. 'Did you find out he'd killed his stepdaughter after all? Is that why you murdered him?'

Clara stares into space. Her teeth give out a rattle. She can't keep the defencelessness up, Leigh thinks; her hostility is showing through her furious eyes.

'Right Clara,' Leigh tries again, ignoring the shake of Des's head she sees out of the corner of her eye. 'I'm going to ask you some questions. As you don't seem able to speak, you can nod your head for yes, shake your head for no.'

'Nod if he told you where Gail's body is, shake your head if he didn't.'

Clara does neither. She turns her face away in protest.

From outside comes the rumble of men's voices and the occasional shout. As soon as Clara was brought in, Duane Harding's outraged supporters had assembled in front of the station entrance, a raggle-taggle of men which includes Duane's dad, his cousin, holding onto two Alsatian dogs, and at least three sorry-looking hangers-on, all holding hastily made placards.

'And what are these for?' Leigh says, freeing the keys from her pocket and shaking them in front of Clara. 'Are these for a garage Duane had? Where is it?'

Des clears his throat and presses his knee against hers to shut her up, a touch that Leigh enjoys, even in the midst of her frustration. He's had to bring Leigh into the custody room with him because she's a DS and it's the right thing to do. That, and he has found himself with a staff shortage. Slapdash and Mark II have finished with the druggie they arrested and have disappeared on the trail of the person who threw the cactus out of the Princes Road flat. The fella whose head it landed on is Slapdash's brother-in-law, apparently.

'You will have to talk us through events of Monday morning, I'm afraid,' Des says. 'Or we'll have no choice but to charge you with murder.'

At this threat veiled in politeness, there's a change in body language; subtle, almost unnoticeable, but there – Clara is getting ready to talk.

'I'll speak,' she says in a whisper, 'but I don't want *her* here.'

'This is a murder enquiry,' Leigh says, after exchanging a glance with Des. 'You don't get to choose who you speak to and who you don't.'

There's a loaded silence while they wait in vain.

'What we need to do then, I'm afraid, is charge you,' Des says.

'What you need to do,' Clara says, turning her fiery gaze directly at him, 'is arrest the person who was hanging around outside our flat all last week.'

16

When the Allegro pulls up outside a scruffy house on Earle Road, the reinforcements are already there in the form of two squad cars and four uniforms, truncheons at the ready. Fresh from searching for cactus keepers in Princes Road flats, the two Godfather squad fellas arrive shortly after Leigh and Des, screeching to a halt with blues and twos flashing, warning everyone in L7, including their suspect, that the bizzies have arrived.

Before they'd left the interview room, Duane Harding's wife had finally spoken – and pointed the finger straight at Gail's uncle. She'd said Warren Jones had stood on the pavement outside the Hardings' flat every day for weeks, for hours at a time, clutching Gail's yellow dog and staring through the window.

Leigh has spent the journey arguing that Des shouldn't have let Clara go home because Warren isn't their perp. She has taken Des through what she knows about his life, even though much of her knowledge has come from his sister, Nikki. Warren has been living in little more than a doss house since his girlfriend decided she'd had enough of his drinking and threw him out. Sober, he's a nice fella. Tanked up, he's the devil incarnate. His drink problem has got far worse since Gail disappeared – he idolised his niece. And, as a point of interest (she's been trying to make him sound sane), he's a talented jazz pianist who used to play in the Kinkajou Club on Duke Street.

After the court case, he'd bought Leigh flowers.

Neither Nikki nor Warren blamed her for the acquittal of Gail's murderer.

Still, non-negotiable needs must and here they are, acting like *The Sweeney*, ready to storm inside and arrest him. The front door is open and the Godfather squad fellas barge into the house, yelling '*POLICE!*' – they love all this drama. While Slapdash and Mark II thunder up the stairs and start terrorising the occupants of the first-floor rooms, Leigh darts up to the top floor, leaving Des hobbling after her with his bad knee. She's the only person who knows where Warren's room is – owing to a description Nikki once gave of an attic – although she's not certain he still lives here. The last time she'd seen Warren, when Leigh was on maternity leave, he'd been on the cathedral steps, welcoming sunrise in with a bottle of cider.

Leigh and Des pass by doors which are open into dingy rooms. In one, a young fella in a stripey hat is wrapped in a worn quilt, smoking a cigarette. In another, two fellas with their heads covered in blankets have their hands up to the bars of an electric fire, even though the temperature outside is in the 80s. The smell of landlord neglect in the house makes Leigh want to gag. She is hot and hungover and the keys she took from the evidence room are digging into her thighbone through the front pocket of her jeans.

Warren's room is at the front and Leigh can see his bulk in there. His meaty hands are groping a table piled with jazz LPs, and he's trying to push himself up from the floor. Des gives a brief warning knock and goes inside. His entrance causes Warren to fall backwards and crash against a mirror on the wall. Their hesitation gives him the opportunity to push past them and gives Leigh the opportunity to let him bolt.

Warren is not lightning fast, owing to being unsteady on his feet, and he doesn't get far. Mark II easily intercepts him as he reaches the landing.

'Oi,' Leigh shouts as Slapdash smashes him up against the wall. Warren's a big lad, but he's putty, all flab and no muscle. 'Go easy.'

Outside on the street, Nikki's brother drunkenly protests his innocence and then blows Leigh a kiss as he's bundled into a squad car. He has no shoes and socks on and his enormous belly protrudes from the bottom of his t-shirt.

Leigh's heart breaks at the sight of him.

'Let's search his room for the murder weapon,' Des says as the Godfather squad fellas screech away in their Ford Zephyr.

They get back to the station ahead of their suspect, having found nothing of interest among the squalor of Warren's digs: no murder weapon or signs of blood.

'Nikki didn't say anything about Warren going around to the Hardings' flat?' Des asks as they wait for Callum to get him booked in.

'I asked her if her brother had had any contact with Duane Harding since he was acquitted, and she said no.'

This is the truth, at least, but Leigh feels a disquiet when she remembers Nikki's hesitation at the mention of her brother's name.

'What's Nikki's alibi?' Des asks. 'You didn't mention it in the report.'

That's because Leigh hadn't asked, but she isn't going to tell Detective Inspector Chung that.

Mercifully, she is saved from answering when the double doors swing open. Their heads turn to see their star suspect weaving his way up the corridor, arm in arm with two uniforms. Callum is limping behind, one hand on his bloodied nose, the other grasping his knee.

'The pissed-up bastard lamped me one,' he says. 'And he stuck the boot in.'

When Warren reaches Leigh, he shouts her name and asks after the baby. Then he shoves his face into hers and gives her a sloppy kiss, as if he's forgotten he's assaulted a police officer.

'I want Leigh in with me, she's family,' he says, not helping matters.

When they'd seen Nikki's brother on the cathedral steps, Kai had been fascinated by this dishevelled giant, and had blown an appreciative raspberry back his way.

The uniforms practically throw him into the custody room.

'Can you put him in the cells, please,' Des says. 'I think we should leave him overnight to sober up.'

Callum arrives back from the gents' a few minutes later, having cleaned himself up. His nose is still bloodied but there's little point in going to the Royal Hospital because the casualty department is still in chaos.

'I'm fine, thanks very much for asking,' he says, as he follows Leigh out of the station after their shift, letting out a groan with every step he takes.

'I didn't ask,' Leigh says and she sees his lips tremor – fighting a smile.

As Callum hobbles down the corridor, he's greeted with a little cheer by an officer coming up the other way. 'Well done, mate,' the fella says as he passes by, assuming he's been injured on the front line. Callum doesn't dissuade him otherwise.

'Milk it for all it's worth,' Leigh says, 'I would.'

As they reach reception, Callum tells her his nose feels okay, but his knee has taken a battering.

'As I said,' Leigh says, 'I didn't ask.'

17

Later that night, Leigh is horizontal on top of the mattress in her brother's old bedroom, Kai's hot little body resting on her chest. She's taken off her shoes and all her clothes and is now lying on the unmade bed in her bra and pants. She's taken the baby's nappy off too, not caring if he wees on her. The window is open and the room is filled with muggy night air.

Peace, at last.

She had spent the journey home arguing with her mum in her head about where she'd been last night. But she needn't have bothered because the house had been empty when she got in, prompting her to run through the rooms, shouting *'Mum?'* It was only when she'd switched on the kitchen light that she'd found a note by the kettle, saying, *'Back late, don't wait up.'*

Leigh drinks in the baby's touch. He is in soft clean clothes and smells of lavender and baby oil. Kai snuffles on her chest and when she glances down, she sees his eyes are wide open. He's wearing a serious expression, looking at her with his intense Zen-like gaze.

If only he wasn't such hard work, she thinks, he'd be really cute.

She stretches her legs out and lets the pillow take the weight of her heavy head. There must be better ways of doing things than this. Maybe she could move back to the Isle of Man, become a bobby on a bicycle, investigate stolen sheep and missing brothers. But who would look after Kai when she was pedalling around the island? She'd have to take Min with her, and Des's three sisters, too.

Having hit an unsurmountable obstacle, the dream fizzles out. Leigh looks out of the window, up to the same square of night sky her brother looked out on in the 18 years of his life. James had loved the planets and the stars; he'd wanted to be an astronaut from an early age, and had applied to Keele University to study physics. She wonders if Kai will love the stars too. She does a calculation in her head. Her baby will reach the age of 18 in 1999, at the turn of the century – they'll probably all be living on the moon by then.

Living on the moon sounds appealing, and she'd also consider Venus, the planet of love. She remembers James once saying a day there lasts nearly 250 earth days, which would certainly suit Leigh, and Des too – they might have a chance of fitting everything in. Before she made her almighty balls up at the Burundi Club, Leigh and Des had often talked about making a new life and had mulled over other careers. They had discussed the possibility of them both becoming nurses, a job Des would be well suited to, whereas Leigh – not so much. (*Don't you have to be caring?*' Des had teased her.) Neither of them wanted to be part of a racist police force and spend their entire lives among the aggro of the city centre streets. But they may as well have been planning to move to the moon. Because Leigh never moves towards what's good for her, she only moves away from it.

Kai mouths the air, searching for something to suck on.

'Greedy,' she tells him, 'you've already had dinner.'

The mealtime reminder seems to do the trick, because he gives up bobbing his head around and settles. Leigh shuts her eyes but immediately opens them again. She doesn't want to go to sleep. She doesn't want to miss any moments with her baby. She gazes around the corners of her brother's bedroom, at the dusty cobwebs collected on the ceiling, and remembers the mess of 45s on the floor, the posters on the walls and the jumble of jackets hanging from the hook on the back of the door. This room used to be painted blue but now it's a dull mauve that echoes the colour of the storm-filled sky.

Leigh basks in the breaths of her baby against her chest. This is his life, for now, she thinks, snatched cuddles with the strange and almost always horizontal woman who calls herself mummy, before being put to sleep in a crib decorated with a bed skirt her mum had knitted in a hideous shade of purple.

To her side, in his usual place in her blind spot, the James of her imagination makes his presence felt. Tonight, he has the definite look of the sulky teenager about him; a smelly, moody adolescent who makes no eye contact, as if he's got something to hide. Or maybe he's upset about her missing his birthday.

On 2 August, it will be the seventh anniversary of the day James went missing. Since then, time has passed in a stretch that simultaneously feels both gigantic and tiny. What has she been doing during those years? Quite a lot, when she thinks about it. She's become a police officer and a detective and she's had a baby. As she often does, Leigh thinks about what James would be doing now, if he was still here. He'd probably be a graduate, with a good job, a relationship, a flat of his own. The James in the room with her now is stuck in a time loop, packed full to the brim with hormones. He shuffles his feet. He plays Lynyrd Skynyrd too loudly for everybody's liking. Does he know that he had an accident in the bay? Or are there other, more hopeful options? Should she tell him that in his last week, he met a blonde girl called Anke, so it's not all doom and gloom?

Leigh looks up to the stars and thinks of the untraceable Dutch girl who James met on his camping trip. Her brother had stayed on after his friends, Geoff and Trey, had come back to Liverpool. Nobody's sure, but it's become the generally accepted belief that her brother chose to be left behind to spend more time with Anke. The Dutch girl and her friends had gone home by the time James was reported missing. They had paid cash and hadn't left an address with the farmer who ran the campsite. Anke probably doesn't know a thing about it. Leigh has always imagined her living her life in a boxy beige house where she brings up her picture-perfect children while holding down a professional job. She imagines her having made all the right choices after a last summer fling on the Isle of Man.

The idea Leigh often has that other people are problem-free attaches itself to a new target – Josephine, the Bolsover Beauty. Leigh bets the Nottinghamshire DI has her life all sorted. She bets she wakes up each morning feeling radiant and does 40 laps of the university swimming pool before she comes to work, feeling refreshed and ready to start the long day. Leigh thinks of Des's smile and wonders if he likes her. So what if he does? she thinks with more rebellion than she actually feels. There's no reason why Des shouldn't fancy a woman 20 years older than himself.

Her thoughts of the station lead her back to the Duane Harding murder case, even though she's been trying to block it out.

'Where do you think Gail is?' Leigh asks imaginary James, who is now wedged between the wardrobe and the wall. But it's all lost on her teenage brother. He's just hanging around. And anyway, she can hardly ask a bit of a kid to help her solve cases. He can't even solve his own.

Leigh gets up, gently carries Kai into her room and puts him in his crib. She goes downstairs to the kitchen and drinks Min's cold soup straight from the Tupperware container. And then she goes into the living room and opens the cabinet in the corner, where a variety of bottles have sat for years. She pours herself a drink and takes it upstairs to her childhood bedroom, where, in a soft voice, she tells Kai all about her plans for them both in 1999, whispering to him in the dark with sherry breath.

18

'Where were you last night?' Leigh asks her mum when she arrives down in the kitchen the next morning, babe in arms.

'I could ask you the same question about the night before last,' her mum says, her expression changing from a frown to a smile when she sees Kai.

Leigh's mum is wearing a summer dress from the catalogue and her newly set hair looks nice, if a little austere with its tight curls. She has just put out her umpteenth cigarette of the morning, judging by the full ashtray.

'I was working,' Leigh lies, retrieving a clean body suit from the drying rack with one hand.

'Min phoned up first thing this morning,' her mum says, making it sound like a complaint. 'She was going on about some soup being too hot. The baby's too young for soup, Leigh.'

'The soup was for me,' Leigh says. 'And it was tasty.'

'Where is it then?'

'I had it last night.'

The Tupperware container is still on the side.

'Where did you say you were last night?' Leigh asks again as she ransacks the kitchen tops, looking for a sterilised bottle to take with her to Min's.

'Seeing a friend.'

'What friend?'

'Never you mind what friend. I'm entitled to a life of my own, aren't I?'

Leigh looks around for the baby sling. She's late again, desperate – Kai had had another restless night, unsettled by all the messing with his routine.

'Will you hold him while I put on my shoes?'

'That baby is being passed from pillar to post,' her mum says, making no move to take him.

Her mum is entitled to a life but Leigh, it seems, is not.

She straps the baby on and leaves.

Leigh has already lost count of the number of days she's been back at work. She thinks it might be four or five but it feels like a hundred. As she approaches Admiral Street station and sees what's waiting for her, she feels entrapped again, fully immersed in the misery of people's lives; fully immersed in misery, full stop.

Duane Harding's supporters are outside the station again.

She can see the line of angry men being held back by a lone uniform behind yellow tape. The turnout has been affected by the thunderstorm overnight because there's a smaller number than there was yesterday – half a dozen protestors holding placards it must have taken them all of five minutes to make; corrugated cardboard ripped from the sides of supermarket boxes and stuck to brooms. The Alsatian dogs are there, too, looking longingly at a fella stuffing crisps into his mouth. These warriors of justice like to make a day of it, keeping office hours and bringing with them packed lunches and eight-packs of beer. Yesterday, when they'd left, the pavement had been strewn with plastic wrappers, cigarette butts and dog poo.

Leigh turns to go through the car park and enter the station through the back door. But then she thinks, bollocks to that.

In the mood for a fight, she puts her chin up and moves determinedly towards the protestors, swerving past the Ford Cortina parked on the pavement – Duane Harding's supporters arrive in one vehicle, attempting a Guinness World Record for the number of tossers in a single car.

As she approaches, she expects angry shouts and jeers. But, apart from one pantomime villain hiss, her presence is met with a hostile silence. She deliberately slows her pace as she moves past the line, baiting them with her presence, defiant in her right to walk where she pleases. She catches eyes as she marches past, recognising Duane Harding's dad, who fixes her with a hurt glare, and the dead man's cousin, who's wearing a cowboy hat. None of them have a job to go to but there aren't any jobs anyway. That's what this is all about, she thinks – a protest on behalf of emasculated mankind, a revolt against having no money and no future. It's a protest against the misery of their existence.

When Leigh reaches the end of the line, one of the Alsatians wags its tail. As she extends her arm and lets it nuzzle her fingers, her eyes pass over a fella who looks like Jesus, holding a dirty placard with the word JUSTICE written on it, and meet those of a Teddy Boy with a duck's arse hairstyle, who smiles and lifts a thumb in her direction, as if he's there to support Leigh.

'Someone's got a fan,' Callum says, walking into the station behind her. 'There's no accounting for taste.'

Leigh glances back to look at the Teddy Boy, who is still grinning in her direction. Is he insane? He must be, to be standing in the rain on a Toxteth street, protesting the innocence of a dead child murderer.

Warren is ready for them in the custody room. He's still cuffed, although there's no need for that now: the idiot of yesterday has been replaced by a teddy bear, albeit a sad smelly one who's been left in a toy box for years.

'All right, lad?' he greets Des, and then mouths 'Sorry' at Leigh.

Nikki's brother is still in his scruffs, not having had a chance to put on fresh clothes before being dragged from his bedsit yesterday, although he's been donated a pair of slippers which are too small for him. Des does the preliminaries – introductions and caution – and gets straight down to business by asking Warren why he'd been hanging around outside the Hardings' flat.

'I just wanted to know where our Gail was,' Warren says, echoing Nikki's words when Leigh went to see her. 'I hold my hands up, lad. I did go round to his a couple of times, stood outside the house. I wanted him to see, to be reminded. I didn't want him thinking Gail had been forgotten. I knocked a couple of times, that's it, lad.'

Warren doesn't fight back tears, he lets them flow. After two years, finding Gail's body is the best the family can hope for. They have long given up hope that she's alive.

'I don't like the thought of that bastard on the other side with our Gail, when I'm not there to look after her,' Warren continues with emotion. After years of working in smoky jazz clubs, he has a croak of a voice, as if it's cracked with age when he's only in his 30s.

'You're not thinking of joining her, are you Warren?' Leigh asks in a gap between his sobs.

Warren shakes his head and squawks his sister's name – he'll stay on this earth for her, but it's difficult. And then the maudlin talk starts – no family, no house, no job, a life not worth living – and goes on until his tears leave splashes on his *Feeling Groovy* t-shirt. His tears are as sloppy as he is, the perfect complement to his flabby belly, lank hair and monobrow. He and Nikki have different dads – her good looks must have been inherited from the paternal side.

'I do need to ask you, if you don't mind, where you were during the early morning of the sixth of July, between three o'clock and five o'clock,' Des says.

'Is that when Harding was done in? I can't remember, lad.'

'Come on Warren, think,' Leigh says.

'In the Moly in Kenny?' he queries, looking crestfallen. 'I couldn't tell you for defo, but I usually go early doors.'

This is a distinct possibility: some of the establishments in the Kensington area, including The Molyneux, host all-nighters.

'Did Duane Harding answer when you knocked?' Leigh asks, wanting to get off the subject of Warren's flimsy alibi.

'He come to the door once, but he never opened it.'

'Can you explain, please?' Des says.

'Yeah, I can explain, lad. He come to the door and spoke through the wood and then the letterbox flapped up so he spoke through that. But it was like he wasn't talking to me cos I didn't know what he was on about. He goes, stop phoning here and I goes, I never phoned you, lad.'

'Please go on,' Des says.

'I kept quiet on the doorstep cos I realised, after a bit, that he thought he was talking to some other fella. He goes, I've told you to piss off. You're not getting no money out of me, lad, if that's what you're after.'

'Are you certain?' Leigh asks.

'Defo,' Warren says. 'Then he stopped talking cos he must have copped onto the fact he'd got the wrong person.'

Warren had thrown himself against the door like a battering pole, two, three times, and then given up begging for information and gone away.

'She was there, the new wife,' Warren says. 'I could hear her, in the background, going, who is it Duane? And he's like it's no one, love.'

'Why didn't you tell us this before?'

Warren splutters. He attempts to take a sip of water but the paper cup he's been given is already empty.

'What? And tell you I'd gone round there? I'd already nearly got nicked for punching the bastard outside the court room.'

'You could have come to me,' Leigh says.

'Going to the police didn't come to nothing, first time around,' Warren says. 'Sorry, love, I know you did your best.'

Warren glances from Leigh to Des as it dawns on him that he might have told them something important. Before he gets a chance to say more, Des announces they're taking a break. This may have been one of the softest murder investigation interviews ever, but one thing is clear.

Warren wasn't the only person hanging around outside the Hardings' flat.

19

'What are you thinking?' Des asks Leigh on the corridor, looking disheartened.

'Warren's not our perp,' Leigh says, with some relief.

Nikki must have kept quiet about Warren's activities in case he was accused of the murder. Leigh doesn't blame her for not having much faith in the law.

'He can't remember where he was on Monday morning but he can remember the details of a conversation through a door?' Des says, sensibly.

'Anyone can see he's genuine,' Leigh says. 'I mean, what he said about Duane Harding being on the other side with Gail. I felt that. And it means someone else was hounding Duane Harding, calling him up, asking for money. *That's* our perp.'

'I think it's a good idea if we visit Clara,' Des says, 'to see if we can get her to speak. We can ask her what she knows about threatening phone calls and unwanted visitors at the door.'

His eyes are flickering in the way they do when he's worried.

'We'll solve this, you know,' Leigh reassures him with more verve than she feels.

'What would you think if you didn't know Nikki and Warren?' Des asks, not really taking in what she's said. 'If you hadn't been involved in the original case?'

Leigh's support has been rewarded with this hint that she's blinkered, but then Des is good at hinting. When he was off work with a bullet in his leg, he'd implied that she was over-involved in Gail's case because of what happened to James. Gail's disappearance had brought her feelings to the fore, that was true, and of course she had thought of her brother – how could she not? But other than that, it hadn't influenced her decision-making and his comments are something she still feels a teeny weeny bit resentful about.

'The same,' Leigh answers, after a long pause. 'Someone killed him because he killed a child.'

Their conversation is interrupted by the arrival of Callum. He's still sporting a red nose and, to Leigh's sadness, Warren has been charged with aggravated assault – a charge Leigh and Des didn't mention during the interview with him.

'I paid Duane Harding's former workplace a visit,' Callum says. 'It's a dump, if you ask me. The fellas at the garage hadn't seen him since he left, but his boss said he'd never believed that Duane would hurt a little girl. He said he'd had a hard time since being released. He'd tried to make a go of things, but it had affected everything.'

'My heart bleeds,' Leigh says.

'His boss reckoned that, after everything that had been in the papers, some nutter vigilante could have believed Duane was guilty.'

'He *was* guilty,' Leigh says.

'Thought he was acquitted?'

'Yeah, due to lack of evidence. He hid Gail's body and wouldn't tell us where it was.'

'Touchy,' Callum says.

'Rude,' Leigh counters.

'Can you keep this professional please,' Des says, 'if you don't mind.'

Leigh is infuriated by Callum in general, but he has a point about vigilantes. While lots of people who knew him thought

Duane Harding was innocent, strangers mostly looked at the facts and decided they added up to him being guilty.

After a brief discussion about where to start, they split up: Des and Callum to visit Clara Harding at her friend's house and Leigh to visit the local shop to buy a can of Tizer and return to the station to start the gigantic task of tracking down any known vigilantes. Kevin is assigned to checking out Warren's shaky alibi, a task he accepts with a good deal of head-nodding. The Godfather squad fellas are nowhere to be seen. Leigh had seen them earlier, in the major incident room, putting all their energies into finding out who threw the cactus out of the Princes Road window rather than helping solve the murder case. Des is having difficulty keeping them in line and they're never where they say they will be.

Leigh picks up the solitary telephone in the meeting room and puts in calls to countless police forces, asking for information on any recent crimes involving suspected vigilantes. She's met with the reply that it could take several days to get the information – doesn't she know the North West forces are involved in policing the rioting?

She puts the phone down and slumps back in the chair. Even if she moved to Venus, where she would have 250 hours a day at her disposal, she still wouldn't be able to cross-reference every index card in every CID department in the country, and vigilante crimes aren't recorded as such, they're down as ABH, GBH, that sort of thing. And why should she want to? Who actually wants to find Duane Harding's killer? Not even Des is that keen; he only wants to solve the case so it doesn't reflect badly on him.

The only thing Leigh is interested in is finding Gail's body.

Later in the afternoon, she telephones the fella who runs undercover at HMP Walton, to see if he can chase down his informants. He's not around, so she leaves a message for him and calls Walton Prison directly.

'We're don't know of any groups operating out of the prison,' the governor tells her, 'but we've got a category A prisoner who was assaulted last night, hit on the head with a stone in a sock. His name is Victor Rivera and he was convicted of the murder of a 5-year-old boy a year ago. He was recently moved from Wakefield, been in three prisons so far. He's moved around for his own safety.'

'What, did they think he'd be safer at Walton?' Leigh asks.

'He was kept in a wing away from other prisoners so we're not sure how it happened. No one saw it and the prisoner won't give a name.'

It's common for inmates who hurt children to get beaten up and nobody notices, not even the prison officers, some of who stand by and allow it to happen. In prison hierarchy, men who abuse or kill kids are the bottom of the rung, on a level even below a snitch. That code is especially strong among Liverpool prisoners, particularly in the gangland fraternity.

'I can arrange for you to speak to him,' the governor says. 'You might get more out of him that we have.'

Leigh knows this is a long shot. Unless this inmate has a death wish, the chances of this scumbag grassing on whoever beat him up are very slim. And why would that person target Duane Harding outside the prison? But she arranges a visit anyway – it's not as if they've got anything else.

She comes across Des in the car park, just arriving back from seeing Clara Harding. They leave Callum standing there and drive away in the Allegro together.

20

Victor Cole Rivera, born in 1912, is four years into a 19-year sentence for murder that he won't live long enough to serve. The details of his crime are too odious for Leigh to think about, but they involve a 5-year-old boy, a filthy flat in the East End of London, and an assortment of despicable men prepared to throw a fiver into a pot.

He shuffles into the dark room, head stooped, eyes on the floor, the picture of abject misery. When he slumps down in a chair at the other side of the table, Leigh gets a good look at his injuries. Despite being recently discharged from the hospital ward, he resembles a crash test dummy which has been sent at speed into a wall: most of his face is blue and his receding hairline is obscured by a deep gash. He's separated from the other prisoners in a segregated ward, but he isn't safe anywhere. They still found a way to get to him.

'I'm an innocent man!' he says, glancing up to see where his words land, assessing which one of them is the weakest link. 'Tell them, will you? Why won't someone tell them?'

'We're not here for that,' Leigh says.

'We want a friendly chat about a cold case,' Des says, more gently, although he can't keep the steel out of his voice. 'You're not a suspect.'

Leigh glances at Des, whose expression betrays nothing. Neither of them wants to breathe the same air as Victor Rivera for long, but he's much better than her at hiding what's going on in his head.

'Who did this to you?' Leigh asks.

Victor Rivera snivels. He pulls at the neck of his t-shirt. He scratches at his sides. Then he reaches for the packet of cigarettes on the table and takes one out with an exaggerated shaking hand.

'I'm living in hell,' he cries. 'I'm in hell.'

'You must have seen who did this to you,' Leigh says. 'Give us a name, a description.'

The convict looks around with frightened eyes and then settles his gaze on the prison officer standing against the wall. There's no real protection in here – some of the screws make it their business to tell inmates about the heinous crimes of men on the segregated ward. Leigh considers asking the prison officer to leave – Victor Rivera will be cautious about being seen snitching.

'I thought you'd come to help me,' he says. 'I thought I could rely on officers of the law.'

His hands shake as he puts a cigarette to his mouth and takes it away again. Beneath the injuries, he is a grey man, in his late 60s, thin, balding, nondescript. He doesn't light his cigarette. He puts his head in his hands and weeps.

Leigh looks on, incredulous. '*Watch yourself,*' the governor had warned them before they came in. '*He's good at pulling the wool over your eyes.*' She can't imagine how anyone on earth would fall for this hammy performance. Victor Rivera wallows in self-pity, presenting himself as the hapless victim of circumstance. She's amazed he thinks he's pulling it off.

As she sneaks another look at Des to see how this is going down with him, a shout from somewhere in the prison sends their interviewee jumping into the air and then burrowing down so he's almost under the table. Brave in a filthy flat, Leigh thinks, not so brave in the hellhole of Walton Prison.

Although she has been here many times before, she'd still been surprised by the sheer misery of the place: the lack of sunlight, the peeling yellow brick, the smell of unwashed clothes, the burning eyes of men who rarely see a woman. On the way through the main hall, she'd looked up at the balcony, checking she wasn't being watched by Mikey Killen, the drug dealer she'd once had an unfortunate one-night stand with. It was another time she'd let Des down, jeopardising their newly fledged romance *and* the investigation into the murder of Mikey's half-brother, Robbie. Since then, Mikey's been sentenced to two years for possession, Stan having succeeded in his mission to nail him but not for the more serious crimes he'd wanted.

'They're going to kill me,' Victor Rivera sobs. 'I won't be the first, and I won't be the last!'

'Who's they?' Leigh asks as she sits forward, a move that causes Victor Rivera to flinch. She sits back again when he doesn't answer, hears Des sigh – this is a waste of time.

'You don't have to name names then,' Leigh says, 'just tell us what happened.'

'If you could give us a name?' Des says at the same time.

They're talking over each other, like they used to when they first became work partners; a little over six months apart, and they're all out of rhythm.

'And then we'll see if we can help you.'

Victor Rivera finally steadies his hand enough to light the cigarette. He sucks on it so hard it crackles.

'There's a hitlist,' he says, dramatically. 'If you're on the list, then you're a dead man walking.'

After a follow-up meeting with the governor, during which Des hadn't pushed hard for Victor Rivera to be moved back to Wakefield or anywhere else, Leigh and Des sit in the Allegro, facing the high wall of the prison. Leigh feels contaminated. She's longing to hold her baby and keep him safe.

'We need to get hold of that list,' Des says, 'Duane Harding might have been on it.'

'What are we thinking? A hitlist drawn up by prisoners sympathetic to victims' families? And they're targeting them outside the prison as well as inside? Getting messages out through former jail mates or visitors?'

'It would be an easy cause to recruit to,' Des says as he lights a cigarette and the car fills with smoke. 'They think they've got the moral high ground; doing the world a favour. Plus, if they refuse to cooperate, they could be accused of being on the paedophile's side. It's something, at least. And it might lead us to other people who hate paedophiles.'

'That would be the whole world then?'

'We do have a rather large pool to swim in.'

Leigh nods in half-hearted assent. Des had told her on the way that nothing new had come of the visit to Clara Harding: Warren had stood outside the flat a few times and might have knocked once. They'd had a few silent phone calls, that was all. She's still refusing to say anything more about Monday morning, although Callum had been pleased to learn that she'd been back to the flat to collect the cat. Des has decided to leave her be while they work on the case.

He's asked for a printout of any phone calls made to the flat but, apart from that, they've got zero leads and a city full of people who wouldn't be unhappy to see a child killer dead.

'There might be no connection whatsoever to this hitlist,' Des says. 'But we'll see if Victor Rivera decides to squeal on who beat him up.'

This, vaguely promised by the governor, who didn't look as if he was that arsed about it. No one wants to help them nail Duane Harding's killer. Even Leigh doesn't want to help.

Without being fully conscious of it, she shoves her hands up her shirt and hugs herself. The rain had been heavy overnight but the morning sunshine through the windows on Dunbabin Road had fooled her into coming out without a cardigan.

'Are you cold?' Des asks. 'It has got a little chilly since the storm last night.'

Leigh nods, thinking, this is what we've been reduced to – talking about the weather.

'Shall we go back and find out what Kevin's found?' Des says, retrieving his suit jacket from the back seat.

'Yep,' Leigh says, feeling the brief touch of his hand as he stubs his cigarette out in the ashtray and drapes his jacket over her shoulders.

Although she's pleased at this thawing towards her, she wriggles around in her seat, suspicious. There's a distinct smell on the collar, not his usual aftershave, much sweeter, like perfume. As Des pulls away, she sniffs loudly to let him know that she's noticed.

Back at the station, after entering through the back to avoid the protestors, Des goes to update Stan while Leigh buys a can of Tizer from the vending machine and listens impatiently to the news from Kevin that Warren is still missing a corroborated alibi for the morning Duane Harding was murdered. She's already late to get Kai and she's got to type a report on one finger before she leaves.

'That's great,' she tells Kevin, hoping that whatever he's telling her is indeed great because she's not listening. Her mind is occupied with Kai's diminishing nappy supply.

'Nobody recalls seeing him in The Miller,' Kevin says, as she wonders if she'll catch Kwik Save before it closes, or if Min has some spare nappies lying around.

'Sergeants Shimberg and Davies are out,' he continues, alluding to Slapdash and Mark II. 'They're still knocking up all the residents of the flats on Princes Road.'

Leigh thinks they have better things to do, like get on with the mountain of jobs Des set the squad on the first day. She types her report quickly and badly and is on her way out of the meeting room when the phone rings, a sudden noise that brings her around from her nappy preoccupation. Kevin shouts after her and she reluctantly turns back, thinking it's a return call from one of the many police forces she'd contacted earlier, or Min, still worrying about the soup being too hot. Or, most likely, her mother, wanting to plague the life out of her. Kwik Save is going to be well shut by the time she gets there.

'Who is it?' she asks the trainee.

'A woman,' he says, shrugging his shoulders.

Leigh sits down with a sigh, rests the Tizer on her belly, and takes the receiver from him.

'Serious crime squad,' she says, deciding it's her mother and wanting to establish that she's not available because she's working.

'Am I speaking with Leigh?' a female voice says. 'The policewoman, Leigh?'

'That's me,' Leigh says, thrown by the accent.

'I'm calling from Utrecht in the Netherlands,' the voice says.

'Yes?' Leigh says, her brain trying to catch up.

'My name is Anke,' the voice says, 'and I need to talk to you about your brother.'

Leigh stands up in response to this thunderbolt. A shiver moves down the back of her neck. Is this Anke, the girl her brother had got to know on his camping trip? *The* Anke, who she's thought about so many times in the last seven years, wondering where she is and what became of her?

'Hello? Hello?' Leigh says, as if she can't hear when the line is clear.

'Yes, I am here,' Anke says.

'My brother?' Leigh says.

'Yes, do I have the correct person? You have a brother called James?'

'Yes, I do,' Leigh says, unable to breathe. 'Go ahead.'

21

Shaking, stunned, amazed, Leigh puts the phone down and runs through the station corridors, in search of Des. He's one of the few people who really knows what she has been through with James – her grief, her hopes, her tendency to see apparitions – and he's the only one who will understand, no matter the situation between them.

She finds him in the car park, walking side by side with Josephine, the Bolsover Beauty. The two of them are deep in conversation, oblivious to the noise caused by a burned-out car being towed away nearby, oblivious to the occasional shouts from the merry band of Duane supporters out front.

When Des sees Leigh marching towards them across the concrete, he immediately moves away from his new best friend and rushes towards her.

'Is Kai all right?' he asks, in the panic-stricken manner of a new parent.

'Yes, yes!' Leigh shouts. 'I need to talk to you, now.'

'I was just talking to ...' Des says as if he's going to start explaining himself.

Not only does Leigh not want to hear it but she has more pressing things on her mind. By the time she's blurted out her news, her heart is pounding against her chest.

'She said she'd prefer to speak in person, she wouldn't say what it was over the telephone,' she finishes breathlessly.

'Are you certain it's her?' Des asks.

Leigh hesitates. She's suddenly unsure of the veracity of the call. Is this person someone pretending to know James? They'd received a fair few crank calls over the years.

'It's her,' Leigh tells Des, rashly deciding she is certain. 'She wants us to meet. I've got to go to London. She says she's over here for a conference for a couple of days.'

'She's waited seven years to come forward, and then you have to go to her?' Des says.

'Her name is Anke Groot,' Leigh says, shouting over his doubts. 'I've got her telephone number and her address.'

She'd been afraid this Anke would disappear and she'd never hear from her again. The details had been written down on a girlie magazine she'd found on the meeting room table.

'How did she find you?' Des asks, still struggling to take in the information. 'Did she phone Admiral Street? It's not even your usual base.'

'I don't know. Does it matter? I've already arranged to meet her. I've got to find a way to get to London tomorrow.'

Leigh is already trying to work out how she can get time off, thinking she'll bring her leave forward from August.

'I'm sure we can sort something out,' Des says, as the Bolsover Beauty steps around them on her way back into the station. Despite the urgent situation, Leigh sniffs, trying to match Josephine's perfume to the scent on Des's collar.

'What girl?' her mum says, when Leigh gets back to Dunbabin Road.

'Anke, the girl who James met on holiday.'

'I've never heard of any girl.'

'I've told you a thousand times,' Leigh says, shouting already. 'The Dutch girl his friends said James liked. She was staying on the same campsite. The blonde girl. It's *her*. She says she's got something to tell us about James.'

'What? She's phoned up after all this time?' her mum says, sitting at the kitchen table, bouncing Kai on her knee. She's all dollied up, squashed into a trouser suit Leigh hasn't seen for years.

'She says she's been trying to find me.'

'What else did she say?'

'She didn't want to talk on the telephone.'

'I bet she didn't.'

Her mum deliberately turns her attention to Kai.

'Aren't you a sweetheart?' she tells him. 'Yes, you are. Aren't you lovely? Yes, you are.'

Around them, the worktops are untidy with the baby paraphernalia Leigh brought with her at the weekend. Next to her mum's depression medication is a new Avon package which has been ripped open to reveal Lily of the Valley foam bath and a novelty lip balm shaped like an ice cream.

'Are you going out somewhere?' Leigh asks.

'Leave it alone, Leigh,' her mum says, ignoring her question. 'I don't want any upset.'

'I'm going to London to meet her.'

'Who's going to look after the baby?'

'I'll take him with me.'

'You can't go to London with a baby! Anyway, I thought you were short of money. You're always complaining about it.'

'This girl could tell us something about what happened,' Leigh says, thinking she's going mad. Why isn't her mum taking this seriously?

'You need to forget about it and move on,' her mum says. 'You need to leave it alone.'

Leigh is bristling as she carries the baby up the stairs and, one armed, retrieves his bathtub from the side of the wardrobe.

Usually, during Kai's bathtime, all the surprises and frustrations of her day fade. He is so happy, so easily pleased by a moving light, a splash of water in his miniature bathtub, at the face of the strange mummy person who has appeared to bathe him, feed him, and change him into the single nappy she's begged from his Nanny Min.

But tonight, Leigh is preoccupied. Anke is a person she has thought of for many years, a person she has imagined out there in the world, existing under the same sky. After seven years, she had begun to think the girl James met on holiday was a figment of her imagination. But it turns out she might be real after all.

And if it really is her, she desperately needs to talk to her.

Kai guzzles the milk down in record time and Leigh sits up, trying a variety of burping positions and settling for his head on her shoulder, giving him a view of the lurid spiral wallpaper Leigh had chosen in her teenage years. When the baby is winded, she lies down with him in her arms, remembering when, soon after he was born, she'd gone for a woodland walk in Dibbinsdale on the Wirral, where there'd been a wishing well. As she'd thrown in a penny, she'd realised it was the first time in her life she'd wished for anything that wasn't for herself. Her wish had been for Kai to have a long happy life, to be safe, to be without sorrow. She'd only made one wish, even though she had more pennies, believing that one was all she was allowed; that if she made any more, her wish for the baby would be cancelled out.

But now she wants another.

She wants to see her brother again.

As if the Dunbabin Road genie has been summoned up, imaginary James appears in her blind spot. To him, it's still early 1974, and the conversation with his friends about what to do that summer hasn't yet happened; the camping trip to the Isle of Man is still a twinkle in his eye. Leigh tries to think of how the trip came to be, but she can't remember. She thinks about the morning he set off, the clear memory she has of James laying his camping gear out on his bed, trying to work out how much of it he could fit into his small rucksack. Their mum was chatting downstairs to a fella who'd knocked on the off chance, offering to clean the gutters, and the two of them had been alone in his bedroom, laughing about a pair of leather clogs he'd bought from Tuebrook Market – they were the in-thing in 1974. The clogs were too weighty to carry so James had replaced them with an even heavier cricket bat and put the clogs on, intending to wear them on the ferry over to the Isle of Man. He'd pulled them off again when Leigh had told him they looked ridiculous.

In her childhood bedroom, nearly seven years later, she turns away from the apparition and looks down at her baby's beautiful face. His head is nestled in her armpit, his eyes are closed. She turns over his hand and looks at the tiny life line on his palm. Since Kai was born, she has felt a sadness that he'll never get to meet his uncle. Now, she has a tiny, silly hope that he might.

Kai is dozing in Leigh's arms when she hears a car pull up outside. When the front door slams, she leaves the baby on the bed, and gets up to look out of the window. There's a black Bentley parked on the pavement, lights on and engine running. Leigh watches as a fella exits on the driver's side and swaggers around to the passenger door. He opens it with a sweep and her mum totters towards the car, unsteady in kitten heels.

Leigh looks on in stunned surprise. She recognises the older fella who is now taking her mum's hand and guiding her with a protective arm. It is he of the silver hair, sharks' teeth and dapper clothes – he's wearing Pringle from head to toe. She stares in horror as he lifts her mum's hand and kisses her fingertips, watching to confirm what she already knows is true.

Her mum is dating a well-known Liverpool gangster.

Her mum is dating Pat Killen.

22

'He's a criminal!'

'He's a property developer.'

'Don't think so.'

'He's doing up some flats out Picton Road way, says they're beautiful.'

'He's bent! He's been in and out of prison all his life! He's a gangster! He hurts people!'

'He could fix you up with somewhere nice, instead of that dump you insist on living in. It's not fit for a baby.'

'Pat Killen isn't fixing me up with anything.'

Leigh stands in the kitchen, hands on her hips, staring at her mum. It's after midnight and, unable to sleep, she'd run down when she'd heard the Bentley drawing up outside to drop her mum off.

'His son's in prison,' Leigh says, making an attempt to drive her message home.

Mikey Killen – the drug dealing son she'd had the one-night stand with a couple of years ago.

'Mikey's getting out next year,' her mum replies, obviously on first name terms. 'Pat said he never did it anyway, the drugs were planted by your lot.'

'I don't think so,' Leigh says, thinking of the death threats Stan got when he brought Mikey to justice. 'I'll have to tell my boss you're associating with a criminal.'

'It's not you he's taking out.'

'How did this happen?'

'We met at the funeral of that lad, didn't we?'

The funeral Leigh had taken her along to, over two years ago now, of Pat's son, Robbie, the sad culmination of the distressing case she'd worked on with Des. Her mum had been on day release from the psychiatric ward and Leigh had only asked her to come because she was complaining about being left behind.

'That lad?' Leigh counters. 'You mean his son? The one he abandoned to a life of poverty? That one?'

'Pat never even knew he existed.'

Her mum swipes at a moth which had come in when she'd said goodnight to her boyfriend at the door. She lights a cigarette in an attempt to smoke the insect out.

'I didn't want to go to that funeral in the first place,' her mother says, pulling a face like she's sucking a lemon. 'I told you we shouldn't have gone. You didn't even know the lad.'

'It's my fault now, is it?'

'You were the one who dragged me there.'

Leigh is momentarily rendered speechless by her mother's logic, or lack of it.

'I did not drag you there!' she says, finding her voice again. 'Seriously though, how? Has this been going on all that time?'

'I bumped into him again, didn't I? In Blacklers in town. He was out shopping for his grandkids. He lives in one of those lovely houses on Sandfield Park.'

'When?'

'A few months ago, now.'

'A few months ago? Why didn't you tell me?'

'My private life is my own business,' her mum says, as Leigh storms out of the room.

She can't take any more of this. Leigh stands immobile in her bedroom, not knowing what to do next. She checks on Kai in the crib and then she grabs her overnight bag from the floor and starts throwing the baby's blankets into it with force. She slams the door on her way to the bathroom, where she sweeps her toiletries off the shelf and holds them in her arms on the short journey back again. As she enters the bedroom, a disturbed Kai starts to shriek like a parrot. She can hear her mum moving around downstairs, closing all the doors for the night before she comes to bed.

Leigh goes on lashing her clothes into the bag. She can't believe this was the reason for her mum's perms and sets, the visits from the Avon rep, the multiple catalogue orders, the good mood. She'd thought it had been the baby's arrival that had perked her up; that his presence had galvanised her out of her depression. But she'd been perked up anyway – by her new relationship with a retired widower with a smile full of menace and a history of relieving rivals of their fingers and toes, not to mention burglary, exertion, money laundering, weapons trafficking, drug dealing and quite possibly murder.

She's attempting to fasten the zip of her bag when imaginary James appears again. He rolls his eyes at the news their mother is dating a criminal. *I know*, Leigh tells the air, *it's the worst thing that's ever happened to me.*

Although they both know that isn't true.

When she's finishes packing their things, Leigh scoops up the girlie magazine with Anke's details scrawled on it, crams it inside her bag, and struggles to fasten the zip. Riots or not, she's not staying here a moment longer. Riots or not, she's jumping a taxi back to her own bedsit. And then, tomorrow, by hook or by crook, she's going to London.

23

'Home, sweet home,' Leigh tells the baby as the door jams against the unwanted pram.

Still reeling from the events of the day, she squeezes through the cluttered hallway and steps inside with sweet relief. She's missed the streetlight shining in through the grubby bay windows. She's missed the smell of escaped gas. She's missed the LPs she keeps in a crisp box she got from the supermarket. She's even missed the rotting tangerine on the messy table which, tonight, is sending notes of sour citrus into the stale air. Leigh hasn't been to the launderette for two weeks, and everything smells of the Toxteth riots – on the way in, she'd dabbed away a smudge of soot on Kai's face.

She puts her hands on the baby's back and thanks the heavens she is back in her bedsit.

Who cares if Des says it's too dangerous? She's put the chain on the bolt, hasn't she? And the neighbours she shares the house with seem harmless – as well as the Italian fella, there's a hospital porter with a book-lined room, and a bearded pensioner who drinks his way through the day. Who cares if her mum says it's a waste of money and the washing facilities aren't suitable for a baby? Staying with her mother is a fate far worse than any shared bathroom. Still, disapproval weighs on Leigh as she gingerly approaches the stinking milk bottle on the windowsill. She'd acted furtively on the way in, rifling for her keys through the bag full of baby clothes and toys, alert to the watchful eyes of the bad-tempered Italian fella who lives downstairs, irrationally fearing that he'd dob her in for being in her own bedsit.

Leigh slips her shoes off, drops the keys from the evidence room on the table, and transports Kai into the kitchen area, carrying the curdled milk in one outstretched hand. She can smell her socks from five feet nine inches away, even through the aroma of coagulating milk. She puts the baby in his bouncer and sponges stains off her shirt, her only concession to getting ready for her trip tomorrow. After she's washed the milk bottle out with her face turned away, she cuddles up on the mattress with Kai and Great Uncle Bulgaria, where they all play peek-a-boo. But Kai is grouchy after being rudely awakened and only goes along with it for her sake.

The baby finally settles but he's grimacing with wind and she feels a pain inside at having to interrupt his routine again tomorrow. The obstacles to getting to London to meet Anke are almost unsurmountable. She's not sure there's enough money in her bank account for the train ticket. She wonders how much it will cost and eyes the biscuit tin with her rent money in it. Then she eyes the porcelain piggy bank her mum had bought for Kai when he was born. The current balance is one whole penny, made up of two half-penny pieces.

In the past, her dad kept her going by slipping tenners her way, but they're not speaking so she can't ask him for money, even though he has plenty of it. The only contact she's had with him since Kai was born was a letter, expressing his grave disappointment and ordering her to get married. It was one of the reasons she'd turned Des's proposal down, if not the main reason.

She can't ask Des for money either; there isn't much left over from his wages after he's paid for his family's flat and upkeep. And she can't ask her mum because she'd rather die. Leigh strokes Kai in his uneasy sleep. She wonders what price a cute baby would fetch. Probably a pretty sum.

Still fretting about money, Leigh looks around for imaginary James – she could do with a bit of back-up. Maybe he could lend her a quid or two or help out with childcare. Leigh stares into space, willing her brother to appear. But he only ever hangs around at Dunbabin Road, never in her bedsit, despite the presence here of the giant telescope he loved.

As she has on and off since the unexpected phone call, Leigh tries to stop herself from anticipating what Anke might tell her tomorrow. Hope is churning in her stomach and with it, the start of ridiculous fantasies that James has been in Holland with the Dutch girl all this time. She fights this ungrounded optimism with all her might. But among the quiet and peace of her bedsit, and with her baby asleep, she finally gives in and allows herself to dream of a reunion.

It's a hazy affair, not big on detail, and takes place in the bedroom she last saw James walking out of seven years ago. She experiences an overwhelming sense of relief as he walks back in again after his extended camping trip, not looking a day older than 18, not showing any signs of an ordeal, if there has been an ordeal.

Leigh is just dropping off to sleep when she hears a distant bang, a screeching siren, or maybe it's an alarm. She opens her eyes to see a plume of smoke, rising above the chimney tops. She struggles up on her elbows. The fragile peace has not held. Less than two streets way, Toxteth is burning again.

24

They look like a happy family. The good-looking Chinese fella with the slight limp, moving the hand of the adorable baby in a wave, the pale-faced girl who must have some sort of lanky, witchy appeal. ('You're just you,' Des had told Leigh in happier times – all he could come up with as to why he loved her.)

A nice family, if a tad unusual. Some people queueing for the ticket counter give them dirty looks, but others smile, perhaps deciding that Leigh and Des are proof that mixed-race marriages really do work. Leigh imagines that this threesome the onlookers see live in one of the maisonettes in Cantril Farm; ordinary on the outside, extraordinary on the inside, with sweet-smelling carpets and no dust, as well organised and neat as the home of Josephine, the Bolsover Beauty. He most likely has a job in insurance because he's wearing a smart navy suit, even though the sun is already cracking the flags. And she's most likely a layabout because she's wearing a shirt she's sponged the stains off, faded jeans and a crumpled cagoule, having left her only good jacket behind at her mother's.

Leigh writes a cheque for her train ticket at the counter, knowing it will bounce. Behind her, she hears a young couple complimenting Des on Kai's cuteness and asking him whether his wife is travelling with them. Appearances can be deceptive, she thinks. They're not married, they're not even together; they're police detectives, working undercover as a happy couple.

And the lanky, witchy girl is getting on a train in search of her missing brother.

Ticket in pocket, Leigh makes her way back to Des and the baby. When Kai reaches out his arms to be scooped up, her mouth waters. She feels the same pang she gets when she looks at a Des, only a thousand-fold, a million-fold. Leigh gives the baby a loopy smile. She feels chipper, rested, hopeful. Despite the disturbances on the street, she had been so tired that she'd slept through the night for the first time since the weekend. Although she had dreamt of Pat Killen coming at her with a machete; no doubt appearing in her consciousness as a reminder that she has yet to tell Des that her mother is dating a gangster. She hasn't let him know she's back at her bedsit either; insisting on meeting him at Min's flat for the walk to the station this morning.

'Are you going to sleep tonight for your daddy?' she asks the baby. 'Yes, you are.'

'Hope you're going to be okay,' Des says, still unsure this is a good idea. 'I'd have come with you.'

'Would you?'

'Yes, of course. But one of us has to stay here and pretend you're somewhere else.'

Des needs to get to work. Last night's confrontations in Toxteth have sent Admiral Street station into a spin again, despite the unrest being quickly extinguished due to the threat of more teargas. He plans to tell the squad she's back at the Hardings' flat, checking it over in case evidence has been missed. The undercover fella from Walton Prison is already working on tracking down the hitlist. Leigh's planned search of the lock-ups is on hold for now, and she's relieved that the only immediate work to do on the case is going through Duane Harding's phone records. She doesn't want any urgent developments. She just wants to get to London.

Leigh smothers Kai's forehead in kisses. She shoves her cheek against his, nuzzles his head and gets wisps from his combover caught on her lips. Despite the imposition, the baby chortles. On their way past the bombed-out church, they'd sung *I Taut I Taw A Puddy Tat* to him, delighting in the belly laugh he's developed in the space of one day.

She pines until she's on the move, and then the feeling disappears. She's thrilled as the packed train gathers speed out of the city, thrilled further when it cuts its way over Runcorn Bridge, and thrilled even more when the buffet car opens. She eats her way through a grapefruit segment with a cherry on top, two slices of bacon, two grilled tomatoes, a Ryvita biscuit and a roll smothered in butter and marmalade. She's so hungry that the on-board meal is almost worth the month's rent she's paid for it.

25

Leigh stares at the young woman across the table.

Anke Groot is exactly who she was expecting.

Casual but chic in blue and grey, the young woman is wearing sunglasses on top of her head and a hippy necklace dangling from her neck. Her hair isn't blonde though, it's the colour of malted milk biscuits, unbrushed, and tied loosely at the back in a low ponytail. Heads turned when she walked into the nondescript café in a place called Earls Court and found a nervous Leigh waiting for her.

'Leigh?' Anke says, because although they have never met, they recognise each other immediately.

Anke takes Leigh's sweaty hand and shows magnificent big front teeth as she smiles. She looks around the café, considering how to order. Leigh watches in interest as Anke goes to the counter. She'd been a student when she'd met her brother on the Isle of Man in 1974. She'll be in her mid-twenties now but she still looks 18: slight and insubstantial, her cheesecloth shirt baggy on her shoulders and her jeans falling from her hips.

This elongated youth, Leigh thinks, is the result of what? A lovely childhood? A blessed transition to adulthood? Anke had told her on the phone she is a trainee lawyer, here in London for a conference.

'How was your journey?' Anke asks as she arrives back with a tumbler of sparkling water – Leigh already has an expensive cola in front of her. 'I'm sorry I couldn't come to Liverpool. I love the accent there!'

'My journey was great,' Leigh says, still full from a breakfast fit for a queen. She'd managed to find the underground station on the map easily and had strolled through the strange crowded streets, expecting them to be on fire. But there is no sign of the Brixton unrest in Earls Court.

In perfect English, Anke mentions The Beatles, the football, the Mersey, the seagulls; an impression gained of Liverpool from the young woman's day spent in the city seven years ago, on her way back from the Isle of Man. Leigh is drawn in immediately and stifles an urge to show Anke the photograph of Kai in her purse.

'You said you wanted to talk to me about my brother,' she says instead.

Anke nods.

'I am sorry, I didn't know.'

Whatever Leigh has been hoping for, she is already disappointed.

'How did you find me?'

'I read about the terrible case of the little girl in Liverpool, earlier this year. It was international news and we were also interested from a legal perspective. I saw your name and recognised it. Your brother said he had a sister who had joined the police. I did some research, for nostalgia, you know? And then I found out James had gone missing.'

Leigh nods, satisfied with this explanation, although she wishes she'd had time to look Anke up on Interpol or something before she came.

'It is not much, what I have to tell you,' Anke says, finally answering Leigh's question. 'But it is something. Something I remember strongly.'

'Anything you remember is good,' Leigh says.

'You might know this already. Yes, you probably know and I have wasted your time.'

Leigh nods at her from across the table – *go on*.

'Okay,' Anke says, taking a sip of water. 'I will tell you what I remember, about meeting your brother, what I know.'

She had noticed the three boys straight away. Anke and her friends had just arrived and had left their backpacks at the campsite to go down to the beach to cool off – the weather was hot and muggy, how it is today, and the ferry journey long. Two of the boys were larking around in the sea – Leigh's brother and the shy one, the one who didn't speak and whose name she doesn't remember.

'Trey,' Leigh interjects.

Yes, him. They were pushing each other under the waves, attracting stares and smiles. Anke was travelling with a group of friends from home and they had come to the island by chance. They had spent the summer touring and camping around England and Ireland. Her parents had paid. She comes from a good family, where money has never been a problem. When in Dublin, they heard about a pretty island in the middle of the Irish Sea where real fairies lived. So they had got the ferry there on a whim – the last stop before going home. They had arrived early in the morning and found their way to a bay which had been recommended to them. The bay was very beautiful: heather-filled cliffs, quaint cottages, rough water even in high summer. You could hear the waves at night.

'Your brother looked like he was having fun, you know? My memory is, how do you say, hazy, but I have been thinking about it more and more, that first time I saw James on the beach. Especially knowing what I know now.'

'What do you know now?' Leigh says, impatient to find out what she has to say but also captivated by this description of her brother through a stranger's eyes.

'Nothing, a little. Only that he is missing.'

Leigh feels disappointment again as the Dutch woman continues. Anke remembers seeing James, bare-chested and tanned, waist deep in water, and noticing him from a distance, that is all. The others, she remembers only a little. The shy one, he was, how would Leigh call it, mixed?

'Trey's dad is from Jamaica,' Leigh says.

'The big one who was with them,' Anke says, nodding, 'he was waiting on the shore with his trousers rolled up to his knees and a handkerchief on his head. It was like he was the dad. I never saw him in swimming trunks for the whole week.'

This sounds typical of Geoff, James's closest friend from primary school. He always was the sensible one.

'The big one helped us put our tent up, later, but your brother just leant back with his hands on the grass and watched.'

That sounds typical of James, too.

'But I didn't speak to him, not until that evening, after we had all been to the pub.'

The pub was on the side of a hill, dark and cosy, with low, beamed ceilings, and Anke remembers the three boys in there, sitting in a corner seat with pints in front of them. Anke and her friend were on the other side of the room, but the pub was small enough to overhear the boys talking in an accent she found it hard to understand – English, but not English, like Leigh's. James was the most handsome. He had a nice smile. He was sunny, or so she thought at first. She liked boys back then – now, not so much – and there were no other boys of their age on the island. Anke didn't approach James because her friend had no interest in the other two. She doesn't think she ever heard the quiet one speak, he only whispered to his friends.

Poor Trey, Leigh thinks, wondering how he's doing. He was always painfully shy and it had taken much persuading for his parents to allow him to go camping, even though he had turned 18.

'And Geoff, his name was? He was plain, no? A person who didn't have much fun. He spent the evening counting money on the table, stacking up pennies.'

Poor Geoff too. He's always been old for his age. His dad had left when he was young and he'd had to look after his younger siblings while his mum went to work. He's doing all right now, though, has a job as a teacher in a secondary school in Chester.

'Your brother,' Anke continues, 'he kept looking over and our eyes met a few times, but nothing else.'

The two groups had ended up leaving at the same time, after last orders were called. The boys were behind Anke and her friends as they made their way down the narrow path to the campsite. And James somehow fell into step with her.

It was a summer romance, that was all. She was not crazy about him, or thought about him again when she went home. They kissed, yes, nothing more; they hung around together, yes, watched the waves, held hands. He once drew her name in the sand. Anke can't remember all the details, of course, but certain images stay in her mind: James dancing to 'Roll Away the Stone' after they'd smoked the dope the boys had brought with them; James playing cricket on the sands; the two of them staying up until the sky flooded with stars. Nothing out of the ordinary. Good times, you know?

But he wasn't someone who made her heart go boom.

She was not in love.

'Did you tell him that you weren't interested?' Leigh interrupts. 'James stayed on, when his friends went home.'

'I think he was more serious than me,' Anke shrugs. 'I didn't know he had decided to stay until I saw his tent was there in the morning and the tents of the other two had gone.'

'And James, how did he seem to you? You said earlier that you thought he was sunny – at first.'

'Happy, sometimes, but then not so much.'

'What do you mean?'
'He said later he was pretending.'
'Pretending to do what?'
'To be enjoying himself.'

As the week had gone on, Anke noticed James would go quiet in company. When he became like that, he would be far away, inside his head, speaking to nobody, listening to nobody, as if he was in a trance. One morning Anke saw that his eyes were red and swollen. He was always the last one to go to sleep. And he ate very little. She remembers they went to Peel to try the famous crab sandwiches there, and he threw his away, untouched.

Anke has thought of these things retrospectively. She has been trying hard to remember. At the time, she thought he was just a boy, immature, and this was the reason. Now, she sees it in the light of him being missing, in the light of what she has invited Leigh to London to hear.

Leigh's stomach turns in anticipation.

One evening, Anke and James bought a bottle of cider from a little shop in Peel and got tipsy on the cliff-top, just the two of them. They had some more dope, too. James was scaring her, acting like he was on a death mission, going too close to the edge of the cliff. And after that, she shared a story of her father having a nervous breakdown – the pressures of his job in government – so she supposes one thing led to another. James said what he said about pretending to be happy, and that something was on his mind. Of course, Anke wanted to know what this was.

He said he could never tell her, in case it put her in danger. He said in particular he could not tell his sister because she was going to join the police. Anke had pressed him because he looked very unhappy.

'He said something had happened before his trip, a very bad thing.'

'What bad thing?' Leigh asks.

'This is what I asked but he would not tell. He was stoned and drunk but not so much that he lost control of what he said. He gave fragments only, of a bigger story. He said other people were involved, nasty people. He said he didn't know what he was going to do. He said he might have to run.'

Leigh has stopped breathing. She takes a gulp of the cola and leans across the table, towards Anke.

'And then we spoke no more of it,' Anke says, 'and the next morning he was sunny again. And that is how he was for the rest of the time, until the stranger arrived.'

26

'What stranger?'

Anke makes an exaggerated shrug in reply.

'I didn't see this person,' she says. 'We were told about this when we were in the pub one night. That he had been asking about the whereabouts of three teenagers from Liverpool, one called James.'

'What else did you hear?'

'The landlady, she said the gentleman spoke with a Liverpool accent and that he drove a black car. He told her he was a friend who was looking for James. He didn't leave a name.'

'And did she tell this man where to find them? The Isle of Man is a small place. The landlady of the pub would have known that the three boys were staying on the campsite in the farmer's field.'

'The lady said no, she did not. She said the man was older, sinister. He was not the type of person that three boys on a camping trip would know.'

'And this is the Manx Tavern, on the road to Dalby?'

'I don't remember the name. The nearest one to the bay? Then, yes.'

'When? At what point in the week did this happen?'

'Towards the end. I don't remember, but James's friends were still there.'

Leigh is leaning so far towards Anke that her fingers are clasped around the table edge. Since hearing about the stranger, she's turned into DS Borrowdale, barking questions as if she's interviewing a suspect. When Anke starts to fidget at the invasion of her personal space, she reins herself in and sits back.

'Why didn't the police know about this?'

'Perhaps, nobody told them.'

'And then what?'

'I do not think this man was a friend because James, he reacted badly.'

'What do you mean, badly?'

'He was, how do you say, paranoid? Afraid. He ran out of the pub.'

'Did his friends go out after him?'

'His friends were not there.'

'Did you go after him?'

'No, he was gone when I went outside.'

'And did you see James after that?' Leigh asks, thinking of how her brother was spotted by a couple walking down to the beach to see the stars.

'Yes. With the big one. I saw them together, later, sitting by the tent. They were talking, you know? Deep in conversation.'

'Did you talk to him about it after that, about the stranger asking after him?'

Anke shrugs.

'You didn't say goodbye?'

'I was interested only in fun, not complications,' she says. 'Life. It is too short.'

Leigh looks incredulously at the young, glowing woman across the table from her. She is suddenly suspicious. She knows nothing about Anke – why should she believe her?

'Perhaps,' Anke says matter of factly, 'he went over the cliff.'

'Or perhaps he didn't,' Leigh says.

'Your brother,' Anke says, 'he was an unhappy person. Perhaps he was not who you thought he was.'

'My brother,' Leigh says, 'was exactly who I thought he was.'

Leigh gets to Euston station two hours early for her train. She goes into Boots, in search of a present for Kai, and comes out with a dummy – he hasn't tried a pacifier before and she's thinking it might help him sleep. Then she goes into WHSmith and buys a notebook and pen from the newsagents, as well as a can of Tizer and an assortment of chocolate bars. Inside the station concourse, she settles on the floor, a plastic bag between her feet, looking up at the departures board and all the place names and stops along the way. Randomly, she looks for a place called Bolsover on the list of destinations. She sees legs pass by, hears conversations float past: 'I will if you keep on smoking, girl,' says the male half of an older couple temporarily blocking her view; 'Platform 14!' says one of a trio of girls rushing for a train, laughing as they squeeze through the crowds, exhilarated by their own mini emergency. To her right, a man dolefully sweeps the floor of dusty footprints, and to her left, striding through the entrance door are two uniformed officers. Leigh puts her head up, but they don't give her a second glance. Why would they? She isn't DS Borrowdale here, she's a pigeon pecking the ground, hoping for a crumb, or a bedraggled bag lady who wanders from town to town, carrying her life in a plastic bag. This last thought gives her a reckless, fuck-it feeling. She could do anything she wanted here and no one would care. She could carry bollocks banners through the streets. She could sleep in shop fronts. She could catch a train to Bolsover.

Overwhelmed and more than a little tearful, Leigh crams a Marathon bar into her mouth. There are so many things that don't make sense. Why would James stay on the island if he thought someone was after him? Why didn't he just go home with the other two?

And if his friends knew about it, why did they leave him there?

After a theatrical but short-lived bawl, Leigh dries her eyes with her fists. She needs to pull herself together and concentrate on her battleplan. She takes her new notebook and pencil out of the plastic bag and makes a list of everyone she needs to speak to.

Geoff and Trey – the friends James went camping with.

Her mum and dad.

The landlady of the Manx Tavern.

Leigh circles Geoff's name – her top priority. He'd been her brother's friend since their first day at Mosspits Lane Primary School and he knew him better than anybody. If James had a terrible secret, he would have told Geoff, surely? Anke had seen the two of them talking, after James found out that a stranger had been asking about him in the pub.

She goes back through the years, trying to recall how Geoff had acted when he discovered James was missing. She decides he'd behaved as you'd expect, frequently visiting the house on Dunbabin Road to ask for updates, offering to help, being attentive to her mum. He'd demonstrated every sign of being devastated, frequently apologising for leaving James behind on the island and wringing his hands over what he could have done differently. But none of her family had seen him since the Queen's Silver Jubilee street party in 1977, during which, her mum had complained, Geoff had eaten all the cold sausages and most of the mini rolls, and they were the Cadbury's ones, too.

She'll go and see Trey as well. He's only down the road in Toxteth, and although she doesn't know his address now, she thinks his parents still live on Park Road. He always was the quiet one – Anke had got the personalities of James's friends spot on – and he'd been an almost invisible presence in their lives, even before James went missing. After an attentive few months, both Geoff and Trey had kept their distance as the years had gone on. And now, Leigh is wondering why.

The departure of the Liverpool train is announced. Once on her feet, Leigh feels a renewed sense of urgency. She runs through her list in her head: Geoff and Trey, her mum, the landlady of the Manx Tavern.

She doesn't know whose door to beat a path to first.

27

Nearly four hours later, Leigh picks Kai up from Min's and catches the bus to Dunbabin Road, hell-bent on asking her mum if she knows anything about what was happening in James's world in 1974.

Only to find Pat Killen sitting at the kitchen table, drinking coffee and smoking a cigarette. The sight of her mum's new boyfriend stops Leigh in her tracks – she hadn't seen his car outside. She stands in the doorway, carrying a snoozing baby in the sling. She is sweating and so hot her blood is at boiling point.

'Now then, young lady,' Pat Killen says, giving her a wink.

He stands up and takes her hand as she enters the room. She feels a knobbly ring press against her fingers.

'Will you leave, please,' Leigh says, not giving him a chance to schmooze her. 'I've got something urgent I need to talk to my mum about.'

Pat Killen sits down again. Her mum is by the sink, putting flowers in a vase. She's dollied up again: silk blouse with a checked skirt, burgundy rouge, pearl lips.

'What's got into you?' she snaps. 'Pat's come round for a coffee. We've not long got back from a drive out to Otterspool, stopped for a lovely little drink in The Little House in Aigburth Vale.'

Leigh releases Kai from his sling and he stays asleep in her arms – worn out from pulling an all-nighter at Min's.

'Would you like another coffee, Pat?' her mum asks, slotting the last of the red roses in the vase.

'Mum, I have to speak to you.'

She can barely keep the shake out of her voice.

Leigh swears she can see alarm in her mum's eyes, but then she remembers she doesn't know she's been to London to see Anke and she's looking at her like that because she's broken the cardinal rule: don't be rude to guests. Kai takes a breath that indicates he's been rudely awoken and a wail is on the way.

'You're upsetting the baby,' her mum says, reaching out to take Kai from her.

'You've got a beautiful grandson there, Gillian,' Pat says, as Kai starts to yowl.

'This baby's worn out,' her mum says, 'it's no wonder he's crying.'

Leigh goes to the sink, pours herself a glass of water, and downs it in one. When she turns back, Kai is in Pat Killen's arms.

'I've got two grandkids myself,' he's saying. 'I've got the magic touch with the kiddies.'

'Pat's a big softie at heart,' her mum says. 'Look, he's stopped crying now Pat's got him.'

Leigh glares at the man with the je ne sais quoi. He's in good shape for a fella in his late 60s. His faced is tanned, his silver hair is blow-dried, his hazel eyes have a sheen of vigour about them, and there's zero slack below his pointed chin. If he wasn't a ruthless criminal, she might think her mum had done well for herself.

'If they get too hot, they get dehydrated,' Pat tells Leigh. 'Our Mikey's wife Linda used to dress hers in cotton in summer when they were babes. It's them things,' he continues, nodding towards the discarded sling on the table. 'Kiddies can't control their body temperature. Our Linda wouldn't go near one of them.'

'I've told her, but she won't listen,' her mum says.

Leigh gives Pat Killen the daggers. Notwithstanding the gravity of the situation, she isn't going to take parenting advice from a fella with an abysmal track record: one son dead, the other banged up in Walton jail. She flexes her fingers and then curls them into a fist, trying to contain her frustration. Her mum goes to the sink, wets a tea towel at one end and attempts to dab it on Kai's head to cool him down. With a stern babble, the baby makes a grab for the material and pulls it onto his knee.

'How old is he?' Pat asks Leigh.

'Five months,' her mum answers.

'Is he rolling over yet?'

Leigh takes a deep breath. She thinks she's about to explode.

'Both of my grandkids were rolling over by that age,' Pat says, putting down his cigarette so it smoulders in the ashtray. 'And sitting up too. His head's still a bit wobbly, isn't it?'

Bored of the tea towel, Kai makes a grab for Pat's sunburned nose. Trying to squirm out of his grasp, the baby talks to his captor in a jabber which turns into a shriek when he turns his head and sees a shark in his face.

'I've been talking to Pat about getting you a flat,' her mum says.

'I'm all right where I am,' Leigh says. 'And I need to talk to you, urgently.'

'Got a lovely little flat I'm thinking of renting off Picton Road,' Pat says. 'Half the price and better quality than where I've heard you're living now. The finish on it is lovely. Near your mam, as well. I'm going to be clearing near-on 15 grand each on them flats.'

'Nobody asked you how much you were making,' Leigh says.

'Leigh!' her mum admonishes her.

Leigh mutters under her breath that being close to her mum would not be in the flat's favour. It's time to leave because nobody is listening and she is officially losing her mind.

An hour later, Leigh is sitting on the mattress in her bedsit with Kai. She is churning over the past, trying to remember her brother's last months before he went on the camping trip.

Anke had painted James as a dope-smoking fiend on a death mission, but this doesn't sound like the James Leigh knew. He'd told her once that he'd tried cannabis with Geoff, and she remembers one occasion when he'd arrived home in the early hours, acting loud and obnoxious and tripping over his own feet on the way to the bathroom. But didn't every teenager do that? Leigh certainly did. She still does it now.

She attempts to take a break from her racing thoughts. The sky outside is darkening and the temperature has dropped, so she gently places a blanket over Kai. He objects immediately, spitting his new dummy out and kicking out with his fun-size feet. His right foot is bare – he's minus a sock, having lashed it on her mum's kitchen floor in baby protest. On the street outside, a motorcycle races past and then another – police bike units, turning right towards Toxteth. Leigh snuggles down and positions her face so she's nose to nose with the baby. There's danger around them, but this bedsit is her haven, a place for just the two of them. Not even imaginary James comes to Canning Street.

In the quiet, and with the dummy once again plugged into the baby's mouth, her mind takes a deviation towards Pat Killen but then returns to James. She continues her search through the past for the bad thing she had missed. During the summer her brother disappeared, Leigh had been 22, lounging around waiting for a start date for her training, getting high or getting laid, usually at the same time. She'd lost sight of James due to a whole lot of trivial stuff going on in her world, meaning she didn't take much notice of her annoying little brother, particularly one who liked Lynyrd Skynyrd and wore wooden clogs. Even their trips into town together on a Saturday afternoon had stopped, interfering, as they did, with her drug taking and casual sex.

The only thing she can ever remember James being upset about is Liverpool FC finishing behind Leeds in the league table.

But what did she know of her brother's secret thoughts? Anke said James couldn't tell Leigh what was wrong because she'd joined the police. But if he'd talked to her, she could have helped. Whatever it was, she would have helped.

Leigh props herself up on a mound of lumpy pillows, causing Kai to writhe under the blanket. She needs a wee but the prospect of disturbing him is too wearying so she ignores her bladder and continues to search her memory for signs her brother was in trouble. It must have been something to do with breaking the law, if he felt he couldn't tell her, but what could it have been? Drugs? Leigh would have understood.

She glances over to the giant telescope in the corner. Even by lamplight, she can see dust collected on its giant tube. The telescope used to live in James's room, blocking the way to the window, so when he'd packed that day to go to the Isle of Man, they'd both had to stand at the end of his bed to survey the things he'd laid out on there. The memory of James packing is engraved in her brain: the clogs, the cricket bat, which had been signed by Rohan Kanhai and Mike Procter at Old Trafford the summer before, and the Old Spice he'd nicked from the bathroom. Leigh can still see her brother's relaxed, smiling face.

He didn't look worried.

He didn't look unhappy.

And, she concludes, nothing untoward happened earlier that year. James finished his A levels. He lazed around listening to records in his bedroom. He went camping with his friends.

And he never came back.

28

'Did Kai settle down okay?' Des asks at the station the next morning, putting a hand on her shoulder as she tries to grab him before the briefing.

His touch makes Leigh want to cry.

'We'll talk later?' he adds, as the officer who was hit by the flying cactus stops to talk to her in the corridor.

Leigh stifles a yawn as the brother-in-law of Slapdash shares his war story.

'Looks nasty, that does,' she says, faking interest in the scratches around his left eye.

'You should see the other fella,' he says, a little red-faced – sustaining injuries caused by a three-foot-tall prickly pear is not conducive to hero status, and the incident is already infamous at the station. In the meantime, Slapdash is threatening to fingerprint every resident of the block of flats on Princes Road, plus carry out a search for cactus spikes in their living rooms. Leigh thinks there's something wrong with him. There were hundreds more people injured on both sides over the weekend, and he's pursuing a no hope case to wriggle out of doing any real work.

When she finally gets away, she heads for the murder investigation room and takes a seat around the table, peopled by herself, Callum, Mark II, and Kevin the trainee. Slapdash is missing again.

'How did you get on with your secret enquiries yesterday? We're all very keen to hear,' Callum says, his eyes fizzing with mischief.

'It'll all be in my report,' Leigh says as Des starts his recap on progress so far, although he's got competition from the noise outside – Duane Harding's supporters again, waving placards in front of the entrance.

'If you don't mind, we'll deal with each lead separately, take them one by one,' Des says. 'Firstly, we have the vigilante line. Victor Rivera, the inmate who was assaulted in Walton is claiming there's a hitlist going around. The existence of this list has been corroborated by our officer who works the informants in the prison.'

'It's not the same MO,' Leigh says. 'Duane Harding was stabbed and Victor Rivera was assaulted.'

'It's still attempted murder,' Mark II says. 'I reckon the way it pans out is that they're recruited in the prison, pick a name off the hitlist, and then get carte blanche to do what they like with the marks. Different courses for different horses.'

'Isn't it the other way around?' Leigh asks.

'You what? They pick a name and then get recruited?'

'No, horses and courses.'

Out of the corner of her eye, Leigh sees Des's shoulders shaking as he stifles giggles. Everyone else around the table looks at her as if she's gone mad which, to be fair, isn't far off the truth. It's nine o'clock in the morning, she's already blasted on Tizer and she can't remember going to sleep last night. She had roused Kai early to go to the phone box to call James's best friend, Geoff, who had been away on a summer school trip.

'Why would someone recruited by an inmate inside Walton write *Sorry, I had no choice* on the wall?' Leigh asks, experiencing a sugar rush as she swigs more Tizer.

'We're still trying to establish that connection,' Des says, a hand to his mouth to stop his giggles – once he starts, he can't stop. 'Kevin has been looking into any prisoners who are known to have lost children,' he adds, nodding towards the trainee to invite him to speak.

When all eyes in the room turn to Kevin, the blood rushes to his face. He gets stuck in freeze mode for a few seconds before he's finally able to speak.

'The prison, er, doesn't keep records about any, er, prisoners whose children were done away with, killed, murdered,' he says in a squeaky, faltering voice. 'I mean ...'

'Of course they bleeding do,' Mark II barks. 'You just have to talk to the right people. Serious crime have got informants inside Walton too. We'll tell you what you need to know.'

'Kevin has also been looking into fellas convicted of crimes against children in the North West,' Des says. 'Do you mind telling us what you've found out?'

The trainee has gone completely still, like a mouse playing dead. Des encourages him to go on by fluttering his fingers.

'I, er, from the list of paedos,' Kevin says, red-faced and stuttering, 'there's two who've been beaten up in the past year and one fella charged so looking into him is, er, we could look into that. Another went missing last October, he was reported missing by his probation officer, but no one's really bothered looking for him because he didn't have any family because of what he did and had been living ...'

'We need evidence, not some sicko's bleeding life history,' Mark II says. 'Any low life who harms children is fair game, it's part of the code.'

'If you don't mind carrying on please, Kevin,' Des says, flapping his hands but standing his ground.

But Kevin has fallen apart. He swallows repeatedly, his Adam's apple works overtime, and when he speaks, he spouts out a few random unconnected words.

'I, er, that's, there's nothing, er ...'

'For Christ's sake!' Mark II bellows, directing his ire at Des. 'Is that the best you've got? We need fellas on the squad who can string a sentence together, not some girlie here to make the tea.'

'If you don't mind me saying so,' Des says, a hint of steel creeping into his voice. 'I'm leading this investigation and I'd thank you not to talk to one of my officers in that manner.'

'What manner?' Mark II snarls. 'I didn't say nothing to the kid. If he can't take it, he shouldn't be here.'

'Great work, Kevin,' Des says pointedly, and swiftly moves on. 'Next, we've got Gail Harding's uncle, Warren Jones, who is missing a corroborated alibi for the time of the murder. And we've got a mystery fella who Warren claims Duane Harding mistook him for when he talked to him through a closed door. If, that is, Warren is telling the truth.'

'He is,' Leigh says.

'It might be that he's trying to get himself off the hook.'

'Don't think so.'

Des sighs and then explains that Kevin, who's the only one who seems to do any work around here, has got a printout of calls to and from the Harding's flat in the two months leading up to his murder. It shows a succession of calls from a telephone box traced to L7.

'That backs up what Warren is saying,' Leigh points out.

'One more thing,' Des says into an atmosphere you could cut with a knife. 'We need to bear in mind what Duane Harding's father has told us. John Harding is claiming his son said he'd have proof of his innocence soon. That might provide motive, if someone wanted to stop it from getting out. Clara Harding is still refusing to cooperate.'

'We should do her for obstructing the course of justice,' Leigh says, off her head on Tizer. 'And John Harding is talking bollocks.'

29

'The relationship hadn't even lasted a week,' Leigh tells Des when she's finished running through what Anke said – as if the fact James's holiday romance hadn't worked out is the most important bit.

'What stranger?' Des repeats, struggling to take it all in.

'Who knows?' Leigh says. 'Who knows if this Anke is even telling the truth. She could be some random woman who got hold of my name.'

'I wonder what would she get out of that, though? Did she ask you for money?'

Leigh shakes her head and they fall silent for a while, both deep in thought as they walk slowly around the boundaries of Admiral Park. It's all quiet in Toxteth this morning – no protestors or rioters – although the shaggy-haired fella with the film camera is making his way through the streets, filming the aftermath of the riots.

'Do you trust what this Anke had to say?' Des asks.

'She seems credible. And she did describe James and his friends pretty well.'

She turns to view Des. He's wearing a dark suit and sunglasses, smoking a cigarette, and he looks very cool. She doesn't know whether she's drunk too much Tizer, but walking side by side with her ex-boyfriend is making her heart knock.

'What's your instinct telling you?'

'My gut feeling is that there's something in it.'

'Me too. I do think it's all going to be rather hard to look into though. You need to refer it back to the Isle of Man force. It's not as if they've got much to do over there.'

Leigh knew he was going to suggest this – Des is a stickler for rules. And she has thought of it herself – the Manx police were good at their jobs when James first went missing, organising a search of the bay and surrounding fields, launching an appeal for witnesses. But they obviously either hadn't made enquiries at the Manx Tavern, or followed up if someone from the pub had come forward.

'You could put in a call to the Manx Constabulary,' Des suggests, looking into the distance towards the shaggy-haired cameraman, 'ask them if anyone reported this stranger.'

'I could, but that might stop me from doing my own investigations. I'm going to telephone the Manx Tavern, once I've located the Yellow Pages. The landlady is probably still there. I've already tried Geoff, James's best friend, but, apparently, he's on a school trip in Wales and he's not back until tomorrow. *And* I need to get hold of the passenger lists for the ferries and airlines that week.'

'Hmm,' Des says. 'We can ask his friends what they know, but be prepared – if they haven't said anything for seven years, they're unlikely just to breeze through the details now.'

'Yes, but I'll be able to tell if they're hiding something.'

'If you don't mind me saying so, that won't do any good. They still won't be saying anything, whether you can tell they're lying or not. We need to corroborate the story at the pub. And the passenger lists are a good idea, but it's an impossible job if we don't know who we're looking for. We do need some type of lead first.'

'You know what Anke said?' Leigh says, calling to mind other parts of her conversation with the young Dutch woman. 'She said, "*maybe he went over a cliff.*"'

Des looks pained. She can see his mind ticking over.

'I don't like to say it,' he says, about to say it anyway.

'James threw himself off?' Leigh says. 'There was no note in his tent. He wouldn't have killed himself without a note, surely?'

'Perhaps he was worried about this bad thing, whatever it was, and the ending of his relationship with Anke pushed him over the edge. Sorry,' Des adds, 'unfortunate turn of phrase.'

Leigh shakes her head. She hadn't countenanced the possibility of suicide seven years ago and she isn't considering it now. The James she knew was happy and carefree; the James she knew had everything going for him in life and was looking forward to the future.

'She also said,' she continues, 'and I quote: "*He wasn't someone who made my heart go boom. I was not in love.*"'

Leigh hadn't minded the bluntness; it was the brutal honesty of her indifference that had grated. If only Anke had said James was the love of her life and she'd never forgotten him. If only she'd said she'd never stopped thinking about the boy she met seven years ago on the Isle of Man. Instead, James had been something to do, someone to pass the time with; a compensation prize in a romantic desert.

'Life. It is too short,' Leigh mutters in a silly accent Anke didn't have, making an exaggerated shrug of the shoulders.

'Sorry?' Des says, absorbed by the shaggy-haired fella with the film camera, who is now being told to do one by the locals. The camera crews are almost as unpopular as the police around here; she's heard one ended up in hospital on Sunday night.

'It doesn't matter,' Leigh says, feeling a little better already. Des had said 'we' and she appreciates the 'in this togetherness' of the plural. She appreciates Des. When they'd first worked together, in 1979, they'd bonded over grief – Des's dad had just died and he couldn't be buried because of the gravedigger's strike.

'I want to know and I don't want to know,' Leigh says. 'I'm scared of what I might find out.'

'I do think it's best not to speculate,' Des says, touching her on the arm, 'it'll upset you, if you think the worst. Try and stick with the facts.'

'One option is that the stranger hurt him,' Leigh says, doing the opposite, 'but the other option is that he got away.'

All morning, hope has again been making its presence felt: magical, deceptive, fantastical hope. One second, she's staving off terrible images about what this stranger might have done to James, the next she's dreaming of seeing her brother again.

'But that can't be right either,' she says, coming down on the side of pessimism, 'because if he ran away, he would have been in contact with me, I know he would. He would have got word to me, somehow.'

They both stop talking to view the cameraman, who is now pointing his lens at the protestors outside the station.

'Anyway,' Leigh says, 'I'm going to need some time off. Can you cover for me again?'

'Um,' Des says. 'I do need you on the case, I'm afraid. We've very short staffed as it is. We'll have to do what we can in our spare time.'

'Can't we come to a compromise?' Leigh says. 'I'm definitely having time off to look into this.'

Des bursts into a smile.

'That's not a compromise, actually,' he says.

In a switch made possible by prior experience in compartmentalising their private lives, they return to talking about the Duane Harding case as soon as they're on the borders of police property.

'I do know you've got a lot on with Kai, and with your brother,' Des says, 'but I read your report from the Nikki

Harding visit and, if you don't mind me saying so, it doesn't say much.'

'There wasn't much to write.'

'What's Nikki's alibi? You didn't mention it in the report.'

'There was no need.'

'I do think there is a need, actually,' Des says, as Slapdash and Mark II stroll in behind them.

'They're a law unto themselves,' Des says quietly.

'And Mark II can't even get his idioms right,' Leigh says, raising her eyebrows.

In the past week alone, they've been told not to court their chickens, that they shouldn't judge a cover by its book, and that words speak louder than actions.

'They think they're the knees' bees,' Leigh says as they watch the two Godfather squad fellas saunter into the station.

Des smiles but he looks tired out. He's been handed the short straw, heading up an investigation that nobody wants to solve, he's being undermined by the Godfather squad fellas, and he's under pressure to get a result. He stops short when the shaggy-haired cameraman points the lens directly at them.

'Actually,' he says. 'I've had an idea.'

Two hours later, they are watching flickering images projected onto an art-covered wall in a Georgian house on Hope Street. The fella operating the Super-8 camera is a lecturer in Social Studies at the university, and shooting images of people less fortunate than himself is his hobby during the summer holidays. His name is Lawrence and he'd been reluctant to share his output with fascist agents of the state, prompting Leigh to give an impassioned plea about how catching Duane Harding's killer could help them find a missing child. He only capitulated on the basis that it won't be used to identify anyone involved in the uprising – as if Leigh and Des could be arsed.

There are hours upon hours of footage, which plays out like a silent and endless movie entitled *Dante's Inferno*. Leigh hadn't realised how many firemen were at the scene – they'd barely been mentioned at the station – but here they are, chasing after lines of fire searing up the road or pointing their hoses at fierce flames. She also hadn't realised the Sally Army were in attendance, serving tea and sandwiches to uniforms at the top of Upper Parliament Street.

There's a long section which shows sick people in nightclothes being wheeled into an ambulance – the evacuation of Princes Park Geriatric Hospital in the middle of the night. And then there's a series of images featuring the charred and the hurt on both sides, sitting on pavements with their heads in their hands, lying injured on the floor, or being stretchered off. '*I was on the frontline when some serious danger happened,*' Lawrence says on one of the occasions he enters the room to check on them. '*I was right on the police lines when they started throwing Molotov cocktails.*' He talks as if he was the hero of the hour, Leigh thinks, but nobody asked him to be there.

As the horror show plays on, and the police start firing tear gas, she trains her eyes on the periphery of the frame. Who they're looking for wasn't involved in the fracas but taking advantage of what was going on. Their host has again disappeared upstairs and they have no idea how to operate the projector, so they just keep on watching as the early dusk on the screen turns into fire-blazing night.

They're waiting for daylight, to see if there's footage of someone near the Hardings' flat the following morning.

But dawn never breaks in Dante's inferno and so, after a long afternoon, they persuade Lawrence to let them take the film away with them, intending to give the job to Kevin and go home.

30

After work, Leigh walks with Kai under the shadows of burned-out buildings. A hot wind is blowing up from the Mersey and the heat is shimmering off the pavements, even though it's past seven o'clock at night. Heading into the heart of L8, her alert system is switched on. She hopes she looks like an everyday woman with a baby in a sling, but being in the police force marks her in a way she can't fathom – she's had people suss out she's a copper just by looking at her.

Leigh's walk takes her up Upper Parliament Street, past her old haunt, the Burundi Club, which she is glad to see is still standing. As she takes a right by the NatWest Bank, she sees the gutted building is heavily policed. Forced to dodge hostile officers and worried residents alike, she makes sure not to catch any eyes. She bends her head and coos at Kai, who is staring at her in his Zen-like way, oblivious to any danger.

The residents of Toxteth have begun to resume their normal routines as best they can, although some of them have been uprooted and temporarily moved to high-rise towers in the city, or to houses off the East Lancs Road, miles out of town. The pavement is peppered with groups of kids dressed in shorts and knee-high socks, a football team on their way home from after-school practice. A couple of the teenagers are being guided across the road by one or both of their parents: the message is that you don't go out alone here or you'll get stopped and arrested.

Leigh walks on towards Lodge Lane. She's already been to see Trey's parents on Park Road, a visit it had taken a while to break free from, owing to the warmth of the welcome, the compliments about the baby, the constant offers of food and drink. Leigh and Kai had been led through the cosy living room, paraded in front of Trey's younger siblings, introduced to the visiting church warden, and Leigh had finally come away with an address.

The warmth of the Hyatt family home is a complete contrast to the tension on the streets outside.

As she walks onto Lodge Lane, Leigh sees the group of lads straight away, sitting on the doorstep of an empty shop front, examining LP covers and drinking beer out of cans. Even though she hasn't seen Trey since the Christmas of 1978, she recognises him by his sloping posture. He's wearing navy from head to toe, a jumper in a lighter colour tied around his neck. After some hesitation – she'd envisaged him alone, preferably inside his flat – she walks in the direction of the group, patting Kai on the back as a security blanket. All three of the young fellas watch as she approaches. Trey looks through her, not immediately recognising the sister of his childhood friend. When he catches her eye, he does what any self-respecting black man in Toxteth would do when faced with an approaching bizzy.

He runs.

Leigh's stride doesn't miss a beat. She carries on walking, making a slight deviation away from the shop front, as if that's what she was planning to do all along. Trey's two mates stay where they are, positioned as if they're on the starting block of a race. Leigh doesn't look back. When she reaches the end of the road, she sees Trey's blue-clad frame disappearing around the corner, still carrying an LP under one arm.

There's no way she's going to chase him. The chances of being misinterpreted around here are too high.

It isn't until she's made it all the way to the Anglican Cathedral that she hears a voice calling her name. She turns to see Trey half running, half walking, in her direction. When he reaches her, he looks around to see if anyone is watching, and then leads the way through the gate of St James's Cemetery.

'If your friends recognised me as a copper,' Leigh says when Trey has nodded a hello, 'just say I was after you. It'll be good for your street cred.'

'I haven't got no street cred,' he smiles.

Leigh doubts this. Her neck strains as she looks up at her brother's old friend, trying to take in his metamorphosis from boy to man since the last time she saw him. He's well over six feet, broad, too, and the face which used to be prone to blushing is decorated with a neat moustache. Back when James knew him, Trey was yet to have his first kiss. She bets he's had plenty now.

'He's a boss baby, he is,' he says, as Kai spits out the dummy he is refusing to take to. 'Is he Chinese? I never had you down as having a mixed-race kid.'

'Why not?'

'You're a Sid, aren't you?' he says, using the shorthand for CID officers. 'You're all racist.'

'I'm not,' Leigh says flatly.

'I seen what went on at the weekend during the uprising,' he says. 'I seen loads of people getting gassed. A woman on our street was scratching her eyes out.'

'The policing of the riots had nothing to do with me,' Leigh says.

'They're not riots, they're uprisings,' Trey says, followed by a harrumphing sound.

As Leigh is wondering when he changed from being painfully shy to being mouth almighty, he puts his head down and strokes Kai's cheek: 'All right, lad?' The baby, delighted to be back at the centre of the universe, reciprocates with a gummy smile.

'Aw, he's boss,' Trey repeats. 'Is your husband good looking?'

'Cheeky sod,' Leigh says. 'Anyway, I don't have one of them.'

'Single mother with a mixed-race kid,' Trey grins, 'you've got more street cred than me.'

The two of them sit down together on a bench, Trey making it ready by sweeping an empty packet of Chipsticks to the floor and then changing his mind and putting the rubbish in a nearby bin – he's a well brought up boy. Leigh shows an interest in the LP he places between them – Syl Johnson's *Is it Because I'm Black*, an old record with a track list of songs she remembers dancing to at the Burundi Club.

'What are you doing nowadays?' Leigh asks. 'Your mum said you left home last year.'

'You've seen my mum?'

'How else do you think I found you?'

'This and that,' Trey says, answering her original question. 'I do my music, been writing a lot.'

'That's great,' Leigh says, remembering his school day prowess on the French horn and also remembering what his dad had said earlier, with a shake of his head, that his son always has ideas which never get off the ground.

Even though Leigh is chomping at the bit to ask her questions, they proceed onto polite enquiries about her mum, her dad, Trey's grandparents, and his older sister, who's married now and living off Aigburth Road. Leigh takes Kai out of his sling so he can use her thighs as a trampoline. She quickly calls to mind the headlines from her time with Anke: James was upset about something bad that had happened, and there was a stranger asking after him on the island.

She takes a deep breath before saying:

'I need to talk to you about James. You know when you went camping? How did he seem to you?'

Trey wriggles beside her. He sits forwards, with his elbows on his knees.

'Dunno, normal,' he says. 'We had a laugh.'

'I've found something out,' Leigh says, not wanting to go too hard, too soon. 'Can you remember that blonde girl, Anke, the one you told us about? The one James liked? She was camping with her friends at the same time you were.'

'A bit, yeah.'

'She got in touch with me, said James told her he was in trouble.'

'You're joking me?'

Leigh fixes her gaze on Trey. He looks – what? It's difficult to tell. He's blushing, but then he's always blushed when talking to women. He's sweaty, but then he's been running. He's lifting his t-shirt out from his chest and complaining about the heat. But then, it's muggy.

'Did James tell you what the bad thing was?' she asks directly.

'Nah, I don't know nothing about that.'

Trey leans over to make a fuss of Kai again.

'Anke said that, during that week, James sometimes looked sad and went off by himself.'

'What else did she say? How did you get in touch with her, anyway? It's been ages.'

'She found me. Phoned me at the station. James mentioned me to her. He told her I was joining the police.'

'What, so she's saying he topped himself? James wouldn't have topped himself, no way. He had everything going for him.'

'I don't think he did that either,' Leigh says, building up to mentioning the stranger. 'This Anke, she told me James said bad people were involved and he didn't know what he was going to do, that he might have to run.'

Trey makes an unfathomable noise.

'He wouldn't tell her that and not tell his mates,' he says.

'That's what I thought. Would he have told Geoff, do you think?'

'Nah, the girl's messing.'

'Can you remember a pub, near Niarbyl Bay, called the Manx Tavern?'

'We went to a few pubs, but I can't remember their names.'

'Have you seen Geoff?'

Trey shakes his head.

'Lost touch ages ago,' he says. 'Don't even know where he lives now.'

After Leigh tells him Geoff is in Chester, they lapse into silence, both of them staring straight ahead at a leaning gravestone featuring an engraved list of orphans.

'Did she say anything else? This girl?' Trey says after a while.

'She said you brought drugs with you and James was smoking dope. I never knew he took drugs.'

Leigh doesn't know why she thinks this is important; her mind certainly keeps returning to it.

'Nah, we never. And he never done drugs.'

Trey fiddles with the sleeves of the jumper hanging around his shoulders. His blush has now spread to his ears.

'Do you remember James saying that someone had come looking for him, on the island?' Leigh asks. 'A stranger, who came into the Manx Tavern asking about him?'

Trey puts his hands to the back of his head. He pulls a face to indicate the ridiculousness of that notion.

'Try and remember anything,' Leigh says, 'anything that you noticed about James that week that wasn't quite right.'

'I can't remember much,' he says. 'It was ages ago.'

'Rack your brains and I'll come and see you in a few days.'

'Nah, you can't come into L8. You'll get killed. And,' he adds, smiling, 'I can't be seen talking to no bizzy.'

'More than your life's worth?' Leigh says. 'Meet me here then, on Friday, same time.'

Trey doesn't say yes or no. He picks up his LP and stands up, towering over her. Leigh is still holding Kai, preparing to put him back in the sling, when Trey surprises her by leaning down and giving her a hug.

'Do you ever think of James?' she asks as he turns to go.

'All the time,' he says. 'All the time.'

Leigh doesn't go home, not straight away. She stays on the bench and points up to the Georgian terraces on Canning Street, showing Kai where he lives. The baby shows no sign of being either interested or tired, so she puts him in his sling and does a couple of laps of the cemetery path.

As she moves through the shadows and patterns of the July dusk, Kai starts to grizzle, complaining that the strange mummy person is no longer pulling silly faces at him. She breaks off from her rumination to sing out loud – even the most contemplative moments in life can be interrupted by *Wheels on the Bus*. But by the time she's gone around the side of the Anglican Cathedral and emerged at The Oratory, she is lost inside her own head again, smiling at the baby on autopilot.

She needs a few minutes to make sense of everything. She has enough experience as a police officer to know when someone is concealing information. As she walks, she thinks about all the secrets that people hide. In her line of work, she finds that people keep things to themselves for lots of different reasons – they're scared of getting into trouble, they're afraid someone is going to come after them, they're protecting someone, or they don't want to get involved.

She wonders which one applies to Trey.

31

'Leigh! How are you, mate?'

'Geoff,' Leigh says, picking up the phone early the next morning to the warm voice of James's best friend.

'Soz I haven't got back to you before, been away on a school trip, a shedload of 13- and 14-year-olds on a trip to Wales – nightmare!'

'Yeah, I bet,' Leigh says, smiling.

Hearing Geoff speak, her suspicions fall away. Leigh pictures him wearing sports gear and slippers while perched on the end of a settee with a handkerchief on his head. She pictures him as he used to be: chunky, round-faced, kind – a Moomin of a person.

'When did you get back?'

'Last night. Anyway, how are things? I heard the streets are on fire in Liverpool! And you had a baby! And got married! I would never in a million years thought you'd go down the conventional path.'

Married? Her mother's shame has obviously travelled as far as Chester.

'Geoff, can I come down and see you?'

'Course you can, mate.'

His voice is still warm, but there's a drop in the excitable volume.

'Today?'

'Today? I'm a bit hectic at the moment, to be honest, mate, school and that.'

'I thought it was the summer holidays?'

'It is, but they keep us busy all year round. No rest for the wicked!'

'Have you got a minute now?'

A pause, minuscule, but there.

'Er, yeah, I've got a minute though, tops. On my way to footie practice, I run a local youth team, six- to 17-year olds. Nightmare!'

Leigh had expected to be making arrangements to visit Geoff, not find out what he knows, but she feels pressurised by the 60-second countdown and dives straight in.

'I've found out some new information about James,' she says, without explaining who it came from – the sand timer has already started to flow. 'I'll explain more when I see you, but I want to know whether James was upset about anything, while you were on the camping trip.'

There's another pause at the end of the line, before Geoff says:

'He was as happy as Larry, mate.'

'Are you sure?'

'What's this about, mate?'

'Did he take drugs?' Leigh asks, still hung up on this nugget of information.

'James never took drugs, mate. No way.'

'Are you sure?'

'You smoked more weed than James did!'

This is true, but it's also something of a theme of Geoff's – how wild Leigh was in her youth.

'The craziest thing he did was getting lathered and farting in my face.'

Geoff has told her this story before, how James had climbed into the wrong tent after drinking too much Bacardi and vomited on Geoff's sleeping bag. Geoff has always believed James had an accident in the bay, and has clung to the idea that his last week had been a happy one.

'I want you to cast your mind back,' Leigh says. 'Is there anything James said about a bad thing happening, anything at all. Did anything happen over there that was out of the ordinary?'

'Sorry, mate. I've got nothing to tell you. The holiday was superb.'

'I saw Trey,' Leigh says, deciding not to pursue the stranger line until she sees Geoff in person.

'Yeah, he told me!'

'Oh. Are you in touch with him?'

'Yeah, I see him loads. We went on a hike in Delamere Forest a couple of weeks ago.'

Geoff breaks off to tell a voice in the background that he doesn't know who's drank all the milk in the fridge.

'Are you all right, mate?' he says when he's back with her. 'You don't sound your usual self. It takes a bit of getting used to, having a baby. My sister had a few problems after she had hers.'

'I'm fine,' Leigh says, a slight edge to her voice – you can quickly go off someone. 'In fact,' she announces, 'I've never been better.'

She's about to return to her visit to Chester, but the sand has almost run through the timer.

'Listen, mate, I've got to go,' Geoff says, after precisely sixty seconds. 'Great to talk to you anyway. Keep in touch!'

Leigh wants to kick herself when she puts the phone down. She should've waited until she could see his facial expressions; it's easy to hide on the end of a telephone line, plus, she's given him time to get his story straight – if he has a story. She glances towards the cot, hears Kai stirring and then settling again; having a lie-in after burning the midnight oil.

She takes a moment to think the conversation over. She's suspicious, but there isn't much to base her suspicions on: the pauses, the proliferation of 'mates', the 'I'm so busy' swerve of her visit to Chester. She wonders why Geoff called her at a time when he couldn't stay on the phone for long. She wonders why he only had a minute when she hasn't spoken to him in years. But then, she thinks, maybe he hasn't got a minute. She hasn't got one either – she's got to get Kai up, fed, dressed and ready to take to Min's. Maybe James's best friend has just moved on. Maybe he doesn't want to be reminded of the tragedy in their lives.

Except. The anomaly. Trey had said last night that he hadn't heard from Geoff in years; that he didn't even know where he lived. And yet, according to Geoff, the two of them see each other regularly. Before Leigh makes a start on her day, she sits for a while, staring into space, not knowing what or who to believe.

32

It's lunchtime by the time she tracks Des down in the Golden Yuen. It's been a busy morning, and not much of it has had to do with policing. She's spent part of her time trying to find the telephone number for the Manx Tavern. But there is no Isle of Man Yellow Pages available at the station, and there'd been no listing when she'd called Directory Enquiries – what sort of pub doesn't have a telephone? And she'd spent much of her time trying to get Des by himself to tell him about her mum dating Pat Killen, the need to do so triggered by walking past a fella with a tanned face and false teeth on her way to work. But her ex-boyfriend has been on the phone, he's been dealing with a determined journalist, he's been flirting with the Bolsover Beauty and, for the last hour, he's been in the Golden Yuen when he's supposed to be taking Kai for their usual Sunday morning stroll in the park.

She finds him at the usual window table, with his packet of Silk Cut in front of him, sitting with Mr Tam's 14-year-old son Eric, who helps out in the restaurant and likes to chat about joining the police force.

'Hi,' Des says, breaking off from the conversation.

As Leigh takes her usual seat opposite, Eric makes himself scarce. For once, he has work to do. Unusually for lunchtime service, one of the tables is occupied: a couple who look like they're from out of town, dressed for a day out touring the ancient ruins of Toxteth. The moustached man is sucking up a line of noodles. The woman is pushing her plate away and lighting a cigarette.

'Have you been up to see Kai?' she asks. 'He's been a bit grizzly lately. He threw his sock off on my mum's kitchen floor the other day.'

She's trying to instigate a conversation that will somehow lead her to telling Des about Pat Killen and moving back to her bedsit, but it doesn't go the way Leigh wants it to and ends with her talking about how Trey had said he hadn't been in contact with Geoff when Geoff said he'd seen him last week.

'That's curious,' Des says.

'He was evasive over the telephone. They were *both* evasive. It's like they're hiding something but it's like you said, I still haven't learned anything new. Anyway, I'm meeting Trey again on Friday. He lives on Lodge Lane now.'

'You shouldn't go into L8,' Des says.

'Yeah, yeah, yeah,' Leigh says. 'We're meeting in St James's Gardens not Toxteth, or at least, I asked him to meet me there. It's not the done thing to be seen with a bizzy. He might not even turn up.'

'Still,' Des says, 'if you don't mind me saying so, it's best to keep away for now, particularly if you've got Kai with you.'

Leigh nods, but she knows she'll knock on Trey's door if he doesn't show.

Mr Tam appears with a menu – there's no fan for Leigh these days, and no banana fritters either. She opens it without thinking and orders the cold milk that's been added since the last time she was here. Then she turns back to Des. The words about Pat Killen rise but get caught in her throat.

'How's Kevin getting on, looking through the footage?'

'He's still going through it. I had to practically force him to go home last night, and he was in at sunrise.'

'Good old Kevin.'

Des smiles.

'If there's anything on there, he'll find it. He's already found out about the fella charged with beating up a paedophile last year, the one he mentioned in the briefing – he's got an alibi. He's been banged up in Strangeways since April.'

The druggie who robbed the young mother on the same morning has also been ruled out.

'At least we've eliminated three people from the potential one million inhabitants of Liverpool,' Leigh says, as their attention is taken away, momentarily, by a growing commotion at the table of the out-of-town couple, to whom Eric has delivered the bill.

'Did you know the Nottinghamshire force had a similar case to Gail Harding's?' Des says, out of the blue. 'A 10-year-old girl, murdered in 1965. Josephine talked me through it yesterday.'

'If you're talking about the Marion Coote case,' Leigh says, bristling at the mention of the Bolsover Beauty's name, 'I already know about it.'

Another little girl missing from home in the middle of the night, another tosser loudly proclaiming his innocence. She had looked up past cases when she'd been investigating Gail's disappearance, and the Nottinghamshire murder 16 years ago had been among them.

'Josephine worked the case,' Des says. 'She was a young sergeant, back then. They picked the perp up pretty much straight away, after his teenage son dobbed him in. She got a commendation.'

'Bully for Josephine,' Leigh says. 'I didn't realise Bolsover was in Nottinghamshire.'

'It isn't, I don't think, but it's nearby. Bolsover's where Josephine lives. Apparently, it's got a castle.'

'Has it now?' Leigh says. 'Anyway, they struck lucky and we didn't. Besides, they had a body.'

Marion had been found by the side of a country road – it's thought she'd been moved from the place she was strangled.

'We should speak to Josephine more about it.'

'Why?'

'I thought it might help,' Des says, shrugging.

'Help with what?' Leigh says as the argument at the restaurant table gets louder.

'What's going on over there?' Des asks.

In an example of terrible timing, or maybe because of the interruption, Leigh decides now is the right time to race through her confession, feeling the need to add her reasons for not telling him before now. She hadn't told him about Pat Killen because she hadn't had the chance. And she hadn't told him about moving back to her bedsit because …

She's not clear on that one so she trails off.

Leigh takes a sip of the cold milk, which is slightly off, and waits for Des to ask her more about Pat.

But it's not her mum's new boyfriend he's interested in.

'I really think it's too dangerous to be at the bedsit,' he says, 'the rioting could kick off again at any time.'

Uprising, Leigh wants to correct him.

'It's my home,' she complains, downing the rest of the curdling milk in one. 'It's where we live, me and Kai.'

'The rioters were stopping ambulances during the first flare-up, to see if there were coppers inside. I know it's difficult, but you do need to take Kai back to your mum's, until things are more settled.'

Des's eyes fly up to the customers in the corner, who have now been joined by Mr Tam.

'No way,' Leigh says. 'And that's an out and out, no, by the way.'

'He is my son, too,' Des says, his eyes fluttering back to Leigh.

'Why are you being so non-negotiable?' she complains.

'Actually, you're the one being non-negotiable. You're only calling me non-negotiable because I'm not saying what you want me to say.'

Leigh marches out of the restaurant, past the table where the argument over the bill has escalated. The moustached man is complaining loudly that Eric had brought the wrong food while Mr Tam is gesturing towards their empty plates. As she storms past the front window, she sees DI Chung approach the table and flash his warrant card.

When Leigh reaches Admiral Street station, having made the journey on foot, she's surprised to see Des's Allegro already parked up, slightly capsizing into a hole in the concrete. It's not like him to park badly, she thinks, as she notices Duane Harding's supporters out front: the cousin in his cowboy hat, the Jesus-like fella feeding one of the Alsatians with a crust from a sandwich, and her biggest fan, the Teddy Boy, who spots her and gives her a cheerful wave.

She pops her head around the door of the murder investigation room, but there's no one in there. The blinds are drawn and the projector is set up but switched off – Kevin is obviously taking a break from looking through the images. Chairs are pulled away from the table, coffee cups pattern the windowsills, and the smell of nicotine and sweat fills the air.

When Leigh wanders into the major incident room, looking for Des, she's surprised to find Stan in there, surrounded by his black-suited Godfather squad cronies. Most of serious crime have decamped and are running surveillance operations from Walton in the north of the city, where she's usually based. She wonders if the DCI has showed up to undermine Des's murder investigation.

She wonders what Stan would say if he knew the man responsible for the death threats against him had been sitting at her mother's kitchen table the night before last.

As she walks towards the serious crime fellas, past Josephine's team of Midlands detectives, the room goes silent in waves, a hush moving from group to group. The usual hum of conversation and camaraderie is missing. In here, it's as smoky and uneasy as the streets of Toxteth outside.

Something's not right.

The slapdash fella folds his arms and gives Leigh a snarky look. Kevin glances up, briefly, before going back to madly scribbling notes. When Callum sees her, he raises his brows. '*What?*' she mouths at him, but he just rolls his eyes.

Stan is on his feet now, making his way over. When he reaches Leigh, he gives her a nod. It's not an unkind nod, it's a *shit's going down* nod, followed by a *what the fuck* head shake. He gestures for her to come with him.

'What are you doing here, boss?' she asks, once they're in the corridor. 'What's happened?'

Stan leads her inside the smelly investigation room and indicates for her to sit down. He's breathing deeply as he plonks himself down on a chair. His face is strained, grave.

'You need to look at this,' he says.

There's a bit of messing about before Stan manages to get the projector running and Lawrence's film begins to roll. The images are in black and white but it's clear they were taken the next morning: the lighter sky they had been searching for yesterday shows up the destruction of the night before. Stan's face is turned towards the grainy images as the gates to Princes Park appear, and then the camera moves to show a view of Duane Harding's flat on Devonshire Road.

And there, on the deserted street at four thirty in the morning, is a clear view of Nikki Harding running away from the murder scene.

33

Leigh doesn't have her bollocks placard with her, but if she did, she'd be waving it in Stan's face.

'No way,' she says. 'There's no way Nikki is a suspect in the murder of Duane Harding.'

'What do you mean, no bleeding way?' Stan snarls. 'She's on the bleeding film.'

He curls his lip so his front teeth are showing but he's not sneering – he's as pissed off about this as she is.

'There's no way she would have killed him,' Leigh says, 'she's desperate to find out where Gail is. And why would she write, *Sorry, I had no choice*? And,' she adds, 'our perp can't be a woman – Duane Harding wouldn't have mistaken Warren's voice for a woman's.'

'Explain what she was doing there then, smart-arse,' Stan says. 'Toxteth's a long way from that caravan of hers in Crosby.'

'It's not illegal to be running down a street.'

'I'll be the one doing the asking,' Stan growls. 'Nikki Harding's in the custody room – we brought her straight in. She's refusing to say what she was doing there – and that screams guilty to me. And we've brought in the pisshead brother with no alibi.'

'There'll be a reason she was there, we just have to ask her what it is.'

'Or we can just get her to cough and have done with this sorry bleeding mess. It's taking up resources.'

'She won't cough because she didn't do it.'

Stan lets out a hiss. He's putting on his usual macho front, but he's upset, they both are.

'There's no alibi for Nikki Harding recorded in your report,' Stan says, eyeballing her. 'And it's not the only alibi being called into question.'

'What do you mean?'

'DI Bennett from the Nottinghamshire force has been reviewing the original case, reckons she's a bit of an expert on missing kiddies. That mate of Nikki Harding's, the one you said vouched for her being in the club all night when Gail disappeared? What she actually said was, she wasn't with her all night and she can't account for lots of it because she was bevvied up.'

'You've got to be joking?' Leigh says, trying to keep her composure after finding out that Josephine has been nosing around in her investigation. 'So Nikki is accused of taking revenge on her former husband for murdering her child *and* is suspected of murdering her child herself?'

Stan lets out a long-exasperated sigh. He knows she's talking sense but he carries on pushing the official line because he has to.

'Harding's old man said his son had evidence that he was innocent. That gives Nikki Harding motive if she was the guilty one in the first place – kill him before he squeals.'

'There's one avenue we haven't looked at,' Leigh says, seizing her chance, 'a bunch of keys were found at the Hardings' flat. They're in the evidence room,' she adds, although the keys are actually in her bedsit, on top of Great Uncle Bulgaria.

'What keys? Why the bleeding hell wasn't this actioned?'

'Let me search again for the lock-ups Duane Harding might have used, see if we can find evidence of this innocence he was talking about.'

Stan gives her a deep stare. She isn't planning to look for evidence of Duane Harding's innocence, and he knows it.

'Clara will know what those keys are for,' Leigh says. 'I'll go and ask her, make her talk.'

'No, you bleeding won't.'

'Okay, I'll go out tonight and try the keys in all the garages in the area – I've already got the list from the original enquiry.'

'Forget it. We've got journos crawling all over the place. The arrest will be front page news by tomorrow.'

'Let me on the interview with Nikki, then.'

'Not a cat in hell's chance.'

'Why not?'

'Because it's not a meeting of bleeding hearts. We need to lean hard on her.'

With that, Stan stands and turns on his mammoth feet.

'Absolute shambles!,' he shouts as he walks out of the door.

In a huff, Leigh goes back to the investigation room, where Slapdash is malingering next to Kevin, whose scribbling has become furious. Mark II has an electoral register in front of him, still tracking down those responsible for the assault by cactus. Callum is at the window, peering through the slats in the blinds, trying to locate the source of shouting from down below.

'I always said women shouldn't be allowed in serious crime,' Slapdash says out loud, for her benefit. 'They get over-involved and they're too likely to stick together. And you have to protect them when you're out on the job. Liabilities.'

'What are you on about?' Leigh says, turning on him.

'I'm saying you've got blood on your hands, love. I always said something about that wife wasn't right. The Notts force solved their case by looking at the most obvious suspect.'

Stan was in overall charge of the inquiry into Gail Harding's disappearance, but it's Leigh who's getting it in the neck because she was acting DI and did most of the work. And because Slapdash is a male chauvinist pig.

'Enough!' Stan shouts as he enters the room.

He gives the nod to Leigh. Out of the corridor, he talks to her in a low whisper.

'Get onto them garages,' he says. 'Go out tonight when it's dark and try the keys in every lock-up in Liverpool. I want to know what he was hiding in there, even if it is proof of his innocence. No warrant. Knock first, say you're in pursuit of a suspect if anyone asks.'

Leigh nods at him, feeling vindicated.

'And take one of the girlies with you, if you want,' Stan adds. 'Go home and get some rest first. It's going to be a long night.'

Leigh's satisfaction in being listened to turns to concern as she heads down the corridor. How on earth is she going to sort out babysitting overnight? She can't ask her mum – she's made it clear Leigh has made her bed and has to lie in it. And she feels bad for overloading Min and fears she's going to wear her out – she's practically Kai's full-time mum as it is.

She's nearly at the entrance when the commotion starts. A uniformed officer appears, seemingly out of nowhere, and wrestles a fast-moving shape to the ground. Leigh looks on in surprise, seeing a halo of blonde hair and flying hands, hearing a barrage of abuse, directed at her.

'He's dead! My husband is dead because of you! I hope you're happy now!'

Clara Harding has found her voice.

She's too angry to be talking sense, but everyone gets the gist. Leigh is responsible for her husband's death because she'd accused him of something he didn't do. Duane Harding's supporters must have either seen Nikki being brought in or got wind of the arrest.

'Get her fucking out of here,' the duty sergeant shouts.

'Where's Duane's garage?' Leigh calls out, as Clara is led away to the custody suite. 'What are the keys for? The ones he left behind in your flat? Is that where he put Gail?'

Clara yanks her head back and stares at Leigh. But it's not a look of hatred, it's a look of knowing; some knowledge in her brain, leaking out of her eyes. And then, all previous gentility gone, she returns to shouting, telling her plans to everyone who will listen, which is everyone here, including frequent visitor Jengo, no doubt recently released from the psychiatric wards which have been fit to burst since the rioting.

She's going to the newspapers! She's going to her MP! She's making an official complaint!

'I wouldn't go out there, love, if I was you,' the duty sergeant says when the reception area falls silent again. He nods to the entrance and shakes his head.

Leigh ignores him and steps outside, where a crowd of Duane Harding's supporters surge forward and surround her.

34

Leigh feels a weight slam into her from behind, a strong grip as she's hauled back into the station, away from the angry faces and placards and barking Alsatian dogs. It isn't until they're safely behind the desk that Des's hands fall away from her shoulders. The reception area is in chaos – the duty sergeant is screaming for the doors to be shut, Stan is belting down the stairs on the bounce, Callum is watching from the sidelines, and a uniform is waving a truncheon around, dodging a flying beer can as he shouts for Duane Harding's supporters to get back.

Leigh is unscathed but shaken. When she looks down at her t-shirt, it's dripping with saliva.

'I'm fine, thanks for asking,' Leigh tells Callum when he appears at her side.

'I didn't ask,' he says, smirking.

Later, after the protestors have been dispersed and a handy line of coppers, plucked from the nearby streets, have taken their places outside the station, Leigh and Des escape to the safety of Great George Square. Ignoring their earlier row, they've already gone through the 'are you okay, no I'm not okay' stuff, resumed their 'move back to your mum's' argument, and had the 'Stan undermining Des about the lock-ups' conversation, and the 'why are they so bloody obsessed with the cactus thrower when there's a murder to be solved' moan about the Godfather fellas.

There'd also been an awkward moment when Des asked the 'what were you saying about Pat Killen' question and Leigh dodged it, hoping her mum's new relationship will blow over.

Now they're onto the murder case.

'I know Nikki didn't do it,' Leigh says as they start their third lap of the square, 'I know it.'

'Can I ask why though?' Des say, taking the packet of Silk Cuts out of his pocket. 'Why are you so certain?'

Leigh is sick of repeating herself.

'She wanted to find Gail.'

'And what if Duane Harding didn't do it? If he had the evidence that would exonerate him, or even if he said he did, it gives Nikki motive.'

'Right,' Leigh says, getting ready to count on her fingers. 'Duane Harding had no alibi – he was at home with Gail all night. He acted like he wasn't arsed when she went missing, and he put Nikki off calling the police. He took his car and disappeared for hours. Why would he do that if it wasn't to destroy evidence?'

'He claimed in his interview at the time that he was trying to protect Nikki.'

'He changed his story multiple times,' Leigh says, already on her fifth finger. 'He said at first he wasn't in the bathroom with Gail but then he said he was – that was after he'd learned we were talking to the neighbours and they could have heard his voice through the walls. He didn't take part in the searches – he carried on working, even though his workplace had offered him the time off.'

'He could have gone to work to keep his mind off it?' Des says, venturing another alternative explanation.

'He was jealous of Gail,' Leigh says too fiercely – she knows Des is only testing out her theories. 'Nikki's grandma backed that up. He was harsh with her. Duane Harding said Gail was difficult. How can a nine-year-old child be difficult?'

Leigh's gets heartache just thinking about it. Every child should be nurtured, in her book; every child should be loved and encouraged and cared for, just like Kai is going to be.

'The cadaver dog!' she says, starting to count the fingers on her right hand. 'It barked by his car. That means a dead body had been in there.'

'I thought the search didn't find anything?'

'It didn't,' Leigh says, billowing the hem of her t-shirt, which is wet where she'd sponged it of spit. They're on Cornwallis Street now and from here, there's a view of a one-bedroom flat they'd once looked around, back when Des used to hold her hand, before she'd plucked up the courage to say no to his proposal, before she'd had one too many wild nights out at the Burundi Club.

'I mean,' she says, 'putting all that together, what would you have thought?'

'I would have thought he acted oddly, but that it didn't amount to more than circumstantial evidence. The uniforms first on the scene didn't see any signs of a struggle, or a clean-up.'

'Everyone cleans the bath.'

'True,' Des says, 'but it was a case of he said, she said. I'm actually surprised it got to court.'

'That's Stan's personality for you. He bulldozed it through.'

And Leigh had been with him all the way.

'Did you ever doubt it?' Des asks. 'Even consider it could have been someone else?'

'Like Nikki, you mean?'

'Maybe Nikki did come home early, like Duane said originally, perhaps she harmed Gail by accident. Duane knows this, he's got evidence, and she kills him to stop the world finding out.'

'What? She carried her out of the flat and hid her body somewhere where it couldn't be found? She doesn't drive. And we searched the flat and the yard, and all the streets and just about everywhere else in the area.'

'She could have got her brother to do it,' Des says, still offering an unwelcome other perspective.

Leigh reaches for another finger on her upturned palm but finds she has lost count.

'Are you convinced yet?' she asks.

'Hmmm,' Des says, with a cigarette still unlit in his hand. 'I was off work at the time of the investigation, so …'

Leigh had frequently discussed the case with him when he was recovering from the bullet hole in his leg, and he'd always erred on caution. Not because he was defending Duane Harding, but due to their low chances of winning the case. But then, Des is evidence mad. Leigh is more a feeling sort of person. And her feeling is that Duane Harding was a murdering tosser.

'Well, I still think he was guilty,' Leigh says as they head back to Nelson Street to see Kai.

'Actually,' Des says, resting a hand on hers, 'if it helps, so do I.'

35

Once inside the station, Leigh marches down to the holding cells. When the detention officer opens the door, Nikki puts her face in her hands and shouts, 'Do one!' When she looks up and sees a friend, she flings herself into Leigh's arms and roars.

'There's no news about Gail,' Leigh says, as she always does.

From the brief glimpse Leigh has got of Nikki's face, Gail's mum looks terrible. She's put too much orange blusher on her deathly pale cheeks, as if she'd quickly attempted to make herself presentable before she left the caravan.

'Nikki,' Leigh says. 'You've got to tell me why you were on Devonshire Road that morning.'

'I can't.'

'Yes, you can. You've got to.'

'I can't!' Nikki says, juddering.

'Just tell me what you were doing there. Whatever it is, it can't be worse than getting charged with murder.'

Leigh attempts to hold Nikki at arm's length but she just tightens her grip.

'And you should have told me about Warren going round to the Hardings' flat,' Leigh says. 'It's like you're both trying to make yourselves look guilty.'

'Our Warren went round there to beg Duane to say where Gail was,' Nikki sobs into the neckline of Leigh's t-shirt. 'He just wanted Duane to say where he'd put Gail. Is he going to prison?'

'Not if someone backs up his alibi for the morning Duane was murdered, although he did punch a police officer.'

Nikki nods her understanding.

'All you need to do is tell me what you were doing there,' Leigh says, giving it another go, 'and then you can go home.'

'Aw, I would if I could, Leigh, but I can't.'

'Who are you protecting?'

'No one!'

'Warren?'

'No!'

'Okay,' Leigh says, having got precisely nowhere. 'Sit tight. I'm going to get you out of here.'

In the still of night, Leigh is outside a row of run-down garages in the Dingle with her girlie of choice, Des. He shines the torch with laser beam accuracy while she attempts to slot each key on the bunch into the locks. She's inserting them all in turn but she keeps getting confused as to which ones she's already tried. Having decided against involving Callum or Kevin, and with Kai in the care of the Godsend that is Min, Leigh has taken Des up on his offer to come along. Leigh suspects his real aim is to keep her safe but she doesn't need protecting, no matter what Slapdash said about her being a liability. Still, she's glad of his company. She's always glad of Des's company, even if the passenger seat of the Allegro is still pushed forward and she saw him today in animated conversation with Josephine. Has he even told her they've got a baby together? Doubtful. Has Josephine even noticed Leigh exists? Again, doubtful. Perhaps she's vaguely aware of her, in the same way you're aware of a bothersome fly that buzzes around in your face now and again.

They work in silence, trying each lock methodically, making completely sure none of them fit. Des's Allegro is parked at the end of the alleyway with its headlamps off. In fact, he'd driven around the entire estate without lights after a jam-butty car had slowed next to them, perhaps thinking Des was taking Leigh somewhere secluded for a quickie.

She can only wish.

Leigh moves to the next garage and rams the skeleton key in the lock. Stan had told her to knock on each door first, but she hasn't bothered with that because there aren't any people around to ask. It's past two o'clock in the morning, the roads are empty of traffic, and the area is eerily deserted. The lack of a warrant isn't a problem either – if one of the keys opens a door, they've found the place.

None of the keys open a door.

'Maybe we should have sent Kevin,' she says, 'he can find things no one else can.'

Des smiles in acknowledgement as he leans against a shutter, resting his bad knee. He reaches into his pocket and pulls out an aspirin, which he swallows without water. Leigh takes a swig of Tizer and then moves along the row, trying to control her nerves. Stan hasn't charged Nikki yet, but the arrest of a woman will be all over the front pages of the newspapers by morning, and a journalist contact of Des's has told him Clara has already done an interview with them. Everyone at the station is bracing themselves for tomorrow. And for dealing with all the people who'll come out of the woodwork to say all sorts of rubbish.

Leigh tries the lock on the last garage earmarked for tonight's search. The key goes in, but it doesn't turn. They get back in the Allegro and drive to Blundell Street for the next round of attempts. After Blundell Street, they go to Highbank Drive, Crown Street, and St James's Place. They carry on working through the night and by the time they've finished their fool's errand, it's sunrise, and the morning papers are already on the stands.

36

POLICE DETECTIVE'S BROTHER IS MISSING

By a staff reporter, Liverpool Standard, Monday 13th July 1981

A detective who led the investigation into the disappearance of Gail Harding has a secret heartache – her own brother has been missing for seven years.

Detective Leigh Borrowdale, who works for the serious crime squad, is mourning the loss of her only sibling, James, who vanished during a camping trip on the Isle of Man in August 1974.

The revelation comes after the news that a woman has been arrested on suspicion of murdering Duane Harding, the missing 9-year-old's stepfather. Mr Harding, formerly a car mechanic at Richardson's garage, was found stabbed at his Toxteth flat on 6 July this year. Two years earlier, he had been charged with Gail's murder but was exonerated of any involvement after the high-profile case collapsed in court.

Now, supporters of Duane, led by his grieving widow, Clara, are alleging Merseyside Police made grave mistakes in the inquiry into Gail's disappearance, including failing to follow up on vital witnesses and clues.

'All Duane ever wanted was for Gail to be found,' said Clara, who met her late husband while he was remanded on bail. 'But certain police detectives were blinkered from the start. They mounted a personal vendetta against Duane which distracted them from finding the person who was really responsible.'

Slim brunette Miss Borrowdale was the acting detective inspector on the investigative team Clara accuses of not pursuing a main suspect, getting too involved with members of Gail's family, and being certain they knew who was responsible, despite a lack of evidence.

'Knowing what we know now, the enquiry was always going to be complicated by emotions,' said Clara, who stood by her man throughout. 'Duane could never have hurt a fly. No one believed he'd harmed Gail, including some police officers I spoke to. We welcome the arrest which has been made.'

The disappearance of Gail Harding from her Devonshire Road home, on 28 September 1979, caused shockwaves throughout the Merseyside area. Gail, who had just started her second to last year at Toxteth County Primary School, was last seen in her bedroom at around 9 p.m. by her stepfather Duane, who was babysitting while his then wife, Nicola Harding, enjoyed a boozy night out with friends. When Duane woke in the morning, the back door was open and Gail was gone. Her body has never been found.

It's highly unusual for anyone to disappear without a trace, and yet, in an eerie parallel, that's just what Detective Borrowdale's brother did.

James was just 18-years-old when he vanished on the evening of 2 August 1974. The teenager, from Dunbabin Road in Childwall, had been on a summer camping break with friends before going to university that September. The trio of Liverpool teenagers had been staying on a campsite in a farmer's field in Niarbyl Bay, on the west coast of the Isle of Man.

On the night of the last confirmed sighting, dark-haired James was spotted taking the path down to the beach late at night. He was wearing shorts and a t-shirt and his feet were bare. He was reported missing more than a week afterwards, and while the reason for this delay is not known, it's thought that there was initially little concern for his safety by his family and friends. James was an 'independent spirit', and a 'bit of a loner', according to friends. His father, who is a property solicitor in Liverpool, described him as an 'ordinary boy', something of a brainbox who preferred astronomy to chasing girls. He was planning to study physics at Keele University and was due to start that September.

In the early hours of Saturday 10 August, eight days after James was last seen, 30 officers began to comb the bay in the hope of finding some clue to his whereabouts. The Isle of Man Constabulary launched an appeal for witnesses but although calls were received and they followed up on various sightings, including one of James working in a café on the Isle of Man, and another of the teenager looking under the influence of alcohol or drugs in Liverpool, the leads came to nothing.

As time went by and the young man failed to return home, various theories emerged. The first, and perhaps most obvious, is that he fell prey to natural elements. The beauty spot is surrounded by cliffs and the oceanic water is known to rise fast, running a risk of being cut off by the tide. Another theory is that James meant to disappear. Police say this is unlikely, given his belongings, including his shoes and return ferry ticket, were left behind in his tent.

Merseyside Police declined to comment. A spokesman for the Isle of Man Police, which still has the case on their books, said: 'The file is still open but we are not pursuing the matter as actively as before. We are keeping an open mind.'

After seven years, the disappearance of James Borrowdale remains a tantalising and almost forgotten mystery.

37

'Tantalising?' Leigh yells towards the corner of the Golden Yuen. 'A tantalising and almost forgotten mystery? James isn't forgotten to me! I've never read so much bollocks in my entire life!'

'Oh dear,' Des says.

Leigh lobs the newspaper at him – she'd bought it on the way to the restaurant and skim-read it as she walked.

'Who wrote that garbage?'

'May I?' Des asks, retrieving the newspaper from the floor.

'Fill your boots,' Leigh says moodily, plonking herself down in a chair opposite. She watches Des's face as he starts to read, waiting for his expression to show the same outrage she feels.

'What does he mean, "the reason for this delay is not known"?' she says, stopping Des before he's even got started.

Des nods his head towards the newspaper, which is now spread out on the table in front of him.

'I'll let you read it,' Leigh snaps magnanimously, pointedly turning away and gazing out of a cracked window pane towards two Chinese men talking under the green awnings.

'I'm going to find that journalist and arrest him,' she says, immediately interrupting again. 'It's illegal.'

'Um,' Des says, looking up, 'I don't think it is, actually.'

'It is! It's slander! I need to go and buy all the other copies, so nobody else can read that rubbish.'

'There's not a lot you can do, I'm afraid.'

'Did you read that bit about how we didn't report him missing?' Leigh says, repeating one of her main grievances. 'No, it's not known why there was a delay because the journalist didn't bother to frigging ask.'

'You couldn't have done more to find him,' Des says, kindly, 'but, if I may ... I haven't finished reading yet.'

'And sightings? What sightings? He knows nothing! Nothing at all!'

Des looks up from the newspaper when some local youths start larking around on the pavement outside. Leigh wonders if he's on alert because there'd been some trouble last night: as well as the broken window pane, she'd noticed damage to the doorframe on her way in.

'Excuse me,' she complains, placing a finger on her brother's name, 'you're meant to be concentrating your attention here.'

Des deliberately keeps his eyes on the newspaper, despite a loud bang as one of the youths crashes into the front window.

When he's finished reading and the pavement is clear outside, Leigh picks up the newspaper and holds it at arm's length. Luckily, the youths have set fire to a bin at the end of Nelson Street. She strides out of the restaurant, chucks the newspaper in the bin, and watches the pages burn.

'Go home,' Stan says when Leigh gets back to the station.

She's hanging around in the car park, knocking back Tizer, as her boss gets out of his car with a face like thunder.

'I'm not going home,' she says, 'I've got things to do.'

Like track down the journalist and kill him.

'Go home and be with your baby,' Stan says, locking his car door and heading towards the back entrance. 'Take the week off. I'll see you get paid.'

Leigh is left standing on the concrete.

'And don't beat yourself up about the Duane Harding fiasco,' he shouts back.

'I'm not,' Leigh shouts after him as he disappears through the doorway.

A few minutes later, she's still in the car park, trying to clear her head, when Kevin appears and beckons her inside – there's a phone call for her. She dumps her empty can of Tizer in the bin and follows him inside the murder investigation room.

'Drugs?' her mum says when Leigh picks up the receiver. 'My son never touched drugs in his whole life!'

'I know,' Leigh says, agreeing only because she's trying to mitigate the damage.

'Pat said not to, but I said I should phone the police.'

'The police? I am the police.'

'I mean the real police.'

Leigh can hear Pat Killen's voice in the background. Despite her disapproval of him, she's glad he's there. She's worried about her mum's fragile state of mind; fearful she'll go back to how she used to be and start trying to top herself again.

'I'll sort it out,' Leigh announces.

'Leave it, Leigh, you've caused enough bother as it is.'

'I didn't talk to that stupid newspaper!'

'Well, someone must have done.'

'Don't answer the door, or the phone,' Leigh says. 'And do not talk to any reporters.'

She can already picture the headline – mother of missing teenager is dating convicted criminal.

After she's left work, Leigh picks Kai up and walks to Lodge Lane. She bangs on Trey's door and gets no answer. And then she goes back to her bedsit, packs an overnight bag and all the baby's things, and heads to the ferry terminal.

38

When the *Lady of Mann* has sailed out to open sea, Leigh escapes the smoky lounge and steps into an almighty gust on the top deck. Kai is slumped low in his sling, protected from the weather, so she can stand in the full force of the wind without disturbing his sleep. Face wobbling, she stands next to the creaking lifeboats, watching the seagulls gliding in the air currents, hoping the blast of air will blow away her tiredness.

The ferry is quiet, at least up here, where the only other passengers are two women handing a blubbering toddler back and forth between them and a family of four, whose anoraks rattle in the wind. Leigh hadn't been able to book a place on the first ferry to leave that afternoon and had had to wait. But at least it had given her time to call Des and leave the address of the boarding house she's staying in; she wouldn't normally have bothered but he's got a right to know where his son is. During the brief conversation, Des had again tried to persuade her to pass the information on to the Isle of Man police. He'd also suggested again that, on her return, she goes back to stay at her mum's.

Leigh would rather jump overboard and be carried away by the waves.

The family of four make like moon walkers past her, trousers billowing. She kisses the baby on the top of the head, where there's still a spot of guilt-inducing cradle cap, and puts a hand over his face to shelter him. An image of Victor Rivera comes unwanted into her head, followed by a wave of fear that the world is a bad place. She folds her arms around Kai and decides to keep him strapped to her forever.

If only that was possible, Leigh thinks. She has got what she wanted – time off work to be with her baby – but not in the way she wanted. She'd wanted to lie on the mattress in her bedsit, staring at him for hours. She'd wanted to wander around Calderstones Park under the monkey puzzle trees. She'd wanted prolonged cuddles instead of snatched ones.

But instead, she's taking him to the Isle of Man, to search for a stranger.

Night has fallen by the time Leigh checks into the Ellan Vannin guesthouse in Douglas. She attempts to get a comb through her hair and leaves Kai's paraphernalia in the spartan room, minus the dummy, which has now been discarded since the little prince has decided against it. She can barely afford the room rate and had toyed with the idea of staying with her cousins or with her two barmy uncles in Sulby. In the end, though, she'd decided against – her cousins would interfere, and her uncles live in a creepy house with no electricity or gas, miles from anywhere on the Point of Ayre.

The ocean still moves beneath her feet as she walks with Kai along the twinkling promenade. The sight of the seaside capital where she spent so much time as a child fills her with maudlin nostalgia. On this very beach, she'd built sandcastles, ridden donkeys, and swam too far out in the sea, all with her little brother tagging along. As teenagers, they'd once hired a boat and rowed to St Mary's Isle. In an early sign of the recklessness that marks out the Borrowdale siblings, they'd misjudged the tide and had to be rescued by a lifeboat crew.

Leigh breaths in the fresh coastal air.

She feels closer to James here than anywhere.

She continues her walk along the seafront and reaches the harbour. Leigh is feeling a little lonely – she doesn't want to do this by herself. She thinks about the wishing well in Dibbinsdale and feels greedy for yet more wishes. And then she goes into a pub on the seafront, orders a pint of lager, and downs it in one before they tell her babies are barred. She returns to the guesthouse, feeds Kai, stares at him in wonder, and is asleep by 9 o'clock.

By morning, some form of mystic isle magic has occurred. When she comes down for breakfast, Des is standing in the guesthouse hallway, wearing the crumpled clothes he's slept in on the overnight ferry.

'I hope you don't mind,' he says, 'but I thought I could spare a day to help.'

'I don't mind at all,' Leigh says.

39

Des looks nervous as he stumbles over the lumpy field, carrying Kai in the sling. At the far corner, a wild ram, one of a handsome pair, is sharpening its horns on a boulder.

'Are they aggressive?' he asks, walking away from the sheep with his head turned in their direction.

'Unlikely,' Leigh says, reverting to her country girl past, 'a spot of headbutting, perhaps. You might want to look out for the stamping of hooves.'

She smiles to indicate she's joking. The rams aren't even looking their way.

'Is it far, do you think?' Des asks, when he's reached the safety of the field's boundary.

It was something he'd asked repeatedly on the 30-minute drive across the island in the hire car – over Knockaloe Moar, and through St John's and Glenmaye. Despite being born here, Leigh had become confused by the winding roads and it was only by chance they'd spotted the sign for Niarbyl Bay and seen the red-brick building of the pub, far up on the hillside. It's surely the place they're looking for – it's the only establishment for miles. Clueless as to how to reach the Manx Tavern – there didn't seem to be a tarmacked road – they'd parked in a recess by a gate and set out on foot. The climb is proving to be hard work. They've been tramping through countryside for what seems like an age and don't seem to be getting any nearer. The wind is strong and the sky is full of purple and black clouds. Above their heads, some seabird is screeching in protest at their presence.

When Leigh takes her eyes from the sky, she sees the shine of Des's hair disappearing through a gap in a hedge. Since they've arrived, he's been operating at a distance from her of at least four feet, more if he can. It's a contrast to the last time they were on the Isle of Man, in the June of 1979, when they'd been newly in love and had spent hours in the bedroom of their holiday cottage with the curtains drawn. Back then, she'd assumed the last sighting of her brother was on the path down to the beach. She's now not sure if this was the case.

They exit the next field to a cliffside view of the glittering sea. Leigh stops to stare at the beauty of Niarbyl Bay, thinking there should be flowers, something to mark where James once walked. Maybe she should have brought a cuddly toy, like the one Nikki Harding carries around in lieu of her only child.

Leigh thinks about Nikki for a few moments: remanded in custody, suspected of murdering her tosser of an ex-husband. Leigh and Des don't talk about cases outside work if they can help it, but Des is finding his troubles difficult to contain. Before they'd set out, he'd bitten his thumbnail as he'd told her he'd been in the interviews with Nikki, during which she had cried and constantly chewed her lovely long hair. Her brother Warren, as helpful to the cause as ever, had caused a commotion at the station after being brought in pissed and shouting his head off.

Leigh can't bear to think about it. And so she doesn't. She pushes Nikki out of her mind before she goes down a rabbit hole of possibilities. She turns and sees Des on the ground behind her, changing Kai's nappy. She lets him get on with it, remains standing on the hillside, facing the sea, getting battered by the wind. She pictures the three lads here, as Anke had described them: James, larking around with Trey in the waves; Geoff, sitting on the shore with a hankie on his head. She gazes down at the patch of sand on the stony beach, wondering whether that's where James drew Anke's name. Her eyes sweep the cliff and settle on a random spot at its edge, where she places James and Anke in the August of 1974, drinking cider and getting high. Leigh turns away as the narrative plays out in her head – James going too close to the edge, acting like he was on a death mission; James telling Anke about the bad thing that had happened.

His postcard home said he was having a great time.

She does a 180-degree turn, trying to work out the geography and the best route to take to the pub. And then she sits down on the rough heather next to Des and Kai. Des blows raspberries into Kai's face, Leigh points out the seabird now hovering above, although why she thinks the baby's interested in birds is anyone's guess. When they've had their short break, she leads them up a narrow track towards the pub. As they climb to the final summit, a limping Des glances around for unseen threats in the summer hedgerows and then looks up to the heavens. He's here out of duty, she thinks. He's here because some things transcend Leigh's misdemeanours. Her thoughts are interrupted by the loud call of the seabird travelling with them; it's making an alarmed shriek as the light changes. Silver clouds have inserted themselves among the bruised ones, giving the sky a pre-thunderous glint.

They finally reach the Manx Tavern by taking the path where James once fell into step with Anke. From the side, the pub looks almost derelict. A couple of the upstairs windows are boarded up with wood and the brick is partly obscured by a palm tree that's seen better days. Once around the front, despite the pub sign that creaks in the wind, they are welcomed by golden lights shining through the net curtains, a contrast to the darkness above, where thunder is now rolling across the sky.

Atmospheric or creepy – take your pick.

Inside, while not exactly welcoming in atmosphere, the pub is warm in temperature; a coal fire is burning brightly in the grate, even in July. It's not long after opening time and two solitary men are sitting on barstools, their backs to an incongruous slot machine which flashes in vivid colours. This isn't a tourist pub; it's a place frequented by the proper Manx, rural people who now share the island with the rich who've moved here because it's a tax haven.

The fellas at the bar appraise them carefully, particularly a hobbling Des; it's not multiracial here, although she had spotted a Chinese restaurant in Douglas. But then she hears one of them greet the baby, calling him *babban*. Everyone loves Kai – he's their bridge to good community relations, even in a remote pub which doesn't welcome many incomers through its doors.

Leigh stares at the corner seat where Anke said James and his friends had sat with pints in front of them. And then she turns back to the bar. In case a cute baby isn't enough to warm the locals to them, she offers to buy the two fellas drinks – Mrs Rockefeller all of a sudden – and is relieved when they shake their heads.

'I'll shout Malane,' one of them says.

The woman who appears from out back has long grey hair that reaches her waist. She's wearing a dress with a lacy collar and a full skirt, as if she's ready for a dance. She has a gentle demeanour, expressive brown eyes and an otherworldly presence. Her hands are dirty, her teeth are yellow and black.

She is very old and very beautiful.

The woman greets them in Manx – *moghrey mie*, meaning good morning – unusual, as the language is becoming extinct. There's a silence while Leigh and Des gaze at her, a quiet Kai breaks it by letting out a deep giggle. He slept all the way through last night and is the only one of the three of them who's refreshed. In the unexcitable and unimpressed manner Leigh recognises in inhabitants of the Isle of Man, the woman doesn't make a fuss of him.

'I'm Leigh and this is Des – and that's Kai,' Leigh says.

'Malane,' the woman says, her expression suggesting she's wondering why this visitor feels the need for introductions before ordering beer.

'Hi Malane. We're here about a boy, well, he was 18, he went missing here, seven years ago.'

'You're the sister,' Malane states unnervingly.

Leigh nods and Malane nods back.

'I remember your brother, the Manx boy,' she says, causing a shiver to go up the back of Leigh's neck. 'He was a fine-looking boy, as brown as a berry. They were staying on the Quayle's campsite over there. I see all the incomers every August when they come flooding in. I recognise faces for a week and then they're gone, replaced by new ones.'

'A girl who was camping at the same time,' Leigh says, 'I spoke to her. She said a stranger came looking for my brother in this pub.'

Malane nods again. To the side, the two locals are quiet, listening in.

'He knocked on my door,' Malane says, 'between the lights.'

'What did he say?'

'He was from Across,' Malane says, meaning the UK mainland, 'and I didn't like the look of him. He said he was trying to find his friend from Liverpool. It was a lie with a lid on because he didn't seem the type to be friends with a young boy.'

'What did this man look like?'

'Short, fair-haired, the look of a goblin about him.'

Somewhere out to sea, a clap of thunder sounds in the sky. Behind the bar, Leigh notices a wooden cross bound with sheep's wool, there to ward off fairies. The little folk on the Isle of Man are not the cute creatures with pretty wings of children's books, and the people here don't take any chances.

'I didn't tell the fella the boys were staying on the campsite,' Malane continues as the electricity flickers on and off. 'I kept my counsel on that one.'

'Did the fella walk up here? Was he on foot?' Leigh asks, remembering the car that Anke had mentioned.

'He was in a car, big and black.'

'How did he get up here in a car?'

Malane points to a road outside the pub that they hadn't known was there; a tractor is parked against the hedgerow.

'That's my tractor,' the fella next to her says, apropos of nothing.

'You don't remember which night it was, do you?' Leigh asks, attempting a one hundred to one shot.

'That, I don't,' Malane says.

'Did you tell the police about this?'

'The police never came to ask.'

'Anything else you can remember?'

'I'll tell you this. The stranger asked if we had any rooms to stay the night in and I said no, we didn't. I told him there was a guesthouse up the coast by Fenella Beach and he could try his luck there.'

'Do you know the name of this guesthouse?'

'That I do. The Ballabeg.'

'Mrs Kneale runs the Ballabeg,' the local fella chips in. 'She's run that place for years.'

When the fella has given her directions, Leigh glances around and locates Des, standing by the fire with Kai, smoking a cigarette.

'Thank you,' she tells the landlady/magical creature behind the bar.

'Slane,' Malane says.

'Slane,' Leigh responds.

'*Goodbye*', she interprets for Des as she turns his way.

'The day is still with you,' Malane calls after her.

40

Leigh is burning to get to the Ballabeg guesthouse. She talks about the stranger all the way back down the hill.

'Will it be okay to drive in this weather?' Des asks, spooked by the coastal wilderness, the angry sky, the cracks of thunder and, finally, the fork lightning which strikes the Irish Sea just as they reach the car.

'We'll be fine as long as we have rubber tyres beneath us,' Leigh says, suddenly an expert on the elements.

'Is that a real thing?' Des asks as heavy rain pounds on the roof.

'Yeah, yeah, definitely a thing.'

'Between the lights,' he says, as he winces with pain after the long walk. 'What does that mean, exactly? I couldn't make head nor tail of most of what the woman said, I'm afraid.'

'It means the time between starlight and sunrise.'

'Twilight?'

'I think that's between dawn and the sun rising? Between the lights is between night and morning, it's a sort of no time.'

'Is there such a thing?' Des asks, starting the engine and putting the windscreen wipers on fast mode.

'There is on the Isle of Man,' Leigh says. 'I think she meant the stranger arrived when the pub was shut.'

'We better get out of this layby,' Des says, 'it might flood.'

He looks her way as he reverses the car. Leigh checks the back seat at the same time and their heads come together briefly – the closest she's been to him since he arrived. Kai is transfixed by the blurry view from the car window, demonstrating the same amazement he'd shown when Leigh had taken him to one of those new automatic car washes, before her Mini broke down.

'And what did she mean about the day being with you?'

Des had obviously been listening more closely than Leigh had thought.

'It was an encouragement. She was saying I'm in time to find out what happened to James. The day is still with you.'

The car wheels score through deep water as Des pulls away and attempts to light a cigarette at the same time. He opens the window a smidgen and rain spits through the tiny crack.

'We'll have a hard time tracking down this stranger, I'm afraid,' Des says, 'and we do need to check with the Isle of Man force. I can't see a scenario when the police wouldn't have made enquiries at the pub – the appearance of this stranger seems to be common knowledge. And we're in danger of withholding evidence.'

Des is obsessed with the Manx Constabulary.

'No one has ever mentioned the Manx Tavern, except Anke,' Leigh says. 'They thought at the time that James had had an accident. That's what everyone thought because James left all his stuff behind. Everyone was just concentrating on the search of the bay.'

'Do you trust Malane's account? Could she be hiding something?'

'Nah,' Leigh says. 'It's just the way she is, the way things are around here. She's got no reason to make it up. I liked her.'

'I wouldn't be surprised if she caused this weather.'

'She hasn't got magical powers,' Leigh says, smiling.

'Are you sure?' Des says, smiling back.

The journey takes far longer than it should, owing to the torrential rain and Des's careful driving. He's never been a fast driver but they're crawling along the winding road so slowly, a long line of headlamps is stretching behind them. The experience is akin to driving along the bottom of a riverbed. Once, helpless among the elements, they lose their way and come to a stop altogether.

'What a place,' Des says, when they finally pull up outside the Ballabeg guesthouse. Leigh can remember the B&B overlooking Fenella Beach from childhood drives past with her dad, and the bar stool fella's directions were good, enabling them to eventually find the place with almost zero visibility.

'What do you mean?' she complains. 'It's not the island's fault the world has decided to end.'

They get soaked on their dash to the seafront entrance, Des sheltering Kai under his flimsy jacket – neither of them has brought coats – and arrive at the doorstep with water filling their shoes. The afternoon sky is as black as night.

There's no one in reception so they sit side by side in the cramped hallway. Des is tense around the shoulders from gripping the steering wheel and has a selection of leaves in his damp hair. Kai has worn himself out with all that window gazing and is asleep on his chest. Leigh waits with impatience. There's a vacancy sign on the front door and a framed Manx saying hanging on the wall. *Ta'n festyr çheet orrin ooilley.* The shadow of death comes to all. The mirror in the hallway is covered with a cloth, the ever-present threat of evil spirits entering through the glass during a thunderstorm.

Leigh finds herself infected by the superstitions that don't impose on her life in Liverpool but her mum holds onto, once blaming James's disappearance on the fact she'd turned away a woman selling heather. As if all she'd needed to do was reach for her purse and the tragedy would have been averted. Leigh glances at Des, who's looking up at the Manx sayings with a frown on his face. He's superstitious, too; he has his own set of omens to look out for and had once refused to view a flat on Park Road because its street number was four.

Eventually, the landlady appears. Her welcome is frosty, bordering on hostile.

'We're full,' she says, viewing the bedraggled strangers dripping water over her hallway tiles.

'Mrs Kneale?' Leigh says, standing up.

'That's my name,' the woman says.

Leigh shows the landlady her warrant card, mainly for time reasons – they need to be at the ferry terminal for half past six. Des has to be back at the station tomorrow, although she keeps her doubts that any ferries will be sailing to herself.

'We don't want a room,' Leigh says. 'We want to know if you keep a ledger of guests. I'm trying to trace someone who stayed here in August 1974.'

Mrs Kneale has a vexed look on her face. Leigh wishes she hadn't shown her warrant card because she feels like an imposter, impersonating an officer of the law. She knows she's off jurisdiction here and should have checked with the local police before asking any questions.

'Have you had the guesthouse long?' she asks, ignoring her conscience.

'Why are you asking?' Mrs Kneale says.

'I wanted to know whether you were here when James Borrowdale went missing from Niarbyl Bay.'

'And why do you want to know that?'

'It's true that I am a police officer,' Leigh says, feeling forced to admit why she's here, 'but I'm following a lead for personal reasons. James was, is, my brother.'

'You're Alan Borrowdale's girl,' the landlady says. 'My sister used to be in the same motorcycle club in Ramsey. Come here so I can take a look at you.'

Leigh obediently steps forward so Mrs Kneale can study her.

'You look more like your mammy than your daddy,' she says when she's reached her verdict, 'there's nothing of you. You should be resting up after you've had a baby.'

Everything about the landlady is sharp – her nose, her teeth, her chin, her mind.

'Thirty years this guesthouse has been in the family,' she adds, answering Leigh's initial question now she knows of the Borrowdale family.

'So you were here when James went missing?'

'I was, yes.'

'We heard a fella was looking for him, during the week he was here,' Leigh says. 'We heard he stayed here the night.'

'Is that so?' the woman says.

'He drove a black car. He was fair-haired, goblin-like.'

'Goblin?' the landlady says. 'Goblins are barred here.'

Leigh turns to look at Des, expecting to find his shoulders shaking, but he's busy talking to a couple who have burst in through the door, and is telling them all there is to know about the baby and the origins of his name.

'The answer to your question is no, we don't keep details,' Mrs Kneale says, folding her arms. 'We're cash only. Always have been and always will be.'

'Thanks anyway,' Leigh says, as the couple at the door laugh delightedly and, she suspects, drunkenly, at something Des has said. 'It was on the off-chance anyway.'

Mrs Kneale is still viewing her sharply as Leigh steps out into the whipping rain, feeling crushed. Did she really think it would be that easy? That luck would be on her side and a small B&B overlooking a sheltered cove would miraculously keep records of everyone who had ever stayed there? She waits on the drenched pavement while Des finishes his small talk about the Toxteth riots. There's no chance of tracing the stranger now, she thinks. Like James, he has disappeared between the lights.

41

Three hours later, they're back at the Ballabeg guesthouse, all ferries having been cancelled for the night due to strong winds. They'd tried a number of B&Bs on the seafront in Douglas, but everywhere had been full, the rooms taken by other passengers while Leigh was running around trying to find formula milk and buying a tiny red TT races t-shirt for Kai, and Des was telephoning the station to explain his late arrival tomorrow morning.

'We've just had a room come available,' Mrs Kneale says when she sees them, 'so it's just as well you came when you did.'

Leigh wonders how this can be. There are two cars parked on the road outside.

'Oh,' Des says, his eyes darting towards Leigh. 'We need two rooms.'

'He's a bit young for his own room, isn't he?' the landlady says, nodding curtly towards Kai.

Leigh hears the rain pelting down outside – the journey back from Douglas had been even worse than the journey there.

'That's fine,' Leigh says.

'Breakfast is between six and eight,' Mrs Kneale says.

As she hands over the key, the landlady runs through a list of rules. No guests in the room, no smoking in the room (although Des can smoke in the lounge), no televisions or radios on after 10 p.m. Strictly no goblins allowed.

Out of the corner of her eye, Leigh sees Des's shoulders start to shake.

The room is cold, the atmosphere not helped by icy blue walls and sparse furnishings of pine. There's a plug to heat Kai's milk, and a kettle, but no cups or tea or coffee. The only attempt at decoration is a plastic plant. The beds are twin, so at least there'll be no awkwardness about the sleeping arrangements. While Des is in the lounge, smoking a last cigarette, Leigh shows Kai around.

'No partying after 10 p.m., and no inviting your goblin friends round,' she tells him, before drawing the curtains on the stormy night. She checks the radiator for heat – it's stone cold – and then switches on the lamp, which immediately makes the room cosier.

Des is gone for some time. When Leigh has fed the baby and put him to sleep in the cot Mrs Kneale has set up in the corner, she closes the door quietly and tiptoes down the stairs, picturing a cosy chat with Des in the lounge. She finds him smoking on the doorstep, sheltering from the rain under the porch. He turns towards her and smiles but she can't read his expression.

'How are you feeling?' he asks.

'I don't know,' Leigh says, even though she does know.

So many things are going through her head.

Des slips an arm around her and squeezes her shoulder. Leigh leans into him. She is nothing but her own worst enemy – she closes in for a kiss. Des breaks away immediately.

'I can't,' he says, putting a hand on the door to push it open.

'Why? Why can't you?'

'I'd like to, but ... sorry, I just can't. Sorry.'

And with that, he goes inside.

Leigh paces around the lounge for a few minutes. Her mind replays Des's words: the rejection in 'I can't'; the promise in 'I'd like to'. She decides to focus on the most hopeful option. But when she goes upstairs and opens the door to the room, Des's head is already under the covers, his damp shirt draped over half of the cold radiator.

Leigh shivers in her bra and knickers as she lays her clothes on her side of the radiator. She ventures over to the cot, scoops the baby up, and carries him back to her bed. She'll need a little hot water bottle to keep her warm.

Kai asleep in her arms, Leigh sits up in bed, listening to the wind buffeting the windows and Des's measured breathing. He always drops off immediately, irritating the life out of her because it highlights the fact it takes her ages to fall asleep. She feels her stomach sloshing – the ham salad sandwich she ate while waiting at the ferry terminal – and tries to push down disappointment. She doesn't know what she expected. A little chat, perhaps, during which they'd laugh fondly about the landlady and the frosty welcome. Or a heart to heart, during which they'd talk about *things*; things like how he feels, how she feels, about what's going on in the silences.

Des shifts in his solitary bed, turning his back to her. The wind lifts the rain and cracks it against the windows. Leigh gazes down at her beautiful baby and tenderly strokes his combover. At one time, she'd entertained dreams of moving to the Isle of Man, picturing her little family living in a remote cottage with a sea view. But now she realises that, even if Leigh and Des had stayed together, that could never have been. Des is too much of a street kid – the countryside frightens him. Instead of being calmed by the peace and quiet, he can't relax. Or maybe it's her company. If they can't talk when they're romantically stranded on an island in the middle of the Irish Sea, when can they?

Still, despite the circumstances, she finds some comfort in the three of them being in the same room while a storm rages outside. It feels safe for Kai, to be away from the dangers of the city, and, for a night at least, he's no longer being passed from pillar to post. She suddenly wishes that her and Des were staying here as old people, having spent a lifetime together. If they hadn't moved to the island at some point over the intervening years, they could have come for a week's stay every summer, during which they'd visit the house she was born in and take a trip to her grandparents' old farm in Glen Auldyn. They'd spend time with her cousins to fondly recall her barmy uncles and stay full board at a B&B (like this one, but definitely not this one), with evening meal included – queenies in garlic butter and a glass of white wine – and keep photographs of their moon-dwelling child in their purses; quiet, satisfied, secure in the knowledge that they had lived an ordinary, happy life and had no regrets.

Leigh sucks back tears and inhales deeply. She's on the turn, about to enter a vortex. How could that life ever have come to fruition while her brother is still missing? That imagined happy future was snuffed out in 1974, when James didn't come back from his camping trip.

Sitting in her lonely bed, staring at the plastic plant, Leigh feels her mood spiral to an even darker place. The deep well of grief she tries to lock away overwhelms her. She feels trapped, not in this room, but in her own body, in her own life. She wonders whether there's a nightclub she can go to, the Manx version of the Burundi Club. She slips her legs out of the bed and gently carries Kai over to the cot. When the baby's settled, she turns towards her clothes on the radiator.

On Fenella Beach, at 1 o'clock in the morning, Leigh lets the torrential rain smash against her skin and run into her mouth. She lets it drench every single inch of her.

The rain hurts. It whips her face and the top of her head and her shoulders and hands. It attacks from the left, landing a punch in her ear; it attacks from the right, plastering her hair to her face.

She lets it beat her to a pulp.

This is more like it, she thinks. This is the equivalent of 10 bottles of Marsden's Ale on a Friday night, only better! Much better! She wants to be washed away and bashed against a rock. She wants to be shipwrecked off the coast and sink wordlessly down to the ocean bed.

She wants to be obliterated.

Leigh stands on the beach in the deafening rain and lets the violent slaps roll her head from side to side. She can't see. She can't hear. She can't breathe.

'Bring it on,' she shouts at the sky. 'Come on then! Give me what you've got!'

Squelching, panting, staggering, hurting, she hollers into the darkness; a battle cry against life and all its bollocks. No one can hear her – there's nothing here, no sky and no sea and no dimensions. She's the last known inhabitant on a lunar landscape, far from earth.

And she has finally lost her mind.

'Evening,' Mrs Kneale says when Leigh comes through the door of the guesthouse.

42

Leigh wakes to sunshine and the sound of the sea. She's slept heavily and feels better for it.

There's no sign of Des and Kai, and the bed next to hers is neatly made. She gets up and draws the curtains to a view of the stony beach she'd stood on in the rain last night. This morning, it looks like a completely different place. The sky is clear, there's a view of lush hills, and she swears she can see a seal's head poking out of the calm water.

Shivering, Leigh goes across to the radiator and puts her hands on her jeans and t-shirt. They're no drier than they'd been when she'd thrown them on there last night, and water has seeped into the carpet below, soaking the fibres. She looks helplessly around the room. She can't put her soggy clothes back on and she has no idea what she's going to wear. Leigh goes to the window again, scanning the beach for Des and Kai. Maybe Des can go out and buy her something to put on; there's a clothes shop on Michael Street in Peel that might open at 9 a.m., although she has no idea what time it is.

She ventures out of the room in her underwear, locates the bathroom, and steps under a trickle of scalding water in the shower. She washes her hair with the guesthouse-supplied shampoo, which smells of grass. The aroma of kippers being cooked downstairs permeates the first floor.

When she emerges, a small towel barely covering her, she comes face to face with the landlady.

'You were busy last night,' Mrs Kneale says, eyeing her sharply. 'I saw you go out to the beach and I thought to myself, what on earth is that girl doing? I was going to send a search party out.'

'I went for a walk,' Leigh says, fronting out her embarrassment. 'My clothes got wet. I can't put them back on and I don't have any others.'

'Stay there,' Mrs Kneale says.

Leigh watches as the landlady disappears into a room at the end of the corridor and comes back holding a blue tartan dress with a profusion of lace around its collar, similar to the trimming on Malane's dress yesterday.

'Your brother's not out there,' she says, nodding towards the sea beyond the window, 'not now.'

'I wasn't looking for him,' Leigh says, 'I was getting some air.'

'We won't speak any more of it then,' Mrs Kneale says.

Leigh is the only person waiting for breakfast, despite the landlady saying there was just the one room available last night.

She sits by the window, at the only table set, taking in the view. On the pavement outside, the drunk couple, looking worse for wear, are lifting suitcases into their car. The woman is wearing a seaside Kiss Me Quick hat. Beyond them, on the beach, Des and Kai come into view. Des is carrying the baby without the sling, smoking a cigarette, looking troubled.

When the couple's car boot slams and they tear away, Leigh looks around the breakfast room. It's a nice room, the best in the house. Bay windows let in the morning light and a framed Manx saying above the fireplace reads: *Traa dy liooar*. In Manx, it means *There's time enough*; there's no rush. Next to the fireplace is a display cabinet packed with bric-a-brac, including a Manx doll wearing a similar dress to Leigh. She wonders if the rough material is making the doll's skin itchy too.

Leigh is ravenously hungry. From where she's sitting, she has a view into the kitchen and can see Mrs Kneale slamming a frying pan on the stove and then cracking an egg. Soon, there's the sound of oil spitting and the room fills with the smell of smoked fish. When breakfast arrives, Leigh savours every mouthful, even though the eggs taste of kippers, the kippers are full of bones, and the bonnag served with the breakfast is sweet and stale.

Des and Kai arrive back just as she puts down her knife and fork and is taking a sip of steaming tea. Des had been silent in bed last night but he's noisy now, slamming the door shut and stamping his feet on the mat. He pops his head into the breakfast room and gives her a look which turns into a double take. The tartan dress is simultaneously too big and too short. She has teamed it with her sand-covered boots, which she's wearing without socks.

'The landlady lent it to me,' she explains, smiling at Kai, who reaches his arms out towards her.

Des doesn't reply. He is simmeringly quiet and she's getting fed up of this.

'Where did you go last night?' he asks.

'What?' Leigh says, responding to his accusatory tone as she takes the baby. 'I can go for a walk if I want, can't I?'

'Kai woke up in the night, crying.'

'Welcome to my world. That's what babies do, they cry in the night.'

'I know, I didn't mean ... your clothes are soaked.'

'I went for a walk on the beach.'

Des sits down at a nearby table and she sees his expression softening. He looks again at the dress and raises his eyebrows.

'It suits you,' he says.

'I might wear it when I go back to work. It gives me the edge I think I need.'

'Talking of edge,' Des says. 'Stan wasn't too pleased when I called him. He's unhappy about me taking time away from the investigation.'

'Why? It's not as though we've been enjoying ourselves.'

Des gives her a quick smile.

'Anyway,' he says, 'there's a ferry sailing at 11.'

'You need to sign the visitors' book,' Mrs Kneale says, producing a hard-backed book from behind reception.

Leigh leaves the cash for the room and the keys on the counter and opens the book to read the latest entries. The ink is barely dry on the rapturous review written by the drunk couple: *All the comforts of home and more!* Leigh wonders what their home is like, and what *more* they are referring to. *We shall return!* The entry finishes, causing Leigh to experience a pang of regret that she isn't living their joyous life. She takes the pen from the landlady's hand, tempted to write, *None of the comforts of home – and less!* But then she remembers she'd be stranded at the Ballabeg guesthouse in her bra and knickers if Mrs Kneale hadn't leant her the hideous dress, which she's promised to return by post. She writes: *An experience we'll never forget!* She adds the exclamation mark to make their visit sound like one of significance.

Leigh feels Des's touch on her arm – time to go. She's closing the visitors' book when something occurs to her. She swings around to locate Mrs Kneale. She finds the landlady in the kitchen, carrying a plateful of kipper bones to the bin out back.

'Do you keep these?' she asks, holding up the visitors' book as she follows her into the yard.

'I do, that.'

'How far back do they go?'

'I've got them dating back to when we first opened.'

Leigh stares at the landlady in disbelief. She'd said she had no record of anyone who stayed at the guest house when, in fact, she's got a whole library of records in the form of old guest books.

'Can I see them?'

'You can have a look if you want,' Mrs Kneale says, wiping her hands on her apron, 'but you'll not find anything but great comments in them.'

Leigh involuntarily pulls a face: she isn't looking for bad write-ups. But Mrs Kneale hasn't noticed. She is leading her back inside and through the hallway, where Des is waiting at the entrance with Kai, itching to get off. Leigh gestures with her head that he should follow her. Once in the front room – an office of sorts – the landlady flings open a cabinet to reveal the spines of navy-blue books on the second shelf.

'Mind you put them back where you found them,' she says, and is gone.

'We do rather need to leave,' Des says as he comes in.

'Help me, then,' Leigh says. 'The landlady has guest books going back years in here.'

Des looks at his watch.

'We'll have to come back another time, I'm afraid,' he says.

'No chance,' Leigh says.

She pulls the books out while Des perches on the edge of the armchair, re-arranging Kai so he's facing forwards and can see the strange mummy person. The baby's grizzling now, tired out with all his socialising during their stay and ready for a nap. She immediately finds the guest books aren't arranged in any order – as if Mrs Kneale didn't know that Leigh would one day be here, wanting to know the name of the goblin-type man who stayed seven years ago.

'Have a look in this one,' Leigh says, handing one of the books to Des.

There aren't many to get through – the entire guest history of the Ballabeg guesthouse is contained in around a dozen books. One by one, Leigh throws them on the floor when she finds the wrong dates in them.

'Finally!' she shouts as she finds the book with entries from 1974.

But when she turns to the end, the last comment is from June that year.

'Bollocks,' she mumbles.

'Leigh,' Des says.

'Bollocks, bollocks, bollocks!' she says defiantly, thinking he's admonishing her for swearing in front of the baby.

Des says her name twice more and on the third repeat, he shouts it.

'Leigh!'

She looks up at him, shocked into silence. Kai starts to cry. The visitor book she'd handed to him is open on his knee.

'I've found an entry for 31 July,' he says. 'It's the only entry for that week.'

Leigh clambers up and attempts to take the book from Des. He hangs onto it, turning it so she can read the entry he's found. Her eyes swirl around the page and he places a finger where he wants her to look. The look on his face is frightening her.

The entry is dated 1 August 1974 and the comment by the date is short. *Here on business.* The place of origin is named as Liverpool and there are initials in the right-hand column, written in capitals.

'H.E?' Leigh says, locking eyes with Des. 'Who the hell is H.E?'

They don't speak much on the journey to the ferry terminal in Douglas, their fevered speculation over with, for now. Trying to reassure her, Des had stressed that this might not mean anything; that this H.E. person might not have anything to do with James. Leigh isn't reassured.

'It could be this H.E. was just on business,' he says, speaking his thoughts aloud as the car climbs the mountain road.

'There isn't any business in Peel,' Leigh says, looking into the back seat to check on Kai. Apparently no longer tired, the baby is gazing as if in a trance at the greenery passing by the window.

As they begin their slow descent down a flooded road and Douglas comes into view, Leigh's mind is alive with her brother's last months in Liverpool. '*Here on business*,' this H.E. had written in the comments section. Why would this person follow James to the Isle of Man when he could have come to Dunbabin Road? What business did H.E. have with her brother? Was James up to no good? She goes through all the first names she can think of that begin with H. She recalls what Anke said about the lads bringing drugs on holiday with them. But then she thinks, that can't be. James was a grammar school boy who liked to gaze at the stars. His idea of a wild time was dancing to Lynyrd Skynyrd in his bedroom while wearing a pair of unfortunate wooden clogs.

Leigh clutches the visitors' book on her knee and sweats in the woollen dress. Des might be cautious, he always is, but she knows she's onto something. If this H.E. harmed her brother, she's going to get him. After seven years, he might think he's got away with it, but *Traa dy liooar*. There's time enough.

The day is still with her.

43

Leigh is sick. So sick she can barely lift her head from the pillow. So sick she has been lying in her own sweat, delirious and barely conscious, for the best part of – she can't be sure – a few hours? A week? A century? Her body aches, her tonsils are sharp blades, her mind conjures up unpleasant hallucinations which occasionally feature imaginary James and frequently feature Mrs Kneale from the Ballabeg guesthouse. Leigh thrashes around under a thick blanket, unable to breathe, as hot as if she's been sentenced to wear the landlady's tartan dress for eternity. Her sickness has a similar effect to standing on Fenella Beach in the pouring rain, but it's not nearly as good.

Min comes in frequently to tend to her, or to vacuum the bedroom she's insisted Leigh share with Des's two younger sisters, Maylin and Lisha. Leigh is too out of her head on Lemsips, cabbage broth, and Gan Mao Ling to care, but Lisha frequently complains about grunting noises when she tries to sleep. During the day, when the girls are at school, Min sits Leigh up to drink broth and tells her off for going out in the rain, in an all hope is lost way.

Min thinks Leigh is dying.

In that event, she will take the baby, of course.

In the first days of her sickness, Leigh is sometimes aware of the smell of smoke from Des's cigarette. He occasionally brings Kai to the door to look at her but won't bring him any further in case she's contagious. He keeps his distance too, out of recent habit, or in case he gets what she's got and has to take time off from work. As she comes round from her delirium, she becomes more attuned to the activity in the flat – chopsticks clicking on plates, Kai chuckling and screaming in delight, Maylin practising her violin, a sound far worse than Leigh's grunting.

She gets to know when Des is in the flat and when he's not. She wonders where he goes on the nights he's late home.

After a few centuries, Leigh is recovered enough to be moved to the living room, where she sleeps on the settee, wearing one of Lisha's brushed cotton nighties and a dressing gown that once belonged to Min's dead husband. She finally gets to spend time with her baby, although again, not in the way she wanted. When he's asleep, she looks at the pictures in Chinese newspapers and reads a dog-eared *Woman's Own* magazine, the Christmas edition. She becomes something of an expert on Ceefax. In between watching TV programmes which appear on the screen in no particular order – *Rentaghost, Match of the Day, Monkey Magic* – she sees a repeat of the *Newsnight* interview with Clara Harding, during which the fragrant widow describes the romantic meeting in a prison visiting room with her husband-to-be and says she will never give up fighting to clear the name of the man she loved. The interview lasts 25 minutes and she doesn't mention Gail's name once.

Also, during the week: torrential rain in the Far East causes the Yangtze River to overflow and, in Mexico, a panda is born, the second child of Ying Ying, who accidentally crushed her first one. There are a host of obituaries for Liverpool in the newspapers and the riots in L8 get up and running again, prompting Min to barricade the front door. Des manages to find someone who was sober enough to remember Warren in The Miller, and Nikki Harding is released under investigation. Evidence tying Nikki to the murder scene has been impossible to find, although all the gossip about Nikki is coming out of the woodwork, as Leigh knew it would.

News of a total solar eclipse best seen from Russia is overshadowed, at least as far as Leigh is concerned, by the distinct lack of news about Des's promised enquiries into the stranger with the initials H.E.

On the home front, the Hondo supermarket runs out of rice flour, Maylin miraculously passes her grade 2 violin exam, Lisha cries over the existence of school sports day, Des's older sister, Jia, visits with her husband, and the summer holidays begin. The visitors' book from the Ballabeg guesthouse still sits in Leigh's bedsit, along with her unpacked bag and the tartan dress which has yet to be returned to Mrs Kneale. Geoff goes unvisited in Chester, the keys to the lock-ups go untried, she misses the planned meeting with Trey at Cathedral Gardens, and she avoids phoning her mother, to whom she hasn't spoken since the telephone call about James's alleged drug taking.

Leigh stays at Min's flat as the sunny skies become overcast. She stays there as Ying Ying makes up for past mistakes, Michael Heseltine arrives to resurrect the city from the dead, and preparations for the marriage of Lady Diana to Prince Charles fill the news bulletins. She stays until she feels well enough to call Stan at home, who tells her gruffly to hand it over to the Isle of Man force. She stays until her mind has recovered enough to resume its relentless churning and Des has brought her a six pack of Tizer, which perks her up no end, and a notebook, in which she writes down her ideas as to why this H.E. was pursuing James.

Drug debt? she writes. *Witness to something he shouldn't have seen?* Leigh spends the rest of her time at Min's flat engaged in manic scribbling that would give Kevin a run for his money. Until, one day, smelling faintly like Mrs Kneale's fishy hands, she gets dressed in Maylin's parachute pants and jelly shoes, leaves Kai behind, and travels by bus to her mum's house in Dunbabin Road. There, as she'd hoped, she finds Pat Killen sitting at the kitchen table, wearing a Sunday tracksuit and a shark's smile.

'Pat,' she says, as she takes a seat opposite, 'I need your help.'

44

Leigh's first day back at work after sick leave, and she walks into the major incident room to the deafening sound of wolf whistles, cheers and insults. She's wearing Mrs Kneale's tartan dress and she looks ridiculous.

Which is just how she wants to look.

'Didn't know you had legs,' a smart Alec shouts, keen to carry on the mirth after the furore has died down.

'Hilarious,' Leigh says.

She proceeds with dignity through the room, which is full of unfamiliar faces and is as packed as it was on the first day of the rioting, the out-of-town detectives chatting animatedly to their new best mates from Liverpool. She knows they've been on numerous drink-ups together; nights out that she wasn't invited to and wouldn't have been able to go if she was.

Leigh finds Des sitting at a desk at the back, surrounded by the piles of documents and statements that have accumulated about the rioting. He breaks into a grin as she approaches.

'It still suits you,' he says.

'I'm wearing it as a protest,' Leigh says.

The dress weighs heavily on her. It smells of fish. Leigh is a martyr to the cause of The Missing. That, and she couldn't find any clean clothes to put on this morning.

'If you don't mind me saying so,' Des says, his shoulders beginning to shake, 'there might be more constructive things you could be doing.'

'Like what?' she asks, but Des isn't listening.

'DI Chung! Sorry I'm late!'

DI Josephine Bennett's vibrant voice sounds out from behind them and Leigh looks around to see the dazzling smile of the Bolsover Beauty.

'Shall we?' Josephine says, cocking her head to one side as she perches on the desk with her back to Leigh.

'*Shall we,*' Leigh mimics childishly behind her back.

Des's shoulders give out one last shake before he says:

'I did mean to say before, and I'm sorry if I didn't, but, as you know, Josephine's been looking through the paperwork on Gail's case and she's going to give us the lowdown on the Marion Coote investigation, on the off chance something there might help.'

The qualifiers are back – Des is obviously nervous in Josephine's presence. He calls over Callum and Kevin and they all gather chairs around the desk.

'Just sit back and enjoy the circus,' Callum whispers in Leigh's ear after looking her up and down with a smirk on his face. To his side, Kevin has his notebook out ready.

'Okay! Let's do this!' Josephine says, still a little high from her hello to Des. 'As you know, I was part of the team who were successful in bringing a prosecution for the murder of 10-year-old Marion Coote, who disappeared from her home in Broughton Vale, Nottinghamshire, in 1965. I was a new recruit back then,' she adds, in case it's not clear she doesn't look her age.

'Never?' Callum says, the devil in his voice.

'Marion was found by the side of the road,' Josephine continues with a fading smile, 'she'd been strangled, and we think she didn't die there – she'd been moved. The perpetrator was arrested within two weeks and he's now serving a life sentence. The death penalty would have been sought, but it had been paused at that time. Although our case did prompt a debate in the House of Commons about the sense in that.'

Leigh folds her arms and listens with mounting frustration – she's missing *Monkey Magic* for this. She gazes up at her rival, partly in admiration, partly through green mist. Josephine talks as if she's being interviewed for a job and needs to stress her expertise – as if the articulate words and the immaculate dress sense weren't enough to convince them. That's where she's been going wrong, Leigh thinks. You have to big yourself up, not storm out of rooms slamming doors. You have to speak without shouting. You have to wear grown-up clothes, rather than Manx national costume.

You have to use 'I' instead of 'we'.

'I was determined, from the start,' Josephine continues, 'that Alfred Woods was our man, despite there being only circumstantial evidence in our favour and despite him not being picked out of a line-up of suspects.'

'A line-up?' Leigh pipes up, driven to point out the differences. 'You had a witness then?'

'I had a young witness who didn't come good,' Josephine says icily. 'But I pressed on. And I soon found another witness – the perpetrator's 13-year-old son, whose testimony secured the conviction.'

Poor kid, Leigh thinks. As if it wasn't bad enough having a murderer for a father.

'I had no doubt about the guilt of our perpetrator,' Josephine continues, making out she caught the killer alone, rather than being a lowly DS on the case. 'He was seen with Marion that night. An item belonging to Marion was found at his home. Fibres from his pit coat were found on her clothes. He had been seen the week before, looking through the windows of Marion's family home. He protested his innocence, but I knew we had our man.'

'There was no doubt about Duane Harding's guilt either,' Leigh says, a thorn in DI Bennett's side. 'We were just unlucky.'

'I don't believe in luck,' Josephine smiles.

Leigh pulls at the sleeves of the tartan dress. Despite the weather turning cold, she is hot, hot, hot, and sitting on the skirt is making the collar tight around her neck.

'Anyway, why are we talking about this?' Leigh asks. 'We're not looking for anyone else for Gail.'

'The DCI has asked me to advise DI Chung,' Josephine says. 'And so that is what I am doing.'

Leigh eyes skim past a scribbling Kevin and fix on Stan's temporary office. A detective from the public order side of things is in there with the DCI. Whatever he's telling him, it prompts the boss to haul himself to his feet, pick his trousers out of his backside, and march out without a word.

'There's a lot more to this case than meets the eye,' Josephine is saying now. 'The original case has bearing on Duane Harding's murder and the answer lies there. Crack one, and you crack the other.'

'We cracked it already,' Leigh says, being slowly strangled by the collar of her dress.

'As a result of my experience,' Josephine continues as the door slams behind Stan. 'My advice is this. The rumoured hitlist circulating Walton Prison isn't worth pursuing because of the mismatch in modus operandi. Duane Harding claimed he would shortly demonstrate that he was innocent of the crime he was accused of. Nikki Harding might not have wanted that evidence to come to light. Her brother, Warren Jones, was present outside the Hardings' flat in the week preceding the murder – his intention might also have been to keep Duane quiet. My experience tells me you need to act swiftly and decisively. By all means rule out other possibilities, but keep within a timescale of 48 hours. After that time, re-arrest Nikki Harding and charge her with the murder of her ex-husband.'

A few minutes later, at the end of the corridor, competitive streak activated, Stan is back from his public order emergency and screaming at Des. Leigh catches the gist of it as she nears them – he's kicking off over something he overheard Josephine say.

'If you don't mind me saying so, I am leading this ...' Des tries to say, but the DCI bellows over him.

'Nobody tells my officers what to do, except me. Don't get some out-of-town totty to step up to the plate because you've got frigging nothing.'

This, despite Stan sanctioning DI Bennett's involvement.

'All right love?' Stan says when he sees Leigh. 'You're with Shimberg and Davies, on the Princes Park cactus assault.'

'I would rather like DS Borrowdale with me,' Des bravely responds.

'She's one of my officers,' Stan growls. 'She works for serious crime, not piddling, small-scale CID. She *works* for *me*.'

Leigh catches Des's eyes. This is how it goes, how it's always gone even before Stan blamed Des for abandoning Leigh and the baby.

'I'll tell you something, lad,' Stan continues, pointing to Leigh. '*She* shouldn't even be working. *She* should be at home, with her kiddie.'

'She's a detective,' Des counters.

'I am here, you know,' Leigh says. 'And lovely as it is to have you two argue over me, I do have a mind of my own.'

'Not when you work for me, you bleeding don't,' Stan says.

45

Still knocking back Tizer to ease her occasional barking cough, Leigh gets on with the boring job she's been given – collate all the paperwork so far on the assault by cactus. She's still sniffly but at least she's on solid foods now and her hallucinations of Mrs Kneale have abated. She'd finally got back to her bedsit with Kai last night, feeling satisfied she'd set something in motion, at least, by asking Pat Killen to see what he can turn up about any local drug dealer with the initials H.E.

Leigh flicks through the index cards, thinking there's more important things to do – like find Gail Harding. She's sure Stan has only put her on this to spite Des. If Nikki is charged, it will officially be game over as far as the Duane Harding investigation is concerned and, after the waste of time that is the prickly pear enquiry, Stan wants her on public order. She stares into space, not wanting to be here. She's uncovered that her brother was probably being pursued by bad people and now she's supposed to act as if nothing's happened.

Last night, when she'd asked Pat Killen for his help, he'd wanted to know why she was asking. She'd stressed that she wasn't asking as a police officer, but as a sister. Pat had said precisely nothing, which she had taken to mean 'What do you take me for? I'm not a grass,' and, straight after that, her mum had come bustling in, demanding to know what they were talking about. Without missing a beat, Pat said he'd been trying to persuade Leigh to take the flat up Picton Road way. 'She won't listen,' her mum had said, 'she never does.'

And then Pat had taken a wad of notes out of his pocket and slid them across the table for Kai. 'He doesn't want that,' Leigh had said, before slipping it into the pouch on the baby's sling. She'd put the money in Kai's piggy bank, but she'd been tempted to keep it for herself – her rent is due and all she's got to offer the landlord is a fiver in her biscuit tin and a handful of Manx coins left over from her trip.

Leigh runs her fingers along the carousel and listens to the noise of Duane Harding's supporters outside. There's been nothing more about James in the newspapers, thank goodness, but the press has gone wild about the arrest of an unnamed woman and the protestors have stepped up their campaign. No wonder the worms have crawled out of the woodwork – it had been all over the front pages and the hints had been heavy that it was Nikki who'd been brought in.

Desperate for a result, the squad have started treating uncorroborated reports as factual. The mythical hitlist of fellas who've hurt children has been abandoned and they're putting all their eggs into one vulnerable little basket. The graffiti on the living room wall of the Hardings' flat isn't even in Nikki's handwriting – they've already checked. She wonders how Nikki is holding up. She knows Gail's mum didn't kill Duane Harding, but even Leigh has to admit that things don't add up. Whatever it is that Nikki's hiding, it will be to do with protecting someone – she's always been loyal to her friends and family.

Leigh looks up as Des, Callum and Mark II enter the room, fresh from being 'in with the Notts force' – meaning Josephine – for further discussions.

'That Josephine's not just a looker, is she?' Mark II says. 'She's got us two cases wrapped up in a single arrest. Killed one bird with two stones.'

Des catches Leigh's eye and she sees his shoulders rise. With a hand over her mouth to hide her smile, she stands up and leaves the room in a hurry. Des follows her out. They hurry down the corridor together, getting as far away from Mark II and his mixed-up idioms as possible before giving their giggles full reign.

'What's so funny?' Callum asks when they get back.

The afternoon passes in a monotonous administrative haze, punctuated only by the guzzling of Tizer, the scratching of the skin on her neck where Mrs Kneale's dress is rubbing, and Des nipping in and out of the room to flick through evidence to help him prepare the case against Nikki.

When he comes in for a third time, he finds Leigh gazing out of the window at Duane Harding's supporters. She recognises the usual bunch of merry men, including the fella they've nicknamed Jesus in his usual place at the end of the line, resting the bottom edge of his JUSTICE placard on the top of his head. It's an attempt to shelter from the downpour which inadvertently forms the sign of a cross over his face. Next to him is her number one fan, the Teddy Boy; dressed today in a pastel-coloured jacket and a bootlace tie. He lets his placard drop when he spots her through the window and blows her a kiss.

'I obviously have a secret appeal only certain fellas can see,' Leigh tells Des when he appears at her side.

'I see it,' Des says, turning to her.

Flirt, Leigh thinks, smiling.

She wonders whether Des's growing warmth towards her is because of James – he's always kind when it comes to her brother. Or whether he's paying her compliments because he's moving on and feels sorry for her. Still, she smiles to herself as he's replaced in the room by Callum, who arrives with a shed-load of papers relating to the investigation Leigh is now excluded from.

At teatime, Callum gets his butties out of his pocket – two slices of white bread with a neon orange filling, sweating in a polythene bag; a packet of crisps – prawn cocktail, crinkle cut. Leigh takes a break and sits next to him.

Leigh dips her hand into the packet balanced on his thigh. He slaps it away.

'Bring your own,' he says, putting a crisp in his mouth and crunching loudly and with relish.

A couple of out-of-town detectives wander in to say goodnight and Callum gives them a wave; mates after the drink-up they'd all been on last night. She's pretty sure Des was at the drinks too. When she'd left Min's last night with Kai, she'd seen him checking his reflection and smoothing down his hair. She keeps meaning to examine him for signs of a hangover this morning.

'In Nottinghamshire, we are perfect,' Callum says when the detectives have gone, jokily alluding to their smugness about solving their case. 'In the middle of nowhere, we have commendations coming out of our arses.'

Leigh grins and takes another swipe at his crisp packet.

Desperate both to hold her baby and take off the stupid dress, she is on her way out of the door, intending to head to Nelson Street, when a CID detective runs in, waving a piece of paper. He's followed by the two out-of-town officers, who are yet to leave the station, and Slapdash, who has obviously been shirking somewhere in the shadows.

'What's this?' Leigh says, snatching the piece of paper out of his hand and putting it on the table.

'Undercover came good,' the CID fella says, looking pleased as punch – he obviously hasn't heard that the investigation has moved on. 'It's the list of fellas who've done crimes against children. They're being targeted out of Walton Prison. Some doozie typed it up – it was found during the search of a cell. Got the marks' addresses on it too.'

Leigh joins the scrum around the table to look at the list, which is typewritten on yellowing, dog-eared paper the size of a paperback book.

'Duane Harding's not on it,' Slapdash says, with a note of triumph. 'Looks like we've got the right person with the ex-wife.'

Leigh stares at the list, a shiver extending down her back, arms and legs. When the Slapdash fella leans across and splays his fingers over the paper, she forcibly peels his hand away.

'Someone's had their nose put out of joint,' he says, stepping back.

'Shut up!' she yells, unable to control herself as blood pounds in her head. 'Just frigging shut up!'

'Someone's really got the hump.'

He is saved from being flattened only by Leigh's distress. She reads the names on the list: Leonard Carey, Henry Clarke, Abraham Romi, but her eyes keep returning to the second name, as if she can't trust what they're telling her.

'Frigging hell,' the CID officer says. 'There's DECEASED written next to two of them.'

Leigh looks away and lifts her head towards the buzz of the harsh strip light above. The others haven't noticed yet, but she's going to have to say it out loud any second now. Any second now and she'll have to break out of her fearful state and tell them that, half way down the hitlist, sandwiched between the two dead people, is her brother's name.

46

Leigh runs all the way to Chinatown as if she's being chased by a monster, its big feet threatening to pound her to dust down the hill. She picks up pace past Cain's Brewery, running for her life, only stopping when she reaches the safety of Nelson Street, the start of the road being too narrow for a Yeti to get through.

She wants to see Des, to lean on him, to hear his voice and let the words trapped inside come tumbling out. Before being chased through Liverpool, she'd searched the station for him, going in and out of every room.

Leigh heads down the street in the direction of the place where he's likely to be – the Golden Yuen.

She stops on Nelson Street to cough her guts out. Around her, steam is escaping from restaurant doors and lines of dried ducks dangle from steel. The restaurants are mostly empty on this Tuesday night, two or three tables filled in some, others with no custom at all, but the smell of delicious food still fills the air and the interiors look bright and inviting under the darkening sky.

Sensing her baby's presence nearby, Leigh looks up to Min's flat and sees a golden square of light in the front room. It comforts her, knowing they'll soon be together, the three of them, on this most terrible of nights.

Leigh pulls at the collar of her ridiculous dress, readying herself to fake a smile for Mr Tam. A group of student types pass by, wandering from menu to menu, their outlines silhouetted in the illuminated windows as they stop to read the boards. She hears one of them, a late adolescent boy with a mop of curls, say: 'This is our kid's favourite Chinese, he comes here all the time.' Leigh judders through her open mouth, her tears set off again by this casual mention of a sibling and ordinary nights.

She wishes this was an ordinary night. She yearns to be part of this place; part of her baby's life. But she's stranded again on the lunar landscape of Fenella Beach, a distant rocky planet where the only other inhabitant is a frightening monster, waiting for her at the end of the road to pulverise her into the ground.

Her only hope of survival: Des.

Leigh is about to cross the road when she sees them, sitting opposite one another at the window table. The lighting is low, but plates upon plates of half-empty food are in clear view. The Golden Yuen banquet: char sui wonton noodle soup, spare ribs with a grated fish topping, fish ball stew, chilli and salt chicken with water chestnuts. And duck, always lots of duck.

She stands at the other side of the street, her bare legs and the hem of the tartan dress patterned with the pink and red lights of the restaurant's neon sign. Through the cracked window pane, the traitor Mr Tam is hovering over the table, smiling beatifically as he serves the tea. Des is paying the bill, waving a cheque. Then he leans across to light his companion's cigarette and, in the small light of its glow, Leigh sees Josephine, the Bolsover Beauty, sitting in her place, opposite Des in their favourite restaurant.

Bollocks, she thinks. Frigging, wanking, bollocks.

She watches them for only a heartbeat longer. She has to go: at the end of the street, the monster is waiting for her.

'Bring it on,' she says out loud as she turns and heads towards oblivion, leaving her baby behind.

Back at her bedsit, spared from obliteration for now, Leigh changes out of the stupid tartan dress. She takes her hair out of the bobble and lets it hang loose. And then she grabs the rent money from the biscuit tin and heads out to the Burundi Club.

47

The telephone is ringing, shrill and loud. Leigh wakes up in a beer-induced muddle and fumbles her way across her bedsit to pick up the receiver. The sky through the bay windows is pitch black; the alarm clock tells her it's just past midnight. She is expecting to hear Min's voice at the end of the line and her body is already aching with guilt – how could she leave Kai behind?

'Leigh? Where are you?'

It's Des, not Min, and his tone of voice makes her immediately contrary. She's just answered her phone. Where does he think she is?

'My mum's stayed up late, she thought you were working, but you must have left the station hours ago.'

'You've been at the station all this time, haven't you?' Leigh says, playing silly buggers – she knows full well where he's been.

'I've just got back.'

In the steely, quiet voice he gets when he's angry, Des goes on demanding an explanation. She didn't pick Kai up or phone to let his mum know, he says. She can't just leave the baby with his mum like that. And where has she been?

He sounds a little tipsy too, although she'd only seen them drinking tea in the Golden Yuen.

There are lots of things Leigh could say to him. Such as: how would you know if I was working late? You were too busy making eyes at Josephine over the Golden Yuen's special buffet, £4 a pop. You disappear all the time without telling anyone where you're going – you've only just got home now.

And anyway, what business is it of yours?

You let me down when I needed you.

But she can't find the words, not about that, or about James and how her world has been turned upside down, so she puts the phone down and falls back into bed.

Less than 15 minutes later, Leigh is on her way to Chinatown, seized with a desperate longing to hold her baby. It's all she can think about – she has to get Kai right now or she might never see him or touch him again. The feeling, a yearning as strong as grief, carries her through the quiet dark streets, propelling her down Upper Duke Street, past the Anglican Cathedral, and onto Nelson Street, where she stops to bark out the remnants of her cough.

'Leigh! Are you okay? Are you okay? You're late, very late. I was so worried!' Min says, rapid-fire as she opens the door with Kai wriggling in her arms.

'Sorry I didn't phone,' Leigh says, not able to wait for Des's mum to hand Kai over. Her hands are on him already, tugging around his tiny waist.

She can feel her brother in him.

Kai grizzles and sticks a finger in her face. When Leigh gives him the loopy grin reserved just for him, he smiles and whoops. He's wearing the TT races t-shirt they bought him in the Isle of Man.

Now on her fourth 'sorry' to Min, she's still drinking in the baby when she sees Des, hanging around on the stairs with all the warmth of a high-end refrigerator. He hasn't heard the news about James, she thinks. She'd thought Callum might have phoned to tell him but, of course, Des has been out.

'You go to bed, mum,' he says, not sounding squiffy at all, as he arrives in the hallway and then steps outside.

'Thank you!' Leigh calls after Min.

'See you tomorrow!' the saintly woman shouts as she walks up the stairs, pulling her dead husband's dressing gown around her.

And now it's Leigh and the baby and Des, facing each other on the bright street – the lights of Chinatown are burning long after the pubs have shut. Leigh retreats a little. She's back in her usual black jeans and top, but they haven't been washed for a month and she smells like a dead body; a putrid mixture of exhaustion, illness, grief, and the Burundi Club. She carries on looking at Des with glistening eyes. If she opens her mouth, she thinks, she'll cry. If she tells him about James's name on the hitlist, it will come out as a howl.

It isn't until she sees a change in Des's expression; a thawing, a puzzlement, that her words finally spill out.

'I want to keep working,' Leigh tells Stan at the station the next morning, an attempt to pre-empt his orders for her to go home. 'I want to be part of this.'

'Not a bleeding chance. You're not going anywhere near it,' Stan says, as she knew he would.

'At least tell me what's going on, boss, what happens next.'

'It's on our turf so I've passed it to local CID.'

By local CID, he means Des.

'They'll run it from here, get the Isle of Man force to send over your brother's case file, for starters. Get the prison doing their bleeding jobs properly, put pressure on the inmate who had the hitlist in his cell.'

'Who is it?' Leigh asks, thinking of the initials H.E. 'What's the name of the inmate?'

'Never you mind.'

'You need to chase the other names on the list down,' Leigh says, full of fear about what they might find.

'That and all,' Stan says. 'Chung will keep you up to date. We'll tell your parents when we've got something to tell. You can go home.'

'I need to keep my mind off it,' Leigh says. 'I don't want to go home.'

'If you must stay,' Stan says, being kind in his own way, 'but only because we're short-staffed, I want to know our case against Nikki Harding for her ex-husband's murder is watertight. The vigilante line has been ruled out because Duane Harding's not on the hitlist.'

'I know he isn't,' Leigh says, biting her lip. 'But we already know the case against Nikki isn't watertight.'

Stan makes an exaggerated point of looking at his watch, a reference to time running out before a charge is made. He doesn't mention the cactus assault.

'Right now, Nikki's the only one in the frame,' he says.

'She didn't do it.'

'I'm sick of you telling me who didn't bleeding do it,' Stan shouts. 'Find me the person who did bleeding do it.'

48

Back in the incident room, Leigh wonders where to start in finding the person who did bleeding do it. The only way she can get through the day is by blanking out James's disappearance and concentrating on freeing Nikki. She's snapping open her third can of Tizer that morning, hoping for a sugar rush to focus her distracted brain, when Callum sidles up and hisses in her ear.

'I need to talk to you,' he says, making it sound like an accusation.

The DC grabs her arm and leads her by the elbow into the empty murder investigation room.

'There was a woman in reception just now,' he says, 'giving the duty sergeant down the banks about her kid being arrested and chucked in the cells on Sunday night.'

'So?' Leigh says.

She wouldn't be the first mother to show up at the station demanding justice this week.

'She cornered me, said she had something to say about Nikki Harding's alibi. Her name's Elaine Yewande and she wants to talk off the record. She's waiting for you on Admiral Park.'

Leigh's heart sinks. Someone else eager to lay the boot into Nikki.

'What has she got to say?'

'Don't have a clue. She was going on about how Duane Harding should have been chucked out of his flat after what he'd done and how her 17-year-old kid's been banged up after the rioting when we left a pervert on the street.'

A woman after my own heart, Leigh thinks.

'Why don't you go and speak to her?' she asks Callum.

'Busy,' he says. 'And I'm handing you a lead on a plate, here. This is when you show some gratitude.'

'Yeah, yeah, yeah,' Leigh says, heading for the playing fields next to the station.

Leigh recognises the woman straight away, even though she's got an orange and black scarf wrapped around her head. She's a friend Nikki often talks about, and Leigh has seen her before at the caravan in Crosby – another mum who has lost a child.

Elaine is pacing in front of the far fence, head down, taking short draws of her cigarette. When Leigh reaches her, she pushes the headscarf back.

'This doesn't go any further, right?' she says. 'No one finds out I've talked to a bizzy.'

Elaine glances around and then moves towards the fence – a futile attempt to hide in a wide-open space.

'Nikki was with me, that night,' Elaine says.

'What night? The night her ex-husband was murdered, or the night Gail disappeared?'

'The night her bastard ex-husband was done in,' Elaine says, cracking her fingers now her cigarette is finished.

Great! Leigh thinks. The answer she's been looking for has miraculously landed at her feet.

'Where?' she asks.

'In my flat. Watching your lot beat up our kids on the street.'

'And your flat is where?'

'I haven't come here to be interrogated.'

'Do you want to come into the station?' Leigh asks. 'If you make a statement, to say Nikki was with you, she can leave straight away. Probably,' she adds, remembering the footage of Nikki on Devonshire Road which proves she wasn't in anyone's flat.

'You're joking me, aren't you?' Elaine replies. 'I'm not signing nothing, right? So don't even try to talk me into it.'

'Why are you here then? We've got nothing if you don't go on record.'

'Listen, love,' Elaine says sharply, 'I'm telling you this out of the goodness of my heart.'

'Goodness of your heart? You're going to allow Nikki to spend the rest of her life in prison because you won't talk?'

'Don't go shouting at me,' Elaine says, although Leigh hadn't realised she was. 'I'm just telling you she was with me, so you can let her go now.'

'It doesn't work like that.'

'Nikki said you were all right,' Elaine says, her expression indicating that her friend had been wrong about that. 'You should be out there looking for Gail, not arresting innocent women.'

'I know,' Leigh says. 'And I am looking for Gail.'

Elaine stares at her. Her look doesn't scream approval.

'I've told you she was with me,' she resumes, 'now call off the investigation into Nikki and let her go.'

'I'm not in charge,' Leigh says.

'Listen, love,' Elaine says. 'I've got a fella in a wheelchair, one kid dead, and the other banged up with a mouth full of broken teeth after your lot arrested him on Sunday night. I'm petrified here, I can't sleep, I can't eat. I've either had a breakdown or I'm having one or I'm about to have one.'

Leigh nods in sympathetic recognition. Elaine is the type of woman she likes, the type who's weathered the storm of life because she's had to. Her youngest son had been only 16 when he'd died during a high-speed police chase through

Wallasey Tunnel. Now her other son is in custody. This woman stands before Leigh hurt and strong, shaking and resolute.

'Anyone else with the two of you?' Leigh asks, clutching at straws.

Elaine shakes her head, already backing away.

'I shouldn't have come here,' she says. 'I don't trust none of yous. You're all the same.'

'Okay,' Leigh says, putting her hands up in surrender. 'Off the record and it won't go any further. And I'll see what I can do about your kid.'

Elaine brings a match to a fresh cigarette with one quaking hand and then starts to speak, throwing light on the mystery of why Nikki was running past the crime scene on that early morning.

'What did she have to say?' Callum asks when Leigh gets back to the investigation room.

'It was nothing,' she replies. 'Time waster.'

49

The curtains are drawn in the upstairs windows when Leigh pays a visit to Dunbabin Road that lunchtime. She knocks gently and, when there's no answer, lets herself in using the key she keeps in case of emergencies. She steps into the porch, slips on the post, and notices a pair of brown leather brogues – slick with polish, freshly heeled – on the shoe rack. Pat Killen's checked jacket is hanging on the coat stand and his packet of Benson & Hedges and lighter has been left behind on the nesting tables. Leigh listens into the quiet and immediately hears the springs of the bed creaking upstairs. Her first instinct is to turn around and head back out of the house. But she doesn't because, out of the corner of her eye, away from his usual haunting ground of the bedrooms, imaginary James is gesticulating to her in the hallway. Anke's words go through her head – '*Maybe he's not the person you thought he was*' – but this James doesn't look capable of hurting anyone, particularly a child.

'Whatever you've got to say, you can say it in front of Pat,' her mum says when she emerges a few minutes later.

She's swinging her hips as she walks across the kitchen to switch on the kettle. There's a glow to her that Leigh failed to achieve last night at the Burundi Club; a night cut short when she got spooked by suspicious eyes.

It's a glow that Leigh doesn't want to take from her.

'This is important, mum,' she says. 'It's about James.'

Her mum sighs heavily as she slots two white slices into the toaster for Pat, now seated at the kitchen table, waiting to be served breakfast. He, like her mum, is in a dressing gown and his feet are bare. Imaginary James leans against the washing machine and puts his fingers down his throat.

Leigh sits down, deciding to say what she has to say in front of Pat, from whom she hasn't heard a word since asking for his help. But she doesn't know how to put it, how to be gentle. She should have waited for Stan to deal with it when the time came, but the urge to know now has got the better of her. If something bad had happened, she figures, James might have confided in someone close.

'James was on a list,' she says, 'and the other people, who were also on the list, some of them are dead, or died.'

To the uninformed ear, this sounds odd, out of context. She starts again.

'Something we came across,' she says. 'It's a hitlist, we think, circulating Walton Prison.' She takes a deep breath before saying: 'We think it's a list of people who harmed children.'

It's the first time she's said this out loud, and the only way she's got her words out without crying is by speaking in a frozen voice which is more than a match for DI Chung's refrigerator.

'What are you on about now, Leigh?' her mum says. She's leaning against the kitchen cabinets and her dressing gown is gaping open at the front, showing a leg. The glow is yet to wear off but it's fading fast.

'What's this list for?' Pat asks, lighting a Benson & Hedges.

'We think the people on it are being targeted by vigilantes inside the prison. Two of them might already be dead. They've got 'deceased' written next to their name, but James doesn't.'

Pat nods. He understands, straight away, that the kind of rough justice she's suggesting is possible, more than possible. He knows how these fellas work, being one of these fellas himself.

'Can you imagine any scenario, any at all, when James might have hurt a child?' Leigh says, cringing as she says the words.

Her mum drops the toast onto the dish rack, where a couple of Kai's bottles are drying. She retrieves a slice and attempts to butter it, but the knife slips from her hand and clangs into the sink.

'My DCI will be coming to see you,' Leigh continues when it's clear she's not going to get a reply. 'Not yet, but if we find anything more out.'

'You need to think about how other people feel,' her mum says, 'having James's dissappearance dragged up all the time.'

Leigh attempts to stop the whine of, *What about me?* from escaping her lips. But it's too late.

'Have you ever, for a single moment, thought about how I feel about this?' she explodes.

This outburst is followed by a loaded silence. Her mum hurries across the room, deposits Pat's toast on the table and retreats back to the corner. Leigh snatches a slice from the plate and escapes upstairs, wanting to find her diary from 1974 before she leaves this house and never comes back. She opens her wardrobe and rifles through the collection of old shoes, boots and sandals in the bottom, pulling at the diaries until the whole lot falls to the floor in a jumble. She sits on the floor and forces herself to eat the slice of toast, which is thick with butter in one corner but otherwise dry and causes her cough to return. She can sense imaginary James in the room with her, making their secret sign with his thumb. Today, he's the James who was larking around in the sea at Niarbyl Bay with Trey, pretending to be happy; an immature teenager.

She makes herself be still, wills her brother to give her a clue. *'What happened?'* she asks him. *'What the hell did you do?'*

Imaginary James answers with a teenage shrug. *'There's no use asking me,'* he says. *'I'm missing. Try God. Or our mother.'*

50

After having a crisis near Admiral Park, eating three Crunchies in quick succession, and making a desperate, unanswered call from a telephone box to her friend Alice to tell her she can't cope with life anymore, Leigh finally pulls herself together and catches the bus back to the station.

She spends the rest of the afternoon in a stationery room where she can cry spontaneously without being disturbed. In between bouts of sobbing and leafing through her 1974 diary, she emerges to telephone Nikki's grandparents, Dolcis and Matty, to see if they can back up what Elaine Yewande told her, or offer any nugget of information that could help get Nikki out of the cells. Out of desperation, she contacts a few friends of Nikki's who might be willing to talk, off the record.

She puts all her torrential feelings about James into getting Nikki out of custody.

And she gets nowhere.

Later that night, at her bedsit, Leigh places Kai in his bouncer at her feet while she searches for a 50p coin to put in the leccy meter. She's praying the power in her bedsit will stay on long enough to prepare the baby's milk and make a Pot Noodle for her tea.

Having failed to find more than two 5p pieces and an old penny, she fills the kettle and sends it on its last hoorah before the electricity goes off. She's intending to get into bed, cuddle up to Kai, and read her diary by candlelight. She sings to him as she waits: *There's A Guy Works Down the Chip shop Swears He's Elvis.*

The baby isn't impressed.

He knows when she's faking it.

When the ancient kettle has made its long and torturous journey to boiling point, she prioritises hot water for Kai and leaves his bottle to cool. She pours the remainder into the dried noodles but the level falls way short of the magic line. Leigh adds the curry powder and watches the dried vegetables float to the top, impatient for the four minutes' wait to be up – she hasn't eaten since the dry toast at her mum's this lunchtime. After less than 30 seconds, she dives in with a spoon and burns her tongue. '*Yum, yum,*' she tells the baby.

After mother and son teatime, Leigh roams the confined space with Kai on her hip, tidying up. On the floor, under the table, is the bag she took to the Isle of Man, still unpacked, full of her soggy clothes and on top, the tartan dress belonging to Mrs Kneale. She needs to return it, but the postage is expensive and she doesn't have the time to go to the Post Office. The visitors' book has been treated with more care: it's wrapped in a Kwik Save bag to protect it, since it's currently sharing cupboard space with the mice family. She retrieves it and puts it on the table, next to the rotting tangerine, ready to take it to the station for Des.

Leigh switches off the light in the living room because the meter is now dangerously low. She massively regrets spending her rent money on a piss-poor night out at the Burundi Club. Maybe she can rig the meter, she thinks. She's heard of people using a knife or fuse wire. Or she could try a Manx 50p and see how far that gets her.

She puts the thought out of her mind – let darkness commence – and settles down with Kai on the mattress. Leigh breathes in his sweet baby smell and listens out for any bangs or shouts that could signal the start of further rioting. Comforted by the quiet outside, and pleased to have finally stopped coughing, she lies next to Kai with her nose touching his. This close-up view is better than anything on the television, and, as an added bonus, being without the money for electricity saves her from seeing Clara Harding make a further appearance on the screen, slagging off the Merseyside Police.

When Kai has dropped off, Leigh lights the candle and picks up her diary, turning the pages of the eight months before James went missing in the August of that year. The A4 diary, with its bright blue cover, was written when she was 22. It's clear from the few entries that this is no diary of secrets. Leigh hadn't treated the pages like a trusted friend and poured her heart out. She'd made a brief record of what she'd done each day, in case someone from the future wanted to look back and discover what the Very Important Leigh Borrowdale was up to in the winter and spring of 1974. She sounds so green and so irresponsible, it's hard to credit she was waiting for her police training to start.

Leigh listens to the pleasing sound of Kai's rustling and snuffling. Without making any sudden movements that might wake him, she continues reading, fascinated by the self-centredness of this pre-James-disappearance person, this pre-Kai-appearance person, who only thought about herself. It's as if she was someone else entirely; another person living another life.

There is only one mention of her brother in the entire six months. On Friday, 1 February. *James to Keele.* Leigh can't remember anything about the day James went for the university interview, although she'd obviously found the event important enough to record at the time. As Alan's only son and heir, James bore all the weight of expectation of getting a degree, whereas Leigh had been as light as a feather as far as parental ambition was concerned. In early 1974, she'd been unemployed and, when she could be bothered, working cash-in-hand on a market stall. With few prospects or plans and no suitor with a professional job in the picture, Alan had offered to pay for her to do a typing course. Applying to join the police force had been her act of rebellion against his lack of faith in her.

She reads a random entry – 12 February 1974 – a Tuesday, that most humdrum of days. Leigh had spent 'the whole night on the phone to Alice,' talking about what, she has no idea. During the week that followed, she went 'out with the gang' to an unspecified gig at the Moonstone ('*Full of troggs!*') and to a reggae night at the Sink Club ('*Very good, very drunk*'). She stayed in on the Sunday, when it rained.

There's no mention of her parents anywhere. And where was James? Leigh had doted on her brother when he was little, spending hours with him at the kitchen table, helping him with his colouring-in books and his drawings of the universe. But at some time during adolescence, he'd slipped into her blind spot. If she tries hard, she can come up with a few memories from his teenage years. Such as: lying in wait at the top of the stairs to jump out at her, and repeating what she said until she became incandescent with rage. *'Mum! Can you tell him to stop it?' 'Mum, can you tell him to stop it?' 'Shut up!' 'Shut up!'* Predominantly, though, Leigh's memories place James, unseen, behind the door to his dark bedroom, through which Geoff's loud and infectious voice often drifted.

She has telephoned her brother's best friend twice now to arrange a visit and, on both occasions, he had made an excuse, saying he was 'mad busy' and how everything was a 'nightmare'.

Leigh puts Geoff out of her mind and carries on leafing through the pages, both engrossed and pained by the carefree life she used to live. She obviously hadn't taken note of anything unusual that occurred from January to August 1974. The entries stop on 9 August, a week after they realised James was missing. It's hard to believe now that Leigh had carried on as normal when her brother didn't arrive back from his camping trip. She'd been out with 'the gang' on three occasions that week. But they'd thought James was being his usual unreliable self, that he'd probably missed the ferry and hadn't let them know.

They lived in a world, back then, when bad things didn't happen.

She flicks through the empty pages to the end, the rest of the year cancelled out, the events unworthy of record including Leigh becoming a police officer, her dad leaving home for another woman and her mum becoming a shadow.

She has just closed the diary when there's a rap at her bedsit door. She knows it's not Des – she would recognise his knock. Her first instinct is to ignore it and hope whoever it is goes away. But then it comes again. And again.

She opens the door to find Pat Killen standing there, giving her his best shark's smile. He's wearing aviator sunglasses – daddy cool – and his aftershave is competing with the sickly citrus smell coming from the rotting tangerine.

'What you doing in the dark, love?' he asks, peering past her into the candlelit living room.

'I was asleep,' Leigh lies. 'How did you get through the front door?'

'The aul fella downstairs let me in.'

The aul Italian fella who's at least 10 years younger than Pat.

Pat indicates towards the living room with his eyes. Leigh reluctantly swings the door open and he goes in ahead of her, switching on the light. She reaches to turn it off again but then decides she doesn't want to be in the dark with a criminal. She wishes she hadn't asked Pat for help. It means she's automatically in debt to the Killens.

'Them initials you were asking about,' he says, shaking his head and crunching up his face to let her know his enquiries, if there have been any, have come to nothing.

'No names?'

'You're barking up the wrong tree, love.'

'What tree should I be barking up?'

'My advice? Leave well alone. Your mam's been through enough.'

He knows something, Leigh thinks. He knows and he's warning her off. She studies his face as he lights a cigarette. His eyes are hidden behind the sunglasses and she can see her harried, frightened face reflected in them.

'Why would anyone put your kid on a hitlist?' he asks, in the manner of a rhetorical question.

'I don't know,' she says. 'Whoever it is must think he's done something wrong.'

'You're clutching at straws there, aren't you, love? Unless your kid wasn't who you thought he was.'

That phrase again, suggesting Leigh didn't know her own brother.

'He was who I thought he was,' Leigh counters, and then corrects herself. 'He is who I think he is.'

'Wasn't and isn't?' Pat says, flicking ash on the carpet. 'You're out of your depth, love. No good will come of poking around in it. You're best leaving it alone.'

'I'm only interested in James,' Leigh says, in an attempt to get him to tell her what he knows. 'I never asked you anything and you never told me anything.'

'As I said, love, your mam doesn't want it all dragging up again.'

Leigh opens her mouth to speak but then gives up. He's not going to give her anything so there's no point in continuing the conversation. And the baby is becoming restless, disturbed by the presence of a shark swimming in nearby waters.

'You know I can still sort you out with one of my flats, Picton Way,' Pat says, surveying the mess.

'You're all right, thanks,' Leigh says, as the light clicks off and they're plunged into darkness.

Leigh surveys Pat Killen's outline in the moonlight, weighing up whether to act on an idea that's just occurred to her. She stares at Pat for a heartbeat longer before making up her mind.

Life, she thinks. It is too short.

'Before you go,' she says, 'you don't know how to rig an electricity meter, do you?'

51

The next morning, almost as soon as Leigh has arrived at the station, the office clerk pops his head around the door to say there's someone to see her in reception. It's okay to come down, he adds, because Duane Harding's supporters haven't arrived yet.

'Who is it?' Leigh asks.

'A fella called Richard Dunne. Said he heard you were asking around yesterday.'

She knows the name.

He was a friend of Duane Harding's.

And not all of Duane Harding's friends thought he was innocent.

Richard is waiting for her in reception; tall, thin, and stinking of fags. This friend of Duane Harding's is a shy man, a nice fella who reminds her of Des. Leigh had spoken to him as part of the original investigation into Gail's disappearance. He has five children, all girls and, he'd told her at the time that, although he gave Duane the benefit of the doubt, he'd felt uncomfortable having him in the house when his kids were there. So much so that, when Duane had come around before his arrest, Richard had told him not to come anymore. When she'd asked him why, he'd said you never know.

She'd taken that to mean he had his doubts.

Richard greets her with a blush that spreads to his ears. He explains that he'd been working away, on the rigs, and had only just heard about Duane, but he's on on-shore leave now. He'd come to the station yesterday but Duane's friends and family had been outside and he'd prefer to remain anonymous.

'There's something that's been playing on my mind,' he says.

Richard had known Duane for a good few years, as Leigh knows already. They played in The Velmont pub darts team, used to meet every week when the tournament was going on, going around different taprooms in the area for a mid-week night out. They were a good bunch of lads. Most of them had lost their jobs when the factories closed, some of them only a few years off retirement, and it was the only time they got out. They used to have a few beers, a free pub supper, a laugh.

Richard can't say he ever thought about Duane much before Gail went missing. He wouldn't say they were close, but Duane got on with everybody and always bought the first round because he was working when the others weren't. Over time, Richard got to know Nikki a bit too – he always thought Duane was punching above his weight there. That's why he's here today, for Nikki, even though his missus had said not to get involved.

The darts team lads all liked Duane, and they stood by him, after it all kicked off. They couldn't believe he'd harm a little girl – he'd always painted himself as a family man. During Duane's trial, the darts team lads went to the court to support him – Richard had seen a couple of them outside the station yesterday, still behind him now.

'Duane was convincing, 100 per cent,' he says.

'Not 100 per cent, though,' Leigh says as she snaps open a can of Tizer and Richard lights a roll-up. 'You didn't want him in the house when your girls were around.'

'Not 100 per cent, no,' Richard says. 'You never know, do you? I'm not going to take any chances as far as my girls are concerned. I gave him the benefit of the doubt, but he wasn't coming through my door.'

'Did Duane go back to the darts team after the case was dropped?' Leigh asks, leading Richard towards saying what had been playing on his mind – they've been in the interview room for a good few minutes already.

Richard nods. Duane was among friends in The Velmont, he says – fellas who believed in his innocence and felt sorry for him. And so, after a lot of persuading, he started playing darts again. He was finding it hard, despite being let off, what with the suspicions never really going away. He'd had death threats and graffiti scrawled over the front of his flat. He couldn't get a job for love nor money. Women would drag their children away when they saw him on the street. It's a difficult thing to shake off, being accused of killing a kiddie. But he had Clara in his life, a good woman who worshipped the ground he stood on, and she wanted to prove his innocence, once and for all, put a stop to all the rumours.

They'd been in The Velmont the night before Richard was going offshore, the end of June. The lads looked after Duane when he came in, same as he'd looked after them when he'd been working, so he always had a drink in front of him. After the darts, Richard and Duane had sat in the corner and got talking – Duane was a quiet lad but he was always chattier when he'd had a few jars.

Richard can't remember all of the conversation, but he remembers Duane started saying some weird stuff, like Gail had never liked him, that she used to look at him as if she hated him. He said she never obeyed him and played him and

Nikki off against each other. It sounded to Richard like he was blaming a little girl and he wasn't too happy about that, having five of his own. He remembered wanting to get away from him, but his kids were at their nan's and his missus had come down for a drink before last orders and was jangling at the bar.

'Was that the thing that was playing on your mind, that he blamed Gail?' Leigh asks as Richard finishes his roll-up and starts making another.

Richard puts his cigarette paper on the table between them and shakes his head.

'There's something that's niggling at me,' he says, returning to the night in the pub.

Duane had started getting over the top pally, like some fellas do when they've had a skinful – putting his arm around Richard, telling him what a good lad he was. He'd had too many – he was slurring his words.

'Why don't you want me in your house, lad?' Duane asked. 'Is it because you think I done Gail?'

Richard had squirmed – he'd always managed to swerve the subject in the past.

'How come you won't let me in your house and all these good folks will?' Duane had said, gesturing around at the fellas in the darts team.

Richard hadn't answered. He'd moved Duane's drink away, out of his reach.

'You won't have to worry about your girls and me for much longer, lad,' Duane had said. 'I'm taking one of them polygraph tests.'

'A lie detector?' Leigh asks, surprised.

Richard nods. 'He said it was Clara's idea – she'd been upset about the graffiti outside the flat, told Duane it would clear his name once and for all and enable them to live in peace. Clara had read about these tests in a magazine. She'd paid this fella who had an old one from a hospital to do one on Duane. He said it was for hospital patients, measured heart rate and blood pressure and all that, but it was used in America for trials, to see if people were lying. They strap you up and then ask questions to see if you're telling the truth.'

'And what was the result?'

'That's the thing. The fellas in the darts team were waiting on the result but nobody ever heard back about whether he'd passed or failed.'

Leigh gazes at Richard, her mind ticking over. They don't use polygraphs in UK courts because they're not reliable. But whether the machine was accurate or not, knowledge of Duane Harding failing the test would have given any of his supporters a motive for murder.

'There's something else,' Richard says. 'The last thing he said to me that night was that all you had to do was control your breathing and make sure your palms didn't get sweaty and then you were set. He looked straight at me and said: "I can cheat anything, me."'

52

'Did your husband tell you what he'd done? After he failed the lie detector? If he did, I wouldn't blame you for stabbing him. All that campaigning for his innocence and then you find out Duane was guilty. Or have you known that all along?'

Leigh, addressing these questions to the swiftly brought-in Clara Harding, is attempting to control herself. She's convinced Duane Harding failed the polygraph test and Clara kept it a secret. But she doesn't want to mess this up by being too shouty and she wants to get as much out of their suspect as possible before her lawyer arrives and the interview begins under caution.

She sits back, her body rigid with frustration. Clara isn't co-operating. She has her face in her hands and all Leigh can see is the fuzz of hair around her crown. Des is sitting by Leigh's side, fridge temperature turned up – both of them are bad cops now.

She takes a breath and tries again.

'Duane failed the polygraph test you'd arranged for him, confessed to you that he was guilty and you stabbed him,' she says, although she knows this can't be the case – Clara wouldn't have had time to get rid of the knife.

'No!' Clara cries through her hands. 'No.'

'Took a big risk, didn't you?' Leigh continues. 'Setting up home with the suspect in the murder of a little girl? Why was he sleeping on the couch on the night he was murdered? Did he confess and you didn't want him in the same bed? Did you spend a sleepless night plotting what you were going to do to him? Or did you get someone else to do it for you?'

'Stop!' Clara says. 'Please stop, please.'

She shakes her head vehemently, but she doesn't uncover her face.

'I'll ask you the question I've asked before,' Leigh says. 'Did Duane tell you where he'd put Gail's body?'

The door to the interview room clicks open and a duty lawyer appears and demands to speak to Clara in private. Leigh and Des wait while their interviewee, still with her head down, is led out of the room for a consultation. When they return a few minutes later, Clara's head is up – she's the type of person who needs someone by her side to give her confidence.

The interview begins in earnest.

'Please can you tell us about the lie detector you arranged for your husband to take?' Des asks – they'd decided in Clara's absence that she was more likely to open up when faced with his charm.

Clara turns to the lawyer, as if asking for permission to speak.

'We do know that you organised the test for your husband,' Des says, gently. 'And that potentially makes you a suspect, if you found out something you didn't want to know.'

'Did he tell you to keep your mouth shut about the results?' Leigh interjects.

Clara makes a squeaking sound and then says something in a voice so quiet they both have to lean in to hear.

'I don't know,' she says, one hand cupped around her cheek. 'I thought he did but then he said he didn't, that I was imagining it.'

She gazes at the lawyer, uncertain she's said the right thing. Leigh had thought the woman had fortitude, but Clara needs support from someone else to make even the simplest of decisions.

'Clara's prepared to speak,' the lawyer says, 'but you'll need to seriously consider the legitimacy of any charges against her when you've heard the context.'

'What did he tell you?' Des asks, nodding.

'He did fail the polygraph,' Clara blurts out, 'and I was expecting him to say what he always said, that he was innocent and those machines were rubbish and they proved nothing. He'd always sworn on his life, and mine, that he was innocent.'

'I told you!' Leigh says too vehemently and to no one in particular. 'I told you all along he was a murderer.'

'Lives didn't mean a lot to him, I'm afraid,' Des says, ignoring her outburst.

'But instead of denying it,' Clara continues, 'what he said was, "*Would you still love me if what they said about me was true?*" I asked him what he meant and he said, "*My time's up. I'll have to hand myself in.*"'

Clara hadn't been able to comprehend. She'd asked him where Gail was and what they were going to do, but then Duane said, '*What are you talking about, Clara?*' She'd repeated back to him what he'd said and he said she must be losing her mind.

'When I asked him what he meant about it all being true,' Clara says, 'he told me he hadn't said that and I should go and see a psychiatrist because I needed my head testing.'

On the night before Duane was stabbed, Clara had been plucking up the courage to leave. But she was confused, and she still loved him. It's difficult to just switch your feelings off like that, she tells them.

So she didn't leave. When Duane got home from the pub, she grabbed the frying pan from the worktop and started cutting up chunks of lard and dropping them into the hot pan.

'You're back early,' she said as Duane approached and put his cold hands up the back of her jumper, making her squeal.

'I'll get your bacon and eggs started, shall I?' Clara said.

She didn't want to touch him, and the lard was sliding around the frying pan as it melted, so she broke free. She was relieved when Duane left her alone in the kitchen and she heard the TV go on in the living room.

When she carried the plate into the living room, she knew at once that Duane's mood had turned. He didn't take his eyes off the television as she put the late-night meal down on the coffee table. Clara sat on the other end of the settee as he ate his bacon and eggs in silence. She watched tensely as the plate slowly emptied, her eyes fixed on the smears of yolk and tomato sauce. When he'd put down his knife and fork, she broke the silence, asking if the bacon was crispy enough, if the eggs were all right for him, if the bread had too much butter on.

She's never been able to stand being sent to Coventry.

Duane grunted in reply and they both stared at the dying minutes of a comedy on the television screen.

'You're quiet,' Clara ventured after a while.

'I'm tired.'

Another beat of silence before he said:

'You could at least have the meal ready for when I come home.'

'Oh. It wasn't too late, was it? You don't usually get in until 11.'

Duane turned to give her a hard, hurt stare.

'Listen,' he said, 'I know cooking isn't your strong point, but you need to get better organised.'

'Yes, sorry. I'll put it on earlier next Friday, get my timing right!'

Duane seemed cheered then. He was always magnanimous after an argument. He leant across and slapped her on the back, as if she was a jolly good fellow, and left the room with a belch, leaving the television blaring. She heard footsteps down the corridor, and then the toilet door shut.

The local news came on the screen, and there was a short update on the unrest in Toxteth before the television shut down for the night. It was over in a few seconds; replaced by an item about the passing away of the president of Cuba. Clara heard the toilet flush.

'What were you watching the news for?' Duane said, standing in the doorway seconds later.

'I wasn't, it was just on. It said there were police in riot gear all the way up the Parli.'

'You seem to know a lot to say you weren't watching it.'

Clara stared out of the window into the night, concerned. On television, the national anthem was playing as the screen faded to a dot. Duane approached the set and snapped off the switch. She got up then, collected the dirty plate from the coffee table, and followed her husband out of the room. He turned right, into the bedroom, and she went into the kitchen to do the washing up. Duane always discouraged her from seeing the news or reading the newspapers – he said it was to protect her, because she got easily upset. But it didn't make any difference. What with the polygraph test and the trouble outside her front door, she didn't need a reminder to feel upset.

'The bacon wasn't too bad tonight, actually,' Duane said behind her.

He hadn't gone to bed, as he'd said. He'd come into the kitchen to compliment her, and to stand behind her with his arms around her waist. She should have reciprocated his embrace, but Clara's anxiety was getting the better of her. She wanted to speak her worries out loud. She wanted him to reassure her that he didn't have anything to do with that little girl's disappearance.

'Duane?' Clara said tentatively as she wriggled away from him and ran the tap. 'You don't know anything about Gail, do you?'

'I can't believe this,' he said. 'Do we have to go through this again?'

'I'm worried, that's all.'

'Oh, for Christ's sake!' Duane shouted. 'Just leave it, will you! Christ! I don't need this!'

And that's all it took for Clara to become uncertain if the fault lay with her and this was just another instance of her worrying about nothing. She turned on the tap and squirted washing-up liquid in the bowl. When she glanced away from the sink, she saw her husband's back disappearing through the doorway.

Clara washed the plate under running water, wincing as the lump of tomato slid into the water and floated like a blood clot. She put some milk on to boil for Duane's usual bedtime hot chocolate and peered out of the window for signs of the police in riot gear.

Later, she could have sworn she saw the fist come towards her in reverse time. As if it had happened the wrong way around, first the smack against her bottom lip, and then Duane's arm, springing out in a straight line, as if it was in recoil. The punch came so fast that she didn't have time to duck or put her hands to her face. In an instant, her bottom lip was split and she was shaking and sobbing with the aftershock.

'What?' Duane shouted. 'You left the tap on!'

Meaning that he was reaching across to turn the tap off with a clenched fist and she got in the way.

'Jesus,' he said, the volume of his voice reduced to a hiss. 'Stop crying, will you? The neighbours will hear you, carrying on like that.'

He reached the door and then turned back.

'I'm going to sleep on the settee,' Duane announced.

Clara held her fingers to her lip, dabbing at the trickle of blood. The milk came to a boil on the gas hob. She used a tissue to wipe her mouth and then went into the living room to serve Duane hot chocolate on a tray.

She'd tried to say sorry, but he'd given her the silent treatment. Clara went back into the kitchen and got everything ready for the morning, closing the blinds, and making sure the front door was locked and bolted. She left Duane in the living room and went into the bedroom to get changed into her nightclothes. She got the duffel bag down from the top of the wardrobe, wondering if she'd ever have the guts to leave.

And then the rioting started outside.

The noise from the street was thunderous. She's never heard anything like it – roars like a football crowd, deafening bangs like it was fireworks night. When she peered through the blinds at midnight, the road was in flames. She was scared the house was going to burn down so she went into the living room to get Duane. He was fast asleep on the settee so she sat on the bed and stayed up, watching the streets burn.

All through the early hours of that night, Clara thought of leaving. But she didn't leave because she didn't have her own money and the housekeeping Duane gave her barely stretched to a weekly shop. She didn't leave because she'd fallen out with her parents and had nowhere to go. She didn't leave because it was dangerous outside.

She didn't leave because she'd never been a confident person. She didn't leave because she didn't know what to do.

She's a worrier, Duane always said so, her mind dreaming up terrible scenarios without a shred of evidence they might come true. And she was punching above her weight with Duane and would never find anyone else. He never tired of telling her she should thank her lucky stars she'd received her first-ever marriage proposal in her thirtieth year, just as it looked like she'd be left on the shelf.

But most of all, she didn't leave because she couldn't face telling anyone she was a beaten wife. She knew it happened to other women – it happened regularly to a woman across the street, who covered up the swelling with scarves and turtleneck sweaters. But not to Clara. She was too ashamed to admit it; too ashamed of her weakness.

She didn't leave because, because, because, because.

And so she stayed.

Clara must have dropped to sleep at some point, because the next thing she knew it was silent outside and a bird was singing. She listened for sounds of Duane stirring from the living room but it was quiet in there too so she'd thought he was still asleep. And then she went into the kitchen and found him there, bleeding on the floor. If the front door was ajar, she didn't notice. She'd definitely locked it before she went to bed. What she said about the intruder wasn't the truth.

There was no man with a balaclava.

'What with Duane saying I was losing my mind, I wondered whether I'd done that to him,' Clara says.

'But you didn't,' Leigh says, fighting her natural tendency towards sympathy. Clara had been looking for stability, for someone to love her, and had found a child murderer instead.

Clara shakes her head.

'And do you know who did?' Des asks, gently.

'I don't know,' Clara says, and starts to sob.

'And, another question, if you don't mind,' Des says. 'Did you mention Duane's confession to anyone else?'

'I don't think anyone else knew about Duane failing the lie detector. He told me not to breathe a word to anyone.'

After getting Clara to write down the names of the supporters she knows, Leigh and Des run to the entrance of the station. But when they get outside, the pavement is empty. Beyond the yellow tape, only the remnants of the protestors remain – cigarette butts and random pieces of cardboard. Leigh exchanges a glance with Des as they go to stand in the middle of the road, turning their heads this way and that, looking for the Ford Cortina.

They've been moved on, not half an hour since, the duty sergeant explains when they go back inside.

As soon as Stan learns the news, he marches into the murder investigation room.

'Every single one of them no-marks who hang around outside have motive!' he yells. 'Duane Harding tricked them into believing he was an innocent man. Hunt them down!'

53

'One of Duane's supporters must have known about him failing the lie detector,' Leigh says, putting four slices of bread under the grill, 'they must have.'

She reaches for the bowl of grated cheese Des has prepared, one-handed, while balancing Kai on his knee.

'Clara hasn't exactly been honest with us, so far,' Des says, smiling at Leigh as she spreads the cheese on the toast and opens the cupboard where the mice family live, looking for clean plates. She puts the toast back under the grill and turns to grin at Kai, who is pummelling Des's thighs with his feet. Today, they'd missed his impressive feat of rolling from his front onto his back for the very first time.

'And whoever knew about it must've been blazing mad he'd spent all that time and effort campaigning for Duane Harding's innocence.'

Leigh breaks off from talking about the case and pulls a funny face at Kai. Her eyes settle on the baby's dad, looking handsome in his apricot-coloured shirt. She feels a pang, but she's leering, so she turns back to the oven to check the progress of the cheese on toast.

They don't go into work stuff much more than that – Des has come home with her because they've got other things to talk about. They're both tired anyway, particularly Des, who has spent the afternoon visiting the homes of Duane Harding's supporters. All of them, so far, have denied any knowledge of Duane Harding failing the polygraph test. Leigh was precluded because of the reaction her face gets when those fellas see it, and had stayed behind to confirm Richard Dunne's alibi for the time Duane Harding was murdered – coming in to tell them what he knew had automatically made him a suspect.

The squad had spoken to most of the merry bunch of men, save a couple of stragglers nobody seemed to know the surnames of – the Jesus-like fella, and Leigh's biggest fan, the Teddy Boy. Duane Harding's dad John hadn't been located either. He was thought, by his wife, to have been on a bender since the previous afternoon, brought on by the loss of his son. Des has decided it's easier to wait for the stragglers to arrive outside the station tomorrow morning and bring them in then.

'Josephine suggested Nikki remain as a suspect until we find out more,' Des says.

'Oh well, if Josephine suggested it,' Leigh says in a snarky tone.

'She was of that opinion, yes,' Des says quietly.

'I saw you,' Leigh blurts out, 'in the Golden Yuen, last night.'

Des doesn't speak for a few seconds.

'Josephine wanted to talk through the Gail Harding case,' he says after an excruciating silence, 'she asked me to meet. I do hang out at the Golden Yuen anyway, so …'

'Talk through the case over a five-course buffet?'

'It was her last night in Liverpool; most of the out-of-town officers are going home today. She was hungry and well, it *is* a restaurant.'

Five courses though? she thinks. Five courses *you* paid for.

Their meals together in the Golden Yuen were always the cheapest on the menu – fried rice and sweet and sour sauce without the pork balls; leftover soup of the day; the odd banana fritter. They'd never eaten the banquet buffet because, with the baby on the way, they couldn't afford it.

'Leigh,' Des says, looking pained. 'Nothing happened.'

He pauses before he provides the explanation he feels he has to make.

'We went straight home afterwards, I was back in the flat by 11.'

It was after midnight, Leigh stops herself saying: the time the telephone had rung in her bedsit. And anyway, why do fellas always say 'nothing happened'? Something *had* happened. A candlelit meal is what had happened. *Intimacy* is what had happened. To Leigh, that's worse than a quick screw on the mattress of a Canning Street bedsit.

When the cheese is bubbling and the crusts are black, they take their meal into the living room. Leigh sits on the bare mattress, where she has a view of the sheets she'd picked up from the launderette on the way home. She puts the baby on one side of her and the soggy slice of Welsh Rarebit on the other, away from tiny grabbing hands. Des sits at the table, angling his mouth to catch the strings of cheese dripping like stalactites off the toast. In front of him is her 1974 diary, quickly snapped shut when they'd entered the room, as well as the bunch of keys she'd signed out from forensics. There's also the visitors' book from the Ballabeg guesthouse, which he's taking with him when he leaves, and two stacks of coins, the result of her counting pennies last night when she couldn't sleep, trying to work out how to make £2.20 last the week. At least the lights are on, she thinks, although she knows Pat's meter fixing is only a short-term solution – she'll have to get the money for a legal electricity supply soon.

'Shall I?' Des says after he's finished eating, referring to the updates on James he promised her.

Leigh glances at her brother's telescope in the corner and nods. *Go on, I can take it.* Even if she's not sure she can.

'We haven't had time to check passenger lists for H.E., I'm afraid,' he says, 'but we're expecting the file on James to arrive from the Isle of Man tomorrow. We'll take another look at witness statements when it arrives.'

By 'we' he means his squad – Des hasn't had the time to look at anything other than the Duane Harding murder case.

'None of the names on the list have previous or have even been questioned for child offences, as far as we can tell,' he says.

'So it's not a list of paedophiles?' Leigh says, relief flooding through her.

'We don't know,' Des says. 'It doesn't mean that those on the list weren't guilty of an unreported crime, or *thought* to be guilty of an unreported crime.'

'No way,' Leigh says. She refuses to believe that her naïve, goofy little brother could hurt anyone, least of all a child. 'It must be something else. But what? What on earth could James have done to end up on a hitlist?'

'It could be a list connected to something else,' Des responds, 'but, unfortunately, we haven't got a clue what. My officers did a search of MERCO and vehicle licensing, but in the end, seeing we had the addresses, we thought it was easier if they just knocked on doors. Two of them have passed away, but the other fella, Abraham Romi, is alive and well and had no idea what my officers were talking about.'

'The ones who had passed away; those were the ones marked deceased?'

Des nods his head.

'They passed away of what?'

'Henry Clarke, he was 22, a student teacher who lived in Old Swan. He died in the April of 1974 after being beaten up when a couple of fellas broke into his home in the middle of the night, armed with wooden bats. It was nasty – aggravated burglary.'

'Did the burglar take anything?' Leigh asks, glancing at Kai and feeling an urge to cover his ears – do babies soak in bad vibes? Will he be damaged if they talk about these horrors in front of him?

'Nothing. It was assumed the burglar was disturbed by Henry.'

'No prints?'

'Gloved up. The perp was never caught and there were no leads from the neighbours.'

'Was anyone ever in the frame?'

'The usual trawl of the usual suspects who liked a bit of house breaking.'

'No H.E.?'

'No.'

'Okay. Who's next?'

'Leonard Carey, he was 78, a former forklift truck driver, died in a fire at his retirement home near Calderstones Park in November that year. His disabled wife managed to escape. There didn't look to be suspicious circumstances. He was a smoker,' Des adds, lighting a cigarette and taking a drag.

Leigh throws her head back to finish the dregs of her after-dinner Tizer. Des is watching her closely through a haze of smoke, gauging whether telling her this information is hurting her. She gets up and rifles through her LP collection, taking out a Smokey Robinson LP, *Warm Thoughts*, and setting it on the turntable. She wants to neutralise the horrible words which are circulating in the air; replace them with a softer sound. She adjusts the RPM and places the stylus on track 3, 'Into Each Rain Some Life Must Fall' and then carefully lifts the now slumbering baby from the mattress and carries him over to his crib. She fusses over the position of his body – no sleeping on your front, little prince – and arranges his blanket over his feet.

'Murders made to look like accidents?' Leigh says, fear in her voice as she throws herself back down on the mattress.

'Maybe,' Des says. 'Maybe not, It could all be a coincidence.'

'Two dead and James missing. That's not a coincidence.'

Smokey Robinson goes on singing, hiccupping occasionally where the vinyl is slightly scratched. The music reminds Leigh of the many nights she's spent with Des in this room, lying in each other's arms with their feet entwined.

'Someone made the list though,' she says, 'someone inside the prison.'

'I'm afraid we haven't been able to find anything more about that. The fella whose cell it was found in, he's a vulnerable prisoner, in that he's spent time in an asylum. He's inside for criminal damage, not violence. It would have been an easy plant.'

'His initials don't begin with H.E?'

'No, they don't, I'm afraid,' Des says. 'We can look through current prisoner names but, if this is suspicious, it's more likely that H.E. was contracted.'

Leigh reaches up, grabs a clean sheet from the end of the bed and, to relieve her agitation, gets up and starts to fit it onto the mattress.

'There must be a mistake,' she says. 'James wouldn't be on any hitlist, he was a kid.'

'It's baffling, but we never know people, not really,' Des says, stubbing out his cigarette and helping her tuck in the corners.

'I did know James, though,' Leigh says. 'I knew my own brother.'

Two hours later, after waiting for Des's sister, Maylin, to arrive to babysit Kai, Leigh and Des are trying the keys in the remainder of the garages in the area between Duane Harding's home and work. They are here at Leigh's insistence – she needs something to take her mind off her brother. And what better than her obsession with finding Gail?

'Bingo!' she says, as the umpteenth key they try opens the lock of a crumbling garage in The Dingle.

Her hands are shaking inside her latex gloves as Des pulls up the shutter, doing his job quickly and efficiently – this is no time to be lily-livered. They exchange a grave glance and inhale simultaneously.

The air is clear.

Leigh and Des step inside and look around. Duane Harding's garage is everything you'd expect from a mechanic looking for a refuge and workshop of his own. It's spick and span, well organised. Wrenches and sockets are stored neatly in an open tool cabinet. A tool belt lies on a long bench running along the back wall. Beneath the tool belt is a box file.

Des shines his torch along the bench while Leigh opens the box file and holds it towards the beam. The file is full of papers, including a collection receipt for photographs he'd taken to Boots to be developed, and a letter that Leigh reads eagerly, but it's just from the DHSS informing him he's entitled to £36.40. The date 2 July 1981 is at the top.

He had been here recently.

Leigh carries on rifling through the papers in the box file and plucks out a single sheet, the words TEST RESULTS at the top. In keeping with what Clara had told them, the test was administered two days before his murder. Leigh's eyes jump down the page. Two questions were asked. *Did you murder Gail Harding? Do you know where her body is?* To each, Duane Harding had answered, '*No*'. The results are at the bottom of the page: *deception indicated*.

'He failed it,' she says, looking at Des. 'He thought he could cheat it and then announce to the world he was innocent, but the scumbag failed it.'

'We need to find the person who administered that test,' Des says. 'And collect those photographs from Boots, too.'

'Forensics?' Leigh suggests.

'We might as well,' Des says. 'He obviously kept this place hidden.'

Leigh stands outside the garage, feeling both relieved and stricken. For nearly two years, she'd been convinced that Duane Harding had hidden his terrible crime in a secret garage.

But now Gail isn't here, she doesn't know what to do next.

54

Early the next morning, before the expected arrival of Duane Harding's supporters, Des drives Leigh to Chester. She is hoping to catch her brother's best friend before he starts the 'nightmare' of another 'mad busy' day. More and more, James's friends are coming across as a bunch of people who haven't got their stories straight, despite having had seven years to do it.

The Allegro enters the darkness of a near-empty Birkenhead Tunnel and moves steadily under the Mersey towards the Wirral. Leigh, too close to the tunnel wall in the passenger seat, clutches the paper bag on her lap – pineapple cake donated by Min after a night spent at the garage overseeing forensics. Or at least, Des had spent the night there – Leigh had gone back to her bedsit to relieve Maylin of babysitting duties. She'd immediately dropped into a deep sleep which had lasted around an hour before Kai woke up and demanded to be entertained.

As they emerge into daylight and Des puts the indicator on to follow the road sign for Chester and North Wales, she takes a wanton bite of pineapple cake. She holds the sticky slice to Des's mouth and smiles as he takes a mouthful. Although (as Des would categorise it) 'nothing happened' last night, something, in fact, had happened. They'd sat in her bedsit like they used to, eating and chatting, with Smokey Robinson turned down low on the stereo. This morning, when Leigh had dropped Kai off, they'd set off together with Min's beaming approval.

'What can I help you with, mate?'

They are a few minutes into their visit to Geoff, sitting on a hard sofa in the kitchen of his shared flat, and have only just got down to business. When he'd finally opened the door, James's best friend had greeted them effusively, giving Des a warm handshake, welcoming him in as Leigh's new husband before touching on her 'wild' past and his amazement that she'd settled down.

In the flesh, Geoff looks just as she'd pictured him over the telephone, minus the handkerchief on his head. He's dressed in a tracksuit which is tight around his bulging middle, and his already thinning hair is in need of a wash. The flat is just as she'd imagined it too: chaotic, studenty, stinky. When they'd arrived, Geoff had closed the door on a room carpeted with clothes, as if suddenly seeing his pigsty through new eyes.

Straight after that, right on cue, he'd said he was mad busy and was on his way out to referee a five-a-side football match.

DI Chung had been forced to make an appearance and show his warrant card.

'We have actually tried to call a few times,' he'd said, the accusation implicit.

Now, after Des has rather formally introduced the subject of his inquiry as 'James Borrowdale', Geoff is looking decidedly sweaty. Or is Leigh imagining that? On the one hand, Geoff seemed genuinely alarmed by the police badge. On the other, he's always on his way somewhere else as soon as Leigh appears.

'I know I've asked you this before,' she says, 'but I really want you to wrack your brains this time. Can you think of anything at all that James might have been upset about when you were on holiday?'

'What's this about, mate?' Geoff asks, even though Des has already told him.

'We've got a witness who says a stranger was asking about James,' Des says. 'It was in the local pub, the Manx Tavern. James ran out of the pub when he heard about this fella, and you were seen talking to James shortly afterwards. I was wondering if he mentioned this incident to you?'

Des is the embodiment of politeness, but he's good at his job and is subtly putting the pressure on, causing Geoff to pull a face as if he's got a sudden twinge in his back.

'Honestly, mate,' he says, his eyes dipping at the serious turn this is all taking. 'He never mentioned anything to me. We had a great time. The holiday was great.'

'What about before he left Liverpool?' Leigh asks. 'Can you think of anything that was worrying him?'

'Nothing,' Geoff says, scratching at his fingers. 'Oh, wait, yeah, hang on a sec. I remember something. He was going for a job interview, some accountants near Belle Vale Shopping Centre. He'd sort of made up his mind not to go to university, but he didn't know how to tell your folks.'

'Why didn't you mention this before?' Leigh asks, her voice trill with the emotion caused by being a rubbish sister who James couldn't confide in.

'I thought you would have known about it, mate,' Geoff says. 'And that had nothing to do with what happened, did it? I mean, he wouldn't have, you know, done anything stupid because of that.'

'We're not suggesting he did,' Des says.

'Describe James to me,' Leigh says when Geoff has wiped perspiration from his face. 'The last time you saw him.'

'We were just waiting for a bus.'

'James came with you, to see you off when you left?'

Geoff nods, but he's looking extremely uncomfortable.

'And then the bus came? The one that goes to Peel Town Hall?'

Leigh is a blow-in from the Isle of Man. She still remembers the routes from her childhood. From Peel, they'd have to get another bus to the capital, Douglas.

'The bus pulled up, I remember that, and I remember sitting on it, looking out of the window. We left James standing there and then he walked across to the Holiday Inn. I remember waving to him as we pulled away. He came with us, to Peel, I think. That was in Peel.'

It sounds simultaneously uncertain and rehearsed, as if he's been over it a thousand times and still can't make his mind up, but James coming with them to Peel is information he's never shared before. Leigh glances at Des. She can feel an idea scraping around in her mind, like a song she can remember the verse to but not the chorus. She almost grasps it, and then it goes away again and all that's left is an empty space.

Leigh cries all the way back to Liverpool.

'Geoff wouldn't lie, would he?' she asks when Des stops at the toll plaza for the tunnel. 'Why would he lie? I've known him forever. He's always been a lovely fella.'

'Actually,' Des says as they head into the tunnel, 'he wasn't in a hurry to help you find James.'

'What are you thinking?'

'I'm thinking he might be a lovely fella, but he's hiding something.'

'I'm thinking that, too,' Leigh says, as her mind accesses the rest of the song and the chorus belts out at her.

'Geoff's account of the last time he saw James was off,' she says. 'As far as I can remember, there aren't any Holiday Inns on the Isle of Man.'

55

Everyone is in place when they arrive at the station. There are officers in parked cars on the street, officers watching from upstairs windows, and officers lurking behind the reception desk. Slapdash and Mark II are hanging around outside the Queen's Arms, looking more conspicuous than they should. The only officer who isn't here is Kevin, who's in the murder investigation room, tracking down the fella who administered the polygraph test.

Detectives and uniforms alike are waiting for the imminent arrival of Duane Harding's supporters.

'What's up with you?' Callum asks when Leigh joins him by the reception window.

'Allergy,' she says, explaining her swollen eyes which are still leaking the occasional tear.

'Allergy to what?'

'To people who geg into my business.'

Callum studies her puffy face in a prolonged manner and raises his eyebrows to let her know he doesn't believe her. Stan had threatened the team with beheading if they blab the information about the prison hitlist around, but gossip spreads fast in the station and everyone will know James is on it by now. The DC kneels to peer through the slats in the blinds.

Leigh crouches down next to him, watching as the Ford Cortina pulls up and Duane Harding's supporters tumble out. They take their places in the line, looking like a downmarket version of The Village People. Leigh takes them in, one by one. Duane Harding's dad, John; his cowboy hat-wearing cousin, Willie; a dishevelled fella with a handlebar moustache; and the Teddy Boy.

The Jesus-like fella is missing.

'He wasn't at the pick-up point,' John Harding says when they drag him, the Teddy Boy, and the two docile Alsatians inside.

'And where is this pick-up point, please?' Des asks.

'Main entrance of Toxteth Cemetery, outside the Lodge.'

Slapdash corners the Teddy Boy, who looks bewildered, as if he only turned up for the sandwiches and the opportunity to leer at women police officers. Mark II escorts John Harding inside, albeit with some difficulty. Thinking he's being arrested and headed that way, he shouts about his rights all the way to the interview room, where his placard advertising police corruption gets caught in the door. Des sends the uniforms out to knock on doors and call on shopkeepers in the area around the cemetery to see if they can locate the Jesus-like fella.

'Check the graveyards,' Callum calls after them, 'he might have risen from the dead.'

While they wait, Leigh visits the cells to find out what's happening with Elaine Yewande's 16-year-old son. But the cells are mostly occupied by uniforms getting their heads down after a night shift and the detention officer tells her that Tyrell is already on his way to youth court. Leigh returns to reception with the impression she's destined to spend her life either looking for the missing or trying to free people from cells.

She takes a left and calls in on Clara Harding in the interview room. Duane Harding's widow is standing by the barred window and jumps when she comes in.

'Tell me what you know about the fella with long hair and a beard, the one with the JUSTICE banner,' Leigh says.

Clara's eyes flicker towards Leigh and away again, towards the view of the terraced houses opposite.

'Where's that nice officer?' she says, meaning Des.

'Come on, Clara,' Leigh says, 'me and you don't have to be mates, but it's in your best interests to tell me what you know.'

'Why do you want to know who he is?' Clara asks. 'I don't understand why you're asking. I need to ask the lawyer ...'

'We're trying to trace Duane's supporters so we can rule them out of our enquiries,' Leigh explains, 'and we can't find him.'

'His name's Tony,' Clara says, without looking up. 'But he would never hurt Duane. He's always been on his side.'

'Tony what?'

'I don't know,' Clara says, 'I don't think he ever said.'

Leigh pumps Clara for more information but gets only scant facts in return. Tony is quiet and funny. He's always been kind to Clara but Duane never took to him. He was only in Liverpool for short bursts – he often went home because he said he had someone to get back for. He speaks with a Midlands accent and used to be a miner but he lost his job.

Clara had met him on the steps of St George's Hall – Tony had driven up from wherever it was he came from just to support Duane. He'd read about the case in the newspapers, he said, and thought it was a terrible miscarriage of justice. After Duane was acquitted, he'd visit their Toxteth flat when he was in town, to talk about clearing his name.

Clara doesn't know this Tony's full name, where he lives, or much about him at all. And, Leigh discovers when she gets back to the incident room, neither do any of the other fellas.

Shortly afterwards, the uniforms call in with a lead. A shopkeeper on Smithdown Road has said he recognises this Tony fella from the description – long hair, shaggy beard, and the JUSTICE placard he carried with him when he went in to buy tobacco in the mornings. The shopkeeper thought the fella was one of those anarchist types who live in a squat on Alderson Street.

Inside the said squat less than an hour later: lots of shouting about the fucking bizzies. When the squad members step inside the door and shout *'Police!'*, they see more than one occupant running out back and clambering over the yard wall. Most stay to fight the good fight and hurl abuse, and some stay because they're too stoned to move. The front room smells of cannabis and amyl nitrate but, other than that, it's more nicely done out than Leigh's own bedsit, with two comfy settees arranged around a tiny television which has *Death news* written in dust on its screen. On the coffee table is a copy of *The Face* magazine with Terry Hall on its cover, and on the wall are a multitude of angry slogans. *Organise to resist! Defiance! Kill the rich! Fuck the state!*

Leigh finds this all a little thrilling. She looks around at the squatters wearing combat gear and black leather, and thinks she has found her people.

None of them look like this Tony fella, though. He might have got wind they're looking for him and had his hair cut by now. Or he might just be having a lie-in – their approach is a tad heavy-handed seeing all he's done is miss his pick-up this morning. As Stan pointed out, they've got no evidence, *'only a woolly back weirdo who didn't show his face this morning.'*

Slapdash and Mark II go through the back into the kitchen, Leigh and Des mount the stairs. Waiting for them at the top is a fella wearing a beret and braces over a vest, shouting that they need a warrant to come in here.

'We're looking for someone, mate,' Des says as he limps towards the top rung.

'Traitor!' the fella grumbles, regaling Des for being a Chinese officer in the police force.

277

'Keep your hair on,' Leigh says. 'We're not searching the place.'

She's about to go into a spiel about how they've got a right to enter without a warrant if they're in pursuit, but decides not to bother. They don't know who they're in pursuit of, or even if it's warranted. And anyway, explaining their powers isn't going to change the fella's mind – Merseyside Police have a reputation in the city that won't be dispelled by her spouting rules.

On the landing, a young Asian lad appears and hovers nervously by a door. He's wearing a red school blazer and Leigh has no idea whether he's run in off the street or if he lives here. He points wildly to a room at the front.

'In there, miss,' he tells her, excitably, and then dashes down the stairs.

The fella with the beret and braces thumps him on the head as he darts past.

'Oi,' Leigh says, 'he's only a kid.'

Des adopts a defensive position and steps inside the room. Leigh follows. It's a box room, what was once a boy's bedroom, painted blue. There's no one in there, but they see the JUSTICE placard straight away, leaning against the window frame. The only others things in here are a mattress, a carrier bag, and a bucket, into which water drops from a caved-in roof. Leigh automatically reaches for the light switch but there's no electricity.

Watched by Mark II, who has advanced onto the landing as if he's holding a gun. Des slides on latex gloves and groans as he gets down on his knees. As he opens the carrier bag, Leigh sees a headline: *Man arrested on suspicion of murder over disappearance of schoolgirl Gail Harding*. Des delves his hand back in, as if it's a lucky dip at a funfair, and pulls out a piece of paper, slotted in between the newspapers. It's a letter, without an envelope, dated *4 June 1981*. Much of it is in block capitals and some of the words have been redacted.

Dear son, lying twat, Shelton,

> I am writing to say I've had a word with him downstairs, as you know we are on friendly terms. I wanted to tell you that I have now SOLD YOUR SOUL, as is my right as your father, so now you are heading STRAIGHT TO HELL. You are a redact words, redact words, redact words. What you have done is redact evil and, when the time comes, Hell's gate will open wide and you'll drown in a pit full of boiling oil and be lashed with iron clubs so you buck like you're in a rodeo. You will be branded LIAR and your LYING mouth will be shut forever.
>
> Your father.
> PS. I am coming to get you as soon as I am freed.

'Parental love knows no bounds,' Leigh says when she's read it out loud.

56

The background searches begin as soon as they get back to the station, the squad checking the Merseyside Criminal Records Office, the Police National Computer, vehicle licensing – anything that could help them to find out more about the fella with the unusual name of Shelton. Leigh organises a warrant to search the squat on Alderson Street. Apart from the placard and the contents of the carrier bag, they had left the room intact, employing a couple of uniforms to secure the scene and apprehend their suspect if he returns.

By the way the beret-wearing fella was screaming at them when they left, she doesn't fancy their job.

There's no progress in finding Shelton throughout the afternoon, so Leigh slips away. She's still on the insurance of the Allegro so she begs the keys from Des and drives to Crosby to see Nikki.

'There's no news,' she says as Gail's mum opens the door to the caravan, referring, as usual, to the search for Gail – she can't tell Nikki anything about the investigation into Duane's murder yet, much as she'd like to.

'I saw Elaine,' Leigh says straight away. 'She came to see me.'

Nikki's face crumples. Leigh resists the urge to offer comfort and keeps talking.

'I know it was Elaine who threw the cactus out of the window of her flat, the one that hit the police officer. She told me. And I know you were there.'

'She only threw it to stop the copper from hurting her son!' Nikki cries. 'The bizzy was hitting Tyrell with a truncheon! Elaine didn't mean to! She's already lost one son …'

'She also told me how you saw the copper writhing around on the ground and went down to see if he was all right, just before a gang of coppers arrived and you had to run.'

Around the corner, up Devonshire Road, past the flat where Duane Harding was lying dead in the kitchen. Less than 10 minutes after Slapdash's brother-in-law laid into Elaine's son, shortly after the back-up arrived. Leigh has already checked the timings.

'The copper's all right,' she says. 'He's back at work. But it's amazing what damage a cactus can do.'

'Are you going to tell on us?' Nikki asks, sounding like a schoolgirl.

'It's an alibi, Nikki. It would get you off the hook. It would mean you're no longer under investigation for Duane's murder.'

'I can't get Elaine into trouble!'

Nikki flings herself into Leigh's arms and sobs. Leigh squeezes her tight and stares over her shoulder. Above *Frog and Toad are Friends*, she can see the motto, *Weak wills wilt*, pinned to the wall. Before she came here, she'd vowed she wouldn't sit on the information about the flying cactus.

But *Weak wills wilt*, and leaving Elaine's flat to check on the copper is such a typical Nikki thing to do. Leigh decides she's been through enough. And so has Elaine.

'Whatever you do,' she says, 'don't tell Des.'

To make the most of having a car, Leigh makes another stop on her way back to the station. As soon as she pulls onto Dunbabin Road, she sees the curtains at number 24 are drawn, upstairs and down. But not, it seems, because her mum is grabbing some afternoon delight. There's no sign of Pat Killen in the hallway today.

Leigh stands in the doorway to the living room. Her mum is flat on her back on the settee. Her eyes are wide open and she's staring at the ceiling. She doesn't look at Leigh, or speak, even though she must know she's there.

Leigh has so much she wants to talk about, but there's no point so she goes up the stairs to her brother's bedroom.

'Accountancy? Really?' she asks the empty space, remembering what Geoff had told her about James's interview in Belle Vale.

When she gets no response, she stands by the window in the chilly room and gazes out at the view of suburbia. She desperately wants her brother's views about what on earth happened to him, but imaginary James doesn't comment. Her brother isn't here and never has been. This is just the empty, neglected bedroom of a boy who's been missing for seven years and is never coming back.

Before she leaves, Leigh looks into the living room again. Her mum is still staring at the ceiling, unable to rip her eyes away from the mock chandelier. Her curly hair is flat against her scalp and the nail varnish is chipped on her toes. On the table by her side is an ashtray over brimming with cigarette butts. On the mantelpiece, the photograph of James has been turned to face the wall.

In past times, Leigh would have turned on the light and shocked her mum into a reaction. She would have argued and she would have cajoled. She would have made sure her mum had shopping and ciggies and anything else she needed. But now, she leaves the room in darkness and drives to Min's to cuddle her baby and ask Des's mum if she can keep him for a while.

Leigh is still at the station, working late, when Des calls her name and indicates for her to follow him out of the room. Her heart is pounding as he leads the way into Stan's empty office, thinking he's going to show her the file on James which has arrived from the Isle of Man. But, once inside, he picks up the phone and nods towards the second receiver. There's an extension in Stan's office and he wants her to listen in on a call to DI Josephine Bennett.

Leigh sits next to him, pleased to be included, but wondering why she is – to take her mind off her brother? So he can prove he's open about his relationship with Josephine? She presses the button to listen in as they wait for the Nottinghamshire officer to come on the line.

'Detective Inspector Chung,' Josephine says in a breathless, post-coital manner. 'Always lovely to speak to you again. How are you?'

Des clears his throat.

'I do have to let you know,' he says. 'DS Borrowdale is listening in on the other line.'

'Best keep it to business, then,' Josephine says, her voice changing from slinky to abrupt, 'if your subordinates are listening.'

Leigh stiffens. She silently mimics Josephine saying the word *subordinates* and sticks two fingers up to the receiver. She's so engaged in making childish gestures that she almost misses what Des is saying:

'I thought it might be worth telephoning you. We've had a development at our end, about the Duane Harding case. We've got a person of interest who's gone AWOL and left a very interesting letter behind. It seems to have been sent from a prison and accuses this person of being a liar.'

'I'm afraid I'm not going to be of much help,' Josephine says, assuming Des is calling her for advice. 'To my mind, it's always the most obvious ...'

'I just thought I'd run it by you, and I know the Midlands is a big place, but the person we're trying to find has been described as having a Midlands accent and I wanted to see if he was on your radar.'

Leigh stops scanning Stan's desk for the three legs of man logo and looks with interest at Des. He's made a good call – she hadn't made the connection.

'We only have a first name,' he continues, 'and that's Shelton, although he calls himself Tony. He joined Duane Harding's band of supporters but nobody seems to know much about him.'

There is a long silence at the end of the line.

'Shelton?' Josephine says eventually. 'Are you sure?'

'Yes, why do you ask? Do you know the name?'

'The only Shelton I know is Shelton Woods. He's the boy who gave evidence against his father at the Marion Coote trial.'

57

'Shelton Woods was 13 years old when he gave evidence against his father, Alfred Woods, in 1965,' Des explains the next morning to a bewildered audience of squad detectives. 'He came forward to say he'd seen Alfred with 10-year-old Marion Coote on the night she disappeared, leading her by the hand towards a path on the edge of the village of Broughton Vale in Nottinghamshire. Shelton was able to describe what Marion was wearing and the sparkly bag she was carrying with her. This bag was found in Alfred Woods' possession, hidden inside his house. Fibres from his pit coat were found on Marion's body. Alfred Woods was a suspect before his son came forward, but it was Shelton's evidence that sealed his fate.'

Leigh takes a swig of Tizer and looks on, impressed: not a single qualifier or hand-dance since the briefing began. Des looks the part, too. He's been up all night and is immaculate in his black suit, whereas she has napped on Min's sofa and looks like a scarecrow. She glances around at the other members of the squad, all present this morning except for Kevin, who has been sent to Boots to collect the photographs Duane Harding had ordered. The audience of detectives appears spellbound by this unexpected turn of events, although that might be because their minds are working overtime, trying to fit the riddle together from the drip-feed of information.

'There was one more witness, a little girl who was nine years old, who said she'd seen Marion at around 6.30 p.m. that evening, talking to a dark-haired man on the street – Alfred Woods has fair hair. This little girl failed to pick Alfred Woods out of a line-up. The Notts Police went ahead and charged him anyway. He pleaded not guilty and he's been protesting his innocence ever since.

'The two children were both witnesses at the trial, one for the prosecution, the other for the defence. The little girl didn't take the stand, but Shelton did – he was the prosecution's star witness. He was convincing, by all accounts – polite and quietly spoken, and he knew the difference between truth and lies. The defence had nowhere to go – they couldn't claim children imagine things because it would've put the testimony of their own child witness in doubt – although they did point out that it was dark, and that Shelton had a difficult relationship with his father, who was known locally as a bit of a psycho. The family lived in an isolated cottage and they weren't on the radar, as far as social services were concerned. The prosecution said Shelton would know his own father anywhere. They put the gaps in his account down to him being traumatised by the experience.

'It took the jury a couple of days to reach a decision. They were out for 48 hours because they were unable to reach a verdict. In the end, the judge allowed a majority verdict and they found Alfred Woods guilty of murder by a majority to 10 to 2 and he was sentenced to a whole life tariff – the death penalty had been suspended by that time so he was lucky, in that sense. He's in Dartmoor now, in Devon. None of his appeals have been allowed.'

When Des has finished his account of the information that Josephine had given him, he runs through what they know about Shelton Woods' infiltration of Duane Harding's supporters, and details the evidence found at the Alderson Street squat: the carrier bag containing a newspaper featuring Harding's arrest, a handful of Fruit Salad sweets, a packet of dolly mixtures, and a vitriolic letter thought to be written by their suspect's father from prison.

'It looks as if Shelton Woods left in a hurry after getting wind of our interviews yesterday,' he continues. "There was no sign of the murder weapon at the squat, so, if he's our perp, he either disposed of it, or has it with him, which means he's armed and dangerous.'

Des pauses to take a sip of tea.

'DI Bennett of the Nottinghamshire force is coordinating a visit to his registered address and a search of that area for him. We've got our officers in Liverpool on alert but there are as yet no photographs available that we can use to ID him.

'As a result,' Des concludes, 'Nikki Harding is no longer a suspect, although we still don't know what she was doing in the area on the morning Duane Harding was murdered. Shelton Woods is now our main suspect.'

This announcement is greeted by a raise of the eyebrows from Callum and silence from Slapdash and Mark II, who are listening, for once. Leigh is the first to speak, and when she does, it's to ask the question that must surely be on everyone's minds.

'Why would the boy who gave evidence against his father want to kill Duane Harding?'

The heated debate that follows covers the hypotheses that Shelton Woods killed Marion and blamed his father, and that he also killed Gail and blamed Duane Harding. This wild and ridiculous theorising comes to an end when Kevin appears at the door, trying to catch Des's attention by waving a wallet of photographs in his hand.

'I collected the pictures from Boots,' he says, when Leigh and Des join him on the corridor. 'You really need to take a look at these.'

58

The three of them stare at the photographs which are now laid out on the table in Stan's empty office. Ten out of the 12 in the roll of film are of cuddly toys, the size of small children, which are nailed to a fence post. Teddy bears mostly, barbed wire piercing the bellies of the smaller ones, although one giant mouse has its own portrait. The mouse is fixed by a stake and duct-taped to hold it in place. A weeping angel hangs from its neck.

'Creepy,' Des says. 'Memorials to children? Or a child?'

'Where's that?' Leigh asks, pointing to one of the other two photographs. It's of an ancient tree, its boughs held up by posts.

'I don't know, I'm afraid,' Des says. 'The scenery doesn't seem familiar.'

Leigh puts her elbows on the table and searches Liverpool in her mind, trying to place an area with dense woodland and rough grass. Her imagination travels to the north of the city, to Fazakerley and Croxteth and the new builds of Kirby, then south to the leafy avenues of Aigburth and the houses of Queen's Drive, where the motorway begins. The motorway leads her to more places, more possibilities: Warrington, Manchester, Huddersfield, and as far as Leeds, where her imagination takes an abrupt turn back to Admiral Street station when she hears Des's voice calling her name.

When Leigh looks up, he is pointing to the last snapshot in the pack.

It captures Clara Harding, smiling next to the macabre stuffed toys.

'That's a memorial for a little girl who was murdered,' Duane Harding's widow says when Leigh rushes into the interview room with three photographs in her hand – one of the cuddly toys, one of the ancient tree and the other of Clara.

'Duane took it last year when we went on a day trip to Sherwood Forest,' Clara continues. 'He said the toys were put there by the little girl's family, near to where she was found on the side of the road. He said he remembered her and how sad it was.'

'What about this one?' Leigh says, placing the snapshot of the tree down.

'That's the Major Oak. It's an old tree, where Robin Hood used to live. But why are you asking me this? Where did these photographs come from?'

'That's you,' Leigh says, putting the photograph of Clara down in front of her.

'Yes, I remember Duane taking it.'

'He took you there.'

'Once or twice, yes. He loved it in Sherwood Forest. He'd been on a camp there when he was a teenager, they used to take the kids who had no money, back in those days.'

'When was the last time you went?'

'I don't know, last September?'

'Why did he take these pictures of the cuddly toys, Clara?'

'I don't know!' Clara cries, glancing around the room for someone to save her. 'I didn't know he had! I've never seen them before!'

'We found them in Duane's garage in the Dingle.'

'What do you mean? Duane didn't have a garage.'

'Don't worry, Gail isn't in there,' Leigh says as she peels the photographs from the table and makes her way to the interview room, where Duane Harding's dad is helping them with their enquiries.

Thinking John Harding will clam up in her presence, she hands over the pictures and communicates her questions through the medium of Mark II, who's in there with him. She stands in the corridor, fired-up, waiting for the serious crime squad detective to report back.

'Yep,' he says when he appears. 'Duane Harding went on a camping trip to Sherwood Forest in the summer of 1965. He was a teenager at the time. John Harding said his son loved it down there, visited from time to time, but that's all he knows – Mr Harding senior has never set foot outside of Liverpool, never mind been down south.'

Leigh's legs are wobbly and her hands are shaking as she bursts through the door of the murder investigation room.

'Duane Harding had ties to the place where Marion Coote was murdered. He was in the area during the same year, most likely at the same time,' she yells at the faces looking her way. 'And these,' she says, holding the photographs aloft, 'are murder site porn.'

Leigh barely has the chance to turn her head as the door bangs open and Stan slams his way into the room.

'The traffic cops have just called in,' he says. 'Sighting of a fella standing on the slip road to the M62 with his thumb out. They spotted him when they were driving over the Rocket flyover, said they thought it was Jesus standing on the roadside. Our suspect got into an articulated lorry, heading south.'

In the nanosecond before the squad leap into action, Stan yells: 'What are you waiting for? Get out there and bleeding nab him!'

59

It's a Saturday night that's all right for fighting.

Leigh and Des get into the Allegro to the sound of shouts and the crack and thud of fists – a brawl spilling out onto the streets from the Pelican pub to the soundtrack of 'Runnin' with the Devil' by Van Halen.

'*Get a bleeding move on!*' Stan's voice shouts in their ears.

They've been microphoned up in case of immediate danger and are now at the mercy of an unseen dictator, controlling them from a hidden room inside the station.

Sirens wail both ways down the street, one set towards the Pelican and numerous others towards the suburbs, where the motorway begins.

'Revenge for Marion Coote?' Leigh suggests, as the lights of the ring road flash by.

'Maybe,' Des says. 'Josephine's reviewing their files on the Marion Coote case – see if Duane Harding was on their radar. We don't know if Shelton Woods even knew Marion. They weren't related.'

'We need to organise a search around Marion's roadside memorial for Gail – immediately!'

'Shall we catch this Shelton first? If you don't mind? He might lead us to Gail.'

Galvanised by their Lord and Master, who continues to blurt into their ears, Des drives faster than Leigh has ever seen him drive before. But it's still not very fast – Slapdash and Mark II are way ahead of them in the Zephyr, as are the squad cars. They cut through back roads to make up for the time they lose when they have to stop for petrol.

'*The truck's turning into Burtonwood Services,*' Stan growls as they approach the Rocket flyover. '*You're all over the bleeding shop. Coordinate yourselves!*'

'Absolute shambles,' Leigh says out loud, as the start of the motorway comes into their sights.

On the M62: a chaos of bright lights and heavy traffic. At least four squad cars speed past at frightening speed, sirens shrieking; on their way to Burtonwood Services, or to set up a checkpoint up the motorway near Stockport – one of the few communications Leigh has been able to decipher through the dodgy radio. It's all very dramatic, but no one has a clear idea of what they're doing, apart from chase a Ford Cargo truck all the way to the Midlands because home is where they think Shelton Woods is heading. The Nottinghamshire force haven't had any joy at his last known address, but they're waiting there in case he turns up. Hopefully, Leigh thinks, they'll have nabbed him before the Allegro reaches junction eight.

Des lives dangerously and moves into the middle lane.

Inside Burtonwood's conical building, a group of lads are sitting in the café, eating fried food and drinking cans of beer. When Leigh and Des walk through the doors, they are already cheering and clapping at the sight of Slapdash and Mark II, inconspicuously pushing their way through the queue at the counter, shouting, '*Police!*' and shouldering people out of the way.

They've already learned from Stan's wince-inducing yells that the truck driver had been located refuelling at the petrol pumps. He'd said their suspect had got out of the cab as soon as he stopped and had promptly disappeared.

Leigh and Des split up and roam the building. The interior of the service station cafe is groovy – a 24-hours-a-day fantasy land, with wipe-clean tables, swirling carpets and an overwhelming amount of Crayola red. As she passes by the counter, she glances at the menu on the wall: gammon and chips for £1.90, a cup of tea costing 17p – the prices in here are daylight robbery. Leigh moves on, into a more formal restaurant, where a waitress in cobalt blue is serving a couple who are the only customers. Des checks the ladies' toilets, Leigh checks the gents. They meet back in the restaurant, where the under-employed waitress asks if they would like a table and Des shows his warrant card.

They are on their way back through the café when she sees him through the window. The outline of a shape, moving in a crouching position on the path around the building. He is thrown into silhouette by the bright lights, but she knows it's him. She can see his long hair. And who else would be creeping around in such a weird way? Shelton Woods sees her, or she thinks he does, because in one hand, he holds up a white carrier bag as a sign of surrender.

And then he's gone.

'Proceed with caution,' the voice barks in her ear, like a second brain.

Bollocks to that, Leigh thinks.

She gives Des the nod and they both run out of the doors and into the HGV-heavy car park.

Leigh bolts after the figure disappearing under the underpass which leads to the Eastbound site. She runs as fast as she can but by the time she's got down the steps, she has to stop to get her breath. She is heavier, wobblier, leakier, than she was before she had Kai and her chest is already heaving with exertion. After a brief pause, Leigh resumes her jog, glancing behind her to see if Des is following her. The tunnel is empty. He's not fast on his feet since his injury, and he obviously hasn't kept up.

When she emerges from the underpass, Leigh locates Shelton Woods immediately, standing on the hard shoulder of the eastbound carriage, waiting for a gap in the traffic. He turns, sees her and launches himself onto the expressway. Leigh shrinks back, her hand to her mouth, as he zigzags his way over three lanes to the central reservation. She makes it to same section of hard shoulder and hesitates. Does she really want to play chicken on a motorway? But the pull of obliteration is a force stronger than herself. She watches a lorry rattle by, its big tyres throwing dirt less than a foot away, and launches herself into oncoming traffic.

After a close shave with a refrigerated truck, Leigh makes it across with a confusion of horns and screeching brakes ringing in her ears. She jumps over a barrier into a nondescript, litter-strewn section of overgrowth, not far from the conical building of the westbound services. This hinterland is uninhabited except for blackbirds feeding on hawthorns and edges onto tractor-marked fields bordered by hedgerows in some places, woodland in others. Beyond where she is now pushing back leafy branches which flick into her face, there is a field of long grass.

Leigh calls for help over the radio. '*Where the bleeding hell are you?* Stan screeches back. '*Eastbound services,*' Leigh says, not realising her mistake. Towards the trees, sheltered by a ragged hedge at the motorway's edge, she senses a presence. There's a split second when she sees a fast-moving shape in the periphery of her vision. Leigh runs at full pelt in the direction of her quarry, twists her head back to look for blues and twos, and hurtles straight into a low hanging tree branch. There's an almighty crack, her ankle twists under her, and she's out for the count.

60

'Are you all right, duck. You need to look where you're going. You knocked yoursen out cold.'

Leigh comes round to the tickle of long hair on her neck. A bearded face hovers above her like a heavenly apparition. *Who is this?* she thinks. *Where is she?* And then she remembers the frantic chase across the motorway.

She's lying flat on her back under a tree on a verge, hidden from view by thick bushes.

And she's in the company of a murderer.

'Here you are, duck,' Shelton says, as Leigh feels her head being gently lifted and lowered again onto bulky material. The makeshift pillow is more comfortable, but a twig is digging into her shoulder blades, like a sharp finger in her back. Her companion touches her ankle to check for a break and she winces.

'I won't hurt you, duck,' he says. 'I don't go round hurting people, willy nilly.'

Leigh thinks of the frenzied way he'd stabbed Duane Harding and wonders if that's true. She tries to sit up but she has a headache to rival a hangover caused by 10 bottles of Marsden Ale at the Burundi Club, so she slumps back down again. The branch that took her out hangs above her – the

Mohammed Ali of trees – and above it is a purple sky and a cluster of stars.

Shelton's face interrupts the view of the Great Bear as it floats above her once again. They nicknamed him Jesus at the station, but right now, he looks like a character straight out of the Old Testament. She tries not to panic as she thinks of the letter his dad wrote to him, calling him a liar, alluding to what he'd done.

But she can't see any rage in him.

His eyes are kind.

'How many fingers am I holding up?' Shelton asks, wriggling a handful of chubby digits in her eyeline.

'Seven,' Leigh says.

'Can you remember your name, duck?'

'Leigh,' she says, as a disembodied voice screeches '*What the fucking fuck?*' from somewhere in the overgrowth. She must have dropped her radio when she ran into the tree branch.

'I'm Shelton.'

'I know who you are and I need to arrest you,' Leigh says, from her position flat on her back. 'We know you killed Duane Harding.'

'Thought you must do,' Shelton says. 'Or else you wouldn't be dodging six lanes of traffic trying to catch me.'

'You're not the only one who wanted a child murderer dead,' Leigh says, thinking, *go on, talk.*

'That's not why I did it.'

'Why did you, then?'

'Are you trying to get a confession out of me?'

'You've just confessed.'

'Have I? I must have missed that.'

Leigh can hear his humour-laced voice to the side of her. She lifts her head and surveys her twisted ankle through wonky vision. She gets a glimpse of Shelton, sitting against a tree trunk, wearing shorts and a t-shirt – he'd parted with his jacket to cushion her head.

'Why don't you run?' she asks as her head finds the floor again. 'I'd run, if I were you.'

'I will, duck, in a bit. I'll see you're all right first.'

'They'll be here to arrest you in a minute.'

'You reckon, duck? I reckon they won't, because they've all run the wrong way. Keystone Cops, if you ask me.'

There's a crinkling noise, causing Leigh to lift her head again. It's coming from a carrier bag he's clutching in one hand. Through the white plastic, she can see the shape of groceries - a square box that looks like cereal, a couple of sachets of Rise and Shine. He puts his hand inside and takes out a packet of fruit pastilles.

'Bit of sugar is good if you're feeling faint,' he says. 'Are you a sucker or a chewer?'

'Chewer.'

'Sucker,' he says, popping a pastille into her mouth and grinning. 'I like the green ones best.'

'Red,' Leigh says.

Go on.

'Do you want to tell me why you murdered Duane Harding?'

'Not really.'

'We know about your dad, what he did to Marion.'

'My dad is one evil bastard.'

'So I've heard.'

'Honestly duck, I kid you not. My old man is possessed. He's like that Jekyll and Hyde but without the good side.'

'Just Hyde then?'

'Is that the evil one? Then yeah, him.'

'And which one are you?'

'You what?'

'Jekyll or Hyde?'

'A bit of both, I reckon. Started out as one, turned into another.'

'Are you going to tell me why you stabbed Duane Harding?'

'Nope.'

'Right,' Leigh says, attempting to get up. 'I'll be off.'

'Suit yoursen,' Shelton says, giving her a smile.

After the blow to her head and the twist to her ankle, he knows she's not going anywhere.

From an unspecified place on the forest floor, her second brain, still separated from her body, yells *Fuck, fuck, fuck.* Recovering a little now, Leigh sits up and reaches behind hers, but the radio is too far out of her reach.

'I want to know why you killed Duane Harding,' she says, 'because I want to find his stepdaughter, Gail Harding. Remember Gail? She's the little girl who went missing from Liverpool two years ago.'

'I know who Gail is, duck.'

'Tell me before they get here and arrest you.'

'They won't be catching me. I could live out in the wild for weeks and survive. I was a right little Robinson Crusoe, growing up.'

Leigh scrambles around, searching for the twig that was digging into her back. She feels like Robinson Crusoe herself, shipwrecked on a verge while the traffic thunders along the motorway just a few feet away.

'We found a letter from your dad, you left it behind in the squat. It said you were a liar.'

'I am a liar, duck.'

'It must be hard,' Leigh says, watching as he splits open the foil wrapper of the fruit pastilles, 'having a dad who's a child killer.'

'I don't,' he says, putting a red sweet in her hand.

'What?'

'I don't have a dad who's a child killer.'

'What do you mean?'

When Shelton doesn't answer, Leigh puts the sweet in her mouth and turns towards him so she can see his face. Notwithstanding her aching head, she feels increasingly uneasy and, for the first time since she's been here, she wonders if she's ever going to leave. She feels a phantom baby on her chest and thinks of the last time she'd seen Kai, early this morning; the feel of his smooth baby skin as she'd planted a sloppy kiss on his cradle cap.

At least she won't have to worry about paying her rent, she thinks, as she lies back and turns her gaze to the sky, searching for the constellations she learned from her brother, long ago.

'What's your old man like?' Shelton asks.

'Mine? He's all right,' Leigh says. 'Fair to middling.'

'Mine's an evil bastard.'

'You said.'

'I had a life worse than a dog, with him.'

'And you're telling me this, why?'

'I was just telling you about my dad, so you'll understand.'

'Understand what?'

'Why I had no choice.'

'That's what you wrote on the Hardings' wall. *Sorry, I had no choice.*'

'That's right, duck, I didn't.'

61

It was just Shelton and his dad at home. His mam had done a runner when he was a nipper. He hardly ever saw her after that and the last he heard, she was shacked up in the nearby town with a bloke who looked like Alvin Stardust. Growing up, he'd always pictured his mam as a timid little thing, someone who'd had no choice but to leave because her husband was a nutter. But it can't have been that, because she'd refused to take him in when his dad got sent down, and he's never heard from her since.

Leigh gazes up at swarm of gnats, hovering above her like a cartoon character's cloud of scribbles. She can hear a quiver of emotion in his voice, cutting through the tone of amusement he is telling his story with.

'Do you think people can be possessed?' Shelton asks, immediately moving on.

'By what?'

'By a demon.'

Leigh doesn't reply. Her head is pounding and her ankle is killing her, but she's wondering how to take him out. She leans on her elbows and her eyes fix on the plastic bag and scan it for the outline of a knife.

'Me dad reckoned he was.'

'Possessed?'

'He said there was a demon living inside him and it came out when someone upset him.'

'A bit like Carrie?'

'Who's Carrie?'

'Doesn't matter.'

The problem, Shelton continues, was that his dad got upset over nothing. Alfred took every single thing the wrong way. If anyone laughed, it was at him. If anything was in his way, someone had put it there on purpose. The family who had the misfortune to be in the local shop at the same time ordered their kids to cry to annoy him. The elderly neighbour who lived at the end of the lane left his bin in the way to make Alfred walk round it. Shelton remembers that, once, a bloke had come knocking, selling sommat at the door. Alfred had got hold of the bloke by the shirt lapels and slammed him against the wall, saying he'd known he was asleep and had woken him up on purpose. That was the worst thing you could do, knock on the door when Alfred was asleep, because his dad didn't interpret anything as innocent or accidental.

As a result of all this, the demon caused a whole lot of havoc in Broughton Vale, the village near to where they lived. It got Alfred barred from the local pub and sacked from his job at the pit. He never turned up for work anyroad but after he got laid off, he hated everyone who had anything to do with mining – and that, by the way, was everyone in Broughton Vale. Alfred would go out at night and press his face against the neighbour's windows. He'd put lumps of coal and spent matches through their letter boxes, like the worst kind of kid on mischievous night.

And then he'd come home for a spot of devil worship.

'Honestly duck, I kid you not,' Shelton says, although Leigh hasn't spoken. Her fruit pastille has been quickly mashed and chewed, but Shelton is still sucking his – she can see it on his tongue as he talks.

'My old man had a chest covered in pentagrams he'd carved hissen with a knife. He'd have blood running down his torso and he'd say the demon did it to him, like he said the demon was responsible for everything he did. You believe that sort of thing, when you're a kid.'

'Did he hit you?'

Shelton splutters at the ridiculousness of this question.

'I always knew when the demon was on its way. I had bionic hearing. I could hear every crack in the walls and every footstep coming up the stairs. I'd listen for the king of rock and roll to start up on the record player.'

Because Alfred always played Elvis to drown out the sound of Shelton's screams.

Nearly 20 years later, on a motorway verge, Shelton again feels the force of those blows. He ducks down with his hands over his head, and then steadies himself by clutching at the roots of the tree. Leigh considers him as he recounts more sickening tales of violence that resulted in broken bones and broken skin. Then she moves her eyes from side to side to get a better view of her surroundings. Towards the back of the thin line of trees is a field, where a small group of sheep huddle at its edge, as timid as deer.

When it got bad like that, Shelton continues, he would just lie on the floor and apologise.

'I used to pretend I had a magic barrier around me, it was see-through but as hard as granite, and it closed around me when I needed it, protected me.'

'Didn't anyone help you?'

'Nah, duck. I never told anyone in the village what went on. And our cottage was in the middle of a field so no one came our way much. And I'm not telling you this so you feel sorry for me. I mean, we never had anything. My clothes were filthy and hanging off my back, my shoes had broken soles which flapped along the pavement when I walked, but money wasn't the problem. It was the fear that was the problem. It wasn't nice, duck, being scared out of your wits all the time. Or maybe it was just me, maybe I'm making a big deal of it. It happens to a lot of kids and they don't end up doing what I've done.'

Maybe it was just me. As if this would have been fine for anyone else and he was being fussy about who he'd got as a parent.

By the time he was a teenager, Shelton had stopped going to school and spent most of his time by the quarry. Back then, he was planning to join the army, and he fancied he was in training. He'd pretend the railway line was an assault course, crawling on his belly, commando-style, along the steel pipe which led from the bridge. There was a derelict cottage on the other side of the quarry, and that, in his mind, was the army barracks. He tried to turn his shitty experiences into positives, telling himself that getting used to extreme temperatures would stand him in good stead when he joined up.

'So, as I said, duck, I was a feral kid. The plantation near the quarry was my little world, my kingdom.'

'Remind me why you're you telling me this?' Leigh asks.

'Because I need to explain how I came to be in the quarry on the night Marion Coote was taken.'

62

It was already night in the middle of the quarry, but there was still some daylight behind Shelton, so he could see them clearly. He'd been hiding out in his den in the old cottage, having spent the day outdoors, preparing for his army medical. He saw Marion first – he knew all the kids in the village, because everyone knew everyone else in Broughton Vale. She was in front of the stile leading into the field by the bridge. Her smiling face was disappearing into the trees as she was led away by the hand.

'And was it your dad who was with her, like you said at the trial?'

'No, duck, it was not.'

'Who was it?' Leigh says, already knowing the answer.

'It was Duane Harding, duck.'

Shelton didn't know his name back then, but he'd recognised him as one of a group of lads doing a camp in the wooden huts in Sherwood Forest. Everyone knew they were there because they reckoned they were hard and they'd come into the village, picking fights with the local lads and chatting up the lasses. There was only a couple of years difference between the lads and Shelton, but the age gap seems massive when you're 13.

Anyroad, Harding must've heard Shelton's steps through the quarry because he stopped and looked around. 'Who's that?' he'd called out. 'Who's coming?' but Shelton held his breath; he was good at making himself disappear. He watched through the bracken for a while and then crept inside his den and hid for hours.

He found Marion's glittery bag in the overgrowth on his way back home. He opened it up and there was a little girl's treasure in it: a comb and a hankie, and a pocket doll. He knew the bag belonged to Marion because he'd seen her with it earlier, when she'd been playing with her friend, Pauline, on the village green. He took it home with him, thinking she'd want it back. He almost put it through the letterbox of her house but it was late by then so he thought he'd take it round the next day.

If he survived that long.

When Alfred came to the door in his pyjamas, Shelton knew he'd woken him up.

Elvis was already singing.

It was the next morning when Shelton found out Marion was missing. Everyone in the village was out, calling her name. There were coppers in lines, walking over the fields with sticks, and there were coppers knocking on doors.

That's when Shelton saw his opportunity.

It has to be remembered that, at the time, he had the indent of a gold ring above his top lip and a nasty bruise over his eye from the night before. He hated his dad's guts. And he was terrified of the demon. So, he had the idea to plant Marion's bag under his dad's bed, make it look as though Alfred had hidden it there. It was a long shot, but worth a punt. He never thought it would go any further; he thought at best it would get Alfred out of the house for a few hours while he was being questioned.

Shelton didn't have to do any more than tell a passing copper about Marion's bag. That was all they needed, and they got that when they searched the house. And, as he said before, his father was not a popular man. Alfred was known for prowling the streets at night and they had witnesses who said he'd been out the week before, looking through windows. The coppers interpreted that for their own ends, said he'd been sneaking a peek at little girls inside the houses.

The demon kicked up an almighty fuss, saying Shelton was going to burn in hell, calling him an effing liar, which he was right about, because he was. Shelton had a scary moment when he saw their next-door neighbour coming out of her house, a baby on her hip and two toddlers clinging to her dressing gown. Their eyes had met and he'd seen uneasiness in her face, not fear, but close. She must've known his dad had been in that night because Elvis had been blaring out.

But she never said a word.

Everyone in Broughton Vale was glad to get shut of Alfred Woods.

He moved in with his auntie. She wasn't his auntie by blood – she'd been married to his dad's brother before he ran off with another woman – but she was all right, took him in when he had nowhere else to go. There were a few more scary bits, as things progressed. Marion's friend, Pauline, told her mam, who then told the police, that she saw Marion with a man with dark hair late that afternoon. Quite rightly, she didn't pick Alfred out of a line-up because he wasn't the man she saw. But then it was all right because she got all her timings mixed up – first she said it was a Saturday when she'd been playing with Marion, and then she said it was a Sunday. She was only a nipper, whereas Shelton was 13.

'A right grown up,' Leigh comments, responding to the tremor, which is there again in his voice.

He felt bad for Marion's mam and dad, her little sister, too. He'd avert his eyes when he saw them, but it wasn't because of the shame of having a child killer for a dad. It was because he knew where Marion might be and he wasn't saying.

One night, soon after his dad had been arrested, Shelton's conscience got the better of him and he went back to the quarry. He thought if he found Marion by accident, if he just stumbled across her, he could take her back to her family. He only put his dad's old pit coat on to keep warm – it had been hanging up by the front door. He knew the searchers were looking in the wrong place, so he went to where the old pit shaft started, to where he'd seen Marion last. He sunk to his knees, and put his ear to the ground, listening for sounds from below the earth. The shaft looked the same as it always had, except the soil was disturbed around the entrance. He lowered himself onto the ladder and began to descend to the landing stage.

If the residents of Broughton Vale had been watching through their bedroom windows that night, they would have seen the shuffling steps and mud-daubed face of a 13-year-old boy, dressed in his dad's pit coat, carrying Marion across the field from the pit shaft and leaving her on the side of the main road, where she could be found.

The fibres from the pit coat found on Marion's clothes had sealed the fate of Alfred Woods.

63

Shelton had been doing okay. Duane Harding pissed off back to where he came from, his dad got banged up, and he'd felt safe living with his auntie, where he could come to no harm. The years passed and although he never got to join the army, he got a job down the pit when he was old enough and set up home with a nice lass called Debbie in the nearby town. He lived as the son of a convicted child killer was expected to live: in quiet shame. Some in the area were sympathetic and went easy on him; others thought that evil must be inherited and he was cut from the same cloth as his old man. He got set upon a few times by local youths, but he's always been a big lad and handy in a fight, so that was no bother.

He never visited his dad, for obvious reasons. But Alfred soon reminded him of his presence – and what Shelton had done – by sneaking letters out of the prison via his brother, the one who'd been married to his auntie. As Leigh has seen, the letters weren't nice at all.

But apart from that, he'd been doing okay. Aided by a lack of headway in processing the events that had changed his life, he rarely thought about the past. It wasn't that he'd forgotten, it was more like he never knew about it in the first place. From time to time, a prompt, like a girl going missing, or some miscarriage of justice, would bring on bad dreams, but in general, he'd noticed the past as if he was asleep and stirred by some noise; a bang in the night that unsettled him but didn't wake him up.

'*What does okay mean?*' his girlfriend Debbie always wanted to know. In their early days together, Shelton had told her a story about his past that he never elaborated on, any push for more information on her part thwarted by his refusal to talk; a tactic he hoped would suggest some deep suffering that he couldn't bear to think about. He took advantage of the fact she came from Sutton-in-Ashfield and didn't know more than the headlines. He made out he was a man of few words, when, truth be told, the inside of his head was full of words.

But to answer Debbie's question, '*okay*' meant he'd forgotten. He'd forgotten seeing Duane Harding that night. He'd forgotten how Marion felt, lying in his arms, the dark smell of her. He'd forgotten Alfred's raging face in the courtroom. He'd forgotten it all.

Until he saw the newspapers, about the little lass, Gail.

And then, he remembered.

Shelton got the shock of his life when he saw the news on the television about Gail going missing up north. Her mam and her stepdad were on, doing one of those teary-eyed appeals for information. Duane Harding had changed a bit over the years, got a bit porkier, but he recognised him straight away. He knew he was responsible. He knew he'd done it.

After that, Shelton couldn't settle to anything or think about anything else. He couldn't get to sleep and, when he did, he'd wake up an hour or two later covered in sweat. He started watching the television news at six o'clock, nine o'clock and ten o'clock. He started buying all the daily newspapers, driving in his van to different towns, different shops, like an alcoholic hiding their drink habit.

Debbie used to ask him, from time to time, whether Gail's disappearance was affecting him, due to the similarities with his dad, but Shelton would keep his mouth shut. '*Honestly,*' she'd say, '*it's like getting blood out of a stone with you.*'

And then one day, Debbie came back from her barmaid job and said, '*They got that man,*' and Shelton went stone cold.

It's funny what goes through your mind, but he blamed Edward Heath for what happened next. The bloody Tories. For weakening the unions, for causing the unemployment. Because they started laying men off at the pit and he lost his job. And because he lost his job, he had time on his hands. So, one morning, he got in his van and drove up to Liverpool and sat in the public gallery of the Crown Court. He was holding his breath, thinking Duane Harding was going to stand up and say, '*It was me and I did that other lass Marion, too.*'

All through the prosecution's opening speech, Shelton had watched the judge and the jury, noticing every expression. He watched the coppers closely; Leigh too. He felt bad for her because she was up the duff, particularly when she was spot on about Duane Harding. He felt bad for Gail's mum, too, still does, as it happens. But Shelton was only out for himself and pleased when it headed the way of no case to answer.

'It's not like I was gunning for him, Harding was one almighty, evil twat,' Shelton says, handing Leigh another red fruit pastille. 'I was gunning for myself. I was obsessed with finding out if he was going to say anything.'

'Duane Harding was dangerous,' Leigh says, as her radio blurts out more profanities.

'I know what he was but I couldn't risk it, duck. If my old man got out, he'd kill me. And I've got no doubts about that whatsoever. My dad wanted to kill me *before* I got him nicked for a murder he didn't do. It's not like I felt good about myself, but it was a matter of life and death.'

'And then what? How did you come to join Duane Harding's merry band of supporters?'

'I *was* a supporter, but for a different reason from the others. They were all convinced he was innocent. Honestly, they were that stupid. And Duane Harding was a good liar, as you well know, duck.'

'Takes one to know one,' Leigh says and Shelton smirks at her.

Before they took their place in the public gallery, Duane Harding's supporters, including his wife, Clara, had been standing outside St George's Hall with placards. Shelton walked past them on the way in and, when there was a break while the judge thought about things, he stopped to talk to them, trying to get the inside track. Clara took to him straight away – she doesn't have a good radar, when it comes to sussing folks out. And after that, he just sort of fell in with them.

And then Harding got off, so that was all right.

The acquittal was as good a time as any to make himself scarce, but Shelton kept coming back, alternating his time between Broughton Vale and the Alderson Street squat in Liverpool.

'Me and Debbie had split up by then and I was sleeping rough. I forgot Valentine's Day, that was the start of it. Then her birthday. I'd leave the house early and get home late without telling her I was going to Liverpool. I had other stuff going on, and Debbie said she couldn't talk to me, that I didn't communicate.'

'What about Duane Harding?' Leigh asks. 'He must have known who you were. Did he think you'd made a mistake, when you said you'd seen your dad? That he'd got lucky?'

'He wasn't best pleased to see me, duck, I'll tell you that. You should've seen the look on his face when I turned up at his flat. He was shit scared. He must have thought it was all going to come out but he needn't have worried about that – I was right behind him. It was like I was baiting him, punishing him, at the same time as making sure he stayed a free man.

When I first went round, he cornered me, asked me what I was playing at, told me to piss off. When that didn't work, he said I was mistaken; that it hadn't been him I'd seen. And when that didn't work, he offered me money. I said I didn't want money, that I wasn't going to say owt and he better not.'

'Did you phone the house?' Leigh asks, thinking about the calls to the Hardings' flat from a telephone box in L7.

'I did, duck, loads of times. I liked to get him agitated. Making his life a misery was the least I could do for Marion.'

'And Gail,' Leigh says.

Shelton makes a small exhalation.

'Yeah,' he says, looking up. 'Gail, too.'

'Go on,' Leigh says, seeing the sheep scatter, suddenly alert to the sound of movement and voices nearby.

Des and the others, coming to get her.

'I've got to get off now, duck,' Shelton says, up on his haunches, watching the silver beams of torches mingle with the headlamps of speeding traffic.

'Here!' Leigh shouts, letting a flare off in her head that nobody can see.

Shelton crouches next to her, motionless, listening as the voices pass by on the other side of the barrier and the noise fades. She feels his arms under her knees and around her back as he scoops her up.

'Why did you kill Duane Harding?' she asks as he carries her to the verge of the motorway.

'I'll tell you some other time, duck,' Shelton says. 'Look after yoursen.'

He gently lowers her to the ground, and is gone.

Leigh lies on the verge, her nose against the carrier bag of groceries that Shelton had dropped when he ran. She gazes at the tyres speeding past only inches away, and it isn't long until she hears the click of heel taps approaching on the hard shoulder.

64

In past times, Leigh would have insisted on taking part in a search for a suspect, whatever the time of night. But she's got a sore head, a sore ankle, a full bladder, and the love of her life to see. And, so, she willingly allows Des to talk her out of it and support her into a nearby squad car.

She holds onto his arm much tighter than is necessary.

When Leigh gets home, she slots herself between the clean sheets on her mattress, props her ankle up on a pillow, and tells Kai how clever he is to have emptied an entire packet of rice flour over his nanny's kitchen floor today. When Leigh had picked him up, Min had been delighted to have witnessed another first from her grandson – the beginning of his grabbing and lobbing phase.

Predictably, Stan had gone ballistic. '*What the fuck were you doing?*' he'd yelled into her recovered radio. '*I told you to coordinate!*' The officer driving the squad car back to Liverpool was under orders to take Leigh to the hospital because of the blow to her head. But Leigh is a mother and she didn't have time for that.

And besides, her body and mind need a rest from all the chaos.

She puts the baby in his bouncer and makes a late-night feast of mush – apple puree for Kai, minestrone soup for Leigh, eaten with two aspirin – and then she hobbles over to the stereo to put on some music: Teddy Pendergrass, chosen for his soothing properties. She sits with the baby in her arms, looking through bleary eyes at his beautiful, tranquil face. Kai is surely on his last lifetime before being released from the cycle of reincarnation. He's gazing at her with the knowledge accumulated in the hundreds of lives he's already lived. She wonders why he reserves this wisdom for waking times only. When she tries to sleep, he acts like this is all new to him and he's never set foot on this planet before.

She doesn't know how long she sits there, staring at her baby's face.

Des knocks just after midnight.

He doesn't update her on the search for Shelton Woods.

'The witness statements about James arrived today,' he says. 'There's something we could look at following up.'

Leigh props herself up against her brother's telescope and listens. Both the Isle of Man Constabulary and the Merseyside force received a lot of calls after James went missing, some intended to be helpful, some downright weird. James was in Ballasalla, Onchan, Germany, Nicaragua and Santa Cruz, to name but a few.

'My team have done a review of the statements,' Des says, lifting the stylus on the stereo to bring the husky R&B baritone to an end. 'I don't want to give you false hope, but there's one witness, in particular, we consider to be of interest. She reported the sighting to the Isle of Man police and her account fits with what Anke said, about James being on the run. Her name is Heather McCree, nee Cassidy. She said she saw a lad who looked like James in Liverpool and she remembers the date because it was her birthday. She was a nurse, at Alder

Hey Children's Hospital, before she had kids, and she seems credible. She knew James from old, from when they both went to the Holy Trinity Church Hall Youth Club.'

'I've never heard of her. Where did she see him?' Leigh says, trying to recall if she's come across this information before. She'd read many witness statements after James disappeared, but most of them had been reported to the Liverpool, rather than the Isle of Man force.

'Paradise Street bus station.'

'When?'

'The day before the last sighting of him in the Isle of Man. The first of August.'

'No way,' Leigh says. 'There's no way James would have come back to Liverpool and not got in touch. I mean, seven years on the run without a word? No way. *And.* He was seen, the night after that, walking down the beach to look at the stars in Niarbyl Bay. That couple, from Wrexham, Jill and Eddie their names were, they were staying at the campsite. They stopped to speak to him.'

'Why think the Liverpool witness was mistaken and the campers on the Isle of Man weren't?'

Des has a good point – the island would have been flooded with incomers during the summer holidays and the farmer's campsite was full.

'But,' Leigh says, 'James left his tent behind. That's one of the main reasons we thought the campers' sighting was credible. If he left at the same time as Trey and Geoff, why didn't he pack up his tent and take it home with him? Why did he leave it there, still erect, with all his things inside it?'

'To throw everyone off his trail?'

'He was an 18-year-old school kid, not a criminal mastermind.'

They are interrupted by Kai gurgling; restless now Teddy Pendergrass is no longer singing his lullaby.

'Did you speak to this witness?' Leigh asks, as Des takes the baby in his arms.

He doesn't take his eyes off the baby's face as he nods. 'Today. Over the telephone. She was helpful, friendly.'

'So, what happens next?'

'I've arranged for us to go and see her in the morning.'

65

The person who claims to have seen James at Paradise Street bus station lives in Wavertree, on Daffodil Road, a street away from the primary school Leigh and James went to. Leigh hasn't stepped foot on these pavements since she was 11 years old, and seeing the school gates brings on an intense pang of pain.

'You must keep your hat on,' Des's soft, teasing voice says behind her.

She looks back and smiles. Kai has come along too – their first outing as a family since he was born – and his sweet baby presence makes her feel calmer.

Daffodil Road is an ordinary, well-kept street in south Liverpool. Leigh has always liked the straightforwardness of these compact, semi-detached houses. On this early summer morning, the estate looks sunny and bright, and the sound of clanking bottles is coming from a milkman's cart.

Life as it should be lived, in all its uncomplicated glory.

As Leigh shuffles along on her tender ankle, she recovers a forgotten-about memory from many years ago. James had got lost before, on this very road. He must have been around two years old, and he'd slipped their mum's grasp when she was chatting outside the school gates, waiting for six-year-old Leigh to finish school. Leigh remembers little of the almighty fuss that ensued; she only knows from later accounts that James had made it across the busy Woolton Road and was halfway down Heathfield when he was caught by a woman who'd been scrubbing her doorstep. It's only now, as a mum herself, that Leigh understands the sheer panic.

'I can't get over it!' Heather McCree tells Leigh as she ushers them inside. 'You haven't changed at all! Still got your lovely locks!' She takes a handful of Leigh's witchy hair and lets it drop. 'And you're so slim! How do you do it?'

'It's the diet of fags and gin,' Leigh says, adding: 'You look pretty good yourself.'

She can't remember ever meeting Heather before.

'I don't know about that,' Heather says, breathing heavily from the walk from kitchen to living room. 'Put on a little weight.' She pats the bouncy pink flesh of her lower arms. 'A lot of weight actually. But you! Look at your lovely hair! And your lovely family!' she adds, grinning at Kai. 'He's gorgeous! How long have you two been married?'

There's an awkward silence, during which Leigh and Des smile inanely.

'We had to delay the wedding because of work,' says the man who, until last week, hadn't spent more than 20 minutes with her since the baby was born.

'This is the best news,' Heather says. 'I'm so made up you're happy.'

After offering them tea, which they decline, Heather sits down next to Leigh on the settee, causing the cushion to sink heavily and Leigh to rise a couple of inches. Des sits on an armchair, bouncing Kai. Two toddlers run in, in matching clothes, both of them chewing on dummies and one with a rusk in her hand. Kai is fascinated by these twins. Friends of his kind, at last. Des grins at the tiny girls as they dive into a heap of toys next to the settee. He's good with kids, Leigh thinks. Good with Kai. Kind.

When Heather is immediately called away by a knock at the door, Leigh exchanges a smile with Des and takes in her surroundings. From where she's sitting, there's a view of a house with a 'For Sale' sign fastened to its front gate. She wonders what her life would be like now if she'd been a different sort of person and married Des. She briefly pictures herself in another life, a straightforward life in which she isn't a penniless single mother holding onto her freedom by means of sabotage. They might have eventually saved the money for a deposit on a house like Heather's. While Des was at work, Leigh could have been a kept woman, looking after the baby and cleaning the house. She snaps out of her thoughts when Heather comes back in with a dustpan and brush and gets down on her hands and knees to sweep biscuit crumbs from the floor.

Forget it, Leigh thinks. She'd need a personality bypass before she even considered it.

'I'm dead sorry about your brother,' Heather says as she sits again on the seesawing settee, 'I remember playing ping pong with him in the Holy Trinity Church Hall.'

The emotion which has been building up in Leigh since she saw the school gates rises to the surface. She picks up a toy from the heap and plays with its arms.

'I'll tell you everything I remember,' Heather says, 'but I might've been mistaken.'

'Thanks,' Leigh says, squeezing the small pink pig. 'Anything will do.'

Heather had been shopping with her mam that day. It was defo a Thursday and it was defo 1 August 1974 because it was her birthday. She'd been to choose an outfit for her party which was due to take place that night. It was around teatime, dead hot, everyone leaving town at the same time. The roads were rammed, so it took a while for the 78 bus to get out of the station. And that's when she noticed James, sitting on the front seat of the double decker.

She remembers saying to her mam, '*That's James Borrowdale. He used to go to our youth club.*' But she didn't think any more about it.

Until she heard he'd gone missing.

'Was he by himself?'

'Yes, I think so. I couldn't tell you where he got on. We were almost out of town when I noticed him. And we got off the bus before him.'

In Heather's living room, seven years later, Leigh opens her mouth to ask a question, one of many which are firing off in her brain. But their host is in a constant state of doing: picking up a weeble from the floor, fetching cloths to soak up a spillage, wiping the toddlers' mouths, and opening the kitchen door to free an enormous yellow labrador.

In the meantime, Leigh turns the pink pig incessantly, thinking that, if what Heather says is true, they'd wasted all that time searching Niarbyl Bay.

'What did James seem like, to you?' she asks when Heather leaves the room and arrives back with an ashtray for Des and a cake – a Bakewell tart cut into slices. ('*We deserve a treat, don't we?*')

Heather thinks for a moment.

'I'm not being funny, but he looked a bit hunched,' she says, mimicking James's posture by rounding her shoulders. 'A bit out of it? Like he was on something? And, I don't know, shifty, can I say shifty? I don't mean it horribly.'

Leigh slumps into the settee. It wasn't him. She can't remember her brother ever looking shifty.

'I'm not 100 per cent sure,' Heather continues. 'It could have been someone who looked like him.'

'How sure are you?'

'Sixty per cent?'

There's a lull in the conversation as Leigh eats her cake with the labrador salivating by her side and Kai squeals in delight at the sight of a living cuddly toy.

'Were you more certain at the time?' Des asks, the first words he's spoken since the marriage conversation.

'At the time, I would have sworn it was James, defo, 100 per cent. And when I heard he was missing, I told my mam and she said to contact the police. We went into Edge Lane police station and they said the Isle of Man police were dealing with it so we telephoned them as well, just to make sure they knew. I've doubted myself, over the years. I hadn't seen James since I was 13.'

'Did he see you?' Leigh asks.

'I don't think so. He didn't look our way. He had a bucket hat pulled down low, over his eyes.'

'What else was he wearing?'

'A jacket? Trousers? His clothes looked baggy on him.'

'It wasn't him,' Leigh says, crunching the pink pig into a ball. 'It wasn't my brother.'

66

In Calderstones Park, where they go to decompress afterwards, Leigh makes it as far as a bench in the Japanese garden before she has to sit down. Her ankle is tender, not broken (Dr Chung had checked first thing) but she's still feeling battered after being taken out by the tree branch last night. Des is glad of a seat, too. He jiggles Kai around in the sling so the baby's feet don't rub up against the bench slats, and takes a packet of aspirin out of his briefcase. They swallow two each.

Leigh and Des have come here to 'debrief', as Des (never far from his DI Chung persona) put it, but there is nothing much to say, except utter a few miserable sentences on the subject of there being no progress in finding her brother. Heather McCree is only 60 per cent sure it was James she saw on the bus, and that's nowhere near enough to give them grounds to pursue the lead.

Leigh stares at the bright green maples and the stepping stones over the still water. Time and time again, her attention has been taken away from her brother, preventing her from dedicating her time to him. And it's no different now. Des had had the sensitivity not to talk about the murder investigation before their visit to Heather, but now she discovers what he's been holding onto since last night.

The Nottinghamshire police are mounting a search for Gail in the disused mine shaft in the village of Broughton Vale.

'I spoke to Josephine in the early hours,' Des says. 'She's confirmed that Duane Harding was in the area at the time of Marion's murder and they spoke to him, along with the other lads staying at the camp. It didn't go any further after Shelton came forward to point the finger at his father.'

'They let him go to kill again,' Leigh says despondently.

She had missed it, she thinks. All through the investigation into Gail's disappearance, she hadn't even considered that there might have been another victim.

'It took some persuading for Josephine to give the go ahead for the search,' Des says. 'I shared the information you'd given in the squad car last night, about where Shelton Woods had found Marion. It's more than possible that, if Duane Harding was responsible for Marion's murder, he used the same dumping ground twice.'

'It's more than a possibility,' Leigh says, her stomach turning at the thought of Gail, lying unfound at the bottom of a mineshaft for nearly two years.

'We can only wait and see,' Des says, patting her hand, 'but people do tend to repeat patterns of behaviour. They do what they've done before.'

They are sitting side by side, so Leigh has to turn her head to look at Des. His hair is glistening in the early morning sunshine and it's exactly the same colour as the strands of Kai's combover. He had said the same thing to Leigh, when he'd split up with her. *'How do I know you won't do it again? People always repeat the same patterns.'*

He'd thought that she didn't love him, that her actions spoke louder than words.

But Leigh's actions had spoken of other things.

By lunchtime, she is back at her bedsit with Kai. She's been ordered to stay at home by Stan, although they'll need her formal account of what Shelton told her at some point in the day.

Leigh switches on all the lights, including the lamp in the corner. She changes Kai's nappy, puts him in his bouncer and opens the cupboards, searching for food. The cupboards are almost bare and contain a can of Tizer, a tin of spaghetti hoops, a pile of mouse droppings, a fork with bent prongs and a curry-flavoured Pot Noodle.

Enjoying the abundance of electricity, she flicks the switch for the kettle. While she waits for the boiling water to work its magic on the noodles, she takes Kai into the living area. She sits with her back to James's telescope, staring in wonder at the baby's tiny curled fist, amazed at his fingernails and the creases of fat around his wrists. Her own hands look ancient in comparison, sinister like the crone in Hansel and Gretel, her nails rimmed with dust from traffic fumes.

Leigh eats her noodles and then lies down on the mattress to stare at her baby. She tries to recapture the joy she felt on maternity leave, but every time she feels it, right there, in her chest, it slips away. She attempts to shut everything else out and concentrate completely on Kai. But her mind keeps wandering to a place, miles away, a place she has never been to, where they talk funny and call each other *'duck'*. In her head, she goes through what Shelton told her about his little kingdom when he was a child: the quarry, the nearby plantation, the derelict cottage, the bridge, the house he shared unhappily with his dad, the house he moved into with his auntie.

Since she had the conversation with Des about repeating patterns, an outlandish idea has been forming in her mind.

Des has promised to phone her as soon as the search of the mine shaft is complete, although it may take some time. The shaft has to be checked for gas before the officers descend a vertical ladder which leads eventually to a third landing stage, 50 feet underground. As Des had said earlier, he'd given them instructions based on where Shelton had found Marion, but the officers already knew where the entrance to the mineshaft was – everyone knows everyone, and everyone knows everything, it seems, in Broughton Vale.

Except, Leigh thinks, maybe they don't.

Maybe some things can be hidden in plain sight.

Leigh parts the strands of Kai's hair and picks at him like a primate. She floods herself with prolonged cuddles. But her mind keeps returning to the search for Gail and the feeling that Shelton had left something out of his roadside confession – what he was doing in the time between seeing Duane Harding make the television appeal and the court case. Despite being a murderer, Shelton has a moral compass – he'd taken Marion out of the shaft and left her where her family could find her. And he'd carried Leigh to the roadside instead of leaving her in the undergrowth.

Throughout the afternoon, while she's waiting for Des to phone with news, she alternates between play and rumination, continually losing the thread of her thoughts and then finding them again. She hides her face behind Great Uncle Bulgaria and talks to Kai in a silly voice. She thinks of the groceries in the carrier bag Shelton left behind on the verge. She sings her entire repertoire of nursery rhymes. She wonders where Shelton is now – the search for him, so far, has yielded no results. She rolls a Roly Poly Ball until its chime rings in her ears and sucks Kai's unwanted dummy, just to make him smile.

But still, the outlandish idea stays with her, gathering force, gaining certainty.

So when Des finally phones to say there's no sign of Gail in the mineshaft, she isn't at all surprised.

Two hours later – the time it takes Leigh to get Kai ready, buy nappies from Kwik Save, drop him at Min's, and hobble to Admiral Street in the fading light – Leigh is in the station. She's meant to be writing her statement, but she goes straight to the evidence room. She wants to look at the contents of the carrier bag Shelton left behind on the verge.

Two Rise and Shine packet mixes, two sherbet fountains, a half-empty fruit pastille wrapper, the green and red ones missing, and a box of Coco Pops cereal.

Leigh limps into the murder incident room. There's no time to visit Nikki in Crosby and she's not on the telephone, so she calls Gail's great-grandparents, Matty and Dolcis. When Dolcis answers, Leigh doesn't bother with any preliminaries.

'What was Gail's favourite cereal?' she asks.

67

Early the next morning, Leigh and Des walk up the country path, their steps quick but quiet. At the end of the meandering lane, a small unit from the regional crime squad is in place, its officers snaking around the wall at the side of the derelict cottage. Stan and the two Godfather squad fellas are here too, ready to lead the charge. Leigh had thought the Nottinghamshire officers would be clueless woolly backs, but they're efficient, professional. Their guns look shiny and new.

She vaguely takes in her surroundings as they unfasten a gate, wondering what a nine-year-old girl would have made of rural Nottinghamshire. To their left is a field of cows, which Des eyes warily, even though the animals are safely behind a fence. On the horizon, surrounded by corn fields, is the incongruous sight of a row of terraced houses next to a colliery pit head. Leigh doesn't recognise this scenery from the photographs found in Duane Harding's garage, but on the way up from the main road, she'd looked for the fencepost memorial to Marion; the shrine to a much-missed daughter and sister.

Stan had headed off DI Josephine Bennett, insisting that Leigh attend the scene. This is as it should be: she needs an ending to her restless, never-ending search. Leigh had filled in the blanks in Shelton's account even before she'd seen Gail's favourite cereal on the evidence table. She had remembered what Clara Harding had said about him – how he often went home because he had someone to get back for. She had thought about repeating patterns: when Shelton saw Duane Harding on the television, he must have suspected he'd use the same dumping place twice.

And she had dared to hope that Shelton had once again descended the stepladder and gone down the mineshaft, in search of a missing girl.

Since arriving just as the red sun was rising, they have already moved incognito around the quarry and the nearby plantation. They've ruled out the house Shelton grew up in, and they've ruled out his auntie's house too – she has long since moved away to Skegness. There is only one place left.

As they reach the tumble-down cottage, a jet of anxiety spikes Leigh's insides.

She might be wrong.

But she doesn't think so.

The nose of a white van is nudging out of the greenery at the top of the path.

Up close, the cottage is pretty but crumbling. The sweet perfume of wild roses comes from a garden otherwise full of brambles. As Des makes a sweeping motion with one hand – the early morning air is full of bugs – Leigh sees Stan's gnarled face poking around the corner of the wall. The DCI gravely meets her eyes. His look says: '*Brace yourself,*' but the communication between them says more than that. It's an unspoken recognition of everything they've been through on this case; a shared belief that there will soon be a culmination to their work.

Des swats away another midge. Leigh takes a deep breath.

The door goes down with one kick.

Leigh hears Stan yelling his head off before she even steps inside.

'Get down on the floor,' he's screaming, 'get down on the fucking floor!'

She hears the pitter-patter of moccasins as Slapdash pushes past her. He jumps over a paraffin heater and joins the pack, pumped full of adrenaline and rage. 'Stay down! Show me your hands!' he shouts, even though Shelton is cooperating, apologising for not following their instructions in the right way.

'Get your hands out!' Stan screams. 'Put your arms away from your sides. Away from your fucking sides!'

'You're under arrest for murder and kidnapping,' Slapdash says, stumbling over the word murder because leaping in the air has made him breathless.

While Shelton goes on apologising, Des gives Leigh a nod. He pushes open a door to a back room and she slips through it.

The cottage is a shell, full of dust from years of being unoccupied. It's made up of a series of small, low-ceilinged rooms, each one leading into another. Leigh checks all of them, noticing signs that someone has been sleeping on the ground floor – there's a mattress in the back room, over which a smelly brace of pheasants hangs from a ceiling hook.

In the back room is a wooden door leading to a staircase. There are at least a dozen thick bolts on it, which she has to use all her strength to open. The door creaks behind her as Leigh climbs the dark staircase and reaches a bedroom in the eaves, where the morning light is streaming in through the window.

And there, crouched in the corner, hiding her face behind a book, is a girl. The red ladybird dressing gown she's wearing is too small for her now and a flock of birds could nest in her sunflower-yellow hair. Around the bed, on a filthy rug, are more books than Leigh has ever seen in one place, arranged in messy piles and eclectic in subject and age range. On her way into the room, she steps over *Children's Britannica* and a paperback version of *The Day of the Jackal*.

'Nothing to be scared of,' she says as she approaches. 'I'm a police officer from Liverpool. What's your name?'

The girl lowers the book long enough to shout: 'Do one!'

Her face is dirty and her eyes are bright with fear and rebellion. She is 11 now, but she still looks nine years old, pale and undernourished from being trapped in a room and living on Coco Pops. The girl bites her hand. She pushes herself up the wall with her feet, trying to escape.

And then she rests her book on her knees, widens her eyes, and stares at the strange woman in the room.

'What's your name?' Leigh asks again.

The girl looks unsure. She is pubescent and defiant and vulnerable in a nine-year-old's dressing gown. When she finally speaks, in an accent which mimics Shelton's, she says:

'My name's Gail, duck.'

'Well, Gail duck,' Leigh says, sinking down to her knees on the filthy rug. 'My name's Leigh. And I've been looking for you.'

68

In the afternoon, back on Merseyside, Leigh knocks at the caravan in Crosby. She stands with her feet in sand and hears the usual, 'Do one,' coming from inside.

When Nikki opens the door, Leigh greets her with a smile. 'There's news,' she says.

69

'Can't get shot of you,' Shelton says when Leigh visits him in the holding cells the next morning, taking the place of the duty lawyer he's sent packing.

'How's your head, duck?' he asks as he bobs upright up from a horizontal position on the bench, light-hearted for someone with a swollen lip, an injury sustained when he was apprehended yesterday. He's had a shave overnight and, although his hair is still long, his beard is gone and he looks like a different person. Without the facial hair, Duane Harding's murderer is chubby-faced, attractive, with even features which enhance his far-apart eyes.

'What the hell were you thinking?' Leigh asks, although she already knows what he'd been thinking. Shelton has signed a statement confessing to keeping Gail in the derelict cottage. He claims that when he'd found her alive in the mineshaft, he'd panicked. He'd only taken her to a place he knew, until he figured out what to do.

He never figured out what to do.

'I've come to get your statement about Duane Harding's murder,' Leigh says when he doesn't answer. 'Seeing you've refused to give one to our officers.'

Shelton hadn't had much choice but to admit to imprisoning Gail – her presence in the cottage was evidence in itself – but no amount of Stan's overnight intimidation strategies had led him to confess to Duane Harding's murder. That's why Leigh is here, to employ a woman's touch, as Stan referred to it, echoing the words of their former boss, Eugene Murphy, who wrongly believed she had feminine wiles which could win over hardened criminals.

'Tell me about the rest of it,' Leigh says, handing him a packet of fruit pastilles she'd nipped out to the shops to buy. 'After you'd recognised Duane on the television and taken Gail.'

'I didn't take her, duck, I rescued her.'

'You kept her, you didn't let her go.'

'I couldn't let her go,' Shelton says, splitting open the packet in search of green sweets. 'Gail's a smart lass, she was old enough to tell everyone what had happened with Harding. And then my dad would be a free man.'

'I get all that,' Leigh says, exasperated – she'd liked him on the motorway verge, that mad mix of wizardry and hard labour, but now she doesn't. 'How did you come to murder Duane Harding? Talk me through it.'

'They'll free my dad if I sign a statement?'

'Do you want him freed?'

'Not while I'm on the outside, I don't. You can do what you like when I'm banged up.'

'Take your time, I've got all day,' Leigh says, thinking of Kai and the plans she has for them both, later on.

Shelton had been in the pub on the Saturday night, playing darts with the lads. Harding had been there, pissed up, and Shelton overheard him telling a bloke called Richard that Clara had done some fundraising and got the money to pay privately for a polygraph test. Harding had been getting a lot of grief – death threats, vandalism, mams pulling their kids away if they saw him on the street – and Clara thought they'd be able to live in peace after the test proved he was an innocent man.

Shelton had stewed on it all the next day. He was meant to be going back to Notts – he never liked leaving Gail for more than a couple of nights ('*That's big of you,*' Leigh interjects) but he stuck around and, on Sunday night, just as the rioting was kicking off, he intercepted Duane on his way back from the pub, intending to talk to him.

But it was too late.

He'd already taken the lie detector test – and failed it.

'Harding was going to tell everyone, duck,' Shelton says now, 'he was going to come clean. And I had to get him to shut his gob.'

Shelton was out on the streets all night, even partaking in a spot of Molotov cocktail throwing by the Racquet Club. He went around to the Hardings' flat before it got light. Harding had opened the door to him.

'He didn't say owt because he didn't want Clara to know about our little secret. He tried to shut the door but I got my foot over the threshold. I tried to talk him out of confessing, but he kept saying it was all over and he was going to hand himself in. So I took the knife out. I wasn't going to kill him. I'd brought it with me because I was going to threaten him, let him know I meant business.'

Shelton springs up, unable to stay still for the next part.

'But as soon as the knife was in my hand, something gave inside me. One stab would have been enough, but I didn't stop, I went on and on until he was lying dead on the floor. There were some felt-tip pens on the side, so I wrote Clara a message on my way out, saying I was sorry.'

'Why hang around after that?' Leigh asks. 'Why stand outside the station waving a placard?'

'I thought I was better off hiding in plain sight, making out I was the same loyal defender of Harding I'd always been. It would have looked weird if I'd just pissed off, never to be seen again, when Clara had lost her husband.'

'It would have made you look like a suspect,' Leigh says.

Shelton nods. He opens his mouth to show Leigh the green pastille on his tongue. He tries to hand her a red sweet but she doesn't take it from him.

'You know something, duck?' he says. 'All my life, I've had a fear I've got a demon living inside me, like my dad has. And that must be right, mustn't it? Because it came out on the morning I murdered Duane Harding.'

70

Leigh doesn't want a commendation. She doesn't want to touch any of the drinks which are stacked up on the table. She doesn't want to celebrate the successful end of the case. She just wants to be with her baby. And with Des, too, if he fancies it.

But DI Chung has been acting weirdly since they'd shared a kiss last night, their first since Kai was born. Their meeting of lips had been brief, delicious, tinged with caution (his). They'd been standing by a fire escape at the back of Nelson Street, talking through the events of the tumultuous day. Des's hand had been on hers, his face so close she could feel his breath, and Leigh had seen her chance. This time, he hadn't broken away, but there was uncertainty in the pressure he'd applied with his lips, strong at first and then easing off. Leigh's mouth, on the other hand, had displayed the overfriendly welcome of a lonely drunk at a bar. *Stay awhile, have another one, let's have one for the road.* They hadn't talked about the kiss afterwards. They'd walked back to Min's together, grinning inanely. And they haven't spoken about it since. All morning, Des has been engaged in some kind of secret communication with Stan, shaking his head at the DCI and mouthing silent words. Now, he's holed up in Stan's office with him, as if they're the best of friends all of a sudden.

Leigh leaves Shelton's confession in the evidence pile and leans against the wall of the murder investigation room, sipping Tizer and surveying the bunch of outsiders who seem unlikely candidates for workplace acclaim. Slapdash lounges in a chair, shuffling his moccasins. Callum makes some wry remark to Mark II, who, in turn, accuses him of thinking he's the knees' bees. Kevin, for once stripped of his notebook, is standing in the corner, rocking back and forth on his heels. He looks self-conscious, but Leigh detects a flush of pride in his cheeks: it was down to his work trawling through the university lecturer's Super-8 film that they now have the physical evidence to charge Shelton with Duane Harding's murder. They'd been too busy trying to pin the crime on Nikki to notice his white van parked on the street, the number plate showing up as clear as day in the breaking dawn. They need time to prepare the other charges he'll be facing pertaining to Gail, but it's safe to assume that father and son won't meet inside a jail because Alfred Woods will be released.

The first can of Cain's lager is opened, the first bottle of Lambrusco popped. The party in the murder investigation room is sparsely populated – the out-of-town officers have gone home. The protestors have gone from outside the station too, although the pavement is not yet empty – there's a huddle of journalists out there, waiting for pounce on anyone who's prepared to talk to them about the sensational news.

A cork catapults out of another bottle and lands on Kevin to the sound of cheers. Leigh collects her bag, ready to leave. The relief of finding Gail is still flooding through her, but she keeps thinking of Marion Coote's parents, about how one little girl was found when the other was lost. She decides she is never in a position to fully celebrate anything. The problem-free life that's needed to do that is the stuff of idyllic childhoods; the lives that Gail and Marion were meant to be living.

Shelton had cared for Gail as best he could, but his loco parentis skills had left a lot to be desired, meaning Gail is in

Alder Hey Hospital, under observation. She hasn't spoken much yet about her ordeal, but it's safe to assume that, as a murderer, Duane Harding lacked both imagination and skill. He must have thought Gail was dead when he wrapped her in the clothes cover and transported her over 100 miles to the mine shaft in the boot of his car. Mercifully, he can't have held his grip around her neck for long enough and she'd only lost consciousness. And mercifully, he carried his victims down the shaft to make sure they stayed hidden. When Shelton had found Gail on the landing stage, still wrapped in the clothes cover, she had a broken bone in her arm that had since healed in a wonky way.

On the brighter side, having had nothing to do for two years but read books, she is practically a genius.

Leigh tries not to think about Duane Harding, although the fellas in the squad have been busy speculating that he'd been motivated by jealousy and revenge. There are rumours – unsubstantiated, as yet – that the 16-year-old Harding's advances had been spurned by Marion's mum; an incident so low on her radar that she hadn't even thought to mention it to police.

As the celebrations go on around her, Leigh grabs her jacket, searches unsuccessfully for Des, and walks out of Admiral Street station the back way to avoid the press. The streets of Toxteth are quiet, despite being crammed with uniforms day and night. There are all sorts of edicts coming from higher up about dealing with incidents in L8, including staying away from hotspots and not making unnecessary arrests. It means Slapdash and Mark II have had to abandon their mission to bring the cactus thrower to justice, which is a blessed relief. Still, it means she won't be welcome at the Burundi Club anymore, so her nights out picking up random men in a shebeen are well and truly over. *'How do I know it won't happen again?'* Des had asked again after their lips had met during the consoling hug last night. *'I won't need to do stuff like that when James is home,'* she'd said.

Finding Gail has given her renewed hope.

Although CID's enquiries into James have so far come to nothing.

On her way out through the car park, Leigh sees a blonde halo of hair, a slight upright figure being helped into a Cortina by Duane Harding's cowboy cousin. Clara Harding, finally leaving the station after being pumped for information.

Leigh doesn't know why she walks over, but she does.

'I've been a fool,' Clara says, when she's rolled down the passenger seat window. 'Duane fooled us all.'

'Not me,' Leigh says. 'He didn't fool me.'

As she strides away, mightily pleased with her reply, she thinks about what Stan said earlier, about her getting a commendation. She'd told him she doesn't want a medal, she wants to do her firearms training instead.

Leigh with a gun, she thinks. She can't fucking wait.

Shortly afterwards, she's sitting at the corner table in the Golden Yuen, the wad of money taken from Kai's recently smashed piggy bank in the pocket of her jeans. Laid out in front of her: noodle soup, spare ribs, crispy duck, chicken with water chestnuts and fish ball stew.

Life, she thinks. It is too short.

Leigh has blown every single penny on the Golden Yuen special banquet.

Kai is propped up in a high chair by her side, trying his first ever spoonful of egg fried rice. She has already fed him mashed up fish balls but he just spewed the mixture out and is now pounding it into his tray with tiny fists. As Leigh stuffs her face, he picks up a spoon and lobs it on the floor with a belly laugh. The baby has entered his yob phase and finds his antics hilarious. As does everyone's favourite Liverpool nan, Min, who is here with them, beaming with delight at her family, her fancy meal, her afternoon out. Together, they discuss how Kai likes his food, how he can recognise himself in a mirror and blow raspberries, and how he can say, 'Ba' and 'Dee'.

From now on, Leigh aims to be a baby bore.

The plates keep coming, including soup of the day for Kai, chow chow for Min, and banana fritters for Leigh. The baby fists the remainder of the fish balls into a goo but as he's paying, he can do what he likes. Leigh smiles across the table at Min and thinks of her own mum, who's missing out on this due to her troublesome temperament. She hasn't been near Dunbabin Road all week, and any telephone calls she's made have gone unanswered. Leigh pushes away her guilt and keeps on eating.

When her belly is bloated and she has come out in a sweat, she pays the bill by flashing her cash in the manner of Pat Killen. She has just left a generous tip ('*I've come into some stolen money,*' she smiles at Mr Tam) and is taking an After Eight mint from its wrapper, when she sees the Allegro pulling up outside. Des gets out, turns towards the flat but then sees them in the window table. She hears the door to the restaurant open and Mr Tam's warm greeting. She already knows Des has something to say because the grim-cop expression is on his face. Leigh shoves the mint into her mouth as he approaches. She's found a way to reach oblivion without Marston's Ale, bad sex, or a storm on the beach at Peel, and she isn't going to be torn from it that easily.

'Um, can we speak?' Des says, momentarily thrown by the food spilt over the white tablecloth and the speck of fish ball stuck to the cracked window. 'It's about work, mum,' he adds, addressing Min, 'we won't be a minute.'

'We're enjoying ourselves!' Min complains, although her eyes are fixed on her son in a loving gaze. 'Leigh is tired from all the dangerous police work! She deserves a treat!'

Out on the street, with a backdrop of hanging dried ducks, Des insists on holding Kai, who has already run his hands down his face and left an orange smear.

'We've got another sighting of James on the number 78 bus,' he tells her, 'a fella who knew your brother from school.

He's sure it was the same day as Heather's sighting. He said James got off a couple of stops before him.'

Des reaches out a sticky hand to Leigh. She holds it tight before asking:

'Where did he get off?'

71

On the front seat of the double decker bus, with a panoramic view of the city streets sparkling in the sunshine, Des wipes the baby's fish ball-smeared face and then holds Leigh's hand. The number 78 sets out slowly from Paradise Street bus station, the place where both Heather McCree and the new witness had caught the bus nearly seven years ago; opposite the Holiday Inn that Geoff let slip he'd last seen James outside. Back in the day, Leigh and James always caught this bus on the way back from town after their Saturday shopping trips, her brother sitting up front, examining whatever prog-rock 45 he'd wasted his pocket money on that afternoon. *'If you don't me saying so,'* Des had said when Leigh suggested leaving the Allegro at Nelson Street and taking public transport, *'your brother's not going to be on the bus now.'*

Leigh knows this, but she wants to take the journey herself.

The bus takes a detour because there's a march going on in town, transporting them up London Road and away from the burned ashes of Upper Parliament Street towards the outskirts. It carries them past the Mount Vernon pub, near the terraced house of Dolcis and Matty, where Nikki and Gail are going to live when Gail is discharged from hospital. Getting to know each other again will take time, Nikki had said when she'd phoned Leigh from a payphone at Alder Hey. Gail is having to learn to do things all over again, such as cleaning her teeth and using a knife and fork, and she keeps asking where Shelton is.

On the bright side, negotiations are going on to get Warren's assault charge reduced due to intoxication and lack of intent, and he's promised to teach Gail the piano as soon as that's all sorted. In the meantime, Gail is writing her Nobel Prize lecture on literature.

Nikki had laughed through her joy, and through her pain.

She'd even made time to update Leigh on Elaine's son, Tyrell, who is now at home, having been handed a practically unenforceable community order to remove graffiti from the walls of Toxteth.

As they near the Wavertree lock-up, Leigh turns her head towards the hairdresser her mum has frequented since she first got her new lease of life with Pat Killen. She's trying to remember her mum's reaction when James went missing. In the first few days, she'd seemed annoyed that he hadn't come back with his friends. ('*Even James wouldn't be that stupid*,' she'd said.) But this exasperation at her brother's unreliability had soon turned to worry and then to full-blown hysteria. When the panic had subsided, largely with the help of diazepam, her mum took to spending her days lying on the settee, inexplicably wearing her winter coat and shoes. And that's where she had stayed, until Pat Killen's appearance, for the next seven years.

They were the actions of a woman deranged by grief.

None of this makes any sense.

And yet, all of it makes sense.

Leigh recalls the names on the hitlist: Henry Clarke and Leonard Carey, both victims of so-called accidents, both marked DECEASED. But not James. James got away. Heather McCree had described her brother as shifty, anxious, dishevelled. The new witness – the fella who went to school with him – said James was tripping over a pair of trousers which were too long for him, as if he'd borrowed them from someone else.

She tries to put herself into her brother's mind on that August day in 1974. You get off the ferry without your tent or belongings. Your mates get different buses home – Geoff to Old Swan, Trey to L8. They leave you behind and you don't know what to do or where to go next. You've done something bad – something illegal, that you didn't want your police officer sister to know about – and you want to get to a place of safety. Where do you go if you're on the run?

You go where you know.

This is no time for words so Leigh takes Des's hand and squeezes his fingers, radiating all her emotions in a slippery grip. She thinks about how her mum threw away every single thing that belonged to James. She'd always thought it was because she couldn't bear the reminders of her loss around the house. But now she wonders if her mum's clear-out was concealment of a different kind; if her grief was really guilt. Is that what her subconscious has been trying to tell her all along?

After all, imaginary James only ever appears in one place.

The bus takes them to the quiet streets of the suburbs, up the road from where two-year-old James once slipped his reins and mounted his first escape. It takes them past the Abbey Cinema, past the stop where Heather McCree and her mum got off the bus that day, past Dr Singh's surgery, past the familiar sights of Leigh's childhood.

It's no surprise when the primary school comes into view.
You go where you know.
Leigh rings the bell for Dunbabin Road.

Pat Killen is already at the door as Leigh marches towards her childhood home. He is a man skilled at reading expressions and nods gravely as he registers the mix of disbelief, hurt and fury on her face.

'You better come inside, love,' he says. 'Your mam's got something she wants to tell you.'

Acknowledgements

Heartfelt thanks to everyone who has helped me either with this novel or with life in general (or a mixture of the two!)

Massive appreciation to my literary agent, Clare Coombes, whose commitment to making northern voices heard is an inspiration. To Genevieve Pegg, whose enthusiasm as a publisher and editor is a joy. To Jess Haycox and Alice Murphy-Pyle and all the fantastic team at Harper North. And to Stuart Gibbon, former murder squad detective, for his ongoing support in making the police work in my novels realistic (the unrealistic bits are all mine).

To my amazing daughter Lily, my ever-supportive husband Paul, my brother Steve (officially the best brother in the world) and my terrible twin, Michelle. To Vicky, Sharon, Jayne, Elizabeth and Jacy, for words of wisdom and laughs.

Writing a novel set 45 years ago means doing a lot of research. The *Liverpool Echo* archive was an invaluable source of information, as was the *British Newspaper Archive*. For background on the events of 1981, I also read *Walk Through a Storm* by Chris Kinealy (2021). Jon Woods' account of filming the events of Toxteth for ITN was a source of inspiration for a plot point in the novel. If you fancy a holiday on the Isle of Man, Niarbyl Bay is one of the island's star gazing sites and a real beauty spot, despite whatever fictional tragedies may have occurred there. I have bolstered my own memories of the island through information available via the Manx Tourist Board and Culture Vannin, which promotes Manx Culture and recognises the importance of Manx Gaelic as a language.

Thank you for reading *The Silent Places* – and if you've read my first book in the series, *The Departed*, thank you for reading that too. Readers are everything and to know you are willing to spend time with my detectives means the world to me. As this novel is partly set on the Isle of Man, it seems apt to finish with a Manx phrase: *Aigh vie dy row erriu ooilley* – may good fortune be upon you all.